THREE SHOTS TO HELL

Hardy Gibbs gestured to Billy McGee. "Pick the gun up off the floor or I'm going to shoot your balls off. Aim it at me. See if you can pull the trigger. See if you can face a man as well as you rape a woman."

McGee reluctantly picked up the forty-five, turned and pointed it at Hardy. But before he could thumb back the hammer, a big bang split the room, and he pitched backward. Horrified, Monk Flanagan and Danny Murphy stared down at their fallen friend, then at each other.

Flanagan cried out, "Get him!" and they both charged. Another deafening shot, and Flanagan tumbled over on his back. Murphy, skidding to a sudden stop, turned and bolted. Hardy took quick aim and blasted away the back of his head.

Hardy looked around at the saloon filled with men who had witnessed the shooting. He saw the look in their eyes. He looked down at his gun, its long barrel smoking. In three shots, requiring less marksmanship than hitting three rusty bean cans, he had lost his home, his dearest love, his future, his freedom: He had become a killer, an outlaw, a man on the run . . . with only his gun to keep him alive. . . .

THE SHOOTER

THE SHOOTER

Paul A. Hawkins

A SIGNET BOOK

SIGNET
Published by the Penguin Group
Penguin Books USA Inc., 375 Hudson Street,
New York, New York 10014, U.S.A.
Penguin Books Ltd, 27 Wrights Lane,
London W8 5TZ, England
Penguin Books Australia Ltd, Ringwood,
Victoria, Australia
Penguin Books Canada Ltd, 10 Alcorn Avenue,
Toronto, Ontario, Canada M4V 3B2
Penguin Books (N.Z.) Ltd, 182–190 Wairau Road,
Auckland 10, New Zealand

Penguin Books Ltd, Registered Offices:
Harmondsworth, Middlesex, England

First published by Signet, an imprint of Dutton Signet,
a division of Penguin Books USA Inc.

First Printing, April, 1994
10 9 8 7 6 5 4

Copyright © Estate of Paul A. Hawkins, 1994
All rights reserved

 REGISTERED TRADEMARK—MARCA REGISTRADA

Printed in the United States of America

PUBLISHER'S NOTE
This is a work of fiction. Names, characters, places, and incidents either are the product of the author's imagination or are used fictitiously, and any resemblance to actual persons, living or dead, events, or locales is entirely coincidental.

BOOKS ARE AVAILABLE AT QUANTITY DISCOUNTS WHEN USED TO PROMOTE PRODUCTS OR SERVICES. FOR INFORMATION PLEASE WRITE TO PREMIUM MARKETING DIVISION, PENGUIN BOOKS USA INC., 375 HUDSON STREET, NEW YORK, NEW YORK 10014.

Foreword

I knew Hardy Gibbs. Most often he was a quiet young man, yet very personable. I was the only writer on the frontier who witnessed his prowess with a handgun. In the more than twenty years I worked as a reporter I saw many gunfighters, and many who claimed to be, but were not. I never saw one with the quickness and the accuracy of Hardy Gibbs. What set him apart from all others was that he was a marksman. Yes, I would honestly say that Hardy Gibbs was the ultimate gunfighter.

—Henry Burlingame
Harper's Weekly

Prologue

The few onlookers along the rutted street were a bedraggled lot of drifters, hopeful miners, and drovers, and not a single one of them was aware of what had precipitated the standoff. But, to a man, they quickly ducked for cover along the small boardwalk when the shooting began—three shots in rapid succession, two from the young shooter standing alone in the middle of the ruts, and the last one a misdirected bullet aimed at him, which splintered one of the posts in front of the Yankee Dollar Saloon. The lone gunfighter in the middle of the street still stood; two of the three near the saloon door lay flat on their backs, and the third man was edging toward the hitching rack, his hands elevated in surrender. The spectators, those who weren't slack-jawed by this shocking display of gunplay and sudden death, were whispering among themselves, some moving cautiously back toward the saloon, wondering about the fate of the third man, barely a man, with his hands high in the air. Several other witnesses weren't interested in anything more than getting back to the watering hole and washing the cotton wads from their mouths with a good belt of red-eye. They had witnessed an unnerving spectacle.

The buckskin-clad gunfighter offered up only several brief words of explanation to the curious and the stunned who were still staring back and forth at each other and down at the two forms on the planking in front of the saloon. Waving the long barrel of his revolver across the scene, he said simply and quietly, "Horse thieves . . . rustlers."

The brief conversation that followed, the bystanders couldn't hear. But the young fellow with his hands in the air quickly lowered them and unbuckled his gun belt, hurried over and began stripping the saddle from a black Morgan. He then went over to his fallen companions, frisked their pockets and vests, and, along with his own wallet, promptly deposited the contents in a pile directly in front of the street shooter.

The shooter's next words to the trembling man were clearly audible.

"You ride back up the road and tell Mister Bullock there's more than one way of skinning a cat. Tell him Charlie is taking your profit back to the army and the Crow at Fort Custer."

As the youth turned and walked toward the hitching post, the shooter quickly came up behind him and gave him a sound kick in the butt. "Yes, and one other thing . . . in case he or any of your thieving friends take a notion to follow, just tell Mister Bullock I have good eyes in the back of my head, too. I'll drop him or anyone else who dares to follow me, just like I did those two over there."

The young man made a weak protest. "Have a heart, mister," he said pleadingly. "That's a two-day ride. I can't make it by myself . . . hostiles . . . Sioux. They're all around the road."

"Well, that's your good fortune," said the gunfighter. "Fetch yourself a couple along the way and make up the losses you have here. I hear they're paying two hundred fifty dollars for the head of an Indian in Deadwood. And consider yourself lucky. If you had whiskers on your chin, I'd have killed you." Pointing his revolver, the man added, "Now, get riding before I change my mind."

Visibly shaken, the youngster did as he was told. Fumbling at the looped reins on the pole, he finally managed to mount his horse and kicked away, up the worn wagon road to Deadwood.

The shooter, after holstering his revolver, wiped his brow with his sleeve, scooped up the loot from the street, led the black horse over to the livery and disappeared inside. Five minutes later, he came out riding the Morgan and trailing a brown and white Indian pony. Edging up to the porch, he tossed out a ten-dollar gold piece. "Cheaper than Indian heads . . . only worth five dollars each. Bury them and have a drink on Charlie." With a casual wave, he rode off down the road to the south.

All of what had transpired in the last ten minutes puzzled most of the motley group of observers, more particularly several who knew who the man Bullock was—Seth Bullock, Sheriff Bullock, head of the law in the recently declared county of Lawrence, Deadwood, Territory of Dakota. Why anyone, especially a killer, was ordering a horse thief back to Deadwood to a sheriff was more than puzzling—it was confounding and incomprehensible, and one observer, Charlie Rollo, an old-time high plains drifter and drover, knew no explanation for it.

His companion, Red Lockhart, another destitute trail hand, staring at the departing shooter, wheezed, "Well, in all of my born days, I've never seen the likes of that one, never! Thought he was one of us, just a drover, waiting around to catch on with some outfit coming down the valley. Strange kid, always playing on one of those harmonicas, sad-like ... made you feel like something was going to happen, something not too good. Said his name was Charles. Poof, and just like that, slicker'n a whistle, he pulls the shades on those two and runs the other one out of town. And back up to Sheriff Bullock? Now, what do you make of that?"

Though Charlie Rollo couldn't comprehend this either, he did shed some light on the identity of the mysterious gunman. In his dozen years on the frontier, Rollo had seen only two or three men who wielded a handgun with any proficiency at all. At twenty-five paces, most couldn't hit the broad side of a barn, and that was a fact. But this particular man, he allowed, he had seen before, somewhat different in appearance, now with mustache and long hair. Rollo hadn't forgotten that snaky stance, though, the little bend in the knees, and that quick, outward thrust and direct aim of the weapon. "I don't know what to make of it ... that Bullock business, but I'll tell you this. That feller's name ain't Charles no more than my name is Abraham." He carefully stepped around the two bodies, hesitated briefly, glancing at the foamy holes in their breasts. "Look at that, would you?" he said. "Right properly placed, both of them, directly in the middle of the chest."

Red Lockhart didn't care to look. "Said his name was Charles . . . that's what he told me last night. Waiting to catch on with an outfit trailing to Kansas."

Charlie Rollo said, "Charles, my ass! He's a god-damned gunfighter, wanted in Missouri, but that ain't his real handle. His name is Hardy Gibbs. I saw him take down a feller in a card game down at Hays. Bang! That one was smack-dab in the head. Thought his name was Charlie, there, too, Charlie Parsons, only later it turned out he was Gibbs."

"Hardy Gibbs!"

"One and the same," replied Rollo.

"Why, he's The Shooter!"

"That he is, one of the best around, they tell me, maybe the best. Probably put a dozen men in the sod, that one."

"Well, what the hell is he doing up in this country? . . . And how do you know it's Gibbs? And consorting with Sheriff Bullock? Now, come on, Charlie, it don't make a lick of sense. Not a lick."

"No, it don't, I reckon," answered Charlie Rollo. "But it's Gibbs, all right. Oh, hell, I don't know about his face all that well . . . two summers ago, maybe, I forget . . . clean-shaved then, but I don't forget his style, that little goosey step forward, the way he's hunched. He ain't standing loose and hanging like a scarecrow. You saw it yourself. He's a goddamned cat."

"Can't say I did. Happened too fast."

"Well, I saw it," countered Charlie Rollo. "And another thing. That revolver. I suppose you didn't notice that, either."

"Hell, yes, I saw it," Lockhart said. "I saw it belch twice, I did—"

"Seven-inch barrel. No Colt, either, no navy piece, no stubby Frontier Six. It's a goddamned Gibbs Special, and there just ain't many of those pieces around. Damn things cost a fortune."

As they walked into the bar, Rollo glanced knowingly at his companion. "Gibbs Special, a five-shooter, handmade, a two-pounder forty-four . . .?"

"Gibbs." Red Lockhart clucked his tongue.

"That's right," Rollo said with a grim smile. "Gibbs. That feller's grandpaw makes 'em . . . Amos Gibbs."

"And the boy shoots 'em," Lockhart said with a sigh. In a brief muse, he nodded several times. "Hmm, must be a good thousand riding on his head . . . Missouri, Kansas."

"I reckon so," replied Charlie Rollo. And, pointing his nose to the south, he said, "Well, there he goes, Red, a heap of swag in his bag and a thousand or so on his head. You want to follow, take a chance? Get some bounty?"

"No-siree-bob," Red Lockhart replied. "No, I just want a drink, that's all."

"You hear what he said? Said he was taking the profit up to Fort Custer. That'd be up the Bozeman Trail, and I reckon I know that country . . . places to hide along the trail."

Red Lockhart stared at Rollo. "You suggesting—?"

Rollo winked. "I reckon we oughta have a drink, all right, sorta talk things over. Let that boy get on the road a ways, then, mebee mosey out real easy-like."

ONE

Birth of a Shooter

Meramec River, Missouri, May 1877

It was Sunday afternoon; the liners weren't biting, but the catfish were, and Hardy Gibbs and his French-Cherokee second cousin, André LaBlanc, had a good mess fanning the water on a stringer below them. They were at one of their favorite holes about a mile down-river from the LaBlanc farm, a farm given to Paul LaBlanc by Hardy's grandfather, Amos Gibbs, in 1864, the year after Hardy's parents and older sister had been killed during a raid by some of William Quantrill's marauders who believed the homestead to be a halfway house for escaping Negro slaves. (In his later years, Hardy Gibbs always referred to these deaths as outright murders. There were no slaves on the property.) Hardy was seven years old at the time and had managed to escape by hiding in the outhouse, while the farmhouse, barn, and two sheds fell to Quantrill's raiders. Ever since Hardy Gibbs had come to live with his grandparents, he and André, the lone son of Paul LaBlanc, had become more like brothers than second cousins. André's mother, Tess, a half-blood Cherokee, was the niece of Grandfather Amos's late wife, Turtle.

Death had been no stranger to young Hardy Gibbs. His breed grandmother, known affectionately to many on the outskirts of St. Louis as Aunt Turtle, died of lung disease when Hardy was thirteen.

The fact that Hardy Gibbs lived in the big house adjacent to his grandfather's gunsmith and munitions shop in Kirkwood Town didn't deter him from making frequent horseback rides along six miles of rutty pathways down to the LaBlanc farm. It was home away from home, and he was just as comfortable among the cows and cornfields as he was working in his grandfather's small arms plant. When he wasn't helping with the chores, he was hunting and fishing in the river bottom with André and sometimes André's father, the sturdy Frenchman Hardy called Uncle Paul, a farmer and wine maker whose grandfather had first come to the area with the fur trading party of Auguste Chouteau. Hardy Gibbs was more than comfortable at Aunt Tess's kitchen table, where sumptuous meals were always served in great white bowls and dishes, and the smell of fresh cornbread drifted out between fluttering curtains into the farmyard.

But however happy and content he had been in these surroundings, the bonding of family throughout childhood, and the splendor of the Meramec bottom, lately he had become less comfortable in the presence of Julienne LaBlanc, André's winsome, dark-eyed eighteen-year-old sister. Those big dark eyes that in the early years had popped with excitement and sheer joy in the companionship of Hardy Gibbs, now often were heavy-lidded, lowered, and aflutter when Hardy was around; and when he chanced to be alone with her, they quit fluttering and stared directly into his heart.

This disturbed him; it put a queasy feeling in the pit of his stomach, leaving him at a loss for proper words to express himself. It was becoming an embarrassing situation, for after all, as much as he adored her, she was his dear second cousin, with whom he had once run across the glades along the Meramec.

André was amused by her affectionate display. He saw nothing complicated in the matter; his sister had good eyes as well as a warm heart; what better prospect for a brother-in-law than his dearest friend, Hardy Gibbs? Julienne had no Gibbs blood in her, though she and Hardy did share the same strain of Cherokee—only a slight strain, at that. Why, André declared, with only one-eighth Cherokee in him, Hardy couldn't even consider himself a legitimate breed, especially with that dark brown hair and hazel-colored eyes. But, of course, André LaBlanc agreed that there was one slight complication—if Hardy wanted to make a loving woman out of his sister—better yet, a wife—he had only the summer left in which to reach some kind of a decision. Hardy Gibbs, at the wish of his grandfather, Amos, was going to Chicago to an engineering college in the fall, and who knew what might happen while he was away?

Hardy Gibbs was slumped up against the trunk of a sycamore tree, his eyes on his bobber. He wasn't even thinking about the hot, flaky white meat of catfish dipped in cornmeal, butter beans for cornbread dipping, fresh greens, and a glass of cool buttermilk. He was thinking more about Julienne, how she had muddled his mind lately, how she had disconnected his thoughts like a string of broken beads, and about how, if ever, he would restring them. André LaBlanc was stretched out beside him, half dozing, hands behind his head, his shoes off, his cane pole propped against a rock and angling out over the green eddy.

Hardy Gibbs finally spoke. "You realize this is quite impossible, don't you? It's like starting something you can't finish, or doing something and you haven't the slightest notion how it's going to turn out. It's like fooling around with a new cartridge casing—testing it—and not knowing whether it's going to blow up in your face or put the lead in the barn wall."

André LaBlanc said lazily, "You mean like experimenting? Well, everyone has to experiment once in a while. That's how you learn the good from the bad, ain't it? That's how Micheline and I caught on, experimenting, and one experiment led to another, and bang, the first thing we knew, we were doing more than experimenting. Boy, we were doing the real thing, rolling around in the hay like two old rag dolls."

Well, Hardy Gibbs knew all about Micheline Bonet, André's sweetheart. She looked sweet and innocent, but she was really one of those smart ones who seemed to know all of the tricks, a regular downtown woman, and she sure doted on Andy. Hardy and she were friends, always had been.

"Nothing worse than a green persimmon," André went on. "You spit it out and try another. You find one that suits your palate. That's what I did."

"This isn't like eating fruit, Andy," huffed Hardy. "It's not that simple. I wish it were."

"Well, that's the way I look at it . . . life, that is. Take the best bite out of it and spit out the seeds. I don't want any of that bitter stuff."

"Jesus, here I am in a stew, and you're sprawled out there eating persimmons! You're not a lick of help."

André barely turned his head. "In the end, a man has to make up his own mind about these things, Hardy," he drawled. "Besides, you're making too much of it, anyway, putting the cart before the horse. Maybe Julie has nothing more on her mind than tasting a little fruit, herself. Ever consider this? Ever ask her what's she's thinking about? I'll tell you this, if she just wants to spread her legs like Micheline does, I'd damn sight rather it would be you than one of those quarry workers up the road always nosing around and making noise over her. Yes, and my notion is, she'd rather it be you, too."

"Oh, Lord, Lord," moaned Hardy Gibbs. "Why, you're worse off than I am, suggesting such a notion! What kind of a fool do you take me for? Going up and asking her about such things. Holy smokes, she's your sister!"

"That she is," agreed André LaBlanc easily. "She's a woman now, too, and there ain't no mistake about it, the way she's been acting up to you lately. I'm not blind, you know, and when it comes to this love stuff, you don't go trifling with a woman and advising her, even if she is your sister. Boy, they've got minds of their own, and when they set to it, they sure as hell know how to get what they want."

Hardy Gibbs sighed. "My grandpaw would have a fit if he got an inkling of this . . . plans, and all. Dammit, Andy, I'm a year too late. I should have gotten out of here last fall."

"You could stick around and be a farmer like me,"

suggested André. "Maybe you could learn to make wine like Paw."

"I like farming." "There's nothing wrong with farming. It's good honest work."

"Or keep tooling up those pistols and such for Uncle Amos, stick around and marry Julie."

"I wouldn't mind that, either," admitted Hardy, and this surprised him, because he surely hadn't been thinking about marriage. "Grandpaw would, though . . . not the tooling part, the marrying. He has this damn idea—"

"Yeah, I know, you're one of them genius fellas," cut in André. "You're gonna make a factory out of that shop and bury old Sam Colt in the dust."

"A dream, I suppose."

"Could be, though."

"I owe Grandpaw everything."

"I know," replied André. "He's a damn good old man."

"One of those Colt men stopped by again the other day," said Hardy. "Wanting to do some kind of business on that ejector Grandpaw has."

"Uncle Amos oughta just sell out the whole shebang and be done with it. He's getting too old. Get you off the hook, too, get out of that schooling stuff."

"And kill a dream?"

"You, the engineer." André LaBlanc smiled.

"I thought you said lover."

"Your decision, Hardy, your decision." André's lids fluttered, he smiled, and asked, "Ever get hard looking at her?"

"Holy smokes, Andy!"

"First sign . . . first sign you're getting hooked."

Exasperated, Hardy Gibbs stared down at the slow-moving water, the changing shades of green as it made a gentle swirl over the deep hole. His cousin, smiling contentedly, had his eyes closed again. Hardy said, "There's only one bobber out there, Andy. It's mine. I reckon some big-whiskered cat has taken your bobber to the bottom. Yep, that's what I figure. Your bobber is a gone goose."

"What!" Bolting upright, André seized the butt of his cane pole and gave a big jerk, resulting in a big jerk in return at the opposite end of his line, one so hefty that it temporarily pulled the tip of the pole right into the water. "Hot damn!" cried André. "I think we got Big Mama here, Hardy. Be damned if I don't! I can't raise the sucker."

This brought Hardy into action, too. Everyone knew who Big Mama was. Well, at least everyone in the Le-Blanc and Gibbs families, including Adah Gibbs, Amos Gibbs's housekeeper and cook. Adah wasn't really a Gibbs. She was a big Negro with frizzy hair who had come to work for Amos when his wife was ailing so badly. She just stayed on after Grandmother Turtle's death. She didn't have a last name, never had, so Grandfather Amos proclaimed her a Gibbs. She was a religious woman, too, sometimes in a humorous, but always in a practical way. She knew all about Big Mama, the tales the boys had told her. They had almost landed the fish twice. So, in her practical way, she would sometimes raise her hands and say, "Praise the Lord, and let my boys catch that big fish." Hardy, scrambling down the bank, began following the bulldog linen line as it arced back and forth in the water, his anxious eyes searching for a yellowish gray snout, the swing of a giant tail, or even the sight of a dorsal fin, anything that might be an indication of size. Nothing. He stared questioningly at André. His cousin simply shook his head and grunted. "Unngh, unngh, I can't bring her up off the bottom, goddammit! She must be sucking up mud down there."

"Well, if she decides to take off downriver," Hardy shouted, "you're just going to have to go with her, that's all. I told you . . . you just don't carry enough line on that fool pole, and it's all raveled around the end, too."

Once more heaving back on the cane, André yelled, "That's hindsight, Hardy, goddammit! What more can I do? She just keeps hugging the bottom. Whoops, she's moving . . . moving." Ping! And a curling piece of line snapped back directly in his face.

Crestfallen, Hardy Gibbs moaned, "Oh, balls!"

Staring at the broken line, André drawled, "Must be getting rotten . . . snapped it like a piece of thread. Poof!"

"Rotten, hell!" snorted Hardy "I just got you that line last summer, thirty-pounder. That was Big Mama, all right." He sighed mightily. "And the only way we're ever going to get her is find her up against some old log, go down and tickle her, and snatch her out bare-handed."

"Poor luck, just plain ol' fate. We must be cursed . . . true sinners, for certain."

"That's right," declared Hardy Gibbs, climbing back up the bank. "You hit the nail right on the head on that one." And, pointing an accusing finger at his cousin, he went on. "That's exactly what it is, sin. And, it's you, dammit, not me. You lost the fish, probably because of all that crazy talk, downright lustful, about me bedding down with Julie."

"That's sinful? Well, damn my hide, anyways, I always thought it was just kinda natural-like."

As always, Aunt Tess's catfish supper had been a good one, topped off with a big portion of rice and bread pudding covered with cream. With his belly happily content but his mind in a furor, Hardy Gibbs reluctantly refused the invitation as well as the urge to spend the night. He had work awaiting him the next morning, exacting work, engraving maple-wood handles on a pistol for one of his grandfather's customers. However, at dusk, temptation sneaked up on him at the gate, temptation in the gliding form of Julienne, and he went walking away with her toward the old oak grove. Well, he was going to break the ice. He just couldn't go on this way forever, and he knew Julienne felt the same way. He sort of touched up against her, and she sort of touched back, and without saying a word, they were holding hands. Feeling happy, but nervously warm inside, Hardy knew she was waiting for him to say something. He did.

"Damn," he blurted, "we have to talk about this, Julie, the way we've been carrying on, the way we . . . the way we feel about each other. You're my cousin. . . . I like you, maybe even more than like. I can't even explain it . . . but, well, it may get everyone all riled up, everyone except Andy. I don't know what to do."

"Andy?" Julienne said. "Now, what's he been saying to you?"

Hardy Gibbs faltered. Boy, what her brother was saying, he sure as the dickens wasn't going to repeat! He stumbled on. "Says ... says, if we like each other we should 'fess up to it ... live our own lives ... be sweethearts."

Julienne squeezed his hand; he squeezed back, and she said, "I'll 'fess up to it, Hardy Gibbs. It doesn't bother me what anyone thinks, and I think we ought to be doing more than just looking at each other all of the time. You're only my *second* cousin, anyhow, and Micheline says that doesn't amount to a hill of beans when you love someone."

"Love?" gasped Hardy Gibbs. "What are you talking about ... love?"

Turning, Julienne blocked his way. She peeked around him, back toward the farmhouse, then looked back up into the shadows of his face. "Hardy Gibbs, I think I've been loving you in my heart for months now, and the thought of you going away for such a long time is breaking it. I thought you were never going to say anything about us."

"Is there anyone watching?" Hardy asked. "Holy smokes, they must already suspect."

"No, I can't see anyone. Let's hide in the trees. You want to?"

"I want to." And, amid the flickering fireflies and the hum of cicadas, Hardy Gibbs and Julienne embraced and kissed—first a small, affectionate kiss, then another kiss, a most passionate one, and as she pressed her breasts against him, he felt a tremble go through her entire body. In this brief, exhilarating moment, Hardy Gibbs knew he was doomed. He trembled, too.

By the time he rode home on his black Morgan, it was dark, and lamplight was coming through the windows, one streak from the small room behind the kitchen, Adah's quarters, and another from the parlor, where Hardy found his grandfather smoking a clay pipe and thumbing through a sheaf of papers—from the looks of them, legal papers of some kind. Probably the latest Colt proposal. Hardy knew the Colt people weren't interested in the Gibbs five-shooter, despite its light weight, slender barrel, and fine balance. They were having too much success with their new Frontier Six. They *were* interested in Amos Gibbs's recently patented cylinder and ejector that could shuck every empty casing in one fell swoop. Hardy exchanged greetings with his grandfather, then briefly told him of his Sunday outing at the farm and the progress there: how high the corn was, an enlarged coop for the chickens, a multitude of new piglets, how the grapes were growing, Uncle Paul's purchase of a young Guernsey bull, and the escape once more of Big Mama. The last bit of news brought a quiet chuckle from the old man.

"And what about that?" Hardy asked, nodding at the legal papers.

Amos Gibbs chuckled again. "Big print says seventy-five thousand dollars, but there's too much fine print. I have to pick up some freight tomorrow. Crate of tempered steel, rough bores. I'll just drop this mess of words off at the solicitors, let them figure it out." He paused, and pointing the stem of his pipe at Hardy, added, "Less you want to try ciphering it."

Hardy Gibbs quickly shook his head, saying, "No, sir, Grandpaw, not I. Not the whereas this, and the first party this, and second party that. No, sir, that's all chicken hockey to me. I can cipher your marks, tool them, too, but it would take me most of the day to cipher those legal terms. That would be just a waste of our time. That's how those fellows make their money, drawing up all those papers that way, you know. They're smart, Grandpaw. They can do anything, make anything legal, but it always takes another attorney to get the papers figured out." Hardy collapsed in a chair, thoughts of Julienne racing through the murky canyons of his mind. Dare he mention to his grandfather or even hint about this new affliction, the throb in his heart (his aching groin, as well)? No, he thought not. He saw the summer ahead, perhaps a long, hot one. Kisses were only the beginning, and Julienne had as much as said so. She wanted to be sweethearts, just like Micheline and Andy. Micheline had told her that a man and a woman loving each other was the greatest feeling in the world, and the only thing to go getting worried about, was getting caught at it.

Hardy Gibbs took a deep breath. "If you're going into town tomorrow, what about that fellow who's picking up the revolver? What if he comes while you're gone?"

"Humph," grunted Amos Gibbs. "Parsons, I recollect. Jacob . . . Jake, I reckon. Abilene man. Well, have Adah fix him something to eat . . . demonstrate the weapon." His shoulders shook in an old man's silent laughter. "You always seem to impress the hell out of them, and most of them don't know how to treat a firearm in the first place, much less shoot one. Yes, you give this Jake a lesson. I figure to be back afore high noon, anyways, and if this Jake has come all the way from Abilene, he can afford to wait a couple of hours or so. Besides, that's the pistol with the maple-wood handles. He may have to wait, anyhow. On you."

Hardy Gibbs shrugged nonchalantly. "Depends on

what he wants on those handles. His initials, I suppose, and that's sure not going to take me all morning."

Amos Gibbs chuckled. "And a prairie rose."

"Aw, Grandpaw . . ."

"That's what he says in the letter, a goddamned prairie rose."

"Well, that should be worth another fifty—yes, sir, at least another fifty. Holy smokes, it'll take me an extra hour or two to tool up a . . . a damn prairie rose." He stared at Amos Gibbs. "What the hell is he going to do with that piece of steel, shoot it or smell it?"

Grandfather Gibbs chuckled again. "Probably smell it. He's a cattle broker, ankle deep in cow shit and money. Just for you, we'll make it five hundred fifty dollars cash on the barrel head, and you can take the extra fifty."

Hardy Gibbs broke out in a wide smile. "I'll make it a very sweet-smelling rose, Grandpaw, I surely will."

* * *

Hardy Gibbs was up at six o'clock. He was thinking about Julienne. There was one brief interlude in Adah's kitchen when he wasn't thinking about Julienne: when he ate breakfast, when he related to Adah the story about Big Mama. But once again he was thinking about Julienne when his grandfather rode away in the wagon to the freight depot down at Union Station. And toward midmorning, when he was putting the finishing touches on the second damned prairie rose, he was still thinking about Julienne. He was rubbing down the last of the polish on the pistol handle, occasionally pausing to admire the shine, the slick, beautiful maple wood, when he heard a clatter of hooves in the yard outside the shop. Well, he knew right away it couldn't be Grandfather Amos returning from the city so soon, and when he got up from his bench and looked out the doorway, there was this fellow dressed in a gray suit and wearing a small drover's hat, and he was sitting in a black buggy, just sitting there and grinning under his mustache like all get-out. There was a little sign printed on the sideboard—JOHNSON'S LIVERY. But this man wasn't Johnson; this man was Jacob Parsons from Abilene. He had rented the buckboard at Johnson's place in town—early in the morning, too, to get out here this fast. Undoubtedly, Mister Parsons had arrived in St. Louis on the eastbound night train, had stopped over at a hotel, and was up at dawn. He wanted to see his Gibbs Special.

All of Hardy Gibbs's assumptions were right on the mark. Parsons, a very jolly, talkative fellow in his mid-forties, related all of this by the time he had hopped down from the buggy. When he reached the doorway, extending his hand for a firm shake with Hardy, he was almost out of breath. "By gosh!" he exclaimed. "You're not Amos Gibbs, are you?"

"Nope," returned Hardy, "I'm his grandson, Hardy. Amos should be coming along directly. Had to ride into town this morning, but I know exactly why you're here, and—"

"I'm damn glad to be here, I'll tell you, Hardy," Jacob Parsons cut in. He took off his small drover's hat and pointed to the faint stain at the headband. "Look at this, will you? New lid when I left Abilene, brand new. Hot, hot, hot. Not this morning, mind you, but the damn train. Took all of the pucker right out of me. Whooee!"

"Never rode a train, Mister Parsons."

"Jake, call me Jake," returned Parsons. "Get you here and there in a hurry, they do, but damn smoky, hot, and dirty. Stay away from the goddamned things. Best advice I can give you."

"I appreciate that." Hardy smiled. "You care for some breakfast? Coffee?"

Jacob Parsons whacked his hat against his thigh several times, then propped it on the back of his head, saying, "Well, now, Hardy, this is nice of you, and I'm much obliged, but I'll tell you, when I saw the sign yonder, I got so excited I damn near jumped out of the buckboard, and eats sure has hell never even entered my mind."

"I know," Hardy said. "Your revolver."

"Hell, yes!" Said Parsons. "We can have eats anytime. Where's my gun? Where is it?"

Turning, Hardy Gibbs went over to his bench, picked up the Gibbs Special, and after carefully wiping every trace of a fingerprint or smudge from its barrel, frame, and handle, he came back and gently placed it in the outstretched hands of Jacob Parsons. For a moment, the cattle buyer was speechless. His face slowly brightened, almost to the color of the maple-wood handles. He sighed deeply, and his voice finally came back, huskily. "Jesus H. Christ, Hardy! Just look at this! Oh, oh, what a beautiful piece of work! Yes, and my prairie rose!"

Hardy Gibbs quickly shoved a chair in front of Jacob Parsons. He thought the man was going to faint away. Parsons sat and cradled the revolver like a baby, easing it from one hand to the other. He caressed the handle, gently gripped it, and finally slipped a forefinger around the trigger. "Whew!" he gasped, shaking his head in disbelief. "I could have ridden all the way to New York for this. It's far more than I expected." And he gave Hardy Gibbs a helpless look. "I can't wear this ... it's ... it's too beautiful. Why, this should be framed and hung on a wall."

Hardy Gibbs just laughed and said, "Well, it's not for hanging, Mister Parsons ... Jake. It's for shooting. Do you think you can shoot it? Maybe you should test it before you buy it, you know, like checking out a horse, that sort of thing."

"You think I should?"

"I do," replied Hardy. "Come on, I'll get some cartridges ... we'll go out in the back by the barn, check it out a tad."

"I think I need a drink," wheezed Jake Parsons. "A bit of a bracer."

"A touch of white lightning? Will that do?"

"Right appropriate, Hardy. Maybe spoil a bit of coffee with it. An event like this is worthy of a toast, eh?"

There was a small table back about twenty-five yards from the side of the old log barn, and upon this table Hardy Gibbs placed a box of .44-caliber shells. Jacob placed his spiked coffee next to the cartridges. Tacked on the barn wall was a piece of white oilcloth that had several black splotches painted on four corners, and a small black circle had been painted directly in the middle. On top of a long plank at the foundation of the barn were a half dozen tin cans, all neatly arranged about a yard apart, bean cans, and they weren't very big, not more than six inches high and about four inches wide. Two wide-eyed neighborhood boys sat in the shade of a big elm tree to the side of the shop.

They usually came running at the sounds of the first shots, but on this particular morning they had seen Hardy Gibbs arranging the targets; they knew there was going to be some fascinating fun, one of those "demonstrations," as they were called by the older people.

The demonstration began very simply, Hardy Gibbs describing every aspect of the Gibbs Special, its ejector, its double action, the ivory-tipped sight, the hair trigger, its light weight and overall balance, and last, its accuracy—this, of course, dependent upon the ability of the shooter. He said to an eager Jake Parsons, "Just remember one thing . . . don't jerk the trigger. Squeeze it. It gives one fraction of an inch, bam, no more, and when you squeeze it a second or third time, whatever, that cylinder will roll around for you like greased lightning. You won't feel it or even hear it."

Nodding, Parsons walked away from the little table, stationed himself about twenty paces from the barn, took careful aim at the oilcloth, and after a deep breath, fired. Lowering the revolver, he leaned forward and squinted, saw a tiny hole a little left of the center smear of black. "Pulled to the left a bit," he said to Hardy Gibbs. "At least I wasn't high. Didn't pull up triggering it." He was satisfied and turned his head and smiled broadly at Hardy.

Hardy said to him, "Try two quick ones without pulling back the hammer." Once again, Parsons stationed himself, and set off two rounds. "By God, Hardy, you're right," he declared joyously. "Greased lightning . . . jumped in my hand a trifle, but by damn, it felt good." He stared down the lane again at the target. "Left again, both shots, but not bad, not bad at all for a novice."

"You aiming that thing with one eye closed?" Hardy asked. "You realize, if you pull off a fraction of an inch, it's more than likely six inches to a foot off center-target at this range? That's why you want to learn to aim and squeeze off carefully. No margin for error, Jake, not a whit, and keep it at eye level nearly as you can. Last fellow who was in here tried drawing and shooting from his side and he put two holes in the barn roof."

"Well, I sure as hell won't do that," returned Parsons. "But I reckon my left eye is closed, all right. I always close it when I take aim." He stretched out his arm and set off another round, lowered the revolver, and observed closely. There was a small hole, this time slightly off center and to the right. "Hmm," he mused, "not shooting to the left, for certain, and almost in the black."

Hardy Gibbs suggested, "You ought to always practice that way. Use both of your eyes. That's what they're for."

After Jacob Parsons expended his last round, he broke the cylinder and watched the five empties kick away and drop by his boots. When he handed the revolver to Hardy, the two boys who had been silently observing from the side eagerly clapped their hands and yelled, and Hardy, with a small smile, explained to the Abilene stockman that he, himself, used to do that when his grandfather prepared to shoot.

Hardy shoved in five rounds, deftly snapped the cylinder back into place with a flick of his wrist, and stepping forward, told Jacob Parsons to keep his eye on the black smudge in the center of the oilcloth. Then, taking aim and without lowering the barrel once, he proceeded to fire all five bullets. There wasn't a hole in the black center, but Parsons could clearly see that it was ringed almost perfectly by five tiny dark dots. Hardy Gibbs had deliberately made a neat circle of holes around the black center. Parsons shouted gleefully, "By God, that's remarkable!"

While Parsons sipped his coffee and beamed with enthusiasm, Hardy reloaded and fired down the line of cans, sending all but the sixth spinning away, and finally one of the youngsters ran over and kicked it dead with a bare foot. Amid the cheers of the boys, and a shake of the head by an obviously impressed Jacob Parsons, Hardy carefully placed the Gibbs Special back on the table. He said to Parsons almost reverently, "Jake, you own a very fine sidearm. My grandpaw says the first and only rule about a Gibbs is take good care of it. He doesn't want his name tarnished."

Hardy Gibbs saw his sweet Julienne twice during the next week, once when she and Uncle Paul stopped briefly on their way to market; she was going to pick up some material downtown for a new blouse. But Hardy had time to show her some work he was doing in the shop; they didn't look at the work, Instead, Hardy shut the door and they quickly fell into an ardent embrace, kissed, and came out a few minutes later breathless.

On another day, Julienne and André visited on their way home from the post office. In a hurried conversation, she told Hardy that she was going to be all alone at the farm the following afternoon. Uncle Paul and Aunt Tess were heading up the river to gather greens for canning, and André was taking the wagon into town to pick up several sacks of chicken feed and to buy himself a new pair of boots. She didn't care to hunt greens; she intended to sew her new blouse. Did Hardy Gibbs understand? He surely did, and if there weren't much work in the shop, he thought he might go fishing, maybe try to catch Big Mama. Did she understand? She smiled.

With great expectations of catching the big catfish, Hardy Gibbs rode away about noon the next day toward the Meramec, finally circled around the LaBlanc farm, and sure enough, the produce wagon and team were gone and so were two of Uncle Paul's riding horses. Julienne wasn't working on her blouse; she was sitting on the front porch, waiting for him. She had on a pretty dress, bows in her hair, and she was barefoot. Well, as soon as Hardy dismounted and tied Sundown to the porch rail, she hopped down the stairs and kissed him, and without a word, led him into the house.

Hardy Gibbs felt a touch of apprehension, and the first thing he asked was, "When they getting back?"

"If it's like always, in time for milking and making supper," she answered, smiling. "That's about three or four hours. It's like forever, isn't it? Being alone all this time."

"How about Andy?"

"Said he was going to stop at Micheline's, so most likely he won't be here until milking, either."

Hardy Gibbs nervously wiped at his damp brow and stared around the parlor. He didn't know what to say; he didn't have to say anything. Julienne did. "You . . .

you want . . . you want to see what it's like? . . . Loving each other?"

Hardy gulped. "Where? The parlor?"

"Back there." Julienne nodded. "Back in my room. Got it all fixed up for us." Eyes downcast, she suddenly embraced him. "Pull up my dress," she whispered. He did, and she didn't have a stitch of clothing on under it. She was wonderfully naked, wonderfully beautiful.

Then Hardy tucked a hand up under her chin and stared into her lovely dark eyes. They were brimming with tears, and she said, "I love you, Hardy Gibbs."

TWO

Julienne and Hardy

It was July now, hot and humid at times. The days were long. Paul LaBlanc was milking twenty-one cows, most of them Jerseys, and it was a daily chore that kept him and André, and sometimes Julienne, busy every morning and evening. He had a new milk shed built out of stone hauled up from the Meramec quarry, and a new-fangled separator that removed the rich cream from the milk. The milk shed was cool in the hot weather; the cream was stored here, fresh eggs, smoked ham, and bacon, too. Most of the milk went to the hogs, but every other day LaBlanc's cream, and sometimes produce when in season, was trundled by wagon to the Shultz Creamery and nearby Union Market. This was a half-day trip, and most often the first stop en route to market was at the Gibbs place, where Adah was the first customer. She had her own pail for fresh cream, and she bought anything else that suited the needs of her kitchen. She always prepared the best of meals for Amos and young Hardy. Adah never tolerated alcohol on her kitchen shelves; she couldn't abide the devil's brew, but since Amos had a taste for his nephew's grape wine, Adah did buy a jug of it every so often, and promptly stored it out of her sight in the cellar.

Adah was very observant, too, and over the past month had noticed a change in Paul LaBlanc's delivery route. Oh, the wagon always came early in the morning almost every other day—that much of it hadn't changed. And either LaBlanc or young Andy came in to chat and have a cup of coffee around the kitchen table with her and Hardy—Amos, too, when he wasn't tinkering in the shop or gone to town. But now little Julienne had begun to show up, and sometimes she was driving that wagon all by herself. Of course, she wasn't all that little anymore. Her skirts, when she wore a skirt instead of those tight trousers and sharp-toed boots, were getting too small for her. Depending on who the observer was, Julienne was beginning to stick out in the wrong places. Adah noticed this. Adah would, because she frequently bought Julienne clothing and very personal wear when she had an occasion to shop down at Scruggs Department Store. This was not necessarily her idea, but Amos's, who gave Adah the money and told her buy a few extras for his grandniece.

Yes, Adah was very observant. In this past month, she also noticed a change in her young Hardy, at least in one way. Well, he hadn't changed a lick in size for several years, not that. He was a strapping big boy, almost six feet in his stocking feet, handsome, too, and nimble as a cat, not a lazy bone in his body. Not cantankerous or onerous, either, and she often wondered about this, because he had every right to be, his folks being done away by those nigger haters that way. She knew he still had bad dreams about that terrible time in his life; she had heard him howl in the middle of the night a couple of times. Hardy never talked about the nightmares, but Amos had told her. Hardy had been having nightmares off and on since he was seven years old. Adah supposed that coming out of that old outhouse and finding your folks' bodies, a burning house, and your sister shot in the head and lying dead by a smoldering corncrib was enough to give any boy bad dreams.

What Adah had noticed lately, though, was that her Hardy was mostly happy; he was all slicked up like a preacher man in the mornings, never went around till noon with his undershirt showing, had on a clean shirt almost every day; sometimes he wore one of those black-ribbon ties, with not a hair on his head out of place. He never knew when some important customer was going to show up. That's what he said. Her white teeth had flashed at this. Yah, yah, yah, she had silently laughed. She knew it was sweet little Julienne who was chasing his bad dreams away. Land o' Goshen, she sure noticed this, and that Master Hardy, why, he was grinning like a possum. The love bug was about, and that old Amos, either he was as dumb as a swayback mule or he just wasn't paying much attention to his grandson.

Julienne came again on this warm July morning; Adah heard the wagon pull up by the pantry, directly the slap of the screen door, and there she was, standing in the pantry with a pert smile on her tan face, her long black hair tumbling down over her shoulders. She had a basket slung over one arm, eggs, Adah presumed, and in the other, a jug of cream. She was wearing denim trousers and a cotton shirt. Julienne had blue bows tied in her hair at each side, too, but that was no distraction from the two melons pushing out of the flimsy cotton shirt. Top two buttons on that shirt were undone, too.

Julienne LaBlanc was a happy young woman. "Morning, Miss Adah," was her cheery greeting. "Brought the cream and some eggs," and she walked briskly into the kitchen and set the jug and basket on the big oak cupboard. Then, whirling around, she sniffed, and said, "Hmm, biscuits!"

"Yessum, biscuits," Adah said. "You just sit down over there and I'll bring you some. Blackberry jam in that jar, milk in the pitcher, 'less you want some coffee."

"Only a biscuit," Julienne said, pulling back a chair and sitting. "I had breakfast. Up before daybreak, I was." She stared around expectantly, and Adah's big eyes rolled white. Adah said, "Menfolk ain't come in yet. Ain't heard a rooster yet, either. You're early, Miss Julie, right early, you are."

"I have much to do today," was the reply. "Extra things to drop off, and extra things to pick up." She swelled up and smiled broadly. Adah was plucking two biscuits from the oven. "Going to a dance next Saturday night at the Buxton School . . . fiddles and banjoes, so I'm getting me some pretties down at Scruggs."

"Is that a fact!" Adah exclaimed. The two biscuits were steaming, and she gingerly put them on a white plate and placed it in front of the smiling Julienne. Adah grinned and said, "Can't imagine who's taking you to a big dance . . . 'less it'd be Master Hardy."

"That's who it is, all right," returned Julienne proudly. "And Andy is taking his sweetheart, Micheline. We're going to kick our heels, that's what. Two-step, jig, everything."

"My, my, if you ain't a caution, Miss Julie! Yah, yah,

yah." Adah placed her two big hands on the edge of the table and leaned down and clucked her tongue as Julienne knifed one of the biscuits in half. And in a half whisper, Adah said, "When you get those pretties down at Scruggs, you get a nice one to hold back your titties. You don't button up that shirt, they's gonna fall right out on those biscuits."

"Miss Adah!" blurted Julienne, and in a little blush, she dropped the biscuit half and started fumbling at the buttons. "Lordy, they don't show that much, do they? Do they? How embarrassing!"

"Ain't nothing to be embarrassed about, honey." Adah smiled kindly. " 'Cept if Master Hardy comes in and sees 'em that way, he might stick a fork in his cheek 'stedda his mouth. Yah, yah, yah." And, as she turned back to the big stove, she said over her shoulder, "When I was your age afore the big war, I had to tie mine back with a piece of flour sack, yessum, a piece of flour sack."

Julienne LeBlanc let out a little gasp of surprise at this intimate disclosure. "Why . . . why, that was terrible, Miss Adah, simply terrible. I can't imagine such a thing. A flour sack?"

"If you was dirt poor in a briar patch, you could," Adah replied. "Made other things outta those sacks, too." She slid a big black skillet across the stove, then moved the pot of coffee to the side. "Menfolk a-coming, now," she announced. "Master Hardy musta smelled that lilac water on you."

It wasn't both menfolk, it was one—Hardy Gibbs— and he hadn't smelled his sweetheart. He had been in his bedroom on the second floor splashing water in his face from a porcelain washbasin when he heard the clop of her horse. And when he came into the kitchen, he was trying to wipe away the last of that water from his forehead with his sleeve. What he wanted to do was rush up and kiss Julienne all around her lovely neck. With Adah present, he didn't do this. Instead, he politely said good morning to both Adah and Julienne, and sat down beside his love. When Adah turned to the stove to bring his coffee, he quickly gave Julienne a peck on the cheek. In return he got a gentle squeeze in his crotch, and he almost leaped out of his chair.

Directly, Adah placed a cup of coffee in front of him. What did he want for breakfast besides coffee? Biscuits and gravy? He said he would have two eggs, and when Adah went to the pantry, he quickly turned Julienne's face to him and gave her a warm kiss right on her sweet, blackberry lips, and she almost choked on the biscuit she was chewing.

"I can't stay long," she finally whispered. "I've got a dozen things to do."

"Damn, so do I," he said. "I'd like to go to town with you."

"I'd like to have you go with me."

"What all do you have to do?"

"The same . . . buy some pretties, too." Returning, Adah brushed by swaying her long skirt. She was carrying two eggs and a piece of ham. She smiled down at Hardy and Julienne. Julienne giggled and whispered unabashedly to Hardy, "She says I have to get something to hold my tits. I told her you liked to kiss and hold them."

Hardy Gibbs, preparing to sip his coffee, almost dropped it. "You said no such thing!" he whispered back harshly. An impish smile from Julienne, the crack of an egg against the edge of the skillet from Adah, the sizzle, the crack of the second egg, *shhh,* and flop went the piece of ham.

"I love you, Hardy Gibbs," Julienne said.

"I'll meet you on your way back . . . I'll work my butt off, try and get finished."

From the stove, Adah said loudly, "There's one of those bugs in my kitchen. Yassah, I hear him buzzing, buzzing, buzzing."

"A bug?" Hardy said, staring around. "What bug? Where?"

"That ol' love bug. Yah, yah, yah."

It was true. What Adah knew about Master Hardy's romance with his second cousin, Amos Gibbs did not. Since Adah considered Hardy "my little boy," she felt it was her obligation to give him some advice. So after Julienne had clattered away to market in the wagon, Adah, clearing Hardy's plate, and rolling her big eyes at him, said directly, "You better tell Mistuh Amos just what you'n Miss Julie are up to, you hear? And I don't mean going to some ol' dance, either. You been stepping high like a rooster, Mister Hardy. You been strutting and Miss Julie's been prissy as a biddie hen. I been watching."

Hardy Gibbs stared vacantly at his coffee cup and thumbed away a trace of blackberry jam on the rim. With a sigh, he said, "I've been thinking on it, you know. I just haven't—"

"Well, you better do more'n thinking," Adah cut in. "You'n that little girl go getting yourselves all messed up is apt to break your grandpappy's heart, maybe Miss Julie's, too."

"All messed up? Now, how we going to get all messed up? We just fancy each other, that's all. It's . . . just natural."

"You be going away to that school, are you?"

"I am, for sure."

"Ain't taking Miss Julie with you, are you?"

"I can't do that. I wish I could, though."

Adah turned back from the cupboard and said, "You get messed up and don't go to that fancy school, ain't gonna set well with Mistuh Amos. You're never gonna be the big-man boss 'round here. You get Miss Julie with child and go away leaving her behind, and she's gonna be pining, too. Now, I don't like to be making black and white of things, Mr. Hardy, but that's the black and white of it. 'Sides, how's a man gonna do all that learning with the love bug buzzing 'round his head all the time? Sure 'nuff, that's getting messed up. My mama told me once, when a man gets a bite from the love bug, his brains turn to grits and he lets his pecker do the thinking. It's what she called a pecker head."

"Adah. Adah." Hardy Gibbs said wearily, his eyes searching the ceiling. "Holy smokes, Adah!"

"I don't want my boy turning into one of those, you hear?"

Hardy turned and grinned sheepishly at her. "I hear."

Hands on her wide hips, she said, "Then you talk to Mistuh Amos. You listen good to what he has to say about this. And don't you let your brains go turning into grits."

Feeling a little band of sticky sweat around his collar, Hardy Gibbs got up from the table and left for the gunsmith shop. He and Grandfather Amos had some exacting work to do, rifling two barrels. As usual, Adah was right—how was he going to concentrate on business with that damned love bug buzzing all around? He whacked himself along the side of the head just to see if he could feel the sludge of grits rolling around inside. Holy smokes, he *was* in love! How could such a wonderful feeling be so miserable, too? This love was like finding a new toy, wanting to play with it all the time, and scared as hell some kid down the lane was going to sneak in, steal the toy, spoil everything, and make him feel damn miserable. High to low, up the slide, down the slide. This love with Julienne was all very natural, all right, wonderful, too, but it was complicated, complicated as all get-out—and all of the sneaking around they were doing!

Well, sometime later, Grandfather Amos came into the tooling shed, and after some shop talk, he and Hardy set about their work, positioning equipment, taking precise measurements, turning, grinding, watching those little scruffs of steel curling around inside the barrels like tiny snakes. And all the while, Hardy Gibbs's mind was twisting and turning with delicious thoughts of Julienne—terribly frustrating thoughts, too.

Near midmorning, Adah came with two glasses of cool sassafras tea. She hiked her brow at Hardy. His brow had sweat on it. She laughed, yah, yah, yah, and left, and Grandfather Amos lit up his pipe and took a nearby chair, where he began alternately puffing smoke and sipping sassafras tea. Nothing left to do on those barrels but ream them clean and get to the polishing. These weren't for the Gibbs Special; these were for a smaller version, a .32-caliber that could be neatly tucked away in a holster to the side of the breast, out of sight under a suit coat. Inconspicuous, but very expensive at $650. A fellow by the name of Allan Pinkerton had ordered them, with more orders to follow if the revolvers proved satisfactory. Hardy Gibbs didn't hold them in much account—the barrels were four-inchers, only practical at very close range, but old man Pinkerton apparently had a penchant for the unusual. He operated a detective agency of some sort, and his men spent most of their time working in secret, often for Wells Fargo, tracking down bank and train robbers.

Hardy Gibbs, contemplating his tea, swirling it about to bring the sugar to the top, said offhandedly, "Have to get myself a new pair of boots, Grandpaw . . . maybe go into town tomorrow. Fancy boots, I was thinking, a couple of buckles to the sides, that sort of thing."

Amos Gibbs chuckled between his pipe stem. "Fancy, is it? For riding or dancing?"

With a little look of surprise, Hardy said, "Well, as a matter of fact, for both. Kill two birds with one stone. I need a good pair of riding boots, and Andy and I are going to this dance next Saturday night, so I figured I might just use them for the dancing part of it, too."

"You boys are going hoofing? Well, well, that oughta be right pleasurable, Hardy, meet some lady friends that way, enjoy a reel or two."

"They don't do those reels, Grandpaw—not around here, they don't. That's a bit old-fashioned, and we're not looking to meet any lady friends, either. We're taking our own. Andy's taking Micheline Bonet, that girl he's been sweethearts with. Her father's a builder, I think, some kind of a builder, anyhow."

"Anton Bonet. He's a carpenter. Damn good one, too."

"And I'm taking Julie," Hardy said hesitantly. "So what do you think of this?"

And without a pause or second thought, Amos Gibbs replied, "I was wondering how long it was going to take you to pay some attention to that girl. You and Andy leave her out too much. Damn farm can be a lonely place for a young woman. Best thing in the world for Julie, get her out among some of her own kind, have some fun. It's right nice of you, Hardy." He momentarily stared at the bowl of his smoldering pipe. "Saturday, eh? I wonder if that girl needs a new dress, shoes, a bonnet, or a silk shawl of some kind." He looked over at his grandson questioningly. "Miss Adah know about this big dancing affair?"

Taking a final swig of his tea, Hardy set the glass aside and said, "Yes, I suppose she does. She knows everything else going on around here. I suppose Julie mentioned it. Women always talk about these kinds of things, what they're wearing, those 'pretties,' as they call them." And Hardy Gibbs sighed inside, thinking about a dainty pretty holding Julienne's tits. Holy smokes, that Adah! By damn, she knew everything, she surely did!

Hardy heard his grandfather going on. "I reckon I should mention it to Adah, anyways. Have her talk with Julie. Fix that little girl up right proper, and no one can hold a candle to her."

Now Hardy Gibbs was staring down at the floor, the bits of metal, scraps, shavings of all shapes and sizes a muddle, a mess, just like his love-riddled mind. "You know, Grandpaw, Julie and I have sort of taken a shine to each other. We like being with each other, and when

I leave, well, it's something I just can't explain, the feeling—"

Grandfather Amos sat upright in his chair, knocked his pipe on the bench, and the hot ashes went spilling out into the rest of the mess on the floor. "Humph. Sounds like more'n dancing, boy," he said. "Sounds like a little of that love is sneaking up on you. Oh, not that it's bad, mind you, and not that it's good, either. Depends on how serious this thing is. Family, you know, that mixing of the blood."

"Blood? It's not that close, is it? She's what you call distant. Not a lick of Gibbs in her, and just a tad of Grandmaw Turtle."

"Humph. Gone that far, has it? Been smooching and carrying on, have you? Discussing things?"

Hardy Gibbs shrugged and gave his grandfather an innocent look. "A bit, maybe. Nothing bad."

"Never is bad," Amos said flatly. "Always is good, far as I can remember, anyways. Consequences can be a trifle bad, though." Glancing over at Hardy, he asked, "What about your Uncle Paul and Aunt Tess? I suppose young Andy knows all about this, but what about them? They must have a notion."

"I don't know. I don't know if Julie has said anything to them, I just don't know, but I thought you should know, and know my mind, too."

Hardy tried to read his grandfather's face. Amos Gibbs wasn't displeased; he wasn't pleased, either. He wasn't red in the face like he often got when he was angry; he was just stunned.

"Oh, 'spect Tess knows," Amos finally said. "That Cherokee in her. If Julie hasn't told her, she suspects. Your grandmother was that way. Couldn't sneak a damn thing by that woman, God bless her. Injun blood. Those Injuns can read your mind like a book. Know just what you're thinking and what you're up to."

"She wasn't all Indian, Grandpaw," reminded Hardy. "Just half, that's all."

"An ounce of that blood goes a long way, son. Seems like just a speck of it gives you that insight, what your grandmother called the 'seeing within.'" He emitted a long sigh and said, "Well, it appears there's a hole in the bucket, Hardy. You'n Julie have gone and kicked it in . . . talked things over, too, this marriage business?"

"Marriage! Holy smokes, no! We haven't talked about getting hitched up, nothing like that." He momentarily thought of Andy, that crazy idea of his about tasting fruit, finding the best piece, and he said to his grandfather, "We're just sort of testing, finding out if we really like each other, wanting to get engaged. She's willing to wait, you know, me coming back in the summers, finishing up the schooling."

Another skeptical "Humph!" Amos Gibbs finally broke out in a grin. "Gumption. She's got some gumption, she has. Maybe some brains, too, to go along with those good looks. Can't do much about the hot blood in you young ones, can we?"

Hot blood? Hardy flinched. His Julienne surely did have hot blood, and she was doing something about it, too, every darned chance she got. Hardy said, "We're not so young, Grandpaw. She's eighteen now, and hell, I'm almost twenty-one."

Amos Gibbs stood, reached over and placed a hand affectionately on Hardy's shoulder. "When I was your age, my father told me I wasn't dry behind the ears yet. I can't tell you that, son, 'cause you became a man

when you were seven years old, long before your time."
He wheezed fatefully. "Just be careful about this testing, as you call it, eh? Little seeds make powerful medicine. You'll have to look down the line a piece, figure
out if it's more profitable making babies than pistols."
He stopped. " 'Course, I reckon if you was a mind to,
you could do both."

Hardy Gibbs smiled back. "I'd like to try, Grandpaw."

By noon, a few dark clouds were scudding across the
horizon, a sure sign of rain; they were coming north-
northwest, down the valleys of the two big rivers, and
the first thing Hardy Gibbs thought of was Julienne
riding back from town in that wagon. He couldn't remember whether she had a canvas tarp stored under
the seat. She did have a light jacket slung over the
back of the seat, that was all he could remember.
Maybe she would arrive in time to beat the rain, wait
it out at the house or maybe in the hayloft in the big
barn, a perfect place to listen to rain beating down on
a roof, right in the middle of sweet-smelling hay. She
would cuddle up to him in that hay and roll around, do
some of that smooching, but she was too smart to do
anything more in the barn. He didn't want to tell Adah
or his grandfather anything so personal and secret, but
Julienne was a very smart and cautious young woman.
She didn't like to do any serious lovemaking unless
there was some water around, like a creek or a pond,
like in that maple grove down by the old Watson Pond.
The Watson place, what was left of it, was supposed to
be haunted, filled with "haints," as some of the locals
called them—ghosts. Old Emil Watson, the last person
to live there, was found dead on the porch, his head

chopped off, and no one ever found the head or who did such a ghastly thing, either. This was just one of the stories. No one ever went there, not around the house, not even near the pond. There weren't any spooks there, not a one, and all the pond had in it were a few frogs. And in that maple grove right next to the pond is where he and Julienne made serious love the second time, then down by the river four or five times, and then, holy smokes, in her own bed again. But there had to be water around, because she always leaped up and went running away to wash herself and this Indian sponge thing that she wore inside her. She knew all about making babies, or how not to make them. At least, she thought she knew.

Hardy Gibbs was sitting on the porch, eating a ham sandwich and drinking buttermilk, watching the dark clouds coming in. He heard the pounding of hooves on the road, but when he craned around, he saw it wasn't his Julienne; it was a lone rider on a big bay, and when the man got near the gate, he reined up and peered under his hat toward the shop where the big sign said GIBBS—GUNSMITH. Hardy saw his grandfather stick his head out of the shop as the man rode up, and then they were both standing directly under the little porch, making conversation. This went on for a while and Hardy had almost drained the last of his buttermilk when he heard his grandfather call and saw him making a beckoning motion. So Hardy, taking one last look up the road for Julienne, leaped off the porch and went to check out this stranger. He was a prospective customer, all right, but Amos Gibbs was reluctant to do business with him. In fact, Amos Gibbs was red in the face and not too happy to see this man, even if he did have a thousand dollars in his pocket, as he claimed. In quick fashion, Hardy learned the man's name was Richard Biddell, and he made his home around the country in Clay County. Well, the name didn't ring a bell with Hardy, but Clay County surely did. That was where most of the James clan lived—or hid— depending upon who was doing the talking. Jesse and his brother Frank still had a lot of Confederate friends around the area, those who would say Clay County is where the James and their cohorts "lived," and not "hid." Whatever, neither Amos Gibbs nor Hardy con- sidered the James brothers heroes, and they had never been able to determine if either of the men were on the Quantrill raids along the Meramec during the war. But one fact they did know, and both Jesse and Frank had bragged about it. They had ridden with Quantrill, Jesse when he was only fifteen years old. And more than once, Hardy had vowed to his grandfather that if he ever met up with a former Quantrill man who had ridden in the Meramec Valley, he was going to shoot him in the head. Not for a moment did Amos Gibbs doubt the pledge of his grandson, for he himself had vowed to do the same thing.

This fellow Biddell seemed to be a pleasant sort. He explained to Hardy all he wanted to do was buy a Gibbs .44, but during the talk when he said he was an acquaintance of Jesse and Frank James, Amos Gibbs had immediately squelched the deal, not even so much as offering a full explanation, only the excuse that any friend of the James brothers wasn't a friend of the Gibbs. That, said Biddell, would surely exclude a lot of prospective customers.

"My grandfather has a long memory," Hardy finally

said. "Both of those James boys rode with Quantrill. Some of Quantrill's men killed my grandfather's son, daughter-in-law, and a grandchild down on the river below here . . . my parents."

"I didn't know that part of it," Biddell drawled. "I'm sorry to hear it, mighty sorry." He shrugged. "Amnesty . . . the war's been over for more than ten years. I didn't come looking to quarrel over it. Country has to heal sometime."

"Not for us," Hardy Gibbs said testily. And then, point-blank, he asked, "You ever ride with that James bunch, Mister Biddell? They still think the war is on, robbing Yankee banks and all."

Richard Biddell laughed. "Now, do I look like a bank robber?"

Hardy Gibbs returned, "I can't say. Never met one. Never met a train robber, either, but I notice you're wearing a sidearm, there," and Hardy nodded to the right side of the man's coat.

"Habit," Biddell said. "Riding some of these roads never has been safe. Just habit."

Amos Gibbs, his face still red, was lighting up his pipe, and he said in between puffs, "Not many in these parts wear guns anymore, 'less they have good reason. And your name, Mister Biddell, it just has a familiar ring to it, like I heard it somewhere. . . . Can't recollect exactly where, though. Maybe I saw it on a poster, something like that."

Biddell's face fell into a frown. His mouth dragged below his mustache, and he said stonily, "Another place, another time, old man, I'd consider that offensive, impeaching my honesty, and your grandson, here, asking me if I ride with Jesse. A customer is a customer, and it's none of your business where's he from or what he does. You don't play a fair hand here, so I'll spend my scrip on something more worthwhile." And with this much said, he turned back to his horse.

"Wait, wait," Hardy said. "There's nothing more worthwhile than a Gibbs firearm, Mister Biddell. Why, that old Colt you're wearing is a piece of trash compared to a Gibbs. Here, now, hold on, and just let me show you. No sense you riding all the way from town for nothing, no, sir."

"I'm not one for funning, son," Biddell said.

"Neither is my grandson," said Amos Gibbs with a deep frown.

"Hold on," shouted Hardy, who had gone inside the shop. Moments later he came back holding a Gibbs .44. He looked back over toward the side of the barn. Some of those target cans were always scattered around, and he spotted two rusty ones, holes already blown into both of them, and without hesitating, he stepped forward and set off two quick rounds, sending the cans skidding. A satisfied smile on his face, he came back to Richard Biddell, and holding the revolver by its barrel, he offered it to the man, saying, "Here . . . want to try your luck? I've always heard that James bunch can shoot pigeons right out of the sky with revolvers. See if you can hit a couple of dead cans."

"No, thanks," Biddell said glumly. "Like I said, I'm not one for funning or taking part in contests. I don't shoot cans."

"I thought not," returned Hardy, and with a deft flip on the barrel, the revolver turned end-over, its handle coming to rest firmly in Hardy's grasp, the barrel now pointing directly at Richard Biddell. "You shoot bodies?" asked Hardy.

Biddell said coolly, his eyes on the muzzle of the revolver, "That's dangerous business, pointing that thing at me."

Hardy Gibbs nodded. "I agree. It's also dangerous business questioning my grandpaw's recollection. If he's heard or seen your name somewhere, he's not being offensive . . . he's being honest. If he doesn't want to sell you a sidearm, that's his business, too. And you're dead wrong, Mister Biddell. It *is* our business to know who you are. A customer is not just a customer. We're damn particular who we sell to."

Without so much as flinching, Biddell reached up and grabbed the pommel of his saddle, swung up, and seated himself easily. "Some other time," he said. "Good day."

"Anytime," Hardy said, tipping the revolver to his forehead. "That goes for your friend, Jesse, too. Oh, you better find a good spot down the road. It's going to rain."

And as Richard Biddell rode back through the gate, Amos Gibbs said, "I may be an old man, Hardy, but I ain't one to forget names. That fellow is one of the James crowd as sure as I'm standing here. And I've got to sit down. Whew!"

"I'll get you a little snort," Hardy said.

"I'd sure appreciate that."

The rain came, and Julienne LaBlanc came with it, a sheet of canvas over her head, carrying several packages and making a run for the front porch at the big house, and Adah appeared, bringing a big towel and a glass of tea. Julienne drank some of the tea; she wrapped her wet feet in the towel. She wasn't hungry; she was just happy to be on the porch out of the rain sitting beside Hardy Gibbs instead of riding down a muddy road in a downpour. And almost as soon as it rolled in, the rain eased and went sliding through the woods to the south. A few fat robins immediately flew down out of the trees and started snatching up worms in the drizzle.

"Oh, gourds!" Julienne suddenly gasped. "The flour! I put a sack of flour in the back. . . . Go see, Hardy, hurry!" Hardy dutifully jumped from the porch and checked the wagon box. He called back that the flour under the tarp was all right, just one damp spot on the sack where a touch of rain had seeped along the floorboards. No damage.

Julienne was ecstatic. The price of cream had gone up twenty cents a gallon, and on the three cans she had made an extra three dollars. Not only that, she had bought several nice things for herself; a pair of button-up shoes and some personals. And Hardy told her that before Saturday, Adah was going into town with her and buy her a new dress and most anything else she needed. She gasped. "Uncle Amos? You told him? . . . What? What did you tell him?"

"Almost everything . . . everything but the details," he confessed.

"God, what did he say?"

"Well, he wasn't mad." Hardy grinned. "In fact, he was downright understanding. He said you had gumption. No girl worth a bean would wait around a couple of years for the likes of me."

"The gumption part I believe," she said. "Not the bean part."

"Said you were a good-looker, too."

"Really? I didn't think he paid any attention to things like that, always in the shop over there."

"We Gibbses have good eyes."

"You finish your work?" she asked. "If you did, and you want to ride back with me . . . you know, partway or somewhere good, we're wasting time. I can't take all day to get back and have everyone worrying."

"I surely had that in mind, all right."

"I love you, Hardy Gibbs."

And Hardy Gibbs, lover and part-time apprentice gunsmith, leaped away toward the pasture to fetch his horse. He tied it behind the wagon, then joined Julienne in the seat, and while they rode happily along in the moist afternoon air, he told her about the appearance of the man called Richard Biddell, one of the Jesse James gang, at least a gang member in the opinion of his grandfather. She was horrified, and she said she had seen a strange rider when she was going by Tinker's Saloon, just before the rain.

"Damn," Hardy said, "he didn't go in the place, did he? Stop?"

"No, he kept riding right on down the road."

"Good riddance, that one. He was a tad annoyed when he left."

"Maybe there's a reward for him, if Uncle Amos remembers something."

Hardy Gibbs scoffed. "That's asking for trouble. There's a few around here who still think those killers are heroes. Some of them probably would come by later and shoot up our place. They don't like informers.

When you kill a joint snake, you have to destroy its head. Its body joins up again, but you can't do anything without a head. Those road agents are like that, too. That Quantrill bunch, when the Federals killed Bill, the rest of them just crumbled like a piece of stale cornbread."

"No such things as joint snakes," she said. "You never saw one in your life, Hardy Gibbs."

"I like to imagine I did." He grinned. They rode on and ultimately she reined off the muddy road toward the old Watson homestead. Hardy asked, "The old house?"

"I'll pull around in back of it." She smiled. "Hide the wagon in the back, shake out the canvas on that flour, and we can make ourselves a pallet. . . . Dry inside that old house, I'll bet."

"It's a little late, you know. How much time?"

"Time enough." Julienne giggled. "And I won't have to be getting up and running down to the pond, so we have plenty of time."

Hardy stared at her. "What do you mean?"

"Never saw a joint snake, did you?" she replied pertly. "Well, I bought something today I'll bet you've never seen, either."

"A present?"

Julienne giggled again. "A present, in a way. You'll see."

Hardy Gibbs saw, all right, and he couldn't believe what his darling Julienne had done. He was stunned. In the light of a broken-out window, she unfolded a little paper wrapper and showed him his present, or better yet, presents—three little coiled and somewhat transparent membranes. "Holy smokes, where did you get these things?"

"From the potions place," she said boldly. "Told the man I wanted them for my husband, that's what."

In a hushed voice, Hardy Gibbs said, "You're right, Julie, I never saw one of these things in my life. Heard about such things, though, some newfangled thing. Say, how do you know—"

Busily spreading the canvas tarp, Julienne replied, "Micheline told me. They call them skins, lambskins . . . sheepskins. They're made out of intestines. That's where those extra three dollars for the cream went."

"Micheline buys them!" He stared incredulously over at Julienne, who by now was standing on the canvas and slipping out of her pants. "She buys these for Andy?"

"No, silly, she just knows about this kind of thing. She said she found one hanging on the commode once, all washed out. Her father forgot to put it away. She said she saw some more on the dresser, too, all rolled up, and she sneaked one. She and Andy use it all the time now. Have to take good care of them, put a little balm on them so they don't dry out too much. They sure cost a lot. You want to try one? See how it feels."

Hardy Gibbs sighed. "Well, I don't want to waste all of that cream money, that's for sure." He turned. Julienne was standing there naked, grinning at him. He asked, "How do they work? Micheline tell you that, too?"

"She says you roll them on. I guess Andy has a big peter, too, but they stretch right over it. That's what she says."

Hardy Gibbs grimaced. "Damn! You women!"

THREE

The Shooter Confirmed

It was midafternoon when Adah and her pretty young charge, Julienne LaBlanc, headed up Chouteau Street in the wagon toward home. Julienne set the gray mare into a brisk trot; both she and Adah were in a hurry, Julienne desirous of sharing some time with Hardy before getting back to the farm, and Adah contemplating on making supper for Amos and young Hardy. The shopping had gone well and Julienne was happy. She had a new pale yellow gown skirted with ruffles, a matching bonnet and a shawl, and some very expensive undergarments, including a lace-trimmed brassiere, and two plain white ones that Adah had insisted on buying. No use showing the good Lord and everybody else the goodies you got, said Adah, or something like that. Laughing inside, Julienne gently flipped the reins as the wagon left the cobbles and headed south toward the outskirts of Kirkwood Town. She adored Adah, she adored Uncle Amos, she loved Hardy Gibbs, and lately she was in love with the whole wide world. What a lovely summer this was, and another glorious month remained before her sweetheart was going to Chicago. She tried not to dwell on Chicago too much, thinking ahead, thinking about her man leaving. She couldn't

help but think, though, and it was very confusing and
upsetting at times even talking about it. It always put
a little lump in her throat and a pang in her heart.
Adah was consoling, or tried to be. Why, during the big
war, some of those pining women never saw their men
for more than a year—two years, even. Some of those
women, in fact, never saw their men at all—their men
just never came home. And, Adah reminded her, Hardy
was going to have holidays; he could come home, even
for a Saturday or Sunday sometimes: "Folks say those
big old trains are coming and going all the time, taking
only four or five hours to come into Union Station."
Well, Julienne knew the trains weren't coming and going all of the time—she had already checked on this,
and there were only two trains coming and going, a
night train and a day train. This made no difference
because Hardy already said he was going to write to
her regularly and that if she got to feeling really blue,
he was going to figure out some way to come home. All
of this was tolerable, and she allowed that Hardy's going away and making Uncle Amos proud—and making
her proud, too—wasn't going to be so terrible, after all.
Chicago wasn't that far away, and she had gumption,
plenty of it. Helplessly in love, these were her
thoughts, inescapable ones, particularly now since she
and Hardy were enjoying the real special love, the sinful, passionate kind. Sinful? Well, she rationalized
about this. So did Hardy. Nothing sinful about two
people loving each other if they were really in love, was
there? Best kind of sinning either of them had ever
done, for a fact. That's what Hardy said. And Julienne
had to giggle about this.

Adah wasn't talking much on this hot afternoon. She

was half dozing when they came down the lane going by Tinker's Saloon. Long before Julienne reached the saloon, she heard the music, the singing and shouting, and Adah no longer was dozing; she was bolt upright. Julienne said, "Some kind of celebration. Maybe a picnic."

"Ain't no picnic at a saloon, Adah said, her eyes rolling. "Those are menfolk hooting and hollering."

What Adah said was true—about a dozen or so men were gathered outside the saloon; some were playing instruments. From Julienne's vantage point she could see three musicians, one with a concertina and two with fiddles. Two other men, their arms clasped together, were twirling around in dance. And Adah, wagging her head, said, "Land o' Goshen, now lookee there at that!"

As Julienne moved closer, several of the men leaned out and began gawking, probably expecting more celebrants, but when they saw Julienne, they began shouting, and this brought a sharp nudge from Adah. "Keep right on moving, child, and don't pay no mind. They's all liquored up. Boozers, the lot of 'em."

"For that Dennis Riley, I think," Julienne said. "He's getting married tomorrow. Probably a party for him," and she gave the reins a smart jerk, setting the mare into a trot. Despite the quickened pace, two of the men rushed to the side of the dusty road and attempted to hail the wagon, waving their drinking mugs and jumping up and down.

One of the more boisterous ones ran directly in front of the gray mare, barely making it to the other side of the road. Another called out, "Hey, Frenchie, I wanna kiss your little ass! Hey, you sweet wench, come on, have a drink with me!"

Adah, stiff as a plank and staring straight ahead, muttered, "Poor white trash! Pay 'em no mind."

The wagon rattled by, leaving several of the men standing in the middle of the road in a cloud of dust, but they were still shouting and waving their mugs, and Julienne, her jaw hard as a piece of iron, cursed between her teeth. "Black Irish assholes!"

Surprised, Adah stared at her. "Miss Julie, tsk, tsk!"

"Well, that's what they are, most of them, a bunch of bastards, always calling me . . . little sweet bottom. Oh!"

"White trash don't know better," Adah said. "But you ain't talking like a little lady, either. My, my, your tongue."

"Miss Adah, when it comes to those quarry rats, I'm no lady. I'm a little bitch."

"They's full of that ol' devil's juice," Adah said, clucking her tongue again. "And why you calling them 'black Irish?' Ain't no colored in the lot, all as white as cotton balls. Why you do that?"

"I don't know why," replied Julienne. "That's just what some folks call them, black Irish . . . shanty Irish. Maybe they worked in a coal mine before they came to the Meramec. Maybe they're the worst of the lot, black hearts, I don't know. Micks! They don't like us, and we don't like them. They call me froggie, too. All French are frogs. Good thing Andy or Hardy isn't here. There'd be a fight, for certain."

"Andy 'n' Hardy be here, and they'd be no fussing 'round in the first place, that's what," Adah said. "Those fool boys would shut up like backwater clams."

She looked over her shoulder back toward Tinker's Saloon. The dust had settled, but two of the men were now dancing in the middle of the road.

Ten minutes later, Julienne and Adah were pulling up in front of Amos Gibbs's place. Hardy was sitting on the porch, his black Morgan already saddled and tied to a post under the shade of a big maple tree. He was ready to move down the road toward the LaBlanc farm with Julienne, but Julienne, after a visit to the outhouse in back, disappeared into the pantry to wash the anger from her face and get a drink of cool well water from the cistern. When she returned to the porch, Hardy Gibbs, munching on an apple, swallowed and gave her a smile.

Adah had already related the story about the drunks at Tinker's Saloon.

Hardy said to Julienne, "Let those boys get your dander up, eh? You should have run your horse right into that burrhead, given him a good roll in the dust."

"Idiots!" she huffed. "One of these days . . ."

"Who were they?"

"The usual, Riley's crowd. One called Monk, I saw him, and the mouthy one wanting to kiss my ass, Jimmy McGee. Horrid toads, the whole lot of them."

"Flanagan, McGee, and Riley," mused Hardy Gibbs. "Yep, some big mouths, all right." He shrugged and took another bite of his apple. And between chews he said, "Well, Riley won't be much of a problem after his wedding. That girl he's marrying is bigger than he is. . . . Sit right down on him, she will, or hang him out on a clothes pole to dry, if she takes a notion. Monk? Don't know about the rascal, but you're right . . . one of these days I might have to take him down a notch." He grinned at her. "Leastways, they've got good taste, wanting to kiss your bottom that way."

"Hardy!"

Hardy kept grinning, and nodded toward the wagon. "Got your pretties, eh? Adah says, 'Lawd, lawd, you gonna be the sweetest lookin' chile at de ball.' "

"That's for you to decide."

"Already decided," he returned, and he threw the apple core over in front of his horse, Sundown, who immediately nosed it over once, then daintily plucked it from the ground. "Grandpaw says no one can hold a candle to you. Exactly my sentiments, too. Isn't a girl around as pretty as you, Julie, and that's the nut of it."

She laughed and kissed him on the cheek. "Beauty is in the eye of the beholder," she said.

"Maybe so, maybe so," he agreed. "Everyone says my eyes are the best in the valley. Anyhow, my eyes surely don't lie."

"I love you," Julienne said, and tipping her glass, she downed the last of her water. Tracing her lips with the tip of her tongue, she said, "For some darned reason, the ride home always takes me longer than I plan, and Mama's always giving me these funny looks, and Andy, he's always winking at me."

"Cat's out." Hardy Gibbs sighed. "Can't go sneaking about like this forever, you know." Nodding toward Adah's kitchen, he said, "I've been getting an earful almost every day from her. We're just going to have to do something about this."

Julienne got up from the bench and took Hardy Gibbs by the hand. With a little satisfied smirk, she said, "Ask me, I think we're doing plenty about it already. Come on, let's go riding. Too much talking always gets me confused." And as they left the porch, she whispered, "Haven't forgotten anything, have you? . . . You know?" Hardy Gibbs tapped his shirt pocket.

From the pantry window, Adah called, "Suppertime at six o'clock, Master Hardy. You being here? Or you being in the briar patch? . . . Yah, yah, yah."

"I'm being here," he answered smartly. And with a hopeless look at Julienne, he said, "See what I mean?"

Hardy Gibbs and Julienne LaBlanc made the old Watson farm into their favorite nesting place. Julienne had put a broom in back of the wagon on the previous Tuesday, which she used to sweep the front room. She swept out all of the spiders and cobwebs, too, and Hardy, after their last rendezvous, had stayed behind and, with his long knife, cut a pile of green hay in the nearby meadow. He made a fine pallet in the corner of the room that served as a mattress when Julienne spread her sheet of canvas over it. There was a big round table in the kitchen. Hardy wanted to bring it down the little hall into the parlor to put their clothes on, but he couldn't wedge it through the doorway. He thought that was why it had been left behind; someone must have built the thing right there in the kitchen. Hardy noticed another thing about that table—there wasn't a lick of dust on the top of it, and when he called Julienne's attention to this, she just laughed and said probably the spooks and buggermen had been using it.

Julienne was joyously happy, and Hardy Gibbs thought she was funny, sometimes, too, like what she said about the old oak table. She was always making joking remarks about the Watson place, and lately she was even talking to the haints, telling him, "They don't mind us here. . . . Gives them something to talk about when we're gone, watching us carry on this way." Once she said, "Haints aren't any different than we are. They like a clean house." That was the day she was sweeping out the place, and she glanced up at the ceiling and said, "Don't you?" Another time, Hardy remembered how she startled him by looking over at the door after one of their strenuous love bouts and said, "Phew-eee, now, what did you think of that one, Mister Watson? Bet you never saw anything so good in your life."

She had laughed, too, adding, "Before you lost your head."

Julienne had taken to calling the place "Hardy's Hainted House," and every time she left she stuck her head back in the door, saying, "You take care, hear?" Hardy had a notion that some folks wouldn't take kindly to this kind of ghost talk. It was sort of like flirting with the devil, or maybe more like making love with the devil and his friends looking on. What Julienne thought funny wouldn't have been humorous to folks in the valley who claimed to have seen faint lights in the place a couple of nights and had heard these strange moaning sounds. "Couldn't have been us they heard doing all that moaning and groaning," Julienne said with a laugh, "because we just do our moaning and groaning in the afternoons." When it came to ghosts, Julienne didn't have a lick of fear in her, day or night.

Since he now used one of his "presents," Julienne wasn't so fidgety about taking care of herself proper-like after they made love. Now she didn't get up at all, and he thought maybe by buying those "skins" she had played a trick on him, a pretty darned good trick. She wouldn't let him get up, either, not until she had satisfied herself a second time with what she called her "swelling spasms."

So, on this afternoon, they were lying there sort of sighing and breathing heavily when Hardy thought it was about time to make some kind of a decision, an important one. He had been thinking on it, and he said outright, "I'm going to have a word with Uncle Paul, get this straightened out—"

"What!" Julienne's wet brow brushed his cheek. "Paw? You can't go telling him about this! He'll have a conniption! If he knew we were loving every day like this, he'd get his shotgun . . . lock me up."

"Holy smokes, he's not blind. He must suspect something."

"Yes, but nothing like this. Says it's just a sweet rash, I have. Don't scratch it too much and it'll go away. That's what he suspects."

"We've been scratching, all right," Hardy said. "Itch is getting worse, I'll allow, so I'm just going to tell him we're getting engaged, see if he has any objection to it, tell him Grandpaw Amos thinks it's a great idea."

"Engaged!" Julienne cried out joyously, and she rolled over and straddled him with her nakedness, knees to each side of his chest, and staring down, she fell serious. "Listen here, Hardy Gibbs, Uncle Amos said no such thing to you. You can't go telling Papa a lie, dammit!"

"No lie," he said. He tried to elevate himself and kiss one of her tits. She playfully shoved him back. "When I tell Grandpaw we're getting engaged, he'll be glad about it. I already told him this was down the line a piece. Besides, he thinks the sun rises and sets on his little Julie. He surely wouldn't go wanting to make you unhappy, that's for sure."

"How far down the line a piece?" she asked. "Just what are you meaning by this?"

Hardy said, "You mean engaged? . . . Or you mean getting married?"

"You tell me," and then she lowered herself slightly and dangled her breasts near his ruddy face.

"Damnation!" Hardy choked. "Engaged, right away . . . marriage down the line . . . maybe next summer, even. Give you time to get all those nice things stored away in one of those chests. Give everyone else time to get used to the idea."

She giggled happily. "A trousseau. Already got one started. By next summer I can have it filled to the brim. Oh, squash, this is wonderful! Talk to Papa . . . yes, talk to him. You get right to it, Hardy Gibbs," and she buried him with her breasts. "You tell him we're planning on getting married."

Now Hardy was beginning to entertain thoughts other than talking to Uncle Paul, and so was Julienne, who was sliding herself down into a coupling position.

There was a noise. It was like someone moving about in one of the adjacent rooms. Julienne, wide-eyed, bolted up and stared down at Hardy. She cocked an ear and said, "Shhh! Listen!"

Hardy did listen. Yes, there was someone else in the place, no doubt about it, and whoever it was seemed to be sneaking about like he was walking on eggs, not wanting to make a sound. Julienne was snatching up her clothing, her petticoat, giving it a shake, and Hardy whispered, "A ghost . . . a buggerman!" He had to grin· he just couldn't help himself.

"Damn you!" she whispered. "It's not funny!"

He couldn't hurry—not too much, anyhow. Pants, shoes, shirt, underpants, the whole works was all piled up in a mess, so Hardy Gibbs did the best he could—he pulled on his trousers, picked up a board from the pile where Julienne had stacked the trash, and he went gliding down the little hall, prepared for battle. If someone had sneaked up on them, the jig was up, anyway. No use worrying about trying to get dressed. When he looked back, though, Julienne was in a hurry; she was all tied up in a mad whirl of clothing, her arms moving all directions.

Hardy Gibbs, his board at the ready, heard the noise again, a scuffling in the room directly ahead of him. The old door was partly ajar, so with one hand raised, he quietly edged it open with his other. The lonely years had rusted its hinges; it squeaked—sounded more like a wail to Hardy—and suddenly two furry balls of fur shot by him, one going right between his legs. Coons! They scrambled down the hall in the direction of Julienne, and Hardy, once again, couldn't help himself. "Buggermen, buggermen!" he yelled, and he went thundering down the hall in his bare feet. It was a commotion, all right. A shrill scream erupted from the parlor, and when Hardy arrived on the scene, he saw the last of the two big raccoons leaping out one of the broken windows.

Julienne LaBlanc, holding out one shoe, was backed up against the wall. "You devil, you!"

It was nothing more than a country dance at the Buxton School, but Amos Gibbs thought it was an occasion worth celebrating, so he had Adah begin preparing supper for the children. She made a fine meal of chicken and dumplings, and she set the big table in the dining room, brought out a white tablecloth and the best dishes. As Amos Gibbs said, there wasn't anything too good for his children; he loved them all. And, to make it more comfortable and stylish for them, he and Hardy dusted off and pulled out the fancy surrey. After Hardy had harnessed up, he drove over to Micheline Bonet's house to pick her up and bring her back to the house, where everyone was going to meet and enjoy Adah's big meal before going to the dance.

Vivacious Micheline Bonet was all French, her mother a Bouchet, one of the early fur-buying families that had arrived in the Mississippi Valley. Hardy Gibbs thought Micheline was much like her mother, Marie, an attractive woman with light brown hair who laughed and talked a lot and was always gesturing with her hands. If Micheline was provocative and a tad flirtatious, she probably got it from her mother—at least, this is what Hardy thought. Maybe that's just the way French women were, he didn't know. His Uncle Paul wasn't too talkative; neither was his cousin, Andy, and neither one of them used his hands much when he talked. Julienne never did. Micheline and her mother both had this same habit, puckering up their lips, wagging their fingers—their butts, too, when they walked—and they both talked a lot. Hardy liked them. Andy said Marie Bonet was a good cook, plus she was the only old lady he'd ever seen that he wouldn't mind crawling in bed with. Only that wasn't such a good idea, Andy figured, since someday she might be his mother-in-law. Hardy thought that bedding with some woman old enough to be your mother was an outlandish idea. But Andy was right in one respect—Marie Bonet, just like her daughter, was a good looker.

And when Hardy Gibbs pulled up in front of the Bonet house, it was Marie Bonet who sat there on a big swing, waiting. She waved, turned her head to the door, and called out something in French. And after this she said to Hardy, "Allo, Hardy, she's coming right away, eh? You come up here and let me look. A woman likes to look at handsome young men. *Voyons! Quel homme!* Hah, and new boots with the pretty buckles, too! I will save one dance for you."

Hardy Gibbs laughed. "I'd probably step right on one of your toes, Missus Bonet." Standing on the stoop, he stared down at the boots. "Haven't quite got the hang of these yet. Figured a good dance should break 'em in, though . . . or give me blisters."

"A fine carriage, too."

"My Granfather's," replied Hardy, looking back at the surrey. "Never have much occasion to use it anymore."

"For a wedding, eh? Very good for a wedding."

"I suppose." Hardy nodded. Then he cleared his throat. "I hadn't thought of that. Not quite ready yet."

Marie Bonet made one of her little puckers and said, "Ah, but I hear these things, eh, *mon ami*. To be in love, Hardy, a wonderful things . . . to be married, better. This is what I tell Micheline, too. Not ready, not ready, everyone says not ready. Too much love, poof!" and Marie Bonet was fanning her face and making another pucker.

Hardy Gibbs grinned. "When Micheline and Andy get ready, they're welcome to use the surrey. Julie and I are just going to have to wait awhile—" and the screen door swung open.

Out came Micheline, dressed in powder blue gingham. She had a long cloak wrapped over one arm. Her eyes were big and brown, just like her mother's. She turned around once, swirling her skirt, graciously curtsied, and said, "I'm ready, Mister Gibbs, ready for dining and dancing. Shall we?" Handing her cloak to Hardy, she turned her back, and he placed it around her shoulders. She smelled good, like sweet jasmine.

"Yes," Hardy Gibbs said, smiling. "The carriage awaits, and I'll give you a hand up."

Micheline Bonet wagged a finger at him, saying, "No more than a hand, mind you, keep it in the proper place."

"Micheline, Micheline," called her mother, "*Si vous portez cela, vous aurez trop chaud.*"

"No, no, Mama," replied Micheline. "Only in the carriage . . . the dust, I don't want too much dust, eh?"

"We'll ride easy-like," Hardy Gibbs said. "Keep the dust down this way . . . no big hurry, anyway." Helping her up, Hardy said, "She worried about me goosing you, too?"

"No." Micheline smiled. "She said it was too warm to be wearing this. If you'd goosed me, she'd probably fallen out of the swing, laughing."

He swung the surrey around the yard back to the road.

Micheline Bonet happily threw back her head and laughed. "Hardy, you're a vain young man, sometimes, yes, you are, but I like you."

Hardy looked at Micheline sheepishly. "Maybe you're planning on more than dining and dancing."

"Always a possibility," she said. "One I never overlook anymore, just like Julie. She's ahead of me now, though, getting engaged."

Nodding, Hardy then glanced suspiciously over at her. "News surely travels fast around here. No one but Julie and I know this, least I thought no one knew. Only decided it yesterday afternoon, you know. Your mother, she's on to it, too."

"Andy was over last evening," explained Micheline. "He knew. Julie told him first thing after she came back from the Watson place." She leaned around and stared up at Hardy Gibbs, a big, mischievous smile on her face. "That old spooky place where the coons hang out. Buggermen, buggermen!"

"Holy smokes!" And Hardy Gibbs sighed forlornly. "Does that woman tell everything?"

"I thought it was funny," she said. "So did Andy." She laughed outright. "You know what Andy said? He said those coons were probably doing the same thing you and Julie were. Humping in that old bedroom."

"Humph!" Then it was Hardy Gibbs's turn to lean over and stare at Micheline. "How do you know it's a bedroom where the coons were? It's just a room."

She shook her head sadly and made her cute little pucker. "*Mon Dieu*, you think you're the only ones who've ever been in that place? That room is right next to the kitchen, isn't it? Window is all boarded up. Those coons went in there from the kitchen ... the back door. Back door is where the spooks come in at night, spooks like me and Andy. We started making love in that place six months ago." She bent over and laughed. "I think it's funny, ironically funny, because that's one thing I never said a word about to Julie. Andy and I were keeping our place a secret. We even have some candles hidden behind the stove. You might as well know this, 'case you and Julie end up there some night. It's better at night, anyhow, more romantic."

Hardy Gibbs smiled and cursed, "I'll be damned."

She giggled and pinched his arm. "I haven't been in there lately, though, haven't seen your little bed of hay. You may be a little vain, *mon cherie*, but you're very enterprising. I'll try out your bed next time. Maybe tonight."

He gave her leg a nudge with his knee. "It's better than that big oak table. I wondered why it wasn't all dusty. I'll bet you have calluses on your pretty butt. Julie said it wasn't dirty because the spooks were using it."

Hands to the side of her head, Micheline Bonet hollered, "Whooo, whooo!"

Amos Gibbs was sitting in a wicker rocker on the porch; Micheline and Hardy were in the swing. Adah was in the kitchen, covering her hot biscuits and placing them in the warming oven. Julienne and André were late, and Adah's fine supper was ready.

A wagon came by on the road. All looked expectantly, but it clattered on by, raising up a distant cloud of dust, loud voices echoing down toward the house. Some of the Riley wedding party coming from Quarry Town, Hardy Gibbs opined, probably headed for Tinker's Saloon to finish off the celebrating. And Micheline, turning up her nose, said, "Sounds to me like they already have a snootful. I hope they don't show up at the dance, the clods."

"Not likely," Hardy said, laughing. "Another hour and they won't be able to dance, at least not proper-like."

The dust had barely settled along the road when Hardy heard the sound of another wagon. "This must be them," he said, and he and Micheline walked from the porch out into the yard. What they soon saw was a wagon hurtling along the ruts, a gray mare running with her ears back, her mane flying in the late afternoon sun, and the fluttering yellow dress of Julienne, who was flailing a pair of reins across the mare's back. There wasn't a sign of André. *"Mon Dieu, regardez-là!"* cried Micheline, watching the wagon skidding dangerously into the long lane leading to the house. "Something has happened! Where is Andy?"

Moments later, the LaBlanc wagon came to a stop. Screaming at Hardy and Micheline to take care of her brother, Julienne, badly disheveled and emitting great sobs, went rushing into the house and fell into the arms of Adah, who immediately took her into the small room off the kitchen. André LaBlanc, badly beaten and barely conscious, lay in the wagon bed, blood smeared on the planking. Hardy immediately saw that it was coming from a big cut in the back of his cousin's head. One of André's pants legs had been half torn off, and there was a huge red welt on his right leg below the knee. "For chrissakes, what happened?" Hardy shouted. "Can you hear me? Andy, can you hear?"

Micheline, at Hardy's side, was shoving her cloak under André's head.

Amos, a big white handkerchief in his hand, told her, "Here, get something on that cut. Stop the bleeding."

André finally managed to mumble, "Jumped us . . .

swerved into us at the turnoff to the quarry. Monk . . . Monk and Jimmy leaped over and knocked me off the wagon. We gotta go get them, Andy . . ."

"You aren't going anywhere," Micheline said, pressing the handkerchief against the back of his head. "You're badly hurt."

Amos Gibbs, carefully tracing his hand down André's leg, said, "We'll have to check this. Might even be cracked. We have to get you over to St. Joseph's, if it is."

André LaBlanc, turning his head to the side and with tears welling up in his eyes, said, "No, I can wait. . . . Go take care of Julie. She said . . . she said that goddamned McGee raped her. . . . Monk and that Murphy, held her down . . . all liquored up, all of 'em."

The thin cord of despair and horror that had been entwined in Hardy Gibbs's head since he was seven years old began to unravel; it suddenly split apart, sending a blinding flash of red anger spinning before his eyes. This wasn't his recurring nightmare of the past; it was the stark terror, the reality, of the present. The blood of the past oozing out of the limp bodies of his father, mother, and sister was now Andy's, on Hardy's hands, on Micheline. "Raped her!" he gasped. "Jimmy raped her!"

André LaBlanc, biting his lip, nodded and said, his voice choked, "We have to get the little bastard."

Stunned, Amos Gibbs said to Hardy, "Let's move him inside. Careful with that leg." And he moaned. "Oh, my poor little girl."

Hardy, helping his grandfather and Micheline move André into the house, was in a dreadful trance. He saw nothing, he heard nothing; his mind was blistered and

flaked like old lead paint on clapboard. He felt a sickening throb in his stomach, an aching throb in his
heart, and he felt that blinding red pain of anger between his eyes. After resting André gently on the parlor
couch, Hardy turned, looked through the dining room,
saw the white blur of dishes gleaming on the tablecloth, saw the sparkling glasses waiting for the touch of
beautiful lips. He looked through all of this and saw
Adah moving about, a steaming kettle in one hand,
cloths and towels in the other, and he moved toward
her.

Adah's shiny face was sagging. "You go on, Master
Hardy. Nothing you can do here," she said. "Miss Julie
ain't wanting to see you, ain't wanting to see nobody
. . . ain't wanting to see a man for a long time—no
man."

"Tell her I love her," Hardy said. And, wheeling
about, he bolted out the front door, went to the shop,
and got his gun belt.

Moments later, Amos Gibbs hurried onto the porch.
"Won't do any good to go chasing after them, Hardy,"
he shouted. "You let the law take care of this, get hold
of the constable, get word to Shamus."

"Shamus!" Hardy called back. "Shamus won't do a
damn thing, Grandpaw. He's one of them. Their word
against ours, that's what he'll say. And they'll deny it.
How in the hell is he going to prove a damn thing?"
Running for the barn, he yelled, "Don't worry,
Grandpaw, just take care of Andy and get word to Uncle Paul. Micheline can ride and tell them."

It didn't take Hardy Gibbs more than ten minutes to
reach Tinker's Saloon. He didn't ride to the front door;
he rode Sundown around to the back and tied the reins

to the handle of the screen door. He adjusted his gun belt and walked directly into the noisy, smoky long room. The noise suddenly dwindled to nothing more than a few whispers, but someone laughed loudly and said, "Hey, boys, here's Hardy, coming in the back door, by gawd. Have a drink, boy."

Hardy saw Monk Flanagan, Jimmy McGee, and Danny Murphy standing at the middle of the bar with Murphy's sister, Maureen, and another girl whom he didn't know. The girls were giggling. Standing alone at the end of the long, shiny bar, Hardy looked at the barkeep, Bill Tinker. He gave him a quiet hello, and Tinker simply nodded in return. Then Hardy Gibbs calmly said to him, "Put that forty-five you have hidden back there on the bar, Bill. I'd appreciate that. Make sure it's loaded, and just slide it over there to Jimmy."

Surprised, Bill Tinker held his hands up protectively, saying, "Now wait a minute, Hardy. I don't know what this is all about, but we don't want to be doing anything foolish. That gun's private. I don't want any of that kind of fighting in here . . . someone getting shot."

"Just do what I say," Hardy said. "You fetch up that pistol or I'm coming back there myself."

Upon hearing this firm order, the two girls standing with the young men at the bar screamed and fled out the front door. One of the men at a nearby table said, "Don't be a fool, Gibbs. If you have a burr in your britches, this ain't gonna solve nothing. Best you go on home, think it over, get cooled off and settle whatever you have to settle with Constable O'Leary."

"Shut up," growled Hardy. Pointing at Bill Tinker, he said, "Do it . . . now!"

With a hapless shrug, Tinker put a hand into the

shadows and carefully removed the hidden revolver. After staring into the cylinder chamber, he placed it handle first on the bar directly in front of Jimmy McGee, who, white-faced, just stared down at it. And McGee, his voice trembling, finally croaked, "I can't do this. I'll not be having a chance." Eyes flooding, he looked helplessly down the long bar at Hardy Gibbs, and Hardy replied, "You'll have more of chance than you gave Julie."

"That was all in fun," Monk Flanagan pleaded. "Hell, Hardy, we didn't hurt the little breed. Riled her a little, that's all."

"Riled her!" said Hardy. "Holy smokes, you drunken bastards, I can't believe this. You practically killed her . . . destroyed every dream she ever had, you goddamned fools." Moving away from the bar, he gestured with his chin to Jimmy McGee. "Pick it up or I'm going to shoot your balls off. Aim it at me, if you want. Just pick it up. See if you can pull the trigger. See if you can face a man as well as you rape a woman."

Jimmy McGee reluctantly picked up the forty-five, turned, and with a shaking arm pointed it directly at Hardy Gibbs, but before he could thumb back the hammer, a big bang rent the room and he pitched backward and collapsed on the floor. Horrified, Monk Flanagan and Danny Murphy stared down at their fallen friend, then at each other, then finally at Hardy Gibbs, who was now tucking his revolver back into its holster. To Monk Flanagan, he said, "Now it's your turn. Take your time. I'm waiting."

Monk cried out, "Get him!" and both he and Murphy charged madly toward Hardy Gibbs. Another deafening shot rang out, and Monk Flanagan, hit squarely in the chest, tumbled over on his back. Danny Murphy, skidding to a sudden stop, turned and bolted for the front door. Hardy quickly took aim and shot him in the back of the head. Everyone in the place was petrified and speechless, but not Hardy Gibbs. Trembling inside, stomach churning, he said to the transfixed, horrified men, "If anyone ever comes around the property of my kinfolk or even dares give them trouble in any way, he'll have to answer to me. Sooner or later, he'll have to answer to me."

One of the men who had been at the table was now moving toward the body of Monk Flanagan. He looked over at Hardy. "You won't be *around*. You'll hang for this."

FOUR

The Sedalia Shoot-out

Hardy Gibbs had no choice, only his direction. He fled. He fled with the blessings of his sorrowful grandfather, and the blessing of two hundred dollars to help tide him over until he found a safe haven; he fled with the help of Adah, who told Shamus O'Leary and his appointed deputies that Master Hardy had gone into town, probably to Union Station, probably was already aboard one of the night trains; he fled without a kiss or embrace from Julienne, or a handshake and wish of good luck from André. Hardy Gibbs fled west on his black Morgan, Sundown, riding by night up the Meramec River trails that he knew so well, at the first sign of dawn heading north, catching the little roads and paths bordering the big Missouri, and moving along slowly until sunup, when he found a shady place to rest under a big oak tree.

Sleep wasn't easy to come by. Hardy wasn't haunted by the fear of being caught; it was too early for this troublesome possibility. Eluding capture would come later when the printed word went out, when those small posters finally began to circulate and were posted at train depots and on the wall of a marshal's office, even in some obscure little post office. As he vainly attempted to nap, Hardy Gibbs's thoughts were the same ones that had gnawed at him all night—the sad memory of his weeping Julie, Adah caressing her with her big arms, something that Hardy had wanted to do, and the memory of the sickening thuds of those heavy slugs slamming into the bodies of three young men, that last round pounding into Danny Murphy's head. Was this going to be another nightmarish haunt in his life, a companion to the other recurring dream of three bodies splattered with blood, lying there in the ashes and dust of the Meramec bottom?

The killing had been easy, just as easy as it had been for Bill Quantrill's raiders—for a fact, as easy as shooting varmints. But the aftermath had not been so easy. Riding back to the house, he had tried to vomit. There wasn't anything in his stomach to expel, so he had just heaved and heaved. Jesus, hadn't there been another less gruesome way to avenge the scarring of a young woman's soul? No, in his moment of fury, his shattered emotions, his exploding brain, it had been the only way, and even now, as he turned and tossed, mulling it over again and again, he could only conclude that what he had done was just—no, not under written law, the legal law, but under moral law. In three shots requiring less marksmanship than hitting three rusty bean cans, he had lost his home, his dearest love, his future, his freedom; he had become a killer and outlaw.

Hardy Gibbs continued to flee, and on the third afternoon spent four dollars in Jefferson—one dollar for a hotel room, fifty cents for a bath, fifty cents for a good meal, a dollar to grain-feed and stable his horse, and another dollar to buy emergency food to stuff in the gear behind his saddle. Refreshed, moderately wealthy, and somewhat less troubled, he left the river roads and rode due west the next morning, heading for the Kansas border. His luck held for two more days until he was nearing Sedalia. It began to drizzle. By the time he rode into the little town, he was wet, his farmer's straw hat limp and drooping, and somewhere along the line in the slick mud, his horse had thrown a shoe. At dusk he was inside Hoagy Boon's livery trying to shake himself dry and making arrangements with Boon to have Sundown shod the next morning when the smithy came to work. Hardy was also contemplating other arrangements, like purchasing himself a rain slicker, a good jacket, and a new hat. Those new boots with the silver buckles, his dancing boots, which unfortunately he had used for fleeing instead of dancing, were proving to be a boon—at least his feet were dry. As he passed by the mercantile, he peered in the window, saw a woman behind a counter striking up a lantern and a man approaching the door. Obviously it was quitting time. Hardy Gibbs knew the man was getting ready to pull the shades, so he quickly stepped inside out of the rain, declaring what he had come to buy. The man was obliging; so was his wife. She flared up that lantern and went right down the long aisle, pointing here and there, and her husband started picking out wearing apparel everywhere she marked; denim jackets here, coats and slickers there, and, down the line, some hats, and, about anything else a man would want.

Hardy Gibbs bought a waist-length denim coat with pockets at each breast. It came right down to the top of his britches; it didn't interfere with the leather holster hanging down on his right side, or the handle of the Gibbs .44 sticking out of it. "Don't ever let a piece of garment get around your weapon": the words of his grandfather. Amos Gibbs figured if someone was planning on mischief, you couldn't go brushing away at a coat, because making a move like that just might give the fool more time to shoot you. Grandfather Amos knew about these things; he knew everything there was to know about firearms and the men who used them, and he had taught it all to Hardy Gibbs. Though Hardy never gave much thought to this knowledge, the practical end of it, he allowed some of it might stand him in good stead now. And after that shooting at Tinker's he had discovered one thing that his grandfather hadn't thought about, or if he had, he had neglected to mention. That seven-inch barrel that was so great for accuracy was just too long when it came to jerking it out of a holster with any great speed. Hardy Gibbs was enterprising. That's what Micheline Bonet had told him, anyhow. He thought most of this enterprising stuff was just common sense. He knew he had to figure a way to pull out his revolver with more speed.

Hardy Gibbs left the mercantile with the coat, a black rain slicker, two pairs of underwear, a flannel shirt, some socks, and a cream-colored hat, one of those drover types. It was stiff and hard, fine for shedding rain, and when the storekeeper made a little dent in the crown, turned up the edges a bit, and placed it on Hardy's head, it felt good. When Hardy stared at himself by lantern light in the dim mirror, it looked good, too. Hardy was thirty-four dollars less wealthy when he left the store, but at least he was adequately prepared for the long road ahead. He checked in at a small hotel named Borden's. After washing up, trying

on some of his new duds, he went downstairs and had
a good meal of stew and biscuits, and later, by lamplight, he wrote his first letters, one to Julienne, another
to his grandfather and Adah. A man of the road with
a precarious future, he tried to sound nonchalant, as if
he were making out just fine, writing that when he
found a good job and a safe place in Oregon, he would
send for Julienne. It was impossible to put his true
feelings in either letter—that he was troubled and
lonely, that in fact he was downright miserable.

Before he went to bed, he picked up his gun belt
and sat down on the floor cross-legged under the coal-
oil lamp. He slid the Gibbs out of the holster several
times, then sat there pondering. After some time, he
began muttering to himself, tracing a fingernail along
the leading edge of the holster, and he reckoned he
could do one of two things—wear the holster lower on
his hip or modify it, and modifying it was going to take
a lot of doing—not much of a trick in Amos Gibbs's big
shop, but out here, along the road it was certainly a
problem. Well, the first tin shop along the way, he
would look into it. He was going to fashion himself a
breakaway holster, see if such a thing would actually
work.

By morning, the rain had stopped, but by the time
Hardy Gibbs had eaten breakfast and posted his two
letters, he was a little late getting back to Boon's livery.
The blacksmith had already shod Sundown, not replac-
ing just one shoe, but all four—"No use doing a job
halfway" was the explanation. If Hardy got down the
road a piece, most likely one of the other shoes would
have kicked off; better to have a new set than take a

chance. This is what the smithy said, anyhow, and he had shown Hardy the three old ones. They weren't bad, but there wasn't much Hardy Gibbs could say about it now. He was a tenderfoot; he was learning the rules of the road right proper, he was. This town of Sedalia had been an expensive place to bed down, both for him and Sundown. He was saddling up, stowing his new gear, and tying on his new slicker behind the saddle when Hoagy Boon came up and said that a man had come in earlier in the morning asking about him, asking about who owned the black Morgan.

This surprising news put a lump in Hardy's throat and a few goose bumps on his arms. But he acted all natural-like. He just said, "Is that so? What'd the man look like? . . . What did he have to say?"

Hoagy said, "First off, just asked who owned the horse. Looked him over for a mark . . . see if it had a brand." He grinned at Hardy and asked jokingly, "Didn't steal the horse, did you?"

"Nope," Hardy replied. "Had him for five years, now." He finished lashing on his slicker. "What did you tell him?"

"Only told him you called yourself Joseph. Rest is none of my business—his either. He had on a regular suit—vest, too—and he was toting a pistol . . . tucked back under his coat, but I saw it."

"Hmm," mused Hardy, his skin beginning to crawl.

"Well, if you're on the run"—Hoagy Boon grinned—"you can rest easy, 'cuz this fellow wasn't no lawman. I know 'em, the law, can always tell one. 'Sides, they always show me a badge, a star, and this jasper didn't have any mark, and he didn't smell like the law."

"Whiskers?"

Hoagy Boon shook his head, saying, "No. He had a big mustache, though, right black, dandied up on both sides."

Well, right away Hardy knew it wasn't Shamus O'Leary. Shamus had a goatee; he seldom dressed in a suit, and if Shamus had ridden a horse this far, he probably wouldn't have been able to walk, much less go around asking questions. Shamus was a miserable old fart. But Hardy Gibbs, who had told Hoagy Boon that his name was Joseph, who had signed on at the Borden rooms as Joe Hollister, didn't have a notion who this stranger was. He had one notion, though— this man must be a bounty hunter. Shamus hadn't wasted any time; St. Louis County had already put a price on Hardy Gibbs's head.

Hardy, swinging up into his saddle, thanked Boon, reined around, and tipped his fingers to his new hat. He looked down at the livery man, winked, and pointing his chin, said, "If that fellow comes back, tell him Joseph rode that way . . . north." He urged Sundown ahead, hadn't gone ten yards when Hoagy Boon called, "Hey, Joseph . . . your last name . . . wouldn't be Gibbs, would it? Gibbs . . . I remember. That's who this jasper was looking for, some young feller named Gibbs."

Hardy shouted back, "Nope, not my name. Don't know anyone by that name, either."

Sure enough, the cat was out of the bag, and at least one man had grabbed on to its tail. Hardy Gibbs pretended he was just riding easy-like, not a care in the world. Wasn't that way, though; he was sweating under the brim of his new hat, and he felt all sticky in his armpits. Holy smokes, not more than a week, not even out of Missouri, and someone was already following him! Sighing mightily, he nervously rode down the street, threading his way between a few wagons that were now coming and going, freighters, farmers, a buggy or two with women in them, probably in town for shopping, and some children romping back and forth, yelling at each other. He had made it almost to the end of the long street when near the front of another hotel a man dressed in a suit and wearing a white straw hat stepped out and hailed him—not just a regular hail, but his name. "Hardy . . . hey, there, Hardy!"

Hardy Gibbs reined over to the side and gawked. By damn, this was the stranger who was asking about him down at the livery, only it was no stranger. Holy smokes, it was that friend of the James brothers—Richard Biddell! Well, right away Hardy knew Biddell was up to no good, had something in his craw, and he also knew that he himself was at a disadvantage perched on top of Sundown this way, so when he pulled up, he leaped clear of the horse, coming down like a cat on the balls of his feet, and it was a good thing. That damn fool Biddell was shoving away the side of his suit coat, reaching for that old navy Colt. He got it out, but he didn't raise it and aim quickly enough. Hardy just leveled down, fired once, and blew Richard Biddell into the mud and horse manure. A lot of people started yelling; a few women shrieked, and three or four kids came running up as fast as they could. Hardy Gibbs, his heart thumping as it did at Tinker's Saloon, didn't have any back door to run out this time. He kept his wits, though—he didn't bolt for his horse; he took it by the reins, slowly walked by Biddell's body, then over to the boardwalk in front of the hotel, where he calmly hitched the horse, took a seat on the bench under the awning, and waited for a constable or sheriff to arrive. No one approached him, but there were a lot of gawkers staring over at him, then back at the body of Richard Biddell. One man, chewing on a toothpick, finally walked up and said, "That was some shooting, young fellow. That man was out to get you." And nodding toward the boys and men around Biddell, he asked, "What in tarnation was his game, anyhow, pulling a stunt like that?"

Hardy Gibbs shrugged innocently. He didn't feel like talking. He was sick; he felt like throwing up. He finally said, "I don't know. I think he's one of the Jesse James bunch. I reckon he thought I was up to something."

"Jesse James!" the man exclaimed. He turned on his heel and quickly went back to the others with the news. Shortly, a stocky fellow, accompanied by two other men, one dressed in a white apron, came hurrying down the plank walk. The short fellow identified himself as Sheriff McDermott, and he quickly set about his business, talking first to Hardy, then to several men who had witnessed the shooting. It was true, the man who was now sprawled on the ground had been drawing his revolver when Hardy Gibbs was in the process of dismounting; Hardy had only been defending himself. But Sheriff McDermott was dumbfounded. If this man called Biddell thought Hardy was after him, why hadn't he just simply gotten out of town? Why would he dare to attempt a killing in broad daylight? No, it didn't make sense, so Hardy Gibbs, alias Joseph Hollister, was asked to walk back to the sheriff's office; there was paperwork to be done, and McDermott wanted to check his memorandums, a few slips of paper, telegraph dispatches, and letters. There were posters, too, some with the faces of men, some sketched likenesses, others actual photographs. And sure enough, after a few minutes of sorting, Sheriff McDermott flipped one across the desk to Hardy Gibbs, one with Richard Biddell's name on it, and a drawing of his face. Biddell was wanted in Missouri for bank robbery. Hardy Gibbs, a slight tremble in his knees, took a step backward and collapsed in a chair. "Why, that sucker could have killed me."

"He could have done that in the dark of night," McDermott said. "Or from the roadside . . . ambushed you. I can't figure out why in the hell he chose my street . . . everyone looking on. Are you a bounty hunter, Mister Hollister, one of those looking for reward?"

"Nope," Hardy said, shaking his head. "I never saw this man in the flesh, only a picture or two back home when my paw and I went to the post office to get our mail."

"You have a good memory," commented McDermott skeptically.

"I suppose I do," Hardy returned. "Those James boys are always running around our neck of the woods. You get used to looking at all of the posters . . . every time you go into the post office." He stared at the crinkled paper. "That surely is a good likeness . . . five hundred dollars! Whew!"

"Five hundred, says here," replied McDermott. "Might even be more by now. I'll have to check on it."

Hardy Gibbs swallowed hard, thinking back to Grandfather Amos, the day Richard Biddell showed up wanting to buy a Gibbs Special. Amos had been right—this Biddell was a no-account. Grandfather was old but his memory surely wasn't. Hardy asked, "You suppose the scamp has friends around here? Someone else with him? I don't want to be hanging around waiting for a damn reward if some of that James crowd is about. I wouldn't get a chance to spend a lick of it, would I?"

"One of the boys says he came in last night," Sheriff McDermott replied. "He's a loner, all by himself. Played some poker. Called himself Luther . . . Luther something." He looked over at Hardy. "You didn't play poker with him, did you, Joe, get him out of sorts, anything like that?"

"Nope. I came riding in all soaking wet . . . took a chill . . . bought some clothes, went right to Borden's and hit the hay.

Directly, the man wearing the white apron came in with Richard Biddell's belongings—his revolver, billfold, a pocketknife, gold watch, and some folded pieces of paper. The billfold had almost four hundred dollars in it. "He wasn't fixing to rob you." McDermott smiled, thumbing the bills. "He wasn't looking to get back his losings."

"Doesn't look like he was much of a loser to me," responded Hardy.

Sheriff McDermott said grimly, "Depends upon how you look at it." Setting the money aside, he began unfolding the papers, one at a time, and grunting as he carefully eyed each one of them. Finally he looked up at the man with the apron. "Interesting, John," he commented. "You think what I think?"

"I think so," the man replied. "Could be a case of mistaken identity. This Biddell was hunting bounty.

Never figured he'd be the bounty himself. I'd say he had the idea, you, Joe, were one of his targets. That's my opinion."

Hardy Gibbs scoffed. "He robs trains . . . banks, doesn't he?"

Sheriff McDermott said, "Appears he's changed his line of work." Nodding at the papers, the small posters and memos—five of them—McDermott added, "John, here, could be right. This Luther . . . Biddell, must have thought you were one of these men."

"Holy smokes!"

"Only names on a couple of these scraps," Sheriff McDermott said. "These others, well, they don't fit your description, so I can't figure how he got himself so all messed up this way."

Hardy Gibbs badly wanted to reach over and look at the names that Richard Biddell had penned on those pieces of paper, wanted to see if his name was one of them, and just how much he was worth. He didn't. He sighed and stared wide-eyed at the man called John, the one in the apron. "What if he'd shot me? I'm not worth a cent. I'd be dead!"

"Wouldn't be the first time some shooter made a mistake."

Sheriff McDermott finally shuffled all the papers together, then spiked them on a sharp spindle at the side of his desk. "Where you heading?" he asked Hardy. "Where can we get hold of you? . . . The reward, anything else we might be needing to know."

Hardy Gibbs didn't know where he was going—west, that was all—but he knew this wasn't a good enough answer, so he said, "Up to Omaha . . . my stepbrother. He's getting out of the army. Says he's tired of fighting

Indians, all those scraps up in the Montana Territory. Scared him almost silly, so we're taking a long vacation on the way home."

"Well, your brother probably deserves a good vacation," opined McDermott. "From what I hear, he's lucky he's still in one piece, that terrible Custer thing last year." He paused and said, "You're lucky, yourself."

Hardy Gibbs agreed. And once again he said that he had no wish to wait around in Sedalia for any reward; he feared for his life. The sheriff understood, but he didn't know how long it would take to get a draft for the five hundred dollars, maybe two or three days by the time all of the details were properly handled, death confirmation, exchanges on the telegraph, those sorts of things. Hardy Gibbs quickly scribbled out the address for Paul LaBlanc. "That's my stepfather," Hardy explained. "He has a farm down on the Meramec. Just send the draft there. I'll write him a letter before I leave so he knows what's happened, what to expect." Hardy Gibbs knew where that reward money was going—right into the hands of his poor Julienne.

Hardy Gibbs, alias Joe Hollister, bounty hunter by accident, moved out of Missouri as fast as he could, riding the back roads, stopping only occasionally to buy food at rural stores, sleeping in the woods, and finally crossing the Kansas border at Louisburg. When he thought the trail behind was clear, he rode to the northwest, ultimately finding comfort and seclusion in Lawrence. If any of Biddell's cohorts were following, or any of the old Quantrill gang, he doubted very much they would make an appearance in Lawrence. Hardy was sure that the people around Lawrence had longer memories than his own—Quantrill's men had ravaged the town during the war, killing almost one hundred fifty men, women, and children. Who could ever forget something like that? Why, if someone even hinted that he was a friend of those killers, most likely he would be strung up on a pole in the middle of town. They surely wouldn't waste the time of day giving him a trial. That damn war was hard to forget; Yankee or Confederate, it made no difference, it was a rotten apple. And that amnesty thing Biddell talked about, well, that was just a bunch of crap.

Hardy Gibbs stayed two nights in Lawrence. Sundown needed some good rest, and so did he. Hardy didn't wander around too much; he lodged at Carpenter's Rooms. Brewster's Café was handy, right next door, and he stayed away from the saloons. Grandfather Amos always said that the quickest way to lose your edge was by drinking too much liquor. Hardy Gibbs figured he was getting the edge now, the Gibbs Special edge, and he still had a mind to make it better—that holster. So he went to the tin shop on the first morning, made a little sketch of what he wanted—two thin, flat pieces of spring steel, curved just so, with a hole at the end of each of them, a hole big enough to accommodate a small brass rivet. He bought a few rivets and a pair of snips at a hardware store, and that night he carefully cut a narrow strip out of the front of his holster, positioned his metal bands at the top and near the bottom, and made his marks where he wanted the springs fastened. Before breakfast the next morning, Hardy went back to the tin shop and flattened the rivets. The tinsmith couldn't believe anyone would ruin a fine leather holster this way, not until Hardy, wondering himself if he had made a mistake, decided to demonstrate. He took his Gibbs Special from under his belt where he had tucked it, slid it carefully into the newly rigged holster, then, to the tinner's amazement, snapped it out. But Hardy wasn't satisfied; the springs were too stiff, so he proceeded to bend them until they snapped back with only a minimum of pressure. "None of my business," the tinsmith finally said, "but I can't help but ask . . . just why you need that thing this way."

Hardy Gibbs smiled. "Only a fancy." Handing the revolver to the man, he said, "Ever see one of these? . . . Long barrel."

The man, carefully examining the Gibbs .44, replied, "No, never saw one these before. Damn pretty thing, though, and sure as hell feels like a feather in my hand."

"With this long barrel," Hardy explained, "it takes a tad longer to pull it out, see? It's awkward." He took the revolver and replaced it in the holster. "Rigged this way, I won't have to pull it at all . . . just grab the handle, shove it up like this, all in one motion, right up to the level of my eyes." He grinned at the surprised tinsmith. "Just in case I ever have to use it, of course."

"Yes, sir, I see what you mean . . . just in case."

There wasn't any mistake about whose place it was; Hardy saw a big windmill, right next to it a white water tower with the initials J. S. P. and under the initials, a red and pink prairie rose. That Jake Parsons was surely partial to prairie roses, for a fact, and despite how tired and saddle-weary Hardy was, he had to chuckle when he saw that big flower up there. When he rode to the pole gate, a barking hound dog came running out, and beyond the dog alongside the big house, he saw a woman staring at him, her hand up to the brim of her yellow straw hat, shielding her eyes against the late afternoon sun. Hardy held up one of his own hands in greeting; the woman called the dog, and Hardy moved on up the lane, and directly was in front of the porch. The woman was tall; she wore working clothes, regular men's trousers, a blue denim shirt, and had a red bandanna tied around her neck. When she took off her straw hat and stepped back into the shade of the porch, Hardy saw that her hair matched the color of the hat, sort of yellowish brown. He saw one other thing, too—she had a new Winchester rifle leaning against the door frame. Right away he thought he'd better say something, so he took off his drover's hat, nodded to her, and said, "Good afternoon, ma'am, name's Hardy ... Hardy Gibbs, and I'm looking for Jake Parsons. He's a friend of mine."

The blond woman—she was in her late thirties, a bit younger than Jake—stared at him for a moment with her brown eyes, eyes with little squinty wrinkles at the edges, and finally said, "Jake isn't here. I'm his wife. What did you want to see him about? Can I help you?"

Hardy, his wary eyes going over to the dog, replied, "I've been riding the roads for almost three weeks, ma'am. Would you mind if I got down and stretched a bit? ... Would the dog mind?"

Speaking to the side, she said, "Go lie down, Bud."

The dog went over to a spot in the shade and obediently flopped, and she gestured to Hardy Gibbs to dismount, which he promptly did, saying, "I was passing by, on my way west, and since your husband told me once if I ever got to Abilene to stop by and pay my respects, that's just what I'm doing."

"My name is Rose," she said. "What did you say your name was?"

"Gibbs ... Hardy Gibbs." And then it suddenly struck him—prairie rose. This Rose standing here next to the rifle was Jake Parsons's prairie rose! Hardy said, "My grandpaw and I made Jake a revolver last spring. I engraved his initials on the thing, a rose, too ... a prairie rose."

"Good God!" she exclaimed. "Gibbs! Of course." Rose Parsons smiled for the first time—not a big smile, but a pretty one—and she motioned him to the porch. "Come on, sit up here on the swing, young man. I'll get you a drink. You must be hot and tired ... the weather lately, it's been intolerable." She stepped aside as Hardy mounted the stairs, and said, "All the way from St. Louis, are you? My gracious, that's a long ride by horse, Mister Gibbs."

"Been a long, hot one, for certain," he said. Tossing his hat on the floor and unbuckling his gun belt, he collapsed on the big swing. "Whew." He sighed. "This does feel good, Missus Parsons." She went on by, into the house, and directly returned with a tall glass filled with cool tea. He thanked her, took a long drink, then looked back at her and grinned. "Jake been shooting that revolver? He surely took a shine to it."

Rose Parsons gave him another little smile, a sad one, and said, "Jake's dead, Mister Gibbs ... robbed and shot two weeks after he came back from your place ... more than two months, now."

Hardy Gibbs felt like the swing was collapsing right under him. He slowly set the glass aside and searched her face, but before he could say anything, she was explaining, relating the whole story, how someone had shot Jake Parsons in the back while he was coming back from the stockyards late one evening. One of the stockyard drovers had found him dead in his wagon not more than a mile from the farmhouse. His money belt was gone; so was his gold watch and his new Gibbs .44. And no one had a clue as to who had killed him, but she had posted a thousand-dollar reward for information and apprehension of the killer. Her two children—a nine-year-old boy, Timothy, and a daughter, Susan, age fourteen—were staying up at her folk's place in Concordia. Rose said that she had sold the stockyard a month ago but not the farm. She nodded at the nearby rifle. "I keep that near me most of the time . . . and the dog. Friends always stopping by to check on me, see how I'm doing. Can't say I feel too comfortable at times."

Hardy Gibbs wheezed. "By damn," he said, "I'm terribly sorry, Missus Parsons. This . . . this is all hard to believe. That Jake, he was a fine fellow. We had a time that morning before he left. He went away whistling . . . happy sonofagun."

"Call me Rose," she said, sitting on the stoop. "Yes, that was Jake, all right, whistling, yes, and polishing that gun almost every day. Like a pet, it was." With a long sigh, she looked up at Hardy and asked what had brought him west, where was he going. And Hardy Gibbs, after a sigh of his own, told her his trip wasn't by choice, but out of necessity—he was a wanted man. And then, as Rose Parsons had done, Hardy related his own story. After he had finished, he picked up his glass and drained the last of the tea. He was surprised when she said, "The bastards deserved what they got, Hardy. They bullwhipped some fellow in Abilene last year for violating a woman. They should have hanged him instead." She looked over at his horse. "Your black needs some pasture, a little rest. So do you. The Oregon country is a long way from here. Get your stuff and I'll fix some supper, find you a place for the night down in the bunkhouse."

"You surely don't need to bother, ma'am."

"Rose," she said again. "Call me Rose. And it's no bother. Jake told me all about you and Amos. He couldn't get over it, something about all the fancy shooting. Least I can do is put you up for the night . . . hide you." She grinned at that.

Hardy Gibbs was grateful. These were the first kind words he had heard in days. He washed up in a little room down the hall next to the kitchen, a room with a big tin tub in it, and water that came down from a tank, not only into a basin but also into a toilet, thus explaining the tall water tower in back of the house. Rose Parsons also had running water in the kitchen, a large kitchen where Hardy sat and ate a fine supper with her.

Later, after he grabbed his small bundle of belongings, they went down to the bunkhouse. Rose said it hadn't been used for two years, ever since Jake quit droving cattle and went into the brokering end of the business. It was obvious that the bunkhouse hadn't been occupied—it was in terrible disarray, and Rose Parsons was appalled. Cobwebs were hanging everywhere, and the floor was covered with mouse droppings.

"Good God!" she cried, fanning the stagnant air.

"This is horrible!" Slamming the door, she said, "You can't stay in here . . . place isn't fit for the hogs. We'll have to do something about this tomorrow, clean it up, just in case you want to rest up for another day." And with another flourish of her arm, she said, "Come on, we'll put you up in Timmy's room for the night."

That night they sat on the porch and talked. Rose Parsons was a very understanding and sympathetic woman. Just because Jake was gone was no reason she couldn't help Hardy; she knew all of Jake's friends, both down at the stockyards and some out on the distant ranches and farms. She had some influence, too. She was considered a wealthy widow-woman, she said with a laugh. If anyone could help him find a good place to hire on, to work in relative seclusion—out of sight, so to speak—she could, and would be happy to do so if he wanted. Might take a few days, but he was safe for the present. Rose Parsons was certain she could make the arrangements.

Hardy Gibbs, with half of his money gone and no particular destination—only as far away from the law as he could get—told her this sounded pretty darned good, at least for the present, and he was mighty obliged. He went to bed this night with some pleasant thoughts for a change. He thought of Julienne, though, and as usual, relived his last, horrible afternoon and night on the Meramec. Sleep came late, but it was the best one he had had since he fled.

The next morning, Hardy Gibbs awoke to the smell of bacon and coffee; Rose made sourdough hotcakes, too. She wore a pretty white robe and a pair of white slippers; her blond hair was fastened in back by a silver clip of some kind, and she moved gracefully around the kitchen, setting up plates, flipping the hotcakes, and pouring coffee. She didn't eat much. She talked a lot, though, about the farm, Jake, her two children, her folks up in Concordia, and how she had to stay busy and keep from thinking too much about the past. Of course, with a farm this big—a ranch, she called it— there was always plenty to do. No stock around now, but she kept two milk cows for the children, had some laying hens, and four horses. She had a big garden, too, and she said that after they took a ride in the buggy down to the yards so Hardy could get a look at the place, decide if he wished to hire on, he could help her pick some beans and greens for supper. When Hardy asked about cleaning the bunkhouse, Rose Gibbs was outspoken, just like Jake—she said to hell with it. Timmy and Susan weren't coming home right away; for the present, Hardy could stay right where he was. And that was the end of that.

They were just finishing up breakfast, Hardy politely listening to more of Rose's rambling conversation, when a woman came riding up to the back porch in a small buggy—an older woman, but spry, wearing a flowered bonnet and a long calico dress. She hurried right up to the kitchen door, rapped several times, and scurried inside. The basket she was carrying was filled with peaches. When she saw Hardy Gibbs sitting at the table, she stopped in her tracks, raised her brow, and said, "Oh, excuse me . . . I didn't expect company—"

Without hesitation, without blinking a brown eye, Rose Parsons, nodding at Hardy and smiling back at the woman, said, "This is my nephew, Charlie . . . Charlie Parsons. He rode in last night from St. Louis."

Surprised, Hardy gulped once, stood, and made a little bow. Rose said, "This is Mary Ketchum ... I call her Aunt Mary ... lives down below here by the river, one of my good neighbors, always taking care of me."

It's a pleasure, ma'am," said Hardy Gibbs, and he sat back down and stared at his coffee cup. *Charles Parsons? Holy Smokes! Well, why not?*

"I didn't know Jacob had a brother," Mary Ketchum said. "This is a nice surprise."

"Jake's brother passed away when Charlie was a little boy," explained Rose. "One of those unfortunate things ... family never liked to discuss it—"

"My father got shot," piped up Hardy. "Same as Uncle Jake." Then Rose Parsons's eyes widened in surprise.

Mary Ketchum tutted and said, "Such sorrowful happenings in one family. My, my, both brothers going that way."

"Yes," Hardy said, "the Lord works in mysterious ways sometimes."

"Amen, amen," Mary said.

Rose took the basket of peaches, began picking them out one by one, placing them on the table and making some small talk at the same time. She told Mary Ketchum that this was very thoughtful of her.

The other woman replied, "Must have been a premonition, Rose." She looked at Hardy and said, "Your Aunt Rosie makes the best cobbler in Abilene, Charlie. Before this day is over, you'll know what I mean. Cobbler always sets well on a young man's stomach, I allow—leastways, did with all of mine." She took the empty basket, adding, "You have a good visit, now. Rosie needs more visiting around this big place. You know, being alone is a chore in itself. My Fred is on a cane, but he still makes a lot of noise with his clapper-claw." Wagging her head, laughing, she left, calling back, "You ride down and see me one of these days, Rosie. Hear? Good-bye, Charlie. God bless you, son."

As Mary Ketchum's wagon moved away, Hardy Gibbs glanced over at Rose, grinned, and said, "Are you going to make peach cobbler for your nephew, Charlie Parsons?"

"I might." She smiled back. "I might if Charlie milks the two cows this morning."

Shoving back from the table, Hardy said, "That's a fair trade." He went to the window and watched Mary Ketchum swing her buggy back on the dirt road. "That's quite an old gal."

"Yes, she has quite a clapperclaw herself. I'd say before another day or two, everyone around here will know Rosie's nephew from St. Louis is visiting."

"Is this going to be a problem?" asked Hardy.

"Not at all, Charlie," replied Rose. "No, it's probably a blessing for both of us. You aren't Hardy Gibbs, the wanted man, and I'm not Rosie Parsons, the merry widow. Yes, and very likely there won't be too many visitors coming around, knowing you're here."

Hardy Gibbs milked the cows; he went for a ride with Rose down to the stockyards, where he met a few of the boys and the new owner, Sam Blevins. Blevins, a strapping older man in his late forties, told young Charlie Parsons that if he decided to stay in Abilene, a job was waiting for him. Blevins said, "Anyone in the Parsons clan is welcome here. If Rose can't use you up at the farm, by damn, we can down here. . . . Find something to tide you over the winter. If you're riding west across the mountains, it's better to hole up and tackle that trip in the spring. They say the consarned winters over that way are bad ones."

Hardy thanked him. "I'll think about it, Mister Blevins, and I appreciate the offer." But Hardy Gibbs had already thought about it; in his present situation, winter didn't make much difference, for by fall, he envisioned every government wall in Abilene might have his picture on it. This place was just too close to home.

Later, Hardy helped Rose in the garden, a big garden with about every kind of vegetable imaginable in it; he picked and dug, and he pulled weeds. They had a sandwich on the porch, and back in the kitchen, he watched her make peach cobbler. Hardy milked the two cows again that evening, and after a fine supper, he and Rose washed the dishes, then sat on the porch, talked, and waited for the night breeze to come up and blow the heat away. Toward nine o'clock, Rose warmed some water and he took a bath in that big tin tub, and when he pulled the plug, the water went right out through a pipe in the floor. After drying, he wrapped the towel around his middle and went whistling down the hall to Timmy's room. Rose was there, had the lamps lit, and she was removing the big quilt from the bed. Smiling, she said, "You won't be needing this . . . too warm in here. I left you a blanket for early in the morning when it cools off a bit." Folding the quilt, she smiled at him again, and left. Staring around the clean room, Hardy thought she was just like a mother—like he imagined a mother would be, anyhow. Everything was neat as a pin, just like the first night: window open, chair by the bed, blanket folded neatly at the foot of it, one of the lamps nearby, and she had hung his jacket on a peg. Hit boots were set neatly side by side near the door. She had even fluffed his pillows.

Rose Parsons took her bath later, a leisurely one, a very thoughtful and disturbing one. What a terrible quandary she suddenly found herself in, and how could it have happened? Oh, how she had enjoyed the day, every minute of it, from dawn until dusk, just being in the company of this young man, her little nephew, Charlie—his conversation, gentle and disarming, innocently charming. In the period of two nights, regardless of how she had tried to ignore them, she had allowed her thoughts to be solely dominated by Hardy. And to be excited, actually feeling like a young woman, was beyond her comprehension. Yes, Hardy had excited her, put thoughts into her mind that she didn't believe existed anymore, ones she hated to admit. Once, she had laughed at stories about merry widows, exaggerated stories, smutty stories, yet what she was dwelling upon now was no laughing matter. These new thoughts weren't those of a doting aunt, those of befriending a nephew badly in need of help and understanding; they were thoughts of making love with him, how wonderful it might be—if he, of course, entertained such notions himself, and she suspected that he did not. Her continuing, frustrating thoughts were that after two, almost three months, she wanted to be held, caressed, and loved again. She missed Jake; she missed his affection, his loving. She was lonely, and young Hardy Gibbs suddenly had made her aware of how much she really did miss this loving and caring. Good God, he intrigued her, this pleasant, mannerly young man. And coming from the bath that way, his curly brown hair, damp ringlets above his forehead, a wet towel hugging his slender, beautiful body, yes, but not completely hiding everything, his trim, well-proportioned legs, and that large bulge at his crotch. This certainly had caught her eye. Oh, how utterly shameless, the thoughts she entertained about that.

Rose Parsons toweled herself, fluffed her blond hair, turned up the lamp, and stared in the long mirror, turned one way, then another, drew a breath, and held in her stomach; she cupped her breasts. They were full, still beautiful, but a bit of sag there. Her face? She stared at herself; she smiled; she wet her lips and ran her tongue back and forth; she turned and stared at her backside, the gentle curve that disappeared in the crease between her buttocks. Too large? Not really. Jack had called it the "prettiest ass in Abilene."

Hardy—handsome, young Hardy. She was almost old enough to be his mother. Did it really matter? She had nothing to lose and everything to gain, if only she could persuade, entice him, and, my gracious, there was precious little time to be coy about this. Rose Parsons went to her bedroom, worried, wanting, Hardy Gibbs on her anxious mind. She was burning inside.

The next morning, Hardy was up shortly after dawn, and with Aunt Rose still in bed, he went to the pasture, checked on Sundown, then chased the two cows to the barn and milked them. There was a small cellar at the back of the kitchen, a place where Rose stored her canned foods, perishables, and the milk, and this was a good place to take refuge when the violent prairie rollers came swooping in. In this cool place, Hardy poured the milk into a big can, came back up the little stairway, and there was Rose Parsons grinning down at him. The hound, Bud, was there, too, wagging his tail. Rose had on that thin white robe again, but no shoes, and from the way the early morning sun was filtering through the robe, Hardy saw that she didn't have any gown on under it. The way she was standing, hands on her hips, her legs apart, he could clearly see the blurry outline of her crotch.

She said cheerily, "Good morning, Charlie. I never realized you were such a good ranch hand. Sun's barely up. Even made your bed. I went to call you," she hastily added. Turning, she swayed away in front of him back toward the house, her feet a startling white against the dark green dewy grass.

"Woke up early," Hardy said, staring at her backside. She was a slender woman, but one with wide hips and a big bottom—probably, he reckoned, from bearing children, maybe even riding stock. She said she was thirty-eight years young, that's what she said. "Yep, thought I might as well do a chore or two . . . earn my keep around here."

"You don't have to earn your keep," Rose said over her shoulder. "A guest doesn't have to work, but I appreciate the help. One less thing on my mind. You wash up and I'll put some coffee on."

Hardy Gibbs did, and when he came into the kitchen, she was still in bare feet over at the stove, stirring up the fire. The wood was popping in the big black range, and the gray porcelain coffeepot was sitting at the side, still dripping with water. Before long, the drops of water were melting away into steam, some hopping about the stove top in little jigging dance steps. Rose was moving about, back and forth. She had some eggs, she had a big slab of bacon, she had a big loaf of bread. But what she *didn't* have was anything on under that white silk robe.

Carving on the bacon, she said, "What do you have in mind to do today? I have to go into town later . . . pick up a few things, go to the bank. You can come along if you wish. I'd like that. Give you a chance to look over the town, the saloons, the bawdy houses." She laughed, then asked, "You need a few dollars? You running short?"

Hardy Gibbs said, "I have a little left, enough to get by. Besides, I can't take your money. Wouldn't be proper."

"A loan if you need it," she replied. "Pay me back when you're passing through again. It's certainly no trouble. I want you to come back and visit . . . meet my children."

"A bad penny always returns." Hardy grinned. "If I don't get caught around here, maybe I will be back someday. I might have to go into hiding, who knows?"

"I'll hide you, Charlie," Rose Parsons said. "And listen, you're no bad penny." She put aside the knife and gathered up the strips of bacon. After filling the skillet, she wiped her hands thoroughly on a cloth and came over beside him. "You're like a new penny, all shiny and bright. You're good, Hardy, a good man, don't let anyone ever tell you differently. Jake said you and your grandfather were special kind of people. Jake was an excellent judge of people, never misjudged anyone. And after listening to you the past several days, I know the same thing. I'm not wrong, either."

Her hand was on the side of the chair. She was pretty close to him, one bare leg sticking partway out of that robe, a pretty slick leg with just a few little blond hairs glistening on it. She swung herself around and leaned against the table, her bottom against the side of it. "You're smart, too, intelligent," she continued. "This is another good thing about you. When you get where you're going, you'll do well, make no mistake about it. All of this is going to blow over, Hardy, and when it does, and if you still want to go to that big school in Chicago, you drop by here and see your Aunt Rose. I'll see that you get the schooling." She reached over and playfully tousled his hair. "Yes, you're intelligent. You're quite handsome, too. That mustache, when it grows out, will make you dashing." Rose Parsons turned quickly away. She was blushing; she knew it, but she sensed something else. She had stirred Hardy; she had stirred herself, too.

Hardy swallowed hard; the touch of her was a tad exciting, and there wasn't any smell of bacon on her. It was like the smell of roses, prairie roses, maybe, though he had never bent down and smelled one. And when she lowered over that way, reaching out, he saw most of her breasts, full ones, hanging down, sort of jiggling. He thought she must have been some looker when she was younger, like, say, about Julienne's age, probably even had bigger tits than Julienne. He also thought maybe he better cross his legs to try to hide his hardness, or did she really mind? He suddenly had the idea that Aunt Rosie was interested in something more than fixing breakfast, and since he had that old queasy feeling again in his stomach, he thought maybe he was thinking of the same thing. When she turned back to the stove, he saw her touch the sleeve of her robe to her forehead. She was thinking about things, all right.

The coffee started to boil. Rose Parsons turned the bacon, moved it over, and cracked several eggs, and they made that sizzling sound like eggs always do. Maybe Rose Parsons was sizzling, too. Then again, he didn't know all that much about women, especially older women. Maybe older women were different; maybe it was just his damned imagination. Maybe he was getting carried away staring at her nice bottom. Those three weeks on the trail, not talking to any women, young or old, were now beginning to play tricks with his mind, but every time he thought about Julienne, it wasn't about love—it was about her screaming, crying, and carrying on the last time he saw her. That was the worst thing about memories—you always remembered someone the last way you saw them, Julienne crying, his folks, his sister, all sprawled out dead, blood all over the place.

Hardy thought of André, what he had said about Marie Bonet, Micheline's mother, how he wouldn't mind hopping in the bed with her, except she might end up being his mother-in-law. Rose Parsons was the same age as Marie Bonet. Maybe that damned Andy understood women better than he did; maybe older women were just the same as younger women, maybe even better at loving. Hardy Gibbs heard Rose again. ". . . we go to town, I'm going to withdraw an extra hundred from the bank, Hardy. Don't argue about it, I've decided. You take it, pay me back, anytime, but you're going to need a little more than you've got to get across the prairie, up the territories, or wherever you decide to go. Of course, if you want to stay around here for a while, see what turns up, you're welcome. When the children come back, we can fix up the bunkhouse, you know, make it nice, put in a new bed, some curtains, a big rug . . . call you Cousin Charlie."

He sighed. "Until someone comes poking around and calls me Hardy, like that Biddell did. That would be some to-do for you, wouldn't it, trying to explain how you were harboring some criminal . . . a shooter, as you called me. Yes, and after telling old Aunt Mary and all of those fellows down at the yards I'm your nephew. Phew!"

Rose Parsons laughed and came toward him with his victuals. "I never thought much about the consequences," she said, standing close to him. "Like I said, you're a very intelligent young man . . . handsome, too. It makes me get a little confused, I suppose. You know what you have to do, I understand, but it's hard to face reality sometimes, isn't it?"

"Reality can turn damn nasty at times, I know that."

"Sweet, too," she said, winking at him. "You have to think about good things, too; never overlook opportunity, Hardy, the little surprises that come along every now and then."

It had been a long, hot day. Hardy Gibbs couldn't sleep, not because of the penetrating prairie heat sifting into his room, but because he couldn't make up his mind where he was going to ride the next day. And, of course, he kept thinking about Rose Parsons, too, lying in her bed all by her lonesome self. Damn, he had get out of here, though, get moving west. He knew it; so did she. He had that extra hundred she had pressed on him, but before fall set in, he had to cache in on a job somewhere, preferably an obscure somewhere, not Abilene. By now, one of those wanted posters he had been checking along the line might even be circulating, one with his name on it: HARDY GIBBS, WANTED DEAD OR ALIVE. Grandfather Amos had said, "The farthest west, the better, but get out of Missouri and Kansas." Well, here he was still in Kansas and an anxious Rose still wanting him to consider hiring on down at the yards. Yes, and fixing up the bunkhouse, curtains, rugs, and a new bed. A new bed, big enough for two, he supposed.

Hardy watched the bedroom curtains rustle. A little breeze was coming up. He figured it must be getting on next to midnight, and he thought about that pallet on the porch swing. Yes, that little breeze whisking across the porch floor might make the night more tolerable, so he snatched up his blanket, the folded quilt, and one of the pillows, and quietly made his way down the hall, through the parlor, unfastened the latch on the screen door. After a moment, he had his bed arranged where he could stare up at the bright moon and stars. That blanket was of no account, so he put it at the foot of his new bed. Well, he hadn't been stretched out and staring up more than a few minutes when he heard the screen door squeak, and cocking his head, he looked over. There in the shadows he saw Rose. She had on her silk robe. She didn't have any slippers on, again. He could see her bare feet, and those bare feet moved as silently as cat paws right over to the swing. She stood there, part of the moonlight now on her, and that white robe, well, it wasn't cinched up as usual— now it was open right down the front, and just as at breakfast, she didn't have anything on under it.

"You can't sleep, either," she said. "Your mind, it's

buzzing like a bee, I suppose. It's no different with me, Hardy. I had a lot of sleepless nights at first. Finally started getting over them. I heard that's the way it always is. Now you come along and set me to thinking, again. It's difficult to get some things out of your mind. Oh, you do, eventually, then something else always comes along."

Hardy propped himself up on one elbow and tried to see her face, wondered if she were looking sad or smiling. Her dark blond hair was tumbling around her shoulders, but his eyes kept going back to the open robe, her bosom, and she sure didn't seem too concerned about her tits showing, or her pretty legs, either, all bare that way. Tucking the blanket around his naked middle, he asked, "Just what are you thinking?"

"Circumstances," she answered, resting on the swing. "How fate plays games. You and me, how fate comes along, looks down and laughs at us. How we're both in such a lonely fix. It's been awfully lonely around here, even when the children are with me." She moved, leaned down, elbows on her knees, cupped her chin, and said, "What do you think of me, Hardy? An older woman, two years from forty? Do women fade like flowers? Too old?"

"Old? Holy smokes, you don't look old," Hardy Gibbs sputtered. "You're a nice-looking woman, Missus Rose. You surely aren't any faded flower, 'specially . . . 'specially the way you look now."

"You like what you see? . . . Really think I'm nice? . . . Pretty?"

"Can't deny it," he said, swallowing once.

"A woman gets lonely." Rose sighed. "Do you understand? I mean in other ways, too. Do you know what

I've been thinking about? What I need? What I want? You must have sensed it. I noticed this morning. . . ."

Hardy Gibbs sat up. And something else was starting to sit up, too. Clearing his throat, he said, "Yes, I know what you need, Rose."

"Am I too bold?"

"No, I reckon not."

She hesitated, sighed again, and said shakily, "I know this isn't right . . . the best way. It's wrong of me. . . . I'm sorry. Oh, God, perhaps I should go." She knew she wouldn't; she knew Hardy's mind.

"Holy smokes, don't go," Hardy softly protested. "Don't be feeling sorry about it. It's nothing to be ashamed of, either. It's . . . well, it's just natural-like, isn't it? Shoot, I had the same thoughts. Yes, this morning, I was looking . . . thinking about, you know, about us."

"Hardy, my dear Hardy," Rose said softly. "Oh, how I've been waiting to hear you say this." She came slowly forward and extended a hand to Hardy Gibbs. He held it; it was warm, moist. He kissed it. With her other hand, Rose discarded her robe, then came down on her knees beside him. She smelled good. She was trembling, had tears in her eyes, and she sobbed softly. "Oh, how I want to be loved again."

He knew how she felt and he didn't want her crying and feeling so guilty, so he pulled her up close and started brushing a thumb across her cheeks to chase away the tears. Poor damn woman.

She caught her breath and began kissing him all over his face, slowly, and talking in a low voice. "Forgive me, I was so shameless," she confessed. "I just had to try and excite you . . . started thinking how I could man-

age this . . . try not to frighten you . . . make you think
ill of me . . . had to be certain. You know how it is . . .
someone always coming around, looking after me,
wanting to make sure I'm all right. Might walk right in
on us."

Returning her kisses, Hardy agreed. Yep, she surely
was right, wouldn't be too proper if someone came
walking in and found her in bed with her nephew.

She sighed, her hand moving around, and she suddenly whispered, "Goodness! How splendid you are.
Oh, I'm much too bold! My gracious, what you must
think of me."

"A hot loving lady?"

"Yes, yes, oh, yes. I haven't felt this way in ages . . .
haven't thought about anything else but making love
with you all the day long."

Hardy Gibbs mumbled back, "I sort of thought so. It
made a long day for both of us."

Adjusting the pillow under her hips, Rose Parsons
said in a hushed voice, "Yes, this is going to be a very
long night, too. You're going to be my sweet lover,
Hardy, and when I feel like this I'm no lady. I don't in-
tend to let you ever forget your Aunt Rosie. Yes, and
I'm certainly going to change your mind about leaving
this house tomorrow." Moments later, the stillness of
the midnight air was broken by a joyous outcry from
Rose Parsons.

Rose Parsons was right. Hardy Gibbs, fugitive and
lover, did not leave Abilene the next morning; he spent
the early part of it in bed with Rose. The cows had to
wait. He had never known such luxury, such unbridled
yet leisurely loving. How he wished he could have had

such timeless sharing with his wondrous Julienne, and despite the lovely nakedness on the rumpled sheet beside him, he ached inside thinking about it. This night and morning had been a thorough, complete giving of each other. There was a difference, though—with his Julienne it had been true love and loving.

Hardy Gibbs didn't leave Abilene the next day, either. He knew he would soon have to leave—so did Rose Parsons—but they were happy while their lonely but passionate love lasted. Finally, two weeks from the day that he arrived, Hardy Gibbs, alias Charlie Parsons, headed out for the frontier. He was more happy than sad. So was his generous, loving aunt, the Prairie Rose.

FIVE

The Killing
of Brewster Cadwell

As Hardy Gibbs had learned in Sedalia and Lawrence, a livery was the best place in town to hear the latest news and gossip; the train station was the second. Men, mostly old men and drifters, hung around both places, smoking, chewing, and just plain old jawing, and if sometimes they appeared to be sleeping, well, it was the "one-eyed sleep." They never missed much of anything, especially the arrival of strangers. So the first thing Hardy did when he rode into Hays, Kansas, was find a livery and a talkative livery hand who took pride in knowing most everyone's business better than his own. The livery he chose was the bigger of the two, Cordell's. The man to whom he talked wasn't Cordell; it was an old codger by the name of Rafe Standish. By the time Sundown had been unsaddled, curried, and given some oats, Hardy Gibbs had learned the following: The best hotel was the Palace, the one with the fancy women was Dugan's Rooms; Oliphant's and the Palace had good eats. Standish said that if Hardy was looking to latch on with some cow outfit back in the hills, Carp's Saloon was a good place to go. One of the regulars who frequented Carp's in the early evening was Jim Crippen, foreman of the big Carpenter spread, and Crippen knew about all of the other outfits south to Dodge City. More informative and startling: For several years, most of the Carpenter stock had been moving east to Abilene, purchased by a man by the name of Jacob Parsons. Of course, Standish said, some thief had shot Parsons in the back last spring. Just where and to whom the Carpenter cattle were headed in the big fall drive, Standish didn't know. He asked Hardy Gibbs if he were a drover, Hardy replying only when he had to be. Standish laughed at this; next to Indian fighting, working with contrary cows was the worst job in the world, and he said that he had done both.

"I hear tell there aren't any Indians left to fight in these parts," Hardy said, "only up north of here on the high plains."

Surprised, Rafe Standish hiked his brow. "No Injuns!" he exclaimed. "Whoever told you that ain't been riding these parts, then. Why, there's always a few sneaking around, coming up from the Smoky Hills . . . the Arkansas. This is their old stomping grounds, you know: Cheyenne, Pawnee, Arapaho. Sometimes they just up and leave the reservations, looking for the old times. Not many buffalo left around here, though, hide hunters and all, but the Injuns steal a critter now and then. Ranchers been making that new fence these days, quarreling over water rights and such, but the Injuns don't pay no mind. They rip out a post or two, take what they want, and sneak away."

Hardy Gibbs grinned and said, "Well, I suppose if someone came in, took your land, shot all the buffalo, you'd be sneaking around, too, looking for the leavings. I suppose they think they have a right to take some of those critters."

"Humph!" snorted Rafe Standish. "Listen, young feller," he advised, "don't be talking like this down at Carp's place. Likely you won't be getting a job droving. Chasing renegades is part of the job. These ranchers don't like Injuns, not a whit." He gave Hardy a look-over. "Say, what's your name, son?"

"Charlie," Hardy Gibbs answered. "Just call me Charlie."

Smiling, Hardy bundled up his duffel, threw it over his shoulder, and trudged down the street. He rented a room in the Palace Hotel, dusted off his boots, washed up, put on a clean shirt, went downstairs, and had his supper in the dining room. Toward seven o'clock, the time that Rafe Standish told him this man Crippen usually rode in, he went to Carp's Saloon. Carp's didn't look any different than the other small watering holes that Hardy had observed along the way, those dim, smoky domains of the men folk. Whenever possible, he had avoided them. This place surprised him, though; it was already well lit with a dozen lanterns. It was clean, the bar glistened with polish, and it was quiet, only a few men jawing and drinking, another group toward a back corner, playing cards. The bar was well stocked, shiny bottles with slender necks all lined up like soldiers in front of a pretty mirror. Hardy Gibbs didn't drink, couldn't tolerate the stuff; it burned his throat and upset his stomach, and that white lightning Grandfather Amos had stashed away for "medicinal purposes" was the vilest-tasting liquor that he had ever drunk. Amos told him that this was a good thing, the fact that Hardy didn't hanker for liquor; it was a blessing in three ways: Abstinence would save him money, the pain of headaches, and, most important of all, shaky hands. Hardy Gibbs did like wine, though. The grape wine Uncle Paul made was some of the best in the Missouri Valley—leastways, this is what the produce men down at the Central Market proclaimed. They bought every jug of LaBlanc wine that they could get their hands on. So when Hardy Gibbs looked over the long shelf behind the bar, he spotted a large bottle of red wine, and for twenty cents the bartender poured him a glass. He took several sips. It was good, it had a fruity taste to it, but it wasn't as good as the wine his Uncle Paul made. He asked the bartender if one of the men present—and there were not more than a dozen— were Jim Crippen. No, Jim hadn't come in this evening, but it was early; Crippen usually showed up for one or two drinks. He lived at the edge of town, didn't live on the Carpenter place, had a house of his own, a wife, and two children. If business with Jim Crippen was important, Hardy could ride out to the house, probably catch him there if he didn't show up at the saloon.

Hardy said he would wait around for a while, thanked the bartender, and wandered over to the card game to watch the play. Another one of Grandfather Amos's admonitions was about this gambling—he always said that if a man took up gambling right regular, he'd better be good at arithmetic and calculating, play the odds, and not gamble, else he was going to be broke the rest of his life. And Amos said there just weren't that many men around who understood this; they were always bucking the odds, flirting with old lady luck, hoping she'd come along and kiss their ass. That was the nut of what he said, anyhow.

There were six men playing poker, one of them obviously a dealer for the house who asked Hardy if wanted to sit in. Hardy smiled, shook his head, and said, "No, thanks. Cards haven't been running my way lately." He thought this sounded pretty good; he wasn't about to say that he never gambled, tip his own hand that he was in fact a tenderfoot.

Three of the men were older, drifter types; two looked like businessmen, one wearing a fancy tie, and the other had one of those derby hats cocked on the back of his head. The sixth fellow was the dealer. He had on a white shirt and a string tie like the one Hardy owned but seldom wore. For a while, Hardy sipped on his wine and watched. It wasn't until about five minutes later when he moved to the other side to set his empty glass on a table when he noticed the handle on a pistol one of those drifters was wearing. It was poked out resting kind of high in the holster, and right away Hardy could see why—the holster was a tad too short. He wondered why this fool just didn't cut a hole in the bottom and be done with it. It was the second and more studied look that made Hardy's heart take a leap. Even in the poor light, he saw that maple handle and the faint outline of a prairie rose engraved in it. Gibbs felt like going over and slipping that revolver right out, but instead he eased himself up a little closer where he could get a better look.

This didn't make the man wearing the gun too happy, someone standing right behind him staring while he was trying to play stud poker. Turning his head, he frowned up at Hardy Gibbs and said, "If you want to play, boy, get a chair. Don't be looking over my shoulders." It wasn't so much what he said, just the way he said it, more like a gruff order than a polite request.

Well, ever since that terrible mess back home when his brain had exploded, Hardy Gibbs hadn't been quite able to get all the pieces back in place, and instead of backing off, probably going down the street and fetching the law, he did what his quick temper dictated—he reached down and pulled the revolver right out of its holster, stared at it to make sure, then laid it on the table right on top of the man's cards. At the same time he was asking "Where did you get this?" the scruffy drover was saying "What the hell are you doing, boy? Get your goddamned hands off my gun!" He bolted up out of his chair, and it went tumbling to the side.

Hardy Gibbs had to dodge the chair, and retreating toward the wall, he replied, "I don't think it's your gun, mister."

"Well, it's none of your business," the man growled back.

At this point, the dealer half turned, looked back at Hardy, and said, "You shouldn't be interrupting our game, young man. You better get along." Hardy heard a few grumbles from several of the other men, and from the side of his vision, he saw the bartender moving his way, too. So he shouted, "Wait a minute, all of you, dammit, hear me out. That revolver belongs to a fellow down in Abilene by the name of Jake Parsons—"

"Why, you crazy goddamned kid!"

"He was killed more than two months ago . . . shot in the back."

When Hardy Gibbs blurted this out, two of the men quickly shoved their chairs aside and stepped out of the way. The bartender stopped at the end of the bar, too, shouting, "Take it outside. . . . Not in here, by gawd!" But it was too late. The whiskered drifter snatched up the Gibbs .44 and angrily whirled around, pointing it, only to be met with a resounding explosion. The impact snapped his head back like a broken spring, and he crashed on his back directly on the table next to the dealer, who, horrified, gasped and frantically began flicking at several spots of blood and splinters of bone that had spattered his face and white shirt. The drifter had taken the bullet near his left eye, but a small trickle of blood was oozing out one ear and there was a gaping hole in the back of the man's skull. It wasn't a pleasant sight; the blood was turning a little area of the green table into an ugly purple splotch. Hardy Gibbs, feeling weak in the stomach, slumped in a chair at a nearby empty table. Placing his revolver in front of him, he said shakily, "Don't touch him . . . just go fetch a lawman . . . get someone in here, but don't touch him. And don't come near me, either."

No one dared approach, but two men who were at the bar hurried for the door. Another man, one who apparently knew Jacob Parsons, called over to Hardy. "How do you know that's Jake's gun? What if someone else shot Jake and it wasn't old Cad? What if he bought it off someone?"

Hardy Gibbs said, "Now, why would Cad, as you call him, want to shoot me if he didn't steal it from Jake? Why didn't he just say outright where he got it? I know it's Jake's revolver. It's just like mine. . . . Jake Parsons was my uncle."

Piece by piece, the puzzle slowly began to come together in Sheriff Orlan Thomas's office, where, spread out on his cluttered desk, were all of Brewster Cadwell's belongings—the Gibbs .44, Jacob Parsons's initials on it, now badly disfigured by a knife blade, a gold watch with J.S.P. intact, and an assortment of nondescript items, small change, a pocketknife, slips of paper, a pipe, and an empty tobacco pouch. But the damning evidence was the revolver and the gold watch. Hardy Gibbs sat disconsolately to the side, staring out the open door of Orlan Thomas's office and jailhouse, which he thought was better than sitting inside one of those cells staring at iron bars. It turned out that Sheriff Thomas was acquainted with the late Jake Parsons and that Thomas, a man about forty years old, was very understanding, yet also very efficient; he had already sent his deputy to the telegraph office with messages, not only to the sheriff's office in Abilene, but also one to Rose Parsons. Thomas believed Hardy Gibbs's story but was disappointed that he hadn't quietly left the saloon and sought out a lawman. All that Hardy could say to this was that's exactly what he had planned on doing at first, except this Cadwell fellow hadn't given him a chance, and second, he got angry when he saw Uncle Jake's pistol.

Orlan Thomas was tall, dark-eyed, had a fine, well-trimmed mustache, and wore a small drover's hat almost like the one Hardy had on. All through the questioning, he hadn't smiled once, and Hardy thought maybe it was because of his job. Sheriff Thomas didn't have much to smile about, trying to keep the peace, chasing down rustlers and horse thieves, breaking up fights, and jailing ne'er-do-wells. He did manage a smile when Hardy, nodding at the new Colt Frontier

Six on his hip, said objectively, "That thing is too heavy, you know . . . barrel is too short, too."

"Yes," Orlan Thomas agreed, "but I can't afford one of those." He nodded at the Gibbs Special lying on his desk. "Town folk aren't liable to buy a five-hundred-dollar revolver for a fifty-dollar-a-month sheriff." And, staring at Hardy's weapon, he asked, "How did you come by that one?"

"My Uncle Jake bought it."

"I thought so," said Thomas. "What about your holster? . . . Cut down the front that way? You do that?"

It was Hardy Gibbs's turn to grin. Shaking his head, he said, "No, this was Uncle Jake's idea . . . fooling around one day, making like we were gunfighters out by the barn. He thought the barrel was too long. We couldn't do anything about it, so we tried this." He sighed. "Damn good thing I had it this way, isn't it? That fellow already had his gun in his hand when I jerked mine out. Sure surprised me."

"You mean he surprised you," Thomas asked, "or pulling out that revolver so fast surprised you?"

Thoughtfully silent for a moment, Hardy Gibbs finally replied, "Both, I suppose. Practicing is one thing, but shooting a man . . . well, it scares me. I never thought I'd be pulling this thing out to shoot someone." He looked over at Thomas curiously. "Does it rile up your belly when you have to do this? Made me sick."

Orlan Thomas got up from his chair, and with his second grin of the evening, said, "Come on, Charlie, let's go get some coffee."

Well, this surprised Hardy, all right. He got up, though. A cup of coffee sounded mighty good to him, and he said, "You want me to leave my gun belt here?

Am I supposed to be in custody? ... Something like that?"

"Hell, no!" Thomas laughed. "Got yourself a hotel room, don't you? We'll get our coffee, and you can go on back to your room, stay there maybe another day until we get some response on those telegraphs, some confirmation. There's paper out on the killer of Jake, you know."

Hardy Gibbs followed the sheriff out the door. "Yes, my Aunt Rose mentioned something about it when I stopped by a couple of weeks ago."

"She tell you how much?"

"I don't recall," answered Hardy innocently.

"One thousand dollars."

"Whooee!" exclaimed Hardy. "A thousand. Well, I surely would have remembered that."

"With that kind of money, you don't have to worry about hiring on with some outfit," Orlan Thomas said. "Single buck like you can get himself on down to Santa Fe for the winter. Rent some little house and find yourself one of those pretty chiquitas. Sure beats freezing your butt off on the prairie all winter."

"Never even thought of such a thing." Hardy Gibbs smiled.

And, crossing the street, Thomas went on, "Besides being wealthy, your uncle was an honest man, Charlie. A few of the rich ones out here didn't come by their money so honestly. From what I hear, Jake was a hard worker, a good family man. Met his missus, your Aunt Rose, once, too, about a year ago when they came up on the train, cattle business. Right out the same cut, she is, a very gracious lady."

Hardy Gibbs, suddenly feeling warm under the collar, mumbled, "Yes, she certainly is."

The next morning, Hardy slept late, later than usual. New nightly haunts had come visiting, frightful ones holding bloody hands with the other despairing visions dancing down the dark canyons of his mind, dead men with holes in their heads, in the mud, across a green felt table, and he had fought a battle with his pillows until midnight. A knock on the door finally brought him around. In his underwear, and rubbing his head, he wedged the door and cautiously peeked around. It was Orlan Thomas's deputy, a fellow whom he knew only as Clay. Telegraphs had arrived, one for Sheriff Thomas, one for Charlie Parsons, in care of Thomas. The deputy, slipping the message through the door, told Hardy that the bank in Abilene had released the reward money; a draft for it wasn't being wired to the Hays Wells Fargo bank, it was being sent to Sheriff Thomas directly and would arrive on the night train. Clay smiled and said, "Orlan says since you're trapped here another day, come on down to the office and visit if you want." He winked. "I don't think he wants you wandering around town. I hear some folks already are talking about you . . . how fast you whipped your pistol out. Always someone around who thinks he can handle a gun better . . . always friends and relatives of the deceased around, too. They take a different notion about these things—more personal, you know."

"That fellow was a killer . . . a back-shooter."

And then Hardy felt a small chill, along with a brief reflection of horror and brooding anger when Clay revealed that Brewster Cadwell once had been a rider

with Bill Quantrill, that so had his cousin, another re-
puted shooter and robber who lived down at Larned.
"Those old boys still run in packs, all of them kissing
cousins," Clay said.

Hardy Gibbs said glumly, "If he rode with Quantrill,
he deserved what he got." He thanked Clay, quietly
closed the door, carefully checked the chain lock, then
took his telegraph message and went over to the open
window. The white curtains were fluttering; a breeze
was up. A wagon was clattering along the street below,
two soldiers from nearby Fort Hays driving it, and indeed, there were people about, a few gathered in small
knots, laughing and talking, and he didn't doubt for a
moment that some of them were gossiping about him,
maybe some condemning him, too. How was he to
know? He unfolded the piece of paper. It had small
strips of printing pasted on it. It was a short message
and it read:

Charlie. Pleased to hear news. My wonderful young man.
Wish you were here.
  Love,
  Aunt Rose.

After Hardy had reread it, he smiled, sighed with relief, and he wheezed out a "Phew!"

Later, at breakfast, a rotund fellow dressed in a suit
and wearing spectacles came over to Hardy's table and
introduced himself. His name was Henry Burlingame;
he was editor of the Hays weekly newspaper and a cor-
respondent for two New York City publications. He
was also very gracious and mannerly. Would Mister

Parsons kindly oblige him with personal information he could use in a story about the shooting in Carp's Saloon? Burlingame explained that he had already heard several versions of the incident from witnesses, extraordinary versions about Mister Parson's dexterity with a handgun. The journalist said that this was quite rare. He had witnessed incidents of gunfights, had written about a dozen more, and most often the participants were very poor marksmen, sometimes even at close range.

Hardy Gibbs was about to finish up one last biscuit. He even had whipped up some honey and butter together and was ready to spread it. He didn't. He sort of lost his appetite right then and there. He certainly wasn't wanting people to read about him in any newspaper; he didn't think it was proper bragging about how he had killed someone, either. He politely declined Henry Burlingame's request. "I can't tell you any more than what you already know. I'm sorry it happened that way, that's all. Nope, I don't want to say anything more."

"Your dexterity? . . . Nothing? You shot the fellow almost between the eyes! His weapon was already in his hand!"

Hardy gave Burlingame a forlorn stare and said, "A man shouldn't be wearing a sidearm unless he knows how to handle it properly. This is all I have to say. Good day to you." He fished out a dollar, put it by his plate, nodded politely to the writer, and left. His stomach wasn't feeling too good.

When he returned to his room on the second floor, a young woman was busily shaking out one of his pillows. She had clean pillowcases and sheets on the bureau top. She was very polite, too, but she didn't ask any personal questions, only said good morning, calling him Mister Parsons, and asked if he wanted her to stop and come back a little later. No need, he told her. He had only come back to get his hat. He had a few chores to do himself, no sense in interrupting hers. She was a pretty girl, probably no more than fifteen or sixteen. She reminded him of Micheline Bonet when she was about that age, skinny, all wrapped up in a dress too big for her, blonde hair all propped up in a ball on the top of her head with a big pin speared through it. Hardy Gibbs went to the door, hesitated, and looked back at her.

He grinned and said, "What's your name, Miss?"

"Mary Lou."

"Bet you can dance up a regular storm, can't you?"

Mary Lou giggled.

"Good day to you, Mary Lou," Hardy said.

"Good day to you, Mister Parsons."

First, Hardy Gibbs went downstairs and paid another dollar for his room for one more night. He got another polite greeting at the little desk, another smile, and a thank-you from another young woman. A man near the door nodded and said good morning and opened the door. Hardy Gibbs thought all of this was pretty good, all of the attention he was getting. Except for Aunt Rose, no one anywhere along the long trail had paid much mind to him, but he felt a tad uncomfortable about all of this attention, too. Folks had funny streaks in them, for sure, looking up to shooters, men like Jesse and Frank, some of those crazy Daltons. Hardy Gibbs was a tenderfoot, but he knew one thing—too much attention wasn't a good thing, like bees drawn to sweet clover. One bee finds out, and the first thing you know, every damn bee in the country knows. Someone smart comes along and turns Charlie Parsons back into Hardy Gibbs overnight. Being too popular was a good way to get hanged or shot, and he didn't take much to this notion. As soon as that reward money came in, he would sneak out in the black of night.

Hardy went down to the livery to check on Sundown. He received another friendly greeting from Rafe Standish and several other men at the stables. Standish, after his right personal-like "Good morning, Charlie," chuckled once and went on, "Didn't get much of chance to see Jim Crippen, eh? Don't suppose you'll be going cow hunting now."

"I'll be leaving tomorrow," Hardy said. And, recollecting what Orlan Thomas had told him about Santa Fe, he added, "I might go to Santa Fe . . . see about a job down there, a place where it doesn't get so cold."

"Hell, Charlie"—Rafe Standish laughed—"what you want a job for? I hear there's big money on ol' Cad's head. Just ride on down and have yourself some fun."

The other two men laughed at that, one saying, "Shoot fire, son, let 'er rip."

Hardy Gibbs tried to laugh with them, but he didn't think there was anything too funny to laugh about. He smiled, though. "A man can get miserable by himself with nothing to do, you know. I always found working keeps your mind off your worries."

One of the strangers in a big floppy hat said, "What you gotta worry about, wrangler? You're gonna be rich.

Rich man doesn't have worries . . . 'less it'd be too many purty gals."

Hardy Gibbs grunted, and moving on by them into the livery, he said over his shoulder, "That's what my Uncle Jake thought. He didn't have any worries, and that Brewster Cadwell shot him in the back."

He proceeded to give Sundown a good brushing, then led him to the corral and walked him around. What Hardy wanted was a good pasture of green grass, but there wasn't much grass around in the late August prairie heat. He told Standish to fork the greenest hay he had into Sundown's stall, water him, and feed him a few oats that evening. After giving the old man an extra dollar, he left and walked back down the little lane leading into Main Street. He found a good clothing store and bought two new pairs of denim pants, a flannel shirt, and some leather work gloves. He was now well stocked for his journey west to find a new home, maybe that Oregon country, someplace where no one knew Hardy Gibbs or Charlie Parsons.

The rest of the day went slowly; he did visit with Orlan Thomas at the jail that afternoon; he avoided the saloons, had no reason to go to any of them in the first place. He took a hot bath and a long nap, wrote letters to Julienne and Grandfather Amos, and he was just finishing his supper when he heard the whistle of the westbound night train for Denver. It was almost eight o'clock. About fifteen minutes later, there was a knock on his door and he heard Orlan Thomas. "Charlie . . . hey, Charlie, payday! I have a nice fat envelope for you."

With the one hundred Rose had given him and all of the bounty money rolling in, he had made himself sixteen hundred dollars—three times more than a drover made in a whole year! Kicking his fancy boots out of the way, he leaped over to the door, threw it open, and with a broad smile, said, "Come in, Orlan."

Orlan was grinning, too, and standing right beside him was Rose Parsons, all dressed in a pretty suit and matching hat. She, too, was grinning. She reached right up and kissed Hardy on the cheek, saying, "Hello, Charlie."

"Holy smokes, Aunt Rose!"

Orlan Thomas tipped his hat to Rose Parsons, nodded to Hardy, and said, "She thought it would be a surprise, Charlie. . . . Only a half-day ride, and she wanted to thank you personally. See you folks tomorrow."

Rose Parsons had one suitcase; she had rented a room down the hall. Hardy picked up the bag, went down the hall with her. She fitted the key into the lock, opened the door, and they entered. Barely a word had been exchanged. Aunt Rose, smiling up at Hardy, went over and gave the door a kick with one of her pointed shoes. After slipping out of her suit coat, she sailed her hat across the room, turned to Hardy, and said, "Give your Aunt Rosie a big kiss, sweetheart."

It was like old times. Hardy Gibbs didn't leave Hays this night, nor did he sleep in his own bed; he slept in Rose Parsons's room, his dearest Aunt Rosie. Rose was as lonely and passionate as she had been at the big farm. With a pillow under her warm thighs, she moaned under him half the night.

Hardy Gibbs, accompanied by his new friend, Sheriff Orlan Thomas, saw Rose off the next morning on the eastbound train. She would be back home at the big farm in Abilene in plenty of time to relieve Mary Ketchum, her kind neighbor, who was tending the place overnight and caring for the two children, Charlie's "cousins," Timothy and Susan. Sheriff Thomas and Hardy waved as the chugging train pulled out, and Orlan opined that Mrs. Parsons was a fine lady, a very special kind of woman. Hardy Gibbs surely did agree. Thomas also suggested that since the Jake Parsons place was such a heavy burden on his Aunt Rose, perhaps Charlie should consider going back to Abilene instead of Santa Fe and giving her a hand. Hardy told Thomas that he had already given the idea some thought and so had his Aunt Rose, and maybe next spring when the heavy work of plowing and planting came due, he might do this, but for the present—and he grinned sheepishly at Thomas—a trip to Santa Fe was the best suggestion he had ever heard. Maybe there was some pretty señorita down there waiting for him.

Hardy Gibbs had a cup of coffee with Orlan Thomas; he returned to his hotel room, sliced open the letter he had written to Julienne, and added a postscript: "That fellow who tried to shoot me had a bounty on him. Here is five hundred. You put it in the bank and it will make a good nest egg when I find a safe place for us. I write again that I love you. Hardy."

He sighed. And with this done, he made out a new envelope, slipped five one-hundred-dollar bills in it, set his hat straight, adjusted his gun belt, and went directly to the post office. He wasted no time returning to his room. Kicking off his shoes, he stretched out on the bed.

By the time he awoke, dusk was setting in. He washed his face in the bowl on the commode and went down to the dining room, where he had his last meal in Hays. When it was almost dark, he returned to Cordell's Livery, saddled Sundown, and carefully lashed on his belongings. Rafe Standish wasn't around, but over by the corner in the livery there was a small table with scraps of paper scattered about. Hardy Gibbs found a suitable piece, pushed out a cartridge from his gun belt, and with its lead tip scrawled out, "Thanks, Rafe. Heading south. Your friend, Charlie."

Hardy didn't ride south toward Santa Fe; he rode west toward the high plains. No one in his right mind would think of wintering in the territories—at least, this is what Hardy hoped people would think, in case anyone chanced to pick up his trail into Hays. Circling the town, passing the old fort, watching the lanterns light up, and listening to the barks of a few dogs, he headed in the direction of the Northwest Territories.

Riding in on the opposite side of town were three solemn men: Wardell Cadwell, Brevard Cadwell, and John Hartley. They had come to bury their kissing cousin—Brewster—and have a look around.

SIX

The Dead Spittoon

After several nights of riding by dark with only the moon to guide him, Hardy Gibbs came to the little junction town of Oakley, a water stop for the trains running east and west. Adjacent to the water tower was a small station, and below it Hardy saw board fencing and some chutes, all in good repair, and on a side track, three empty cattle cars. There were no critters in sight, and only several people, but cows had been here, and recently. Several piles of fresh manure were right along the railroad tracks. Obviously, someone in the area had one those "spreads," as everyone seemed to call them, because except for the trains taking on water, there didn't seem to be any other reason for anyone building a town at this place. He found out later that roads from all four directions crossed here, that this was the headwaters of the Saline and Solomon rivers, and that to the south were the Smoky Hills and the Arkansas, once the traditional lands of the Southern Cheyenne. Fort Wallace, an outpost built ten years back at the beginning of the Indian wars, was only fifty miles down a trail to the southwest.

At the end of the plank platform, Hardy saw four large piles of hides all bundled and ready for freighting.

They had a bad aroma, like a decaying critter, and they weren't cowhides. They were the hides of buffalo. Hardy Gibbs hadn't seen one buffalo on his journey, and yet here were four piles of hides from dead ones, probably headed to St. Louis. From what Hardy could see as he rode by, they surely weren't fit for robes. That raggedy fur on them wasn't worth a lick.

It was shortly after midday, hot already, and Hardy Gibbs was tired and hungry and needed a good bath. From what he could see of the town, if one dared call it that, finding hot water and some supplies for the trail might be a chore, because there just wasn't much to look at here—one rutted street with about a half dozen buildings, most of them sided with clapboard, a few log houses scattered about. There were only four or five trees in sight, and not a blade of green grass anywhere. Hardy hitched his horse next to the little depot, stepped around several cow pies, and entered the waiting room. The place was deserted, without even a station attendant in the little caged office by the back door leading out to the boarding platform.

Hardy Gibbs turned about and started to head out the way he had come in, and there beside the door was a big wooden board with signs, handbills, and messages tacked all over it, and as he looked them over he discovered a few were advertising for cow hunters, cooks, and mule skinners. Some were advertising for wanted men, too, and as his eyes wandered back and forth, they finally came to rest on a small white sheet that hadn't been there but a day or so, not a fly speck on it, but it bore the name Hardy Gibbs. Emitting a long wheeze, Hardy looked closer. Holy smokes, someone had even tried to draw a picture of him! Well, it was a pretty damn poor one! But the message was clear: "One thousand dollars, dead or alive, Hardy Gibbs, wanted for murder in St. Louis County, Missouri. Contact Laclede Station, County Attorney." Hardy let out another wheeze. That drawing sure as hell didn't resemble him, and he impulsively took out a cartridge, glanced cautiously around, and feeling foolish about it, he quickly rubbed in a mustache on the picture. Still didn't look like him; he ripped the little sheet from the board, folded it, and shoved it in his back pocket.

Nervously whistling a strain of "Tenting on the Old Campground," Hardy Gibbs hastily left the empty station. Holy smokes, he was worth as much as Jesse James! No wonder that Richard Biddell had picked up on his trail so fast.

There was one barn in Oakley. Two men were there, one wearing a leather apron, the other sitting on an empty keg that had been turned upside down. Both of these fellows had their eyes on Hardy as he walked up leading Sundown. The man with the apron tied around his torso nodded. He said howdy; the other man didn't say anything, just spat in the dust, and then stared up indifferently at Hardy. Hardy could see stalls in the barn, a few coils of rope, some harnesses, and part of a stagecoach in the darkness at the back. There was no sign over the building. Even though this place looked like a smithy's shop, it smelled like a livery.

After the fellow in the apron asked Hardy what he was up to, where he coming from, and what he wanted, Hardy explained, and the liveryman, who said his name was Jediah, motioned him into the barn. As Hardy led Sundown to a stall, untied his hot roll, and slipped the bit and saddle, the conversation went back and forth between Jediah and Hardy. The old codger on the keg with the chaw in his mouth didn't say anything. He just listened and frequently spat. Besides learning that north- and southbound stages always changed horses in Oakley, he also found out that the cattle pens and chutes by the depot were new. Anticipating a boom in the cattle market, the railroad people had built them. Several big ranches were now in the country, Jediah told Hardy, motioning to the north and nodding to the west. Colorado country was only forty miles away, only another hundred miles into Denver, and the folks in Denver had a big appetite for beef, especially those miners. The country was growing; Oakley had fifty people and they didn't want to get left behind.

This surprised Hardy Gibbs. Oakley didn't look like it had twenty-five people, and during his long ride from Hays, he hadn't seen a soul—not one cow, buffalo, Indian, or trooper. This "growing" country was about the most lonesome land that Hardy had ridden through since he had fled the Meramec.

The little mercantile that Jediah directed him to was a pleasant surprise. It was well stocked with supplies, dry goods, and almost anything a man traveling the prairie would want. Hardy bought a few more cans of beans, some nigger-heel molasses, coffee, hard biscuits, and a slab of bacon. He also bought a newfangled pannier with straps on it that he could hang over the back of his horse and lash onto his saddlebag. Leaving his purchases behind the counter, he shouldered the rest of his belongings and went two doors up to another small building with a long, shed-like roof. A sign in front simply said, HOTEL. This place, however,

was more like one of those saloons, two swinging
doors, and two windows on each side. As Hardy
walked in, he could see right off that it was more than
a hotel—it was a saloon and a place for eats, as well,
but it didn't have that saloon or eats-place odor. It
smelled like a barnyard. His first thought was that he
should make a quick retreat, go find himself another
place for a bath, but then, from what Jediah told him,
this was the only spot in town where a fellow could get
hot water. And maybe in those rooms in the back the
odor wasn't so bad. He hoped not.

When Hardy Gibbs walked over to the little bar, the
barkeep must have noticed the frown on his face.
The fellow looked like he was eating sour apples, too.
He didn't even say hello or what do you want; he just
stared over toward the corner to the left of the door and
said, "It's them . . . spoiling the place."

Hardy followed the bartender's stare, saw two disheveled men at a table, a bottle and glasses in front of
them. Suspenders were drooping down from their
badly soiled underwear tops, underwear once bright
red but now faded and stained to a yellowish orange
color. One man was almost bald; the other one had
long, scraggly shoulder-length hair. Directly next to his
glass was a pistol, and lodged up against the windowsill
Hardy saw a long rifle, one of those .50-caliber Sharps.
It took him a moment to make a connection—the
hides at the depot, the big freight wagon across the
street with two teams of mules in front of it. Hide
hunters. Well, they smelled exactly like those bundles
stacked up on the freight platform, maybe even worse.

"Worse than a wood pussy," Hardy Gibbs opined,
shaking his head.

"Fixing to take baths," said the man. "Maybe the place will air out after they're cleaned up." He glanced over at Hardy. "You want a drink? Whiskey?"

"Nope," replied Hardy. "I came in for a bath . . . a room for the rest of the day. Been riding at night, a damn sight cooler that way." Peeking over the bar, he asked, "Do you have any wine back there?"

"Used to. Some blackberry wine around here some-where . . . right here it is." And uncorking the bottle, he took a whiff and nodded. "Smells all right." He set up a glass and poured. "My name is Wilson—Will, they call me—Will Hammond."

Hardy Gibbs grinned and said, "I'll put this wine right up close to my nose, Will. Charlie, I'm called."

"I don't like them," Wilson Hammond said, looking over toward the corner, "but I can't chase them out, ei-ther. Got paid for their hides this morning, and they take quick to celebrating. They come in loaded for bear. A few dollars for the bottle, a dollar for a bath, ain't much worth it for the stink they make."

"Troublemakers?"

"Sometimes." He smiled at Hardy Gibbs. "Had a few young drovers in here yesterday . . . bringing in some cows that went out on the rails. They get a snootful, but they don't stink."

Hardy said, "It's your place. If you don't want their business, tell them so. My grandpaw has a business. When a customer comes around he doesn't like, he chases him off."

"Your grandpa doesn't get the likes of those two," re-turned Wilson Hammond.

"They make trouble, get the law down on their butts."

"Law?" Wilson scoffed. "Nearest sheriff around here is back down the rails at Hays. Nearest marshal is down at Dodge City. Hell, that's more'n a two-day ride. There's a few bluecoats still down at Fort Wallace looking out for renegades, not the business of us town folk. No, only law around here is what's on the table over there, a gun, and I don't like getting my place shot up. Ain't worth all that much, but it's all the missus and I have . . . waiting for the boomers to come, maybe settle down."

No constable, no sheriff, no marshal, no law. Hardy Gibbs mulled this over. Under his present circumstances, it was a pleasant thought. At this moment, a young woman came in carrying a basket covered with a white cloth, and one of the hide hunters immediately yowled and made a grab at her skirt. She deftly dodged and kept right on walking and disappeared in the back.

"My daughter," said Wilson. "Lucinda. Oven in the kitchen back there gets too hot, so she bakes the bread at the house."

"Right pretty," commented Hardy Gibbs.

"The missus says it's the breed in her." He chuckled. "My missus is Cheyenne . . . half. Lucinda is a quarter-blood. Don't look much Injun, does she?"

A vision of Julienne LaBlanc suddenly loomed before Hardy's blinking eyes. She was one-quarter Cherokee, and except for those flashing dark eyes and black hair, she didn't look Indian, either. But what was a breed supposed to look like? Red skin? He never had seen a full-blood with red skin. Sort of copper, sometimes, but surely not red. "I have a touch of Cherokee in me. My sweetheart, she's part Cherokee, too."

"You must be from the other side of the big river,

then," Wilson Hammond said. "A few Cherokee are settled down on the reservations now, Kansas and Missouri border, but the old ones where your blood came from never lived around these parts. Met my woman twenty years ago outside of Omaha. She never knew who her ol' man was. Probably some trapper, one of those Frenchies."

Hardy Gibbs grinned. "My sweetheart is half French, too."

"I'll be damned!"

Sipping the last of his wine, Hardy finally said, "About that bath . . . a room?"

Slapping his hands together, Wilson Hammond, said, "Yes, sir, Charlie." He moved to the end of the bar and called his daughter's name. Hammond told her to fix up a room and the tub for Hardy. With a nod and a little smile, Lucinda once again disappeared in the darkness. The fare was two dollars, including supper, and Hardy quickly dug the money from one of his pockets. He had no more than slid the coins across the bar top when one of the hide hunters yelled, "Ho, there, what the hell's going on! That's our hot water we been waiting on. You ain't giving it to that kid there, are you? What you trying to pull on us, anyways?"

Wilson Hammond held up a hand. "Hold on, men," he said quietly. "I didn't think you were ready, having your drinks and all, and this fellow has already paid for a room and a bath. So it's first pay, first served."

"The hell you say!" the bald one grumbled.

But the man with the shaggy hair was bellicose, boisterous. Leaping up from his chair, he shouted, "Bullshit! I ain't taking no second water. I ain't waiting one bit, Mister." Glaring at Hardy Gibbs, he said, "You best get along, boy, or take a seat, let us men get all washed up first. You're a Johnny-come-lately, you are, a little tit-nipper. We been waiting long enough."

"Holy smoke!" Hardy said aside to a startled Wilson Hammond. "They're crazy, getting all excited over a tin tub of water."

"Takes a while to heat the kettles," Wilson returned in a hushed voice. "You want to wait that long? Dammit, no telling what those two might do."

"I can wait," said Hardy Gibbs. And without thinking about what he was saying, or intending to be offensive, he said to the men, "Go ahead, gentlemen, you need that water a lot more than I do. My pleasure, I'll wait."

For one moment it was very quiet. Then the bald man said, "Well, I'll be damned! Now, listen to him, will you! You're asking for a thrashing, talking to your elders like that. You better do as Arlo, here, says—pick up your hot roll, there, and get moving, get the hell out of here."

A little flash of fire suddenly burned Hardy Gibbs behind the neck. Turning, he squared off, staring back at the two hide hunters. The bald man was hitching up his suspenders; the shaggy one was bundling up some clothes on the chair next to him. Aside to Wilson Hammond, Hardy said quietly, "Said you didn't want your place shot up. . . . how about that spittoon can there by that fellow's foot? I'm not letting those two scamps chase me out of here."

Wilson whispered, "You know what you're doing, son?"

"Yep. Getting rid of two skunks who've been stinking up your place." And with that, he called over to the men, "Say, when you get that stuff all picked up, just go on over to the door . . . move out. I'm not going any-where."

"Haw, haw, haw!" the bald one laughed huskily. The scraggly one, Arlo, whirled about, seized the neck of the whiskey bottle, and cursed, "You little sonofabitch—" but that was all he managed to get out between his tobacco-stained lips.

Hardy Gibbs's revolver went off; the spittoon near Arlo's foot bounced two feet in the air, came down, wobbled crazily away, and Hardy's second shot sent it cascading out the door. The bald man, a horrified look in his eyes, collapsed in his chair, and sliding his re-volver back into its holster, Hardy Gibbs leaned back against the bar. "Like I said, this little tit-nipper isn't leaving."

Lowering the bottle, Arlo cursed, "You damn little fool, you coulda shot my foot off! That's a fool stunt if I ever saw one."

Hardy smiled grimly. "Mister, if I had wanted to shoot your foot, I'd have done it. You want me to show you, or do you want to move?"

"Goddammit, he's daft," the bald man said to Arlo. And back to Hardy: "All right, all right, we're moving, but you ain't heard the last of this, boy."

"He's right," snarled Arlo, jerking madly at the cloth-ing, wadding it, angrily shoving it under an arm. Snatching up the revolver on the table, he gave it a hard shove into a badly worn holster. "This ain't over by a long shot."

"That's all right by me," replied Hardy Gibbs. "I'll give you a choice if you want."

"What choice?" the bald one said at the door.

Hardy Gibbs grinned. "You can go out in the street

and wait for me, the both of you, make it over right quick-like, or you can cross the street, get in that wagon, and ride out of town."

"Shit on you!" Arlo cried, turning away. The men crossed the street.

"My God!" a gasping voice came from the hallway. Hardy Gibbs turned his head and there was Lucinda, a hand to her mouth. Another woman, older, eyes wide, was standing beside her; her face was glowing, glowing like shiny copper. He heard a glass clunk on the bar beside his elbow; his wineglass—it was full to the brim.

"Jesus," said Wilson Hammond, "have one on the house, Charlie."

Lucinda and her mother, Blue (called this because Wilson Hammond thought Blue Necklace was too proper), were both very attractive women, and attentive, too. While a thoroughly clean Hardy Gibbs napped in his room, the straw-filled mattress feeling as luxurious as a feather bed, they washed his dirty trail-riding clothes and hung them on a line in back of the hotel to dry. Lucinda also went two doors down to the mercantile, where she retrieved Hardy's pannier and supplies that he had bought earlier in the day. Hardy thought all of this was very kind, and he wanted to pay the women for these chores, but they would have none of it. What Mister Charlie had done, chasing away those smelly hide hunters, was plenty, and with their noses distastefully wrinkled, they both had admitted they were horrified at the thought of those ugly men using the bath. Never had they smelled anything or anyone so bad. And Blue Necklace said if they ever came back, she had already told Will what to do—to shoot that spittoon with his shotgun. This would scare them plenty good.

Hardy Gibbs sat on the front porch in the shade of the plank roof. The bath, the four-hour sleep, and a good supper had revived him. His horse had been watered, well fed, and was now tied to a post in the shade of the building. One of the Overland stages had just rattled away up the dusty road north to McCook with connections to Julesburg, and there was a small haze of dust in the corral next to the stage office where the exchanged horses were rolling and being fed and watered. Hardy didn't see any passengers getting off to make connections with the night train heading into Denver. The depot was still empty, too, but now Hardy understood exactly why—the part-time stationmaster was inside tending bar and jawing with two men. The stationmaster was Wilson Hammond.

The lone street was now deserted, not a resident in sight, not even a boomer coming into town, and Hardy wondered if there ever would be. Lucinda Hammond came out. She was pretty enough to turn a man's head. She had on a clean dress and her hair was tied back and fastened with a beaded leather band, the only thing about her that looked Indian. Lucinda was marrying age, seventeen. Hardy didn't think Oakley was such a good place to fetch a husband. He had told her this when she was folding his clean clothes, but she wasn't too worried. When the boomers started coming, there would be plenty of gentlemen around, and one of the new spreads was only twelve miles up the road. Some of the young drovers were handsome; they didn't have much money, but they were single men, and handsome. Hardy wanted to tell her to keep her legs crossed, but he didn't. Maybe her mother, Blue, had already warned her about young bucks.

Lucinda sat on the bench at the other end. She was staring at the empty street, too, and directly she said, "It's a good thing you been riding at night, Mister Charlie. The trails are like the street . . . lonely. When you ride at night you don't see all of the loneliness."

Hardy Gibbs thoughtfully agreed. "You hear the loneliness out there, though, day or night. The other night down the line I heard howling—coyotes, I suppose, a lonely sound." He grinned. "I'm one of those tenderfoots, you know, can't tell the difference between a coyote and wolf. Might not know the difference if I saw them, either."

"You're joshing," she said, smiling and flashing her dark eyes at him. "You don't look like a tenderfoot. I see them get off the train sometimes. They get out and make a stretch or two, but I see the white in their eyes. They're trying to dust the cinders off themselves, making like everything is all natural, but they're looking around for Indians, desperadoes, or troopers chasing Indians." She giggled. "If that iron horse started moving away and leaving them, they'd likely go crazy with the fright." Her head came down, and she peered over at him. "You don't look anything like a tenderfoot. Father says you're a gunfighter."

Hardy Gibbs's stomach took a small roll. Oh, Lord! He quickly forced a smile, saying, "What a notion! A gunfighter! Holy smokes, do I look like one of those? No one ever said anything like this before. Why, I don't even know what one of those fellows look like. A gunfighter, ha, ha."

"You can't tell by the way they look, Mister Charlie," she said, laughing. "Father has been on the frontier for more than twenty-five years. That's before most white men ever set foot out here . . . before you were even born."

"Before I was a tit-nipper?"

Lucinda Hammond giggled again and said, "You get riled right easy, don't you? Is that what got your dander up this afternoon?"

"Nope," Hardy replied. "It was just the thought of maybe having to take second water. I couldn't abide that."

"Well, I certainly would have heated some more kettles for you," she declared. "Father says in all the time he's been out here, he never saw anyone pull out a pistol as fast as you did."

It was Hardy Gibbs's turn to laugh, and with a little chuckle, he said, "I'll bet he never saw a man kill a spittoon so fast, either."

"He said he never saw a gun like that one," Lucinda went on. "He told us he thought it was some kind of a special thing, that scabbard, too. He never saw anything like that, either."

Hardy Gibbs sighed, then shrugged. He tried to act nonchalant; he wanted to change the subject, maybe get back to how pretty she was, how she could go over to Denver and fetch herself some rich gold miner. He certainly wasn't going to take out his Gibbs Special and explain how it worked and tell her how much a Gibbs was worth. Hardy finally said jokingly, "I practice a lot . . . shooting spittoons. That's called a spittoon fighter, Miss Lucinda."

She laughed again. The conversation turned back to

his direction of travel, up toward the big mountains, and she told him about a good place where he could rest and take care of his horse up on the South Fork of the Republican River; it was on his way. It was an old homestead. The man there was called Curly Robe John, his last name Peltier. His wife had Cheyenne blood. Her name was Blackbird. They used to make fine buffalo robes and boots, but they operated a big farm now. "He likes anyone with French blood . . . anyone with French relatives, or a little Indian blood in them. Mother and I go up there several times a year, and he comes down here about twice a year, too. You stop there and say hello, anyhow."

Hardy Gibbs said if the time was right he would.

About an hour later, dusk set in, and he packed up his belongings, tucked some away in his saddlebag, put the rest in his new pannier, and lashed down the whole of it in back of the saddle. He went back in the little hotel, shook hands with and said good-bye to Wilson Hammond, Blue Necklace, and Lucinda. The women were cleaning the bath and heating more water, probably for the family. Hardy didn't feel much like riding now. He didn't think much of Oakley, but he liked the Hammonds—they were nice people, and except for that ridiculous incident with the hide hunters, his short stay had been a pleasant one. The street was deserted, and he had no qualms about the direction he was riding, north.

He hadn't gone more than a short distance when he heard Lucinda calling out his name. "Mister Charlie, Mister Charlie . . ."

Hardy Gibbs reined up, turned, and she came running up, out of breath. She reached up and handed him a piece of paper.

"Here . . . here," she said. "I found this behind the chair in the bath . . . probably dropped out of your shirt or your britches."

Harby Gibbs gulped once. It was that damn wanted poster with his picture drawn on it. He said lamely, "Thanks . . . thanks, Miss Lucinda. It doesn't amount to much, but thanks."

Lucinda Hammond reached up and grasped the pommel of his saddle. In the dusk, he could see a little smile on her face, her long black eyelashes batting up and down. "Is that you?" she asked. "Or are you looking for him? That picture doesn't look like you. You're more handsome, Mister Charlie."

Hardy Gibbs put his hand over hers. Grinning, he said, "How would you like to make five dollars, Miss Lucinda?"

Her smile widened. She broke into a giggle and shyly pulled back her hand. "I'd rather make a thousand, Mister Charlie."

Still smiling, Hardy Gibbs dismounted, dug into his pocket, and fetched out a five-dollar gold piece. After crumpling the poster, he gave her an unexpected kiss on the lips, and Lucinda gasped, "Mister Charlie!" But before she could say anything else, he pressed the gold piece into one of her hands and the wadded paper in the other. "Here," Hardy said, "save the money for a pretty, and when you wear it, you think of me. Take this piece of paper and throw it in the kitchen fire and don't think of me." He quickly remounted.

Lucinda Hammond, her eyes sparkling like black

gemstones, replied, "I'll throw it in the fire, Hardy Gibbs, but I won't ever forget you . . . not ever."

During the early part of the night, Hardy Gibbs elected to follow the stage road. From what he could determine by observing the North Star, the road most often was heading in that general direction. At times it bent around a few small hills, often coursed along rocky gullies. Hardy was satisfied that he had made the right choice by deciding to follow it, because the prairie wasn't so flat in this particular part of the country. It wasn't so dry, either. He crossed several small creeks and he forded one stream where the water was up to Sundown's hocks. Once, in the middle of the night, he heard several critters bawling. Since he had heard there were a few isolated spreads in the country, he assumed they were cows.

Ultimately, the ruts came to another small river, and in the predawn light, Hardy Gibbs saw a line of big trees along the riverside about a quarter of a mile away. Thinking about some coffee and a little shut-eye, he reined off and walked Sundown toward the trees. It was a good place to camp, all right, plenty of dead branches scattered about, good shade when the sun came up, and at the lower end of the grove, when he looked back upstream, he couldn't see the crossing. Pretty good head of grass along the edge of the water, too, bluestem, enough to fill Sundown's belly, so he unpacked, picketed the horse, and made himself an impromptu camp. Gathering up some wood scraps, Hardy Gibbs also found out he had another fuel source: dried buffalo turds. He had heard Rose Parsons call these turds "chips." When she and Jake had first settled on their place, she said the whole river botton was filled with these chips. Hardy knew these were buffalo chips because they were all humped up and balled in the middle, and he had never seen a cow patty that looked like this, fresh or old. When he had his fire going, he threw on a couple of chips. He was surprised to see that they burned and glowed like a piece of coal, and he knew this is why Rose also called these turds "prairie coal." He had to chuckle to himself. A couple of months back, if anyone had told him that he was going to be out on the frontier burning shit to make his coffee, well, that would have sounded pretty stupid, all right.

It didn't take more than ten minutes for his little pot to come to a boil. He added the coffee, watched it bubble for a minute, then poured in a bit of cold water to settle the grounds. Resting back against the trunk of the big cottonwood, he watched the sun come up. Even with all his troubles, Hardy Gibbs thought it wasn't such a bad world after all. Oh, he was lonely, but shoot fire, a man didn't have to be gambler to kiss Lady Luck's ass. He was a long way from home, didn't exactly know where he was going, but he was alive, and his pockets were jingling. Settling back on his canvas tarp, pulling his blanket up under his chin, he went to sleep.

This was the morning Hardy Gibbs met Willard Colby. In a way, it was kind of funny; in a way it was kind of dangerous, too, or it could have been. It taught him a lesson—just because someplace looks isolated and lonely doesn't mean it is. First off, Hardy thought he was dreaming, hearing music that way, and himself all dressed in white marching up to the Pearly Gates.

It was a dream, all right, but the music wasn't, for sitting there under one of the trees, his horse grazing alongside Sundown by the river, was a young man, his drover's hat perched on the back of his head. Holy smokes, he was playing a mouth organ! Or he was trying to play a mouth organ. Hardy had no idea how long the fellow had been here, but one thing for sure, he had sneaked right up like an Indian without making a sound.

Directly, the music stopped. This fellow slapped the harmonica up against his thigh several times to knock the spit out of it; he grinned over at Hardy and said, "Bet you never heard breakfast music before, did you?"

Shoving his blanket away, Hardy Gibbs replied, "Nope, not music like that. Sounded more like a sick rooster, one with the croup."

"I know," the young man said, "I can't seem to get the hang of this thing."

Hardy stretched, sighed once, and said, "Here, toss it over. Let me show you." The harmonica came sailing over and Hardy handily caught it, whacked it against his own thigh, cupped his hands, and played a tune, "Camp Town Races." After he had finished, he threw the harmonica back, saying, "That's the way you you do it . . . have to fit your tongue over the holes you don't want to play . . . tonguing the harmonica, it's called."

"I'll be!" the man said.

"Just like everything else, it takes practice." Hardy went over behind another tree and began urinating, talking back, asking the drover—for that's what he looked like—how he had managed to sneak up and how long he had been sitting under the tree. The fellow said his name was Willard Colby, said he didn't think Hardy would have heard a herd of buffalo the way he was sawing logs. Hardy introduced himself as Charlie Parsons, and was about to rekindle the fire and heat up the coffee when young Willard Colby said there wasn't any need to do this; if Hardy wanted some coffee, eggs, and fatback, even bread and molasses, he could ride back over that little hill. There was a line cabin, the place from where Willard had ridden looking for stray cows along the river. This was the North Fork of the Solomon. His uncle, Bill Colby, didn't like it when the critters roamed too far—made for too much cow hunting in the fall. Willard didn't know how many cows his uncle had on the range, seven or eight hundred head, maybe more. Willard rode around in his assigned area every day checking things out, looking for signs of rustlers. Always the chance of someone cashing in on another fellow's labor, and there was the Calhoun spread to contend with. It was a neighboring ranch owned by Quincy and Desmond Calhoun, two brothers who were always quarreling with his uncle over water, range, boundary rights, and cattle without brands. Willard said the Calhouns were clever thieves.

Hardy got packed, and Willard said that he might as well get back to the cabin himself—he had been up since dawn and figured it was time for him to eat again, too. It didn't take but about ten or fifteen minutes to reach the cabin. It was set back in a small, sheltered coulee with a few trees around it, but it had a good view of the land below. One could see for miles, and, indeed, there were cows around; Hardy saw fifty or sixty off at a distance feeding on the browning bluestem and buffalo grass.

It was a small cabin with two wooden bunks, one

with Willard's suggans, or quilt, and canvas draped over the hay, the other one vacant. The cabin had a small cooking stove, a table and two chairs, and a few wooden pegs in the wall for hanging clothes. Windows with screens but no glass faced the land to either side. Hardy Gibbs noticed this while they were eating, and he asked, "What do you do about that when winter sets in? I hear when the blizzards come, this country isn't a fit place."

Willard Colby grinned and replied, "I don't stay up here in the winter. No one does. It's crazy enough being a drover. I usually only do this in the summer . . . help out my uncle, get away from town. I'm studying law . . . live in town, Denver, but I'm taking a year off to do some studying on my own. Need more preparation. My father's an attorney, a solicitor." Willard slit open a can of peaches with his knife. "A supply wagon comes up here every week from the ranch, about six miles. Maybe riding at night you passed the ranch, or close by it."

"I heard some cows last night riding up from Oakley."

"Near the ranch, then. You passed it." Spilling out half of the peaches onto Hardy's tin plate, Willard said, "We took some cows over to Oakley three days ago . . . shipped out two carloads on the train."

Hardy Gibbs, spooning into the peaches, smiled over at Willard, saying, "I knew someone shipped some cows. I had to step around what they left behind. I almost had a fight there, too, with two of those buffalo hunters . . . of all things, over a tub of bathwater."

Willard laughed. "That's unusual."

"What," asked Hardy, "fighting with hide hunters?"

"No, them taking baths," replied Willard. "Who won out?"

"I didn't take any second water, I'll tell you that."

"Gadfrey, not fisticuffs!"

"No," replied Hardy with a small smile. "One of them was fat, the other one up over my head. I equalized them. You won't believe this, but I shot a couple of holes in a spittoon." His grin spread. "I suppose that scared the hell out of them. They left."

"Whew!" Willard sighed. "One stout fellow and a tall one? Sounds like those two bounders over on the South Fork a month ago. Either they were drunk or you were fortunate. The tall one, he's Arlo Summerfield. He rustles cows, but no one has been able to catch him at it. Uncle Bill says he's suspected of killing two men, too, but no has been able to prove that, either. Scoundrels, the both of them."

Hardy Gibbs's brow hiked. "Is that so? Well, they just looked like poor white trash, to me. For a fact, they smelled like polecats. Mister Hammond was glad I moved them out. Says the devil always gets his due, the devil in this case being the Indians. He says one of these days some renegades off one of the reservations will get those two. He says all the buffalo in the Panhandle have been killed by hide hunters. I can't say one way or the other, because I haven't seen one of those critters yet, only where they've been."

"The big herds are all above the North Platte," Willard said. "Only a few settlers and still a lot of hostiles about up there. It's no secret, you know, the government's behind it all. Once the government gets rid of the buffalo, the Indians won't have a reason to leave the reservations. There's supposed to be something spiritual about the buffalo, a cultural phenomenon. Kill two birds with one stone. Get rid of the buffalo and destroy the culture at the same time, something like that, a presumption at best."

Pushing his plate to the side, Hardy Gibbs said disgustedly, "That's a stupid idea. I've never heard that before, but it doesn't make sense to me. My grandpaw Amos had a Cherokee wife, half Cherokee. Her people got whomped all over the place, but she never did forget her roots, and she was only half. No, Willard, the only way you can destroy a culture is destroy all of the people, too. That's my mind on it."

"You don't appear to have any Indian in you."

Hardy grinned. "My eyes are dark, aren't they? A little hazel-like."

"What does that prove? My eyes are almost black . . . brown, but almost black. Besides this, your hair is brown."

"I've seen some coloreds with reddish-looking hair," said Hardy Gibbs.

"That's from consorting with whites, too," countered Willard. "And another thing, Charles, you don't have the look of any ranch hand, either."

Hardy Gibbs smiled at his new friend, wondering what he meant by this, if he had suspicions of some kind. "Well, I know what an Indian is supposed to look like," he said. "So, what's a drover—one of these ranch hands—supposed to look like?"

"First thing, your hands," Willard replied. "You don't have a callus on them, not a nick, scratch, burn, or bruise. Second, your clothes. They aren't worn out, torn, or patched. And last, except for that Missouri brogue, you speak adequate English without the necessity of using a curse word every time you open your mouth."

"Did you miss anything?"

"You don't know too much about cattle, either," added Willard. "You don't have any chaps, no decent lariat for roping, and that Morgan, he's too good for stock work, more suited for pleasure riding. You should have a good rifle out in this country. . . . You don't own one. I can't say about that horse pistol you're carrying. I've never seen one of those before." Willard gave the little table a slap and added triumphantly, "No, I don't think I missed much. If I were a true attorney, I might even make a case out of this, but I'm not. Have another year and a half of schooling left."

"What's a drover's favorite cuss word?" asked Hardy.

Willard Colby fell into a little muse and scratched up behind an ear. "I don't know one that a cow hand doesn't use. I've heard words I didn't even know existed, but I suppose 'shit' is the favorite. Shit yes, shit no, shit on you, you're full of shit. A horse isn't a pony, a mare, or a stud, not even a stallion. A horse is simply a shitter, or in more imaginative terms, a brown-assed shitter or a gray-assed shitter, depending upon the color. Sonofabitch, of course, is probably the second favorite word. Anything and everything can be a sonofabitch, even a shitter, a cow, a wagon, a branding iron, a weapon, a shoe, but last of all, another man." Willard smiled across the table at Hardy Gibbs. "We've been talking ever since we left the river. I haven't heard you use either of those words, not once."

"The shit, you say!" Hardy grinned.

"So what are you?" asked Willard. "Or what were you? What do you want to be?"

After a moment's hesitation, Hardy said, "For one thing, I'm lost. I was going to Chicago, Loyola . . . it would be in a few days, now . . . to get some schooling, engineering."

"What! Why, what a coincidence!" exclaimed Willard Colby. "The university? That's where I attend! Gadfrey, what happened?"

"Problems. Very personal." Hardy hesitated. "I don't—"

"No, wait," Willard said, holding up a hand in gentle protest. "Don't talk about it, not if it burdens you, Charles. I'd rather not hear. It's quite obvious it was personal, to give up your study, to abandon such a worthy endeavor, pursuit—"

"Burdens me?" asked Hardy Gibbs, lifting his brow. "It pains me. It hurts. What would you do if someone violated the woman you were going to marry? What would you do?"

Momentarily staring down at his empty plate, then looking back at Hardy, Willard said, "So this is your problem. Well, I would be furious at such a grievous offense. I would have the scoundrel jailed, tried in a court of justice. He would be whipped or hanged."

Hardy Gibbs, without a trace of emotion, said, "I killed him."

Willard Colby enjoyed the company of Hardy Gibbs, and Hardy, feeling secure in this prairie cabin retreat, readily accepted his new friend's invitation to visit for several days. Willard said jokingly, since Hardy was a greenhorn, at least he might learn a little about outriding, something that would stand him in good stead if he needed a job later on. So they began some range riding later that afternoon, discovered a few critters wandering down the Solomon Fork too far, herded them back several miles upriver, stopped at the bankside cottonwood grove where Hardy had bedded down earlier, and proceeded to cool off, taking a swim and continuing their conversation in the water.

A short time later, riding back to the line cabin, Willard came to a halt, put a finger to his lips, then pointed ahead, and Hardy, following the point, saw the heads of a few big birds sticking out of the bluestem and brambles. The closer he looked, the more birds he saw, a flock of at least two dozen, he allowed. Prairie chickens. He had seen some of these birds several times along the trail on the way out. His first encounter was along the Kansas River, when, riding right into a hidden flock, the birds exploded into flight directly in front of Sundown. The horse had bolted, almost throwing Hardy out of the saddle.

"Chickens," whispered Willard, edging his horse back, making a circling motion with his hands. "There's our supper, Charles . . . fried chicken, more palatable than fatback."

Hardy edged Sundown back, too, and he was preparing to dismount, thinking about sneaking up and shooting a couple of the birds, when Willard whispered harshly at him, "No, no! One shot and they'll scatter."

Hardy Gibbs whispered back, "You want birds? I can hit one on the grass . . . catch another one getting up, can't I?"

Tossing Hardy a sour look, Willard said, "Come on, there's a shotgun up at the cabin . . . come back and ground sluice these birds, get ourselves three or four that way."

"That's just extra work," Hardy Gibbs said, and slipping off of Sundown, he drew his revolver—the "horse pistol," as Willard called it—walked up slowly, and pulled down on the first bird he saw. Blam! Feathers flew. So did the rest of the prairie chickens, lumbering up into the late afternoon air like turkeys. Blam, blam! Another chicken folded in the air and crashed, flip-flopping in a death dance, but the remainder of the birds were off and away. Hardy Gibbs turned and gave Willard a hapless shrug. "Held too low on that third one, but two of these things are enough, anyhow. They're pretty big, aren't they?"

"Damn!" wheezed Willard. "By God, not only can you play the harmonica, you can shoot!"

It was the following day, toward noon, that Hardy Gibbs saw his first Indians and working troopers. It wasn't like anything he had envisioned, those bare-chested redmen of the plains riding along majestically, feathers dangling from their hair, lances upright, heading off on a hunt, or maybe to some big ceremony, one of those powwows, as he had heard them called. No, this wasn't an exciting spectacle like that; this was downright pathetic. Up near the river crossing on the way to Oakley, he and Willard were riding along about fifty yards away when a line of soldiers riding two abreast, and a few Indians trailing behind, some mounted, others in two wagons with flapping canvas covers, heaved into sight. He and Willard nudged their horses ahead where they could get a better look. One of the soldiers at the front waved. Willard waved back. The troopers and Indians, however, didn't stop, but kept trotting right on by.

Hardy Gibbs asked, "What's that all about?"

"They're heading back to Hays," Willard Colby said. "Probably runaways . . . out of the Indian territory too long, or unauthorized, hard to say, but the army's taking them home by way of Fort Hays. That's my guess."

Hardy Gibbs stared. What he saw was this long file of soldiers, directly behind them eight Indians riding horses, and behind them three wagons. One of the wagons was filled with supplies wrapped with white canvas: boxes, rations, and camping gear. In the last two wagons there were more Indians, their heads poking out, staring back at him and Willard. Some of them were women and children; none of them looked happy, their mouths all drawn down like stump toads. A few more horses were trotting along loose behind the last two wagons: browns, grays, and paints, all Indian ponies.

As the trailing wagon and group of horses moved by, Hardy said thoughtfully, "Taking them home, eh, Willard? If I were going home, I'd be grinning. They aren't grinning, no, sir. You know what I think? I think this is their home. We're sitting here right smack dab in the middle of it."

Reining around, Willard said, "Perhaps you're right. But if it is their home, they aren't safe in it anymore. That's part of the army's job, Charles, trying to protect them. I hear most of them are friendly. Oh, certainly there are exceptions, but anytime a few Indians of any kind show up, it frightens the wits out of some of the settlers around here, provocations, altercations. It becomes troublesome for everyone concerned. No one understands the other anymore, all because of a batch of poorly written, misunderstood treaties."

"You think they got hog-tied?"

"In a manner of speaking, yes," replied Willard. "That's how the government works, and now it's trying to hog-tie the ranchers, letting all of the sodbusters in, dictating how much range a man can use, making him fence . . . even trying to control the use of the water. One of these days, there's going to be litigation hanging out all over the place like laundry."

"Well, that bodes well for your father," quipped Hardy Gibbs. "Too bad he wasn't here twenty years ago. . . . Indians could have used a good solicitor."

"Perhaps," Willard Colby said, smiling over at Hardy. "You probably could use one, too. Tell you what, Charles, if you ever do go back home and want to face up to that killing charge, you let me know. I'll go to court for you. Won't charge you any fee, either."

Hardy Gibbs nodded appreciatively. "That's surely a kind gesture, Willard."

"What are friends for?"

SEVEN

The Benkelman Shoot-out

Hardy Gibbs stayed at the line cabin three days with young Willard Colby and welded a true friendship; it took him another two days to locate Curly Robe John's big farm on the South Fork of the Republican. Losing his bearing north of Beaver Creek, he wandered too far to the northwest and had to ride down the South Fork four miles before he finally sighted Peltier's spread on a big flat with a line of cottonwood and elm trees bordering it. A few huge golden willows surrounded the big cabin, which had a new addition attached to one side. There were two other buildings: a large log barn and a tall shed sided with shingles, probably a big corn crib. Several fields along the flat below were filled with corn shocks and stubble; there were melons, squash, and pumpkins out there, too, and the sight of this gave Hardy's troubled mind a nostalgic turn. Had there been more trees, bushes, and brambles, a grape arbor, and some milk cows, it would have been as though he were coming home to the Meramec bottom.

Hardy Gibbs got a warm welcome from Curly Robe John Peltier and his wife, Blackbird, a Cheyenne woman who was a good friend of Mrs. Blue Hammond back in Oakley. And, as young Lucinda had predicted, when Curly Robe John learned that Hardy's kin were French-Indian and that Hardy had a touch of Cherokee in his blood, he was immediately accepted as a brother—in this case a son, because Peltier and Blackbird were both in their mid-fifties. Hardy later learned that Curly Robe John, a name bestowed upon him by the Southern Cheyenne, had once lived with them when he was younger, and that during a fight he had killed a man. That fight was over Blackbird; Curly Robe John was banished from the tribe, but he took Blackbird with him for his wife and eventually settled on the South Fork.

During the evening meal, Hardy also learned that Curly Robe was a veteran of the frontier, had trapped in his early days, later became a scout and guide for emigrant trains, and had served as an interpreter for the army. When the buffalo were plentiful, he and Blackbird had fashioned the best robes, coats, and boots west of the Missouri River. John Peltier was born in St. Louis, where his father had been engaged in the early fur trade. Peltier had readily adopted the spiritual beliefs and mysticism of the Cheyenne, who believed in the prophecies handed down by their holy prophets foretelling the coming of the white man. Curly Robe was astute. He wisely filed claim on his homestead, and because of his long friendship with the government, had no trouble in obtaining additional acreage. Curly Robe John and his wife were permanent fixtures on the South Fork of the Republican. It was a lonely place, and a safe place for Hardy Gibbs.

The following morning, Hardy learned that his new host was highly respected and trusted by the Indians, those few who were either on authorized leave from the Indian territory or who had fled and were attempting to go north to the high plains of the Montana and Dakota territories. North of the Geese Going River, there were only a few soldier towns near the newly established reservations for the Lakota, Northern Cheyenne, and Crow, and white settlers were rare in the great valleys of the Powder, Tongue, and Big Horn valleys. However, there was one festering sore that Hardy had already heard about, a notorious illegal gold camp called Deadwood in the Black Hills. White men were crawling about like crazy ants up there, jeopardizing their own safety as well as that of the Lakota—or Sioux, as they were now being called.

Three of the Indians who trusted Curly Robe John and Blackbird showed up early in the morning when Hardy Gibbs was helping John Peltier hitch up a team of mules. The Indians were Cheyenne and were mounted, well packed, and well armed. They pushed four black mules ahead of them. One of the Indians, smiling, holding up a hand in traditional greeting, addressed Curly Robe John, simultaneously talking and making sign. This intrigued Hardy, for in all his time at home, even when he had been a boy and a few of Grandmother Turtle's relatives had visited, he had never seen this sign language. He wondered why they were making these signs, because after a while, John Peltier simply talked back to this fellow in Cheyenne language.

As the Indians unpacked their belongings by the barn, John told Hardy these fellows were heading north; they wanted to sleep in the barn until it was dark because there were soldiers searching for them. When it got dark, they were going to head out, eventually cross the South Fork of the Platte somewhere between Julesburg and old Fort Morgan. The bluecoats didn't like to travel at night. John Peltier, with a wink, said, "Only men who don't want to be seen move like wolves at night, eh?"

Hardy smiled. It was a small jest. Without elaborating or discussing details, he had already told John and Blackbird he was on the run to Oregon and that he was riding by night a good part of the time.

Hardy said to John, "No, if there's a good trail to follow, it just makes sense to ride at night, especially out here. I can't tolerate the heat. My horse doesn't like it too much, either."

"Ah, *oui*." John Peltier smiled, making a little pucker, "I did not think of such a thing."

The three Indians began taking their bundles into the barn, and their horses and the four mules, as though they instinctively knew where to go, began filing off toward the distant pasture down by the river. One of the Indians came out and began trotting along ahead of the stock. His companions soon emerged, too, but they squatted in the shade of the log barn and silently observed. Stringing out the harnesses, Hardy asked, "Where did they get those mules? Strays? Or you think they stole them somewhere along the way?"

With an expressive flourish of his hands, John replied, "No, no, my friend, they did not steal them. They found them, *oui*, out on the range, eh? A wagon, two dead men, buffalo hunters." He chuckled. "They had no use for the dead men. The same for mules, so they bring them to me, a gift. You see, *mon ami*, the bluecoats almost caught them down below. If they catch them with those mules, well, who wants to get blamed for this, rustling mules, eh?"

Hardy Gibbs stood there, a crupper dangling from his hand, staring curiously at Curly Robe John. "Holy smokes!" he finally said, and after a deep breath, he added, "I'll bet those soldiers are the same ones I saw a few days back . . . had a passel of Indians with them, taking them back to the reservation. Those mules . . . I think I saw them, too, at Oakley. There were two hide hunters at the hotel. They had four big black mules just like those." Staring down at the two impassive Indians, Hardy said aside to John Peltier, "If the mules belonged to the hide hunters and these fellows claim they didn't kill the men, who did, do you suppose? Who would do something like this?"

John Peltier, fastening a wooden tree, paused and answered, "Someone who wanted money, not mules, eh? Robbers. My friend, there are many bad men around these days, very big country. They say they saw three riders far away the day after they found the dead ones, eh? They hid from these men. *Oui*, no one is safe, not even a poor hide hunter. Those dead ones, they will rot long before the wagon, and no one will know what happened."

"Well, maybe someone shot those two dirty scamps because they smelled so bad," said Hardy. "They weren't exactly poor, you know. They sold a lot of hides, four bundles. I'll bet they had almost two hundred dollars worth."

Curly Robe John shrugged and grunted. "A man got killed up at Antelope Station last spring. From what I heard, all he had on him was a five-dollar gold piece." He turned and spoke to the Cheyenne again. The third one had returned and was leaning against the barn. After a moment, they all looked at Hardy, nodded, and smiled. One said a few words back to Peltier, who laughed and turned back to Hardy. "I told them what you said, about the soldiers leaving, heading east. They think you are a friend, eh? They make a little joke. They say they don't want your scalp."

Hardy Gibbs didn't see much of a joke in this, but he gamely forced a smile. "Tell them I'm mighty obliged. Tell them I have a touch of Indian in me. That should count a little, you know." He observed the Indians as John Peltier casually talked and finished up with the harnesses. Except for their moccasins and hair, long hair that was parted in the middle and tied at the back of their necks, these Indians were dressed in regular clothing, denim britches, and loose, pullover sack shirts. Two of them owned black broad-brim hats, and only one of the men wore beads around his neck. One thing they all had in common was weaponry. They possessed rifles—two Spencer repeaters and one Henry, both formerly used by the military. When Hardy asked Curly Robe about this, he only laughed. Those rifles were all over the frontier now; everyone owned a rifle, either bought, captured during a raid or fight, or stolen, stolen being the most frequent method of procurement. Cartridges were becoming a problem, though. Since the troopers were now using Winchesters, there wasn't much of a market for the obsolete rifles. Many of the older black-powder cartridges had been on the shelves for ten years or more.

Hardy and John Peltier worked on and off most of the day pulling logs from the bottom, skidding them up to the side of the house, and stacking them where they were handy for sawing. Hardy didn't see anything more of the three Cheyenne until sunset, when Blackbird took them down a pot of stew and some dipping bread. They came out of the barn, carrying bowls and sat together in the fading September sunlight. They weren't eating buffalo and flat cakes; they weren't seated on a robe in front of a painted lodge, surrounded by women and children, the odor of the cooking fire and sweet prairie sage around them. No, they were eating cow, the white man's buffalo; they were sitting in front of an old barn, the aroma of hay and manure around them, and they were staring across the fields of Mother Earth, her face turned upside down. Hardy Gibbs thought the Indians looked pretty damn lonely. Well, he understood part of it. He had lost his home, too.

Hardy awoke the next morning to a familiar odor— bacon and sourdough—and another nostalgic memory suddenly caressed him, one of Adah in her kitchen, her frizzy hair covered with a bandanna, spatula in hand, talking away, flipping his pancakes and thick strips of bacon onto a big white dish, and he was sitting at the table sipping coffee, not only awaiting breakfast, but listening for the rattle of a wagon, anticipating the arrival of his sweet Julienne. The sound, though, was not the rattle of a wagon, but a pattering on the roof. When Hardy rolled out of the bunk and peered outside, the drab, olive-colored landscape had turned into a filmy gray; a mist hung over the river. It was raining. Curly Robe had said at the end of summer, it always rained.

Hardy didn't leave on this day; the whole countryside was socked in, and he knew that riding in the rain all day was as uncomfortable as riding in the prairie heat. However, the three Cheyenne apparently didn't mind the rain. When Hardy, covered by his slicker, went to the outhouse, he saw fresh tracks in the barnyard mud, and he judged that the escaping Indians knew their business. Patrolling troopers and curious white men were unlikely to be about—they didn't like riding in the rain any more than they did riding at night.

The inclement weather was only a minor hindrance to John Peltier. While Hardy sat on the porch, repairing several rifles that Curly Robe had acquired over the years, including a seven-shot Spencer, John and Blackbird harvested a half wagon load of vegetables from one of the fields. Along with some squash and pumpkin, this produce was going down to Benkelman, a small town about twenty miles down the river, a pickup point for freighters running the stage route into McCook. Later, after John had boxed and sacked the produce, he made his tally and figured his income on the load was worth about forty dollars. And, if Hardy had fixed the firing pin on that Spencer, he thought he could get another fifteen dollars for it, thus making the trip very worthwhile. A man could buy a lot of sugar, flour, and coffee for fifty-five dollars, plus some pretty cloth for Blackbird.

By the next morning, only a few patchy clouds were in the sky. It was cool, a fit day for riding, and by nine o'clock, Peltier, with Hardy Gibbs sitting beside him on the wagon, and Sundown trailing behind was on the trail, heading for market. Curly Robe had a big twelve-gauge shotgun cushioned on a blanket directly beside him. This brought about a quick and saddening reflec-

tion to Hardy. Maybe if Andy had carried a shotgun beside him that horrible Saturday afternoon, well, just
maybe everything would have turned out differently.
Yes, if only those boys could have been scared off by a
shotgun, he wouldn't have gone crazy and ended up
killing them.

It took about four hours to get to Benkelman, and to
Hardy Gibbs's notion, Benkelman didn't look much different from Oakley, except that it lacked a railroad station. There were several small buildings, one housing a
general store and post office, another with a TIN SHOP
sign hanging over the door, an implement and tool
store, a hotel-saloon, much like the one in Oakley, and
a freight and market depot where John Peltier and
Hardy were soon unloading the farm produce. John received three dollars less than he had anticipated for his
load, but at the general store he got five dollars more
for the reconditioned Spencer rifle, which probably
had seen its first and only use in the Beecher Island
battle.

Peltier was happy. So after purchasing his staples
and loading them in the wagon, he and Hardy went
into King's Hotel-Saloon to have a farewell drink.
Hardy wanted to make it to Imperial by this night, and
on up to Julesburg the following day, traversing the big
mountains into Oregon before the frigid arctic air came
down from the north country. And if he didn't make it,
he wanted to find a safe place to winter. With almost
five hundred dollars hidden in various places, all the
way from the bottom of his coffee sack to one of his
boots, he considered himself moderately wealthy,
wealthy enough to pay forty dollars a month for room

and board if he had to hole up somewhere along the way.

King's Saloon, unlike Wilson Hammond's at Oakley, had two floors. John Peltier said there were four rooms and a bath on the upper floor. There were only two customers in King's, both strangers to Curly Robe John, but he knew the bartender, a fellow called Corky Joe. After a few words, Corky Joe placed bottles of wine and whiskey and two glasses on the bar. While John and Hardy were tasting their drinks and exchanging talk with the bartender, one of the two strangers left his table, and with a sidelong glance at Hardy mounted the stairs to the rooms on the second floor. The one remaining at the table rested back in his chair and coolly stared, prompting John Peltier to ask Corky Joe if he knew who these men were. The bartender said he didn't recall their names on the register book but they had arrived earlier in the day; they were headed for Julesburg. One of them had asked Corky Joe if anyone riding a black Morgan had stopped by lately. John Peltier, his eyes suddenly shifting nervously, turned and stared anxiously at Hardy Gibbs.

Hardy was turning, too, resting his back flat against the bar, and he said in a low voice to Peltier, "Your Indian friends saw three men riding down below, didn't they? Day after those buffalo hunters were killed? I suppose those scamps did some talking before they shot and robbed. These fellows weren't looking for hide hunters. Those poor devils just got in the way . . . lost their earnings as well as their lives. No, these men are trailing me, John, that's what. Probably stopped at Oakley, too."

"Ah, can you be sure, my friend?" whispered John Peltier.

"I don't know," replied Hardy. "I have a feeling, that's all. You better move over a tad, keep your eyes on that one at the table, and Jesus, John, if he starts to make a move, you holler."

"*Mon Dieu*, there are three of them!" John said. "I better go and get my shotgun."

"No time for that," replied Hardy. There was a clomping as boots echoed hollowly on the stairs, and directly two men appeared, first the one who had been sitting at the table, then another taller, older man, dressed in a vest, white shirt, and black pants. He had a black-handled revolver strapped high on his right hip. The man to his side walked slowly to the opposite end of the bar; the man in the vest took a few steps and stopped in the middle of the room.

Corky Joe whispered harshly, "What the hell is going on?"

Without moving, Hardy Gibbs said, "We'll know in a minute."

With a small smile the tall man spoke. "Finally caught up with the Missouri Morgan and the boy with the silver buckles. Hello, Charlie . . . Hardy."

Hardy wasn't surprised; the surprise had already worn off by the fact that three men had come asking about someone riding a black Morgan. He replied, "If my name is Hardy, what's your name?"

"Name's Wardell . . . Wardell Cadwell. We've never met. You met my cousin down in Hays, though, left him dead and we had to come up and bury him. We're up here to take you home, son."

"Is that so?" Hardy Gibbs said. "Well, I recall that affair in Hays. I recall that Brewster fellow shot Jake Parsons in the back. I recall he tried to shoot me, too. Now, don't tell me you—"

"Charlie Parsons, is it?" The man laughed. "Is this your handle? Let me tell you, boy, Jake never had a brother. Jake was from Boonville, Missouri, same place as the Cadwells. Hell, boy, we all grew up together until the goddamned war came along. We couldn't figure this out. Charlie Parsons. So we took a little trip down to Abilene . . . talked to the widow Parsons, you understand, wondering how in the hell she fit into this thing, vouching for you, her nephew and all. Why, she had this crazy notion we were going to pick on her two kids, so she fessed up right quick."

Hardy Gibbs felt his stomach wrench. Poor Aunt Rose. Those small strings holding his mind intact were beginning to unravel again, and he tried to keep his voice from cracking. "You made a big mistake, Mister Cadwell, bothering that lady—"

"Lady!" Wardell Cadwell snorted, and the man at the end of the bar snickered.

Hardy Gibbs's brain suddenly exploded; so did his Gibbs Special. The first shot hit Wardell Cadwell in the middle of his breast, and he flew backward and staggered once, but before he hit the floor, Hardy whirled and set off a second round, this one at the man at the end of the bar who was frantically pulling at the pistol in his holster. He toppled backward, too, a bullet in his head.

Leaping clear, John Peltier cried out, "*Faites attention!*"

Two more explosions went off simultaneously; the man at the table slumped in his chair and Hardy Gibbs felt the searing burn of a hot poker in his left thigh. The shooter in the chair was coming up, raising his revolver again. Before he could fire it, Hardy Gibbs set off two more rapid shots, and the man jolted back, upset the chair, and collapsed on the floor.

"Holy smokes!" Hardy Gibbs gasped, and grasping his leg, he hopped backward a step and tried to steady himself against the bar. "Damn, John, it hurts like hell." Curly Robe shouted at a wide-eyed Corky Joe, who couldn't believe what he had just witnessed. "Get a chair, *tout suite!*"

Moments later, John Peltier had Hardy's pants cut at the wound, an ugly piece of torn and bleeding flesh high on the inside of Hardy Gibbs's leg, only inches down from his crotch. The bullet had passed through the leg and had spent itself in the wooden bar front.

Corky Joe brought bar cloths, a bottle of whiskey, and a long strip of flannel. He and Curly Robe quickly bandaged the wound and were binding it tightly when four or five of the town folk who had heard all of the shots began to appear in the saloon. They were wandering around, whispering, asking questions, and staring down at the three dead men. Corky Joe told them that the men were killers. There was little use in calling the law; the nearest deputy marshal was forty miles down the trail at McCook. But before the curious had helped Corky Joe drag the bodies outside to the boardwalk, they all knew what had happened. This young Charlie Parsons had killed all three of these men, men who Curly Robe John claimed had bushwhacked and robbed two buffalo hunters several days before.

It seemed to be a truthful story. The dead men weren't destitute. They had over three hundred dollars between them, and further search of their pockets and personals revealed who they were—Wardell Cadwell, Brevard Cadwell, and John Hartley. Hardy said they were part of a roadster gang out of southern Kansas. Additionally, he believed the Cadwell brothers had once ridden with William Quantrill. Since there were no dissenting grunts from the small group, Hardy concluded everyone present was either a Yankee sympathizer or had fought for the Federals.

Someone finally asked what they were going to do with all the money they had found on these men. Turn it over to the deputy when he came up?

Curly Robe John quickly answered this. "No, no," he said. "Put their guns, their belongings on the table, eh? You men take the money . . . *oui*, divide it for the cost of burying these desperadoes."

"We can't do that till the sheriff comes," one said.

John Peltier said, "Well, take the money for making some boxes for them, then."

Everyone stared at Curly Robe John. Then they stared around at each other, and one man finally said, "I think this is a helluva good idea." The rest of the onlookers quickly agreed.

Feeling sick and miserable, his leg thumping away in an agonizing throb, Hardy Gibbs observed most of this in silent awe. Hardy was a killer, John Peltier was a helpful liar, and all of these other people were damn money-hungry crooks. He tried to settle his stomach with another draught of wine. Curly Robe was whispering in his ear—could he ride his horse? Could he ride it only a mile out of town, up the road to Julesburg? Hardy Gibbs didn't know. He thought it would be painful even mounting Sundown.

"You try, eh?" whispered John Peltier. "You let everyone see you ride out of here on that black horse to Julesburg. Other men will be coming here, looking for you, *mon ami*. You make a circle, eh, come back and I meet you up the river road. Then you stretch out in the wagon. Let my woman fix that gash . . . sew it. She knows these things. You hide at Curly Robe John's until you can ride again."

Hardy Gibbs stood, drew a breath, and hobbled to the door. At the door, John Peltier smiled and patted him on the back. "You are a fortunate young rooster. This shot, eh, a little higher, *allons*, maybe the fellow would have turned you into a hen."

EIGHT

Julienne's Recovery

During the weeks that followed the Tinker's Saloon shooting, Julienne LaBlanc, as well as André, looked forward to Micheline Bonet's consoling visits. André, limping about, was recuperating swiftly and was back at his chores. Micheline happily shared in the work at the farm, harvesting garden crops and working in the vineyard. And when the wine making got under way, even Anton and Marie Bonet visited for two days to help with the processing. Understandably, the tragedy of midsummer was never discussed. This was a time of healing; André's limp, his many bruises, were disappearing, but Julienne was a different concern. As everyone knew, mending a wounded heart was a very personal and delicate matter, one that only Julienne herself could resolve, and she had begun this healing in a peculiar way. First, she had Micheline cut her hair.

It was late in August and Julienne had begun riding again, disdaining the wagon, but instead saddling up one of the farm horses and riding up to visit Uncle Amos and Adah. Occasionally she'd detour on the way back for a chat with Micheline and her parents. Micheline Bonet, appalled at this hair-cutting notion, had protested. "I can't do this" she said. "It's crazy. Your hair is beautiful. Why? Where did you get such an idea?"

"The Indians used to do it," replied Julienne. "It was a gesture of grieving for lost husbands ... lost husbands and sweethearts."

"But ... but you're no Indian," protested Micheline. "You're only part, and not much, at that."

"I know, I know," agreed Julienne, "but I want it cut, anyway. I want it cut short, just like Hardy's, so I can part it ... comb it over to the side."

"Ah, but to cut your beautiful hair," moaned Micheline, "no, *je ne peux pas le faire,* no, I can't do it. You'll be like a boy, an urchin of the street."

Despite Micheline's protest, Julienne had persisted, ultimately seating herself on a bench under the big chestnut tree in back of the Bonet house, where Micheline grudgingly trimmed away her long locks. Occasionally, Julienne positioned a hand mirror, turning her head one way, then another, directing the work, and when she finally was satisfied, she smiled up at her dearest friend and said, *"C'est tres joli, Mademoiselle."*

"Mon Dieu." Micheline giggled. "You are quite handsome! I think I could fall in love with you! With a little mustache, you would look just like a man."

Julienne LaBlanc quickly plucked a wisp of fallen hair and placing it above her mouth, she giggled back. *"Violà!"*

This was the beginning of the transformation, a transformation that culminated several days later when Julienne put away her dresses, skirts, and blouses and began variously wearing long pants, bib overalls, shirts, and a jacket that Hardy had left behind. Her brother,

Andy, was amused. Micheline was fascinated, but this blatant display of disguised femininity suited Julienne just fine. If and when she chanced to meet curious people or some of those annoying, resentful quarry workers while she was riding the road or along a trail, she believed they wouldn't recognize her, and if they did, it would give them something more to gossip about.

One morning in early October:

Dearest Julie:

I am safe and as well as can be expected. I hope you received the money I sent from Hays town. What I saved for the road I still have, most of it. It has been my good fortune to meet some kind people. I have continued to make my bed on the prairie when possible. I saw a paper with my name and picture in a town called Oakley. The picture was not very good. My mustache is full-grown now and I wish you could see me and see if you like it. I hoped to be across the Wyoming Territory by now but I was delayed. Some men from Kansas who were relatives of that Cadwell fellow I shot in Hays followed me. I tell you this because I think it will be in the newspaper. They knew my name and were out to get me for revenge and claim reward. This is my notion. I am not happy about it but they are dead and I was shot in the leg. This is nothing to worry about because I am safe and my leg is healing without any infection. I am staying at a farm owned by a man called John Peltier, a real man of the plains. He is true French and was born in St. Louis. His wife is Indian and she is called Blackbird. I may stay here for the winter since this fellow and his wife want me to do this. I cannot ride because of my sore leg. John says if I do leave I should go to Julesburg and take the train west and not ride Sundown anymore. That is how those men followed me, asking about the horse and my boots with the buckles. I took off those damn buckles but I do not want to sell Sundown since he is all I have left of home. If you want to post me a letter you can send it to John Peltier using his name in care of Benkelman station, McCook, Nebraska. Post it downtown and not at Kirkwood. This is safe. No one comes to John's farm except a few Indians who do not like the place they have to live. They are nice fellows. They stay a day or two and leave for the north country. John talks with an accent like Uncle Paul. I wish Uncle Paul and Andy could see this farm and talk with him. He knows a lot about how to grow crops. I look forward to a letter from you with all the news. I miss Grandfather and Adah. I miss you so much I cannot explain it. I always think about you and about how much I love you.

   With all my love, Hardy.

Julienne put the letter on the table and looked across at Adah. Adah had big tears in her eyes as she sat there, her hands clasped to her breast, hanging on every word as Julienne slowly read the letter. This was the third one she had received since Hardy Gibbs fled the Meramec.

Adah, after a long sigh and a brush at her teary eyes, blurted, "Oh, dear Lord, my poor little boy! Oh, sweet charity, God bless him, what's he going to do next?"

Julienne sighed, too. She forced a little smile and said soothingly, "He's all right, Miss Adah, he's all right. One thing he's not going to do is sell his horse. That would break his heart."

"My boy's heart is already broke, Miss Julie, broke when he first came here, broke when he left. It's a regular catchin' sickness . . . everyone gets their heart broke."

Outside the Gibbs house, the maple leaves had already turned yellow, red, and orange, and frost was on the ground. All of the crops at Paul LaBlanc's farm down by the river had been harvested, but LaBlanc and his son, André, were still making a milk and egg run down to the market every second or third day. LaBlanc was selling a little cider, too, and within another month, his grape wine would be ready for jugging. Julienne, however, never went beyond the gunsmith shop anymore, never rode past Quarry Town or Tinker's Saloon, even though a fragile peace had fallen over these places. Hardy Gibbs's rampage, his angry threat to return at any sign of repercussions, had put the fear of God in the troublemakers, those few who were left. And more than a few of the folks in the area, including Constable Shamus O'Leary, believed that Hardy Gibbs was still moving about the Missouri countryside close enough to mete out retribution if he thought it necessary.

These wary people were totally unaware that the young gunfighter Charles Parsons, the one they had read about in several small dispatches out of neighboring Kansas, was one of their own, the killer, Hardy Gibbs. But Amos Gibbs was aware of it, and so was the rest of the Gibbs-LaBlanc clan. The little clan also knew that the Joseph Hollister who had killed Richard Biddell in a shoot-out in nearby Sedalia was Hardy Gibbs; Amos knew it as soon as he had read about the swift shooter. He hadn't been the least bit surprised when a bank draft for five hundred dollars made out to Paul LaBlanc showed up at the post office a week later. But the little group had been stunned and saddened because Hardy's flight west had become so violent. Disbelief turned to rationalization, Julienne leading the way. Her Hardy had been provoked. Had he been guilty of any crime, certainly the law in Kansas would have jailed him. Adah, her big eyes rolling, claimed Hardy didn't have a mean bone in his body. André LaBlanc had been expressively blunt about it—a man was like some poor animal that was always being mistreated. It could only take so much before it was either going to bite, scratch, or kick the shit out of you, and he believed that his cousin had reached the point where he wasn't going to take shit from anyone. Yes, and Uncle Amos shouldn't feel any remorse about teaching Hardy everything about guns and how to shoot them. For a fact, if Hardy didn't know all these things, he'd most likely be as dead as the eight men he had killed.

Adah got up from the table and went over to her stove, where she had some bacon frying. Master Amos, even though he had been dragging his lips a little, never lost his appetite, and he had perked up a bit since Julienne had taken to coming every day or so to help him in the shop. This was Adah's reckoning. Fact was, Julienne had recovered from the summer disaster faster than Master Amos. Took her three weeks before she left the farm and came visiting, another two weeks before she began all that chattering again. Maybe she was close to her old self, but she didn't look it. Adah cried when she saw her little girl. Julienne now looked more like a boy: she was wearing boots and bibs all of the time; she had cut all of that long, beautiful hair, and you could see her ears; her titties didn't stick out anymore; and she always wore one of those big felt hats. For a fact, she looked like Master Hardy's little brother, and sometimes when Adah had those evaluating eyes on her, Julienne looked and acted just like Master Hardy. Adah *knew* that morning about a week ago, when Master Amos was out there with Julie by the barn. Little Julie had one of those pistols in her hand. She was busting up old rusty bean cans, taking to that shooting just like a man. Maybe even Julie didn't know what she was doing, but with Master Hardy gone, she was stepping right in and taking his place. Yas'um, that's exactly what she was doing. What a notion!

Julienne was eating a biscuit with some honey on it. She had some coffee, too, but since she had eaten at the farm, she didn't care for any eggs and bacon. Adah brought over the big blue-speckled coffeepot and refilled Julienne's cup. Julienne was rereading the letter from Hardy, waiting for Uncle Amos to come down to breakfast, and Adah finally said to her, "One of these days, you be getting on the train, Miss Julie, going out to see that boy when he allows it's proper. You just be patient."

"Proper or not," Julienne replied, "I'd go tomorrow, right out to this old farm, this Peltier place, if he asked me. I can read between these lines. He's lonely."

"We're all lonely for that boy," declared Adah, "but you're my child, too, and I ain't going to be letting you get on no train, looking like poor white trash, and your hair that way, short as a possum's back. Best you be thinking about this. Ain't no telling what Master Hardy's going to do next, flipping and flopping around like a doodlebug. You show up looking like this, he's liable to throw you in some big river . . . let one of those Big Mamas gobble you up."

Julienne giggled once, looked around, and said saucily, "I'll bet if I showed up he wouldn't go throwing me in any river, not if I took off these old clothes. He'd throw me in a bed, that's what."

Adah's eyes rolled white and she said, "You hush that talk, hear? Puts grits in your head, and you be doing something foolish and get yourself in a big mess, running away like he did 'afore it's time. Most folks think that ol' train whistle sounds the same, wha-oo, wha-oo, but it ain't so. Has a special sound sometimes, and when it blows for you, Miss Julie, you're going to know it, so best you go on helping Master Amos till you hear the call . . . shoot some of those old bean cans. Yah, yah, yah."

Julienne was a driven young woman. her sustenance was work: work on the farm with her parents and brother, work in Uncle Amos's shop where she was now polishing and helping assemble guns, and on occasion, testing a weapon. She had no time to dwell on the past, that filthy, demeaning afternoon in July when her wonderful summer had suddenly blown away like a tornado in an outburst of violence. She had no time for feminine frivolity, the ruffles, the lace, the ribbons and bows. Despite Adah's gentle chiding, she saw no reason for such vanity. Hardy was gone, and in his absence, however long it was to be, her womanhood had ceased to exist. Besides work, Julienne also found sustenance in Hardy's letters. She read these letters over and over again. As Julienne had told Adah, she read between the lines. Hardy Gibbs's loneliness and love had consumed her, and without him, she had unconsciously but fervently become him.

Those mornings when her father and André went to market, Julienne stayed at the farm with her mother,

Tess, helping with the daily chores. No one was ever
alone at the farm, not since the "Tinker's Affair," as it
had come to be called. There was a loaded shotgun
next to the front door, there was a sign on the fence up
by the road that said KEEP OUT, and there was another
shotgun behind the seat in the wagon. The residue of
the "Tinker's Affair" was resentment and fear on the
part of many in the community. Sentiment had been
divided between those who had applauded Hardy
Gibbs's act of violence and those who had condemned
it. The rash of rumors about his continued presence in
the countryside, particularly after a daring holdup or
bank robbery where the description of the perpetrator
fit Hardy Gibbs, amused some of the area folk, but as
André LaBlanc had wryly commented to his sister, it
scared the shit out of the Irish quarry workers. André
thought that they would be considerably more frightened if they ever found out this gunfighter, Charles
Parsons, or the man who shot Richard Biddell, was actually Hardy Gibbs, and he assumed that sooner or
later, this unfortunately was going to happen. His
cousin, with his unique ability with a handgun, was becoming a plains phenomenon, and one unusually canny
newspaper writer in Hays, Kansas, who had written a
story about the shooting in Carp's Saloon, had gone all
the way out to Benkelman to file another lengthy dispatch. Another story by this man, Henry Burlingame,
had appeared in *Harper's Weekly* under the title of
"Odds, Three to One: The Shooter Wins."

After breakfast with Uncle Amos, Julienne took her
horse over to the barn, slipped its saddle and bridle,
and turned it out to pasture. Her uncle, as usual, was
appreciative of her help. He had several jobs already

near completion, and had received an order from the Pinkerton people for two even smaller versions of the Gibbs Special, .32 calibers. During the past month, Julienne had learned the names of the various precision instruments and tools used by her Uncle Amos, and her dexterity had become invaluable. Amos Gibbs was no longer calling her Julie; he was calling her "partner," and when customers showed up at the shop, he referred to her as "assistant."

Amos Gibbs was in a good mood this morning. He had read the letter that Hardy had sent to Julienne, was aware that his grandson had been wounded, since both news dispatches had mentioned this, but he was now relieved to learn that Hardy was recuperating, that he had found a safe home, however temporary. Shuffling through a few templates, he said to Julienne, "If that man Peltier has an Indian wife, you damn well bet that boy's going to get proper attention. I'm glad he was shot in the leg instead of in the back, that's all. Says he's not happy about that shooting. Well, this is good, too. Shows he has feelings, that he's no troublemaker. When a man starts looking for trouble, he sure as hell is going to find it."

"It seems the other way around," Julienne said. "Trouble seems to go looking for him. That's why Adah says I shouldn't go looking to join him until it's proper. I'd likely cause more trouble." And with a little laugh, she added, "She says I have to wait until I hear the right train whistle, one with a special kind of sound."

Amos Gibbs smiled. "That woman's right. You go gallivanting out there and we'd have two worries on our heads instead of one. You'll just have to wait a piece, wait until he gets over into that Oregon country and settles down and finds some peace of mind. That boy says he's all right. Humph! Truth is, he's still burning inside. That mess up the road set his brain on fire. No, when he finds a good place, one fit for a young woman, he'll be letting us know." Amos cast a sidelong glance at Julienne, grinned, and added, "Can't say you're looking much like a young woman, though."

"Can't say I care to be looking like a young woman," she retorted with a smile of her own. "Micheline says I make a handsome young fellow."

Setting aside one of the templates, Amos Gibbs reached over and picked up a small bundle of drawings. "She and Andy getting any closer to the marrying date?"

"Next spring, maybe. She's hoping I won't leave before then. She wants me in the wedding, standing up there with her."

"Not best man!"

"Uncle Amos!"

Amos Gibbs chuckled and said, "You know, I've been thinking on what I can do for those two youngsters. Andy's a farmer, and Micheline, well, I don't know what she is, but from what your father says, from the way she pitched in and helped out down there after the mess, she knows her onions. 'Course, neither one of 'em can hold a candle to you, partner, way you're catching on here."

"I like it here, Uncle Amos," Julienne said. "It's interesting. It's better than slopping hogs and shucking corn, or turning the handle on that separator."

"Farmer's work is never done."

"You have something on your mind? Something like a wedding gift for them?"

"Yes, that's exactly what I mean," replied Amos, and winking at her, he added, "Sort of a secret right now. Oh, Micheline's father knows. We've kicked the idea around a bit. You being my new assistant, I thought maybe I'd see what you think."

"If I can keep a secret, that is." She smiled. "Of course I can."

Smoothing out the drawings on the table, Amos Gibbs said, "You know the old Watson place? Down the road a few miles, sits in the hollow?"

Julienne LaBlanc suddenly caught her breath. Did she know the old Watson place! She surely did! There wasn't much about the Watson place that she didn't know, except where Emil Watson's head was. She knew every crack in the front room ceiling intimately, and suddenly her mind was awash with memories, both loving and humorous. How many afternoons had it been that she and Hardy had lain there together, staring up, whispering back and forth, making all of those plans? The old Watson place? It gave her goose bumps just thinking about it.

Uncle Amos continued. "Place butts up against your father's property on the upper end."

"Yes, Uncle Amos, I know the place."

"There's a good-sized pond there, always full. Water's downright cool at one end."

Julienne knew this, too.

"You know why?"

She shook her head. No, she had never taken time to think about how cool that water was; she was always in a hurry when she had washed there.

"Lime rock at one end," her uncle explained. "There's a regular spring coming up in that pond. Tap into it and you don't even need a well. Soil is good loam, and in those lower fields, a man can grow about anything he has a notion to. A hundred and sixty acres. Well, I bought it."

Julienne caught her breath again. How wonderful! Yet, how ironic. "You bought it! Bought it for Andy and Micheline! Uncle Amos! Why, this is great!" And she reached up and kissed him on the cheek. "But . . . but that old house?"

"Yes, it's a mess, all right," Amos said. He chuckled and wagged his head. "No ghosts about, but the varmints been using it right regular. Even a big bed of hay in the parlor. That Anton's a funny one . . . said some old bear was making himself a place to bed down for the winter. He's a caution, that man."

Julienne gave a short laugh. "Yes, he certainly is."

"No," Amos Gibbs continued, "we'll most likely make a big shed out of the old house, tear out some of those walls, fix the windows. Make a good shelter for critters. 'Least, this what Anton figures. We took a ride down there Sunday, had us a picnic basket, did some jawing, figured out most of it. Looks like we need a house."

"A new house!" exclaimed Julienne. "Oh, gourds, Micheline will faint away when she hears this! She'll just simply swoon!"

Holding up a warning finger, Amos said, "Wait a minute, now—a secret, remember? We own the property, but if there's no wedding, there's no house to put on it."

"Why . . . why, that sounds almost like an arrangement, a temptation, like you and Mister Bonet are conniving, trying to be matchmakers. Why, I declare,

Uncle Amos, you wouldn't do a thing like that, would you?" Amos Gibbs chuckled, and Julienne, breaking out in a smile, slowly nodded, "Yes, oh, yes, you would."

"I reckon, then, you approve of this, maybe want to start talking to Micheline about the wedding party, her dress, all of those things . . . around Christmas time, maybe start letting your hair grow long?"

"Yes, I approve," replied Julienne. "And what's more, I'll do anything you wish, even let my hair grow again."

"Good. Then it's settled." And placing one of the papers flat on the table, Amos Gibbs said, "Now let's get down to this business." He smoothed the paper with the flat of his hand. "Look here, partner, you see this? Specifications. Specs on the thirty-two-caliber for Pinkerton."

Julienne studied the various configurations on the thin drawing paper, the many notations carefully printed with ink, the delicate curvature of lines, and all of those minute measurements. She understood very little of what she was seeing, but she said authoritatively, "This weapon doesn't pack much wallop, Uncle Amos. It's a lightweight. It won't knock over a stump."

"Humph, not only do you look like your cousin, you're talking like him. Pay attention, now."

Julienne reached up and gave her uncle a quick peck on the cheek. "I'm sorry, that's just what Hardy said about this revolver."

"Well, the boy's right," Amos said. "Compared to the forty-four or forty-five, it is a lightweight, but let me tell you something, if a bullet with a soft nose and maybe a little hole drilled down the middle of it catches a man in the proper place, it usually gets the same results. Of course, with a four-inch barrel, it doesn't get you much for accuracy." Tracing a finger up near the top of the paper, he went on. "What we want to do is extend the barrel here two inches, taper it accordingly, and match it to one of the patterns over there on the shelf."

Julienne looked up at her uncle. "Those Pinkertons want a six-inch now? Hardy said you made it four because they wanted something compact to hide up under their coats in one of those shoulder holsters."

"That's what the Pinkerton people wanted," Amos replied. "That's exactly what they got, and they're going to get two more." He paused, smiled, then said, "You see, partner, we're going to make three of these things, only one is going to have a six-inch barrel, more fit for some fancy shooting, fit weight for a woman. You think you can rule out and modify this drawing? Make a pattern, get the taper right?"

"I'll surely try."

"Have to be damn precise."

"Yes, of course." She gave him a questioning look. "Some woman wants one of these? You have a buyer?"

"No." Amos Gibbs grinned, and reaching over, he gently tousled her short hair. "No, this is for a special little boy, one I used to call my favorite niece, something easy to handle. We're going to make this weapon for you. Say it's your wages, something like that."

Julienne was stunned, and she slumped down in her chair, her eyes suddenly glassy, her heart joyful. She hadn't felt this way since the night before the dance at the Buxton School when she had displayed her new wardrobe for her admiring mother and father, when she had gaily laughed and swirled around the front room on her toes. This was no ordinary gift, one that any other woman would appreciate, or even understand. Hardy Gibbs would understand the significance of this. Julienne took her uncle by the hand. She said, "I love you, Uncle Amos. You always make me feel so special."

Amos Gibbs smiled fondly back at her. He said, "Well, child, I reckon this is because you are special."

Constable Shamus O'Leary was hearing rumors again, that the young killer Hardy Gibbs was about, had come up from the Ozarks, where he had last been seen, that he was visiting his kinfolk, hiding about somewhere in the woods near Kirkwood Town. There was no mistake about it. Sean Laughlin had seen him riding on the lower road toward the Meramec. Constable O'Leary was a dedicated law officer, but for four months these persisting rumors had turned out to be elusive shadows, and he had done nothing more than chase them around in hopeless circles. Shamus didn't doubt old man Laughlin's report; several other people had seen some mysterious happenings, too, so the reported sighting seemed credible. The fact that old man Laughlin had notoriously bad eyesight didn't deter the constable; he and his deputy, Michael Higgins, hitched up a buggy and began taking a few evening rides, for ever since the day that Hardy Gibbs had ridden away in broad daylight, eluding Shamus and his deputized "shoot to kill" posse, the constable had been obsessed with capturing the young man.

Shamus O'Leary wore a derby, was short, rotund, had a florid face, and was addicted to cigars. He always had a stogie tucked in the corner of his mouth; he had a habit of spitting shreds of it to the side while he was talking. Adah claimed that Shamus had spat on her porch that terrible afternoon when he and some of the posse came looking for Master Hardy. She later confessed to Amos that she had shaken her broomstick at Shamus. She had told him to stop that spitting; no, she didn't know exactly where Amos and Hardy were, probably riding down to the train station; no, he couldn't come in her house and go poking around. So it wasn't until this late autumn afternoon that Shamus O'Leary, despite his lawful authority, dared venture back to the Amos Gibbs property, and of all people whom he didn't want to meet, there was big Adah Gibbs standing on the porch, hands on her hips, a deep frown on her face, waiting to greet him. Shamus O'Leary tipped his derby and asked if Amos were about. Adah, guarding her porch, said nothing, simply pointed back to the gunsmith shop, and Shamus and Michael Higgins made a peaceful retreat.

The constable's visit was brief. While he talked to Amos, his deputy casually strolled around, looked over the pasture, examining the barn; spotting several bullet-riddled cans, he pointed his finger at one and got off an imaginary shot. This was the extent of the visit, Shamus O'Leary learning no more than what he already knew—he wasn't welcome. When the two men were well away from the house, Shamus removed his cigar, spat once, and said, "Shit." He directed Michael Higgins to drive toward the lower road, and eventually they approached the forks, one leading to the tiny community of Quarry Town, the other twisting its way across the golden farmland and on down to the river bottom. Since this was the area where Sean Laughlin had seen Hardy Gibbs, the two men followed the farm road to the right; Quarry Town, with all of its hostility, was out of the question.

Chomping on his cigar butt, Shamus O'Leary was dwelling on the thought of riding over to the Paul LaBlanc farm, which was now about three miles away, but with an eye on the lowering sun, he decided it would be too dark to see anything by the time he and Michael Higgins made their return trip. So at the lane leading down to Emil Watson's abandoned farm, he ordered the deputy to swing the buggy around. As they were making the turn, Shamus O'Leary, leaning out to spit, suddenly called "Whoa" and pointed to the ground. Tracks, fresh tracks—and leaping down, he began examining them. Unusual, yes, very interesting; a wagon had been in and out of the place. A separate set of tracks also indicated that someone had ridden a horse in and out of the property, too.

"Now, Mike," Shamus finally said, "what are y'supposing this is all about? Who'd be taking this road to the old shanty below, and why? Do y'have a notion on such a thing?"

"A hidden spot, it is," replied Michael Higgins, "but it's not the season for gathering greens or picking blackberries."

"Aye," agreed Shamus. " 'Tis the season for hiding, though, so best we go and do a little investigating, eh?"

And so they did, winding their way down through the weeds and brambles until they came to a grassy clearing where the old house stood, silently framed by the towering oaks. It was very quiet; a few leaves were falling, and a sudden clatter below brought the men anxiously whirling about. A flight of startled ducks lifting into the air above the pond quickly became silhouettes against the dying sun, and Shamus said sheepishly, "The place is haunted, y'know. Y'can'na shoot a ghost."

Michael Higgins replied morosely, "I don't believe in 'em."

Shamus O'Leary, nervously mouthing his stubby cigar, slowly pushed the front door partially open and shifted his eyes back and forth across the empty room. He was surprised. The litter and debris that he had expected to encounter in such an aged and abandoned house wasn't there. Although splintered and badly warped in places, the floor was immaculately swept— except for that place in the far corner. Shamus O'Leary, stepping carefully, Deputy Higgins directly behind him, walked over, stared down at the pile of hay, then said in a hushed voice, "By God, Mike, someone has bedded down here! Do y'think . . . could it be possible . . .?"

In a whisper, Michael Higgins whispered back, "Aye, 'tis possible. If the lad has been about, aye, he could have slept here a night or two."

Nodding toward the little hallway, Constable O'Leary moved on, once again followed by Michael Higgins. The next two rooms were what Shamus had initially expected, the floors covered with trash, broken glass, and the droppings of varmints. The men continued on. They forced open the door leading into the kitchen, where they abruptly stopped and shared stares of surprises. The kitchen was as clean as the parlor, and it had been recently used, too, for there on the big round table was a shiny tin plate with two forks on it. While Michael Higgins carefully inspected the utensils, Shamus wandered over to the stove, and, lifting one of the round lids, lowered his head and sniffed, then reached down and plucked out a bone, then another. Holding them forth, he exclaimed, "Hah, look at this, Mike! Here we have it! If it's the lad, someone's been feeding him, eh? Chicken bones, aye, and there's more of 'em in there." He pointed to the side of the stove where a few broken boards and branches were neatly stacked. "Had a bit of fire, so it seems, everything nice and cozy, the lad sitting here on the stool, his accomplice on the box, eating biscuits, chicken."

"Biscuits?" asked Michael Higgins curiously. "How would you be knowing this? The table is as clean as a whistle, not a crumb on it, not a crust on the floor."

"Mice," Shamus said. "Aye, the mice, they always come in to clean up, eh?"

"Mice leave little turds, Shamus."

Constable O'Leary wheezed out a sigh of exasperation. "I'm only supposing, Mike, trying to piece this thing together."

"Ah, a bit of sleuthing. Yes, I see." Two empty bottles were on a nearby windowsill, and taking up one and sniffing, Higgins asked, "How do we know it was young Hardy? It could be some of the quarry lads drinking, eating, sporting one of the lasses on the sly."

Shamus huffed. "Because the lads are always talking, that's why. There's never a secret among them. We would have heard of it, wouldn't we?" He rapped one of the bones on the boarded window. "Boarded from the inside, it is," he said. "Now, I ask you, would one of the lads do this?"

"If he was up to mischief, he might."

"Hah, well there y'are, my boy!" exclaimed Shamus. "Why should they be coming up here to do mischief when there's all those places below, and the old shanties in back of Tinker's? Now, I ask y'that? No, I tell you, this is a hideout, I'm thinking, and we'll have to keep our eyes on the place for a night or two."

Heading out the back door, Michael Higgins said, "I'll not be liking that, Shamus."

Shamus O'Leary heartily cackled, "Ghosts? You were telling me you didn't believe in 'em."

"They don't come in the light of day."

"Aye, but if old Emil is still looking for his head, I can'na believe he would be looking for it in the dark of night, either."

Julienne had come out of the tool room just as Shamus O'Leary and Michael Higgins were getting back into their buggy near the front office, but it took her only one glimpse to recognize the fat form of the constable and that black derby perched on his head. Uncle Amos had pretended nonchalance, chuckled when he told her that Shamus was hot on the trail of Hardy, that the constable had received fresh reports that young Gibbs was once again in the vicinity. Julienne, however, knew her uncle was irritated by O'Leary's visit. His face was red; it always glowed when he was angry or deeply annoyed, and even though she shared this resentment of Shamus O'Leary, she had given Uncle Amos a consoling hug, dismissing the constable as a fat buffoon with a brain the size of a goober. This had brought a genuine chuckle from her uncle, and a short time later, after promising to return the next morning, she had saddled up and ridden away in the late afternoon sun toward home.

Julienne, her spirit rejuvenated by the exciting revelations of her uncle—the purchase of the Emil Watson homestead and the impending tooling of her very own revolver brushed away the annoying thoughts of the afternoon visit of Shamus. She didn't want that buffoon intruding in her happy new thoughts; she wanted nothing to disturb the small resurrection that was beginning to mend her shattered soul. Oh, the winter was going to be a long one, but she had much for which to be thankful, the promising future ahead—working with Uncle Amos, the wedding of André and Micheline, and last, but most wonderful of all, a reunion with Hardy in the summer, summertime in the hills of the Oregon country. Gradually, however slowly, she was washing away the dirtiness of Jimmy McGee. No, she wasn't a whole woman, not quite, but she was going to make it; she was on her way. Oh, Lordy, how she missed her Hardy, how she loved him.

In the excitement of the afternoon, Julienne hadn't paid any attention to the direction taken by Shamus O'Leary and his deputy when they left the gunshop office. She didn't really care. Good riddance. She wasn't even thinking about him when she turned off at the forks and headed down the long, winding farm road. She just pulled down her slouchy hat against the setting sun and let the gray mare trot for home. She was at ease with herself, enjoying her little private world, at ease in the saddle, too, until she saw this familiar black buggy swing out of the lane at the old Watson place. It immediately struck her—that idiot O'Leary! He had been snooping around the old homestead, too! It was Shamus, all right. She could see his black derby, the broad-brim hat of his deputy, too, and then suddenly the horse pulling their buggy reared. It shied and the two men hurriedly leaped out. Horrors upon horrors, the deputy fell, and there was a resounding blast. She knew the sound of a shotgun, a *whoom*, not the sharp *blam* of a rifle or pistol, and she could only assume that the deputy, in his fall, had accidentally discharged his weapon. Julienne had no time to dwell on the accident, even why the two men were scrambling for the ditch along the road. Their horse, panicked by the blast in back of it, was pounding down the road directly toward her, the buggy lurching wildly back and forth close to capsizing. Julienne reined quickly to the side as the horse and buggy went hurtling by.

And then she was startled by a shout from down the road. She couldn't see the men, because to her amazement they were hiding in the ditches to either side of the road. "Get off that horse," one commanded. "Get off and put your arms in the air!"

Julienne LaBlanc, stunned and horrified, thought, *My God, has Shamus gone mad!* Now she could make out the forms in the barrow pits; she saw the muzzle of the shotgun poking out of the weeds, and there was O'Leary's black derby stuck up like a fat toadstool above a big rock. Lord, Lord, what was happening here? These men were crazy, and anger slowly began to supplant her horror and fear. But she did as ordered. She dismounted and put her arms up and shouted, "What the hell's the matter with you, Mister O'Leary? You quit pointing those guns at me, you damn fools."

A voice called out, "Hardy Gibbs? Is that you m'lad? You come forward now. . . ."

Hardy Gibbs! Julienne thrust out her head and angrily cried, "I'm not Hardy Gibbs. Can't you see? Look!" And she carefully reached down with one hand

and lifted off her hat. "I'm Julienne LaBlánc. I'm Hardy's cousin from down on the river, Julienne LaBlanc."

At this alarming disclosure—at least alarming to Shamus O'Leary and Michael Higgins—Julienne saw two dark forms slowly emerging from the weeds. The black derby hat swung down off Constable O'Leary's head, and she clearly heard the whack of it as the rotund Irishman smacked it against his fat thigh. Lowering her arms, Julienne grasped the reins of her big mare and strode angrily forward in unleashed fury. "Of all the stupid . . ." she sputtered. "You dumb bastards, you crazy fools, you could have shot me. I can't believe this! Jesus, if I'm Hardy Gibbs you two buffoons are Jesse and Frank."

Shamus O'Leary, waving his derby frantically, said, "Now, wait. Wait, you'll be hearing me out, Miss Julienne—"

"The hell I will!" she cried.

Michael Higgins got in one sentence, saying lamely, "Your cousin's been staying down in the shanty below. We thought—"

"Found his leavings there, we did," O'Leary interrupted. "Bones. Someone's been feeding him chicken, biscuits."

"Oh, you fools!" Julienne screamed. "You stupid fools! My uncle bought this property a week ago. He and Anton Bonet spent most of last Sunday down there making plans to fix up the place, checking the water, making plans to build. If you found chicken bones, they were from the basket Adah fixed for them before they left. Oh, you stupid men! Wait until this story gets around!"

Shamus O'Leary gave her a helpless shrug. "I'm sorry, Miss Julienne, you looked like young Hardy."

Shoving a boot into her stirrup, Julienne hissed, "Hardy, Hardy, Hardy! That's all you're thinking about. Well, forget it. My cousin isn't within five hundred miles of these parts." Dark eyes sparking, she stared down at Shamus O'Leary. "When he hears about this, he may be. He'll probably come looking for you."

As Julienne reined around, O'Leary gave her an imploring look and said, "Would it be asking too much if you'd kindly go down the road a piece? See if you can fetch my horse . . . the buggy?"

Giving her mare a nudge forward, Julienne replied, "Lordy, Mister Shamus, you are crazy!"

NINE

The Oakley Shoot-out

A blustery March along the plains bordering the Rockies gave way to the warming westerlies of April, melting the snow and bringing a renewal of life to the land. Hardy Gibbs stirred with it. The long winter was over.

My dearest Julie:

John came back from Benkelman late this day with surprises for me. He brought two letters from you and one from grandfather. I have read them several times and it is hard to describe how much they please me. I am happy to know you received the beads. They are real Cheyenne beads made especially for you by Blackbird. She says they will be good medicine. She also made me a string but I do not feel comfortable wearing them. I think they are better for a woman so I will save them for you. I surely would like to see your new revolver. It does not surprise me you are becoming a good shot. Amos is a good teacher. I truly wish you'll never have to use the revolver on any of the quarry trash. I have discovered there is a big difference between shooting targets and people. It is not a pleasant thing to kill a man, even if he deserves it. I must tell you in all honesty it makes me sick. The weather is getting better and I have helped John plow two fields. Blackbird is ready to sow. As for myself, I am fine. John gave me one of the mules to use as a pack animal and I plan on leaving soon. John thinks I should take the train west up at Cheyenne but I cannot abide the thought of leaving my horse and not having him when I find a good place for us. You are always in my thoughts. I wish I could be there for the wedding and have a drink of Uncle Paul's wine with Andy. I will write when I get up the line a way. I still have plenty of money. Show this to Grandfather and Adah and tell them not to worry.

Love again, Hardy.

The corn was planted, and Blackbird, her hair decorated with a few dried husks and carrying a handful of kernels, moved along between rows, singing her song, praying to the Great Mystery to bless her fertile fields. Curly Robe John followed, carrying a long pipe decorated with strips of fur and a few feathers, and he was humming. Hardy walked along behind them; he didn't understand what Blackbird was singing, sort of a *hey-yah, hey-yah* sounding song, up and down the scale, and he would have felt foolish trying to hum as John was doing. He would have felt more foolish trying to accompany Blackbird with his harmonica that Willard Colby had given him, although he had played it off and on all winter, occasionally when Blackbird was singing one of her Cheyenne melodies. He knew what this corn-planting ceremony was all about, and since he had become part of the family during his lengthy stay at the farm, participating in it expressed only a small part of the gratitude he owed these two good friends.

Curly Robe John told him that Blackbird always did this, first when the corn was planted and again when the corn was harvested. Although the Cheyenne hadn't planted crops for many years, she wanted to remember and celebrate the customs. The old ones, before they came across the Big Mother River, revered the corn that had been bestowed upon them by the Great Mystery as those who followed revered the gift of the buffalo. Corn was holy; the buffalo was holy. Curly Robe John said it was good medicine to remember this way, to give thanks for these gifts and all of Mother Earth's bounty. Once they had walked the length of this field, they stood in a little circle, whereupon the pipe was lit and Curly Robe, chanting in Cheyenne, offered it to the Four Great Directions. When this was done, he took several puffs and passed it to Hardy. Hardy nodded; he received the pipe stem-first, puffed several times, and handed it to Blackbird, who also smoked. After this was finished, she sighed, smiled happily at Hardy, and gave him a fond pat on the cheek. She loved this young man called Charlie; Charlie had no mother, and she was a barren woman without a son, so she had made Hardy Gibbs her son. John Peltier explained to Hardy that this was the Cheyenne way, family unity, the bonding of love and care for everyone. No one was left alone.

Hardy Gibbs knew this was true, for throughout the long winter months and early spring, these two wonderful people had treated him like one of their own. However lonely he felt, he had little time to dwell upon it; it was no winter of discontent. When he and John weren't working around the farm, sawing wood, tending the stock, and trapping along the river bottom, they were either fishing or hunting. Once they had taken a four-day trip into the snowy Colorado foothills, where they shot two bull elk. They talked and sometimes sang around the fireplace at night. Hardy, an eager student, had learned a few phrases and words of Cheyenne and had become proficient in using sign language, and though he already was knowledgeable in engraving, John and Blackbird taught him the art of tanning and tooling leather. He now owned a beautiful slip-over buckskin shirt and a pair of fringed leather britches that were so perfectly fitted to his legs and middle that they actually felt like his own skin. At Blackbird's insistence, when he tried on his new trail riding garb, tucking the pants into his boot tops and donning his western-style hat, he was no longer recognizable as Charles Parsons or Hardy Gibbs. His dark mustache was full and flowing, drooped at the corners; his hair was long, knotted at the back with a rawhide strip. He was a buckskin-clad man of the frontier, and Blackbird, happily content with the renovation, eagerly clapped her hands. Although she disdained the use of the word "squaw," she cried out, "Squaw man!"

On this brisk spring afternoon following the corn ceremony, Hardy and John, preparing for Hardy's imminent departure, were in the barn, fashioning new shoes for the pack mule when they heard a whinny from an approaching horse. Up above the fields, winding down the lane from the south, was a wagon with two persons perched on the seat, and John calculated it had to be visitors either from Colby or Oakley, the two nearest communities in that direction. Directly, a long "Ki-yi" whooped down the lane, this immediately bringing a smile to Curly Robe John's wrinkled face. It also brought Blackbird out to the porch below, and before John could explain to Hardy, his wife screamed back at the approaching wagon a "Ki-yi" of her own. The visitors, John explained with a smile, were Blue Necklace and Lucinda Hammond from Oakley. Mrs. Blue Hammond was lonely for Cheyenne talk; she had come to visit for several days. Hardy remembered them—how could he ever forget them after the silly quarrel in Wilson Hammond's saloon over a tub of bathwater—but he had never entertained the thought of seeing these people again.

After pulling their wagon up at the porch, the two women began unloading a few bundles and were busily engaged in an animated conversation with Blackbird by the time John Peltier, followed by Hardy, arrived at the house. The unexpected appearance of Hardy Gibbs, the young man they knew as Charlie, shocked both Lucinda Hammond and her mother. Lucinda, black eyes wide and a hand to her ruddy cheek, exclaimed softly, "Mister Charlie? Mister Charlie, is that you?"

With a small grin, hardly discernible under his thick mustache, Hardy replied, "Yep, it's old Charlie, Lucinda. I didn't get too far, did I?" He shoved out his hand and exchanged warm shakes with both Lucinda and Blue Necklace.

"Why, we heard you went north," Mrs. Hammond said.

Lucinda, her face aglow, chimed in, saying, "We didn't exactly hear. We read it in the Denver newspaper. The shooting down at Benkelman. I guess Mama heard, though. Papa read it to her. Papa was right, too. He said you were a gunfighter."

"You don't shoot those tobacco pails?" Mrs. Hammond asked. "*Eyah,* you shoot bad men! They shoot you." She examined him from head to toe. "Ah, but it wasn't bad. You look good, Mister Charlie. You look handsome."

Nodding at Hardy's leg, Blackbird said a few words in Cheyenne which brought a little laugh from Blue

Necklace and a gasp from Lucinda. Hardy Gibbs had no reason to ask for a translation; he knew what she had said. That bullet, as Curly Robe John had said that day, came close to turning him into a hen, but Hardy now surprised himself and the women when he nodded knowingly and uttered a few clucks. Everyone broke out laughing.

There was a large plank table in the front room of the big cabin, and shortly, Curly Robe John, Lucinda, and Hardy were seated while Blackbird and Mrs. Hammond began arranging cups and pouring steaming black coffee. Initially, the conversation was casual, about the women's wagon trip up from Oakley, crops, the condition of the greening range, and the good moisture. But when Hardy asked how Wilson Hammond was going to manage the saloon and hotel while Lucinda and her mother were gone, the talk suddenly turned ominous. A Mrs. Nell Collins, wife of the livery owner, Jediah Collins, was helping Wilson, and Jediah, too, had taken up watch over the place. Fighting had erupted between two of the area ranches, the Desmond and Quincy Calhoun ranch and the Bill Colby spread. Two of Colby's hired hands had been killed. Armed men were loitering in town, some frequenting Hammond's saloon. Until the dispute was settled, Wilson Hammond thought this was an opportune time for his wife and daughter to go visiting. Most of this news came from Lucinda, and when she mentioned that two of Bill Colby's men had been killed, a frightful chill coursed Hardy's body, a dreadful premonition, and he knew before he even asked.

In almost a whisper, Hardy stared at Lucinda and said, "Willard Colby? He wasn't one of them, was he?"

Surprised, she said, "Why, yes . . . yes, he was the first one. Mister Colby was his uncle. How do you know? Did you know him?"

Hardy Gibbs took a long sip of Blackbird's coffee. It was bitter and hot, but it felt cold. Hardy's entire body felt cold, and after a moment, he replied, "Willard was a friend of mine. I stayed with him for a few days up at a line cabin before I rode over here." The harmonica was lying on the table near Hardy's cup. "He gave me that," Hardy said, nodding at the shiny mouth organ. "He couldn't play it worth a lick. Likely, he couldn't shoot worth a lick, either." Staring morosely across the table, he asked, "When did all of this happen? How?"

From Mrs. Hammond and Lucinda, who had learned most of what they knew from Wilson Hammond and in overhearing conversations in the saloon, Hardy heard the grim details. Young Willard Colby and another drover by the name of Martin Simpkins had caught four of the Calhoun men tearing out a section of new wire fencing dividing a section of land between the two ranches. Apparently the Calhoun brothers and Bill Colby had argued over the proper placement of the fence a few days earlier, the Calhouns claiming it was illegal and prohibited their stock from grazing on the new grass along the river bottom. When Willard and Martin Simpkins encountered the Calhoun hands removing the fence, an angry exchange of words ensued, this followed by the shooting. Young Willard, so it was reported, was in the process of dismounting and had reached for his rifle, only to be shot, and Martin, to the back of him, had reined about and bolted away back to the main ranch for help. He was shot in the back, but managed to deliver the news about the shooting. He died later that afternoon. All of this had happened Monday, three days before.

Lucinda Hammond said that late in the afternoon on the day following the fight, Bill Colby and his wife, Emma, had come into town with their nephew's body; it was in a wooden box, and Wilson Hammond helped load it on the night train for Denver. Emma Colby had accompanied the body. After the train's departure, Bill Colby had Wilson Hammond send a telegraph message down to Hays asking for help. The following morning, a reply came up from Hays—a marshal and a judge were coming to Oakley to investigate the matter; they were arriving on the late train Thursday.

"Tomorrow night," Mrs. Hammond lamented. "But my man says what can they do? Decide the boundary line? *Eyah!* What can they do about those two dead boys? My man says who can testify against those killers? Who knows what happened? Bad medicine, I tell you. Tsk, tsk, tsk."

"It certainly wasn't a fair fight." Lucinda Hammond sighed, staring forlornly at the harmonica.

Hardy Gibbs, his eyes also on the harmonica, said, "Fights are seldom fair to the loser."

"That's what that Martin fellow told Mister Colby before he died," she replied. "This fellow, Truscott, he did the shooting. Mister Colby told Papa he's a killer. Those Calhoun brothers hired him to scare off Mister Colby's drovers. Papa says its going to cause a range war, only Mister Colby is going to lose 'cause he only has himself and one drover left over there now."

"*Mon Dieu!*" exclaimed John Peltier in a low voice. "This Truscott . . . Tom Truscott, yes, I know this one."

"You know him?" asked Hardy. "From where? Who is he?"

"Once, from Julesburg," Curly Robe John answered. "He was a deputy up here, *oui,* maybe two years ago. He killed some men, eh? Too many, they say, not good for the town, too much bad talk, so they told him to go away before more trouble comes. A gunfighter. I think once an Indian fighter, too. Ah, this is what I remember. Too many things happening all of the time. Too much trouble."

Lucinda Hammond huffed indignantly. "Indian fighter! That's what one of the drovers told Papa. He made a joke of it when Papa said the marshal down at Hays and some judge was coming . . . said some of those renegade Indians running around up above town would probably get them, too, making believe Indians had a hand in that shooting."

"That's ridiculous." Hardy Gibbs sighed.

"It's happened before," Lucinda replied, and everyone around the table nodded gravely. "Put the blame on someone else."

Hardy was sickened by the loss of his friend, Willard, the man who had been so kind to him out on the range, one who had sympathized with him and had promised one day to defend him if ever the occasion arose. Hardy Gibbs was also appalled at the thought of the killers going scot-free, doing their ill will in Oakley, and perhaps even thwarting the marshal's investigation. He remembered how Willard Colby referred to the Calhoun brothers as a pack of thieves, rustling Bill Colby's shorthorns every time an unbranded yearling wandered away too far. And poor Colby, a man whom he had never met but only knew through the good words of his nephew, he certainly had been hung out to dry, only he and one hired hand now left to look out after that big spread. While all of this saddened and angered Hardy Gibbs, he knew it wasn't any of his business. His business was west, and by the end of the summer, he wanted it finished. He was doing just fine now. It was as Grandfather Amos had said—a man goes looking for trouble and he's sure to find it—but something was gnawing away inside him like a hungry pack rat.

Lucinda Hammond was talking again: ". . . six or seven of them, counting that Desmond and Quincy. Papa says they'll be no boomers coming to settle around our place, not with that kind of trouble going on. What can the marshal do?" She glanced at Hardy Gibbs. "I'll bet those . . . those bastards wouldn't be laughing and bragging if you stepped into Papa's place."

Hardy Gibbs looked up curiously. "Laughing? Bragging?" he said. And a sickening whirlwind suddenly swirled through his mind, one of frustration and anger, the horrible remembrance of those three quarry rats standing at Tinker's long bar, smirks on their dirty faces, and those two girls, giggling and rubbing up against them, little whores, little bastards consorting, bragging about an afternoon's work well done. Hardy's mind splintered like fragile glass, tiny shards piercing the deepest recesses of his brain.

Tipping his cup, he downed the last of his coffee and slid back his chair. "I think I'll go down to Oakley and have a look," he said flatly.

Blackbird gave him an anxious glance. "We'll be having supper soon, my son," she said. "Cornbread. A good stew."

Hardy smiled fondly at her. "Thank you. No, I'm leaving. I'll need a few things for the trail, that's all."

Curly Robe John said hastily, "No, wait, Charlie. It will work out. No use making things worse for yourself, getting involved in this affair."

"I won't unless I have to," Hardy replied. "I'm just going to go down and express my condolences, see if Mister Colby needs any help. Willard was my friend." He went around the table and bent down and kissed Lucinda Hammond on the cheek, and she impulsively turned quickly and kissed him back on the lips.

Hardy, momentarily flustered, said, "I'll stop and see your father, too." He managed a grin for Mrs. Hammond. "Don't worry . . . I won't shoot that spittoon again."

Shortly after dawn, Hardy Gibbs rode down a long green flat where several hundred head of cattle were grazing in the early blue light, and sitting at the end of this flat were several sheds, one large barn, and a house, all surrounded by slat-and-pole fencing. There was activity; a wisp of smoke was curling up from a rock chimney at the big house, and Hardy could see a man walking from the barn followed by two dogs. He carried a rifle. When he saw Hardy approaching, he stopped, but the two dogs came leaping forward, their tails wagging.

Hardy quickly hailed the man by waving a hand in greeting. Yelling "Friend!" and dismounting at a wire gate, he unfastened it and, along with the two leaping dogs, walked up and identified himself—he was a friend of Willard Colby, he had ridden most of the night, he was tired and hungry, and he had come to see Bill Colby.

"You're looking at him," the man said. Bill Colby was tall and angular; he wore a drover's hat and a sheepskin jacket, canvas pants, and stovepipe boots; his mustache was flecked with gray. Hardy allowed Colby was between forty and forty-five years of age. He was mild-mannered, spoke softly, and was obviously dead tired. As the two men walked to the house, Hardy explained how the news of the shooting had come to him, and the fact that he was friends with the Wilson Hammond family seemed to please Bill Colby. Moments later, when they were in the kitchen, Hardy caressing a hot cup of coffee between his hands, Bill Colby, in sudden recollection, was even more pleased.

"Parsons . . . Charlie Parsons!" he exclaimed. "Yes, yes, I knew you were up there with Willard last fall, but the name didn't hit me until just now, son." Slapping his thigh, he grinned. "Benkelman . . . you shot up some of those Missouri bad men." He sat down at the table, took a sip of coffee, and smiled at Hardy. "Willard said you didn't look much like a drover, even talk like one. He said you were a shooter. Well, at the time I had to laugh about that. Willard had a habit of exaggerating at times. Smart as a whip, though; didn't realize he wasn't exaggerating one bit until I read about that Benkelman affair." Colby hesitated, swirled his coffee around, and stared at the cup. In a choked voice, he said, "Damn, I'm going to miss that boy."

At this point, another man came into the kitchen, younger, dressed somewhat the same as Colby, but wearing denim britches. He wore a spur on one of his boots, the first such riding device Hardy had seen on his long trip. His name was Joseph Bemis, and it was true what Lucinda had said—Bemis and Bill Colby were the only two men left on the ranch. After the introductions, Bemis asked Hardy if he had a hankering for eggs, fried potatoes, and fatback. Well, this sounded good to Hardy; he hadn't eaten since noon the previous day. His butt was angry from the long night ride, but his belly was angrier.

During the ensuing conversation, Hardy Gibbs didn't learn much more than the Hammond women had already told him, except that the disputed boundary and contentious fence, one of those newfangled Gates wires with the sharp spikes on them, were within Colby's legal rights. The land was not part of open range, and in fact, the men from the Calhoun ranch were trespassing when the incident occurred. It also was true that Tom Truscott was no more of a cowhand than Hardy. Desmond and Quincy Calhoun had hired Truscott because he was a shooter, and according to Bill Colby, a damn good one, too.

"I'm no drover," Hardy Gibbs admitted, "but I heard you were shorthanded." Smiling, he held up both of his hands. "I have two good ones. Worked all winter about thirty-five miles or so over on the fork of the Republican."

"What's your game, son?" Bill Colby asked.

With a shrug, Hardy Gibbs said, "Oh, I thought after I get a couple hours of sleep, while you watch the place here, Joseph and I could go and fix that fence. I want to go down to Oakley, too, see Mister Hammond. Told his folks I'd do that."

"You want to hire on with me?" asked Bill Colby. "Is this in your game?"

"No, I'm not looking for wages, Mister Colby. Not that I wouldn't mind working for you, no, not at all. I have other plans, to the west, and I'm already six months later than I planned. A couple of days here, this is about all I can spare."

Joseph Bemis brought three plates of food to the table and, with a smile at Hardy Gibbs, said, "I'd appreciate help on the fence, Charlie. I'll feel a helluva lot safer with you there, tell you that."

Forking into his eggs, Hardy grinned back. "Truscott? Well, you just forget Truscott, Joseph."

"Forget?"

"Yep. I'm going to kill him." Hardy Gibbs, with a continuing smile, chomped down on the forkful of eggs.

It took some persuasion on the part of Hardy, but he convinced Bill Colby that it was far safer for the rancher to remain at the ranch than to accompany him into Oakley to meet the marshal and judge at the depot. Hardy gave several reasons for this—first and foremost, since the feud between Colby and the Calhoun brothers had flared into violence, this was no time to leave the ranch unguarded. Second, since the impending investigation would bring the Hays authorities out to the ranch the following day, there was no reason for Colby to jeopardize himself by chancing the hostility that had befallen Oakley. With this agreed upon, and a promise to return either this night or the next day, Hardy Gibbs rode off to keep another promise—to check on the well-being of Wilson Hammond.

When Hardy rode into the little town, it looked almost the same as he had last seen it, one long street, and except for a few horses hitched there and there, not a soul in sight. After what he had learned from Lucinda and Mrs. Hammond at Curly Robe John's farm, Hardy didn't know what to expect, but he was prepared for the worst. At the first building he reined away behind it and rode out of sight until he came to the back of Jediah Collins's livery, which was located directly across the street from the saloon-hotel of Wilson Hammond. As it had been with the Hammond women, Jediah momentarily didn't recognize Hardy. He did recognize the black Morgan, and when he looked at Hardy a second time, a twinkle came to his eyes and he said, "Charlie, isn't it? You forget something? If you did, you came back at a helluva time to find it."

After a short greeting and handshake, Hardy, standing in the shadows of the big shed, nodded toward the saloon-hotel. "Have you been keeping your eyes on that place?"

Pointing to a shotgun in the corner, Jediah said, "Ehyup, that I have. Get the call, I'm ready. How'd you know that?"

Hardy explained that he had talked to Lucinda and her mother a day ago, that he was aware of the problems, and that this was the reason he had returned, to help however he could. Jediah, tossing a look across the street, said that the horses tied up in front of the saloon belonged to Calhoun's men, three of them, who had arrived about a half an hour ago, but Desmond and Quincy were not among them. The two bosses had been at the saloon the night after the shooting; Jediah hadn't seen them since. He gave Hardy a sly wink, suggesting that the two brothers didn't want to get involved personally if any more violence occurred, not with the marshal expected to arrive in several hours. Hardy searched his denims, brought out two dollars, and handed the money to Jediah, telling him it was a dollar for keeping Sundown out of sight in the back stall, and another dollar for watching the front door of the saloon until after the night train for Denver pulled out. With a glance at the double-barrel, Hardy said, "It might just turn out to be real peaceful around here, but don't hesitate to use that thing if you think it's necessary, only, for chrissakes, don't shoot *me* with it."

Jediah grinned. "If you're in the street, I'll cover you. Say, now, where'd you get that purty buckskin shirt, Charlie? Goes right nice with your new hairdo, it does. That where you been all winter, consortin' with hostiles?"

"Ehyup," mimicked Hardy Gibbs.

He backed off into the darkness and disappeared out the back of the shed, and five minutes later was peeking through the back door of the hotel, where he saw Jediah's wife, Nell, sitting on a stool in the kitchen. Entering quietly, he held a finger to his lips and eased over out of sight of the hallway leading into the saloon. He beckoned Nell Collins, and she quietly left her stool and cautiously approached him, unaware of who he was. Finally Hardy talked softly, identifying himself, telling her that he was a friend of Wilson Hammond, that he wanted to see him, mainly to confirm the identities of the three Calhoun drovers inside. She understood, and left. Shortly, Nell reappeared, followed by Wilson Hammond, who was nonchalantly whistling and carrying a bottle of wine.

Smiling nervously, Hammond whispered, "By God, am I glad to see you. When she said a fellow by the name of Charlie was back here, I damn near fell over the bar." He grinned and thrust out the bottle of wine. "Managed to grab this before I fell. Forgot to set up the spittoon, though." He chuckled at this and asked, "For God's sake, what the hell are you doing here?"

Nell brought a glass, and as the barkeep poured, Hardy quickly explained everything to a thoroughly shocked but highly elated Wilson Hammond. Moments later, Hardy Gibbs got his answer—yes, one of the men inside was Tom Truscott. And how, Hardy asked, was he to know which one was Truscott?

"That's easy," Wilson Hammond said. "He's the one wearing two pistols, one on each side."

Hardy Gibbs almost choked on his wine. "Two! Holy smokes, what for? My grandpaw told me once there were a few fools around who toted a brace, but I surely never expected to see one. Most fellows don't even know how to shoot one pistol properly."

"Maybe he's trying to scare someone," ventured Hammond.

"Bull," scoffed Hardy Gibbs. "We'll have to see how good he is, Mister Hammond. He took those boys up above unaware . . . shot that Martin boy when he was riding away for help. That's what Lucinda said."

Wilson Hammond gave Hardy an apprehensive stare. "Look here, you're not planning on going in there, are you?"

"No, no," replied Hardy, waving his glass. "No, I'm going over to the station, try to talk to the marshal when he comes in and see what he plans to do about this mess, maybe get rid of these troublemakers."

"Well, that's a relief. They don't push very easy, but

the marshal, he'll probably tell you it's none of your business."

"Not when I tell him I'm Charlie Parsons, he won't." Hardy grinned. "Not when he finds out all of these Calhoun boys are in an ornery mood, and one of them is a hired gunfighter."

"You don't think that spittoon trick would work again, do you?"

"It might with two of them. I don't think it would impress that Truscott one whit."

Wilson Hammond gave Hardy a friendly pat on the shoulder. "Good luck, Charlie." Picking up the wine bottle, he said, "One drink is enough, don't you think?" He disappeared down the hall.

Hardy Gibbs heard the whistle long before he saw the train. He stirred from his resting place on a wooden crate at the end of the platform and put his harmonica away. There had been some activity in the station. Wilson Hammond, clad in a white shirt and dark vest, had arrived, followed by a woman and two men, apparently passengers transferring from the Overland stage that had come from Garden City late in the afternoon. Stepping from behind the crate, Hardy peered over toward Hammond's saloon-hotel; the three horses were still hitched outside, and he saw Nell Collins in a white apron standing in the doorway. She wasn't watching the approaching train; she had her eyes on the livery across the street, where a rider— another Calhoun drover, Hardy suspected—had just dismounted and was talking to Jediah. A man with an apron emerged from the mercantile two doors down from the saloon; he came hurrying up the dirt street to-

ward the station. Hardy reckoned this fellow was coming to the station to take delivery of merchandise arriving on the westbound.

Directly, the engine slowly huffed past, screeching to
a halt some distance beyond Hardy. The mail car door
slid open, and the clerk inside tossed out several bundles. Two cars down, another door opened, and a dark-
suited porter hopped down, placed a platform below
the door, then stood back. Hardy Gibbs, leaning
against the wooden crate, first saw a portly man step
out, a suitcase in one hand, and tucked up under his
other arm a black satchel. He wore a derby and a dark
suit; this had to be the judge. Behind him, another
derby-clad fellow stepped off, waving a shiny black
walking stick and carrying a small suitcase. Hardy
Gibbs strained his eyes; this man looked familiar, a
face out of the past, but Hardy couldn't recollect
where he had seen him; and then an astonished Hardy
Gibbs watched a third man—tall, mustached, and
wearing boots, a tan jacket, and matching pants—
nimbly hop down. It was Sheriff Orlan Thomas! Hardy
Gibbs blinked both in surprise and wonderment. What
was the town sheriff of Hays doing here? Well, whatever it was, Orlan Thomas began discussing it with
Wilson Hammond, the judge, and the third man, all of
whom had gathered together near the station doorway.
Directly, Wilson Hammond pointed up the platform
where Hardy was standing. Momentarily, Hardy Gibbs
and Orlan Thomas exchanged stares of disbelief before
Hardy finally waved a hand and said, "Hello, Orlan,
welcome to Oakley."

The judge was George Tubbs. He had come with
platforms and would rule on the boundary dispute. The

man with the shiny cane was Henry Burlingame, the newspaper corespondent. He had come to write a story about a range war, but at this surprising reappearance of The Shooter, Charlie Parsons, his story was suddenly of greater import than just a simple range war. The elusive, mysterious Charlie Parsons was himself news. Sheriff Orlan Thomas had come because he was now a U.S. deputy marshal, a position considerably beyond the scope, as well as salary, of a town sheriff. Hardy Gibbs was pleased about Orlan's new job, but not by the presence of Henry Burlingame.

Before leaving for the hotel to take up lodging, the three men quietly talked with Hardy in the vacant station. Since they already knew most of the details in the Colby-Calhoun dispute, there was little he could add, only that his involvement was personal. He had been a friend of Willard Colby and was a friend of the Hammond family, and he was upset that the townspeople were being frightened out of their wits by the Calhoun bunch. It was his contention that when the quarrel over the fence was settled (and he said that he and the one Colby cowhand remaining had just replaced the wire), violence was likely to erupt again. Bill Colby was now badly outnumbered, and once the law left the area, he would be in constant jeopardy, either personally or threatened with the loss of cattle and even his property.

After the situation was thoroughly discussed, Hardy Gibbs asked Orlan Thomas, "Outside of taking care of the fence, what else can you do? You know, do to protect Colby."

"Unfortunately, only what the law says I can do," Orlan replied. "Talk to the Calhoun brothers, all of the drovers, warn them to abide by the law or face the consequences in court. Wait for charges to be filed by Colby."

"What about the Truscott fellow?"

The marshal said forlornly, "Charlie, you know the law as well as I do on that score. Witnesses. I'll have to wait and see if Bill Colby files charges. Dammit, you know what it boils down to—it's his word against theirs, and he wasn't even there when all of this happened."

Judge Tubbs said, "Marshal Thomas will need a bona fide witness to support the state's case if Mister Colby decides to press charges. No jury will decide a case on hearsay testimony, and from what I understand, Mister Colby has no supporting evidence to contradict the claim of self-defense to which Mister Hammond says these other drovers have alluded."

"Yes," Hardy Gibbs said grimly, "I'm well aware of this business of 'it's their word against mine,' this self-defense bull. That may be the law, but by my way of thinking, it surely isn't justice. Mister Hammond says those scallawags are coming and going now like they own the town, laughing and carrying on. They think it's a big joke. That Truscott is a bad apple, Orlan, one bad apple."

"Get rid of the bad apple before it spoils the whole barrel?" said Orlan Thomas.

"You can tell him he's disturbing the peace," suggested Hardy. "Things might simmer down if he just moved along, went somewhere else. Mister Hammond doesn't like it, him sitting over there all afternoon with those revolvers hanging from his hips. It's not good for business. It's downright threatening."

"Oh, come on, Charlie, you know better. If every man who wore a gun was chased out, there wouldn't be anyone left in town, including you. If Hammond doesn't like those men wearing a sidearm, he can make his own rules . . . a house rule. Check your weapons at the bar. Hang 'em on the wall. It's done in other places, you know."

"Hah!" Hardy scoffed. "They'd likely fall over on the floor laughing at something like that."

"Well," replied Orlan Thomas with a tight smile, "we'll just have to wait and see."

"If you don't get him out of town, Orlan, I will."

While Marshal Thomas, Judge Tubbs, and Henry Burlingame were being registered for their rooms, Hardy went over to a table across the room from the three Calhoun drovers, who were involved in some kind of a card game. They had a bottle and glasses at their table, but they weren't drinking much, just sitting there staring at the cards, occasionally muttering and casting sidelong glances at the marshal and his two friends. When the new arrivals finished registering and followed Hammond down the hall to their rooms, one of the drovers finally spoke up, addressing Hardy Gibbs. "Hey, son, those old boys your friends?"

"Nope," Hardy answered innocently. "Just ran into them at the depot over there. One of them says he's a United States marshal, that tall one. Says he's here to settle some business about those shootings up at the Colby spread. Coincidental, it is. I'm riding up there, too, so he invited me in for a drink."

"Is that a fact!" one man exclaimed.

"You mean that he's a marshal or that I'm going up to Colby's?"

The man wearing the leather vest and a brace of pistols, Tom Truscott, spoke up. "We already know what the marshal is up to, boy. I think Caleb here is surprised you're heading for Colby's place, the trouble and all."

"Oh, that." Hardy Gibbs shrugged and went on, "Well, you see, I don't pay any mind to all of the talk I hear. Someone down the line told me Mister Colby needed a few extra hands, six or seven, and I'm the first. He wanted someone right off who was handy with that Gates barbed wire, and since I strung a lot of it down in the Panhandle last fall, I thought maybe this Colby could use me."

"This ain't the Panhandle," the man called Caleb said. "Folks up here don't like all that goddamned wire. Don't you know that's what's causing all this ruckus? Any wire blocks off the grass and water, mos' likely ain't gonna stay up long. Why, you just might get yourself in a peck of trouble riding for old man Colby, mebee even shot."

They all chuckled at this and went back to playing their cards.

"Say, I surely wouldn't like that!" exclaimed Hardy Gibbs. "I don't like the notion of anyone shooting at me."

The three drovers all began laughing hilariously at this, and a startled Wilson Hammond, who had just returned from the back rooms, came over to Hardy's table, frowned down at him, then glanced over the Calhoun men. "What the hell is going on?" he whispered harshly. "What are you telling them? Jokes, for chrissakes!"

"No, I only said the notion of anyone shooting at me scares the hell out of me." Hardy grinned under his black mustache. "Told 'em I was hiring on up at the Colby spread, and they said I might get shot fooling around up there stringing wire. That's all."

"Jesus!"

"Can I have a sip of wine?"

Wilson Hammond wheezed. "Boy, for your age, I've never seen anyone the likes of you!" He hurried away back to the bar, returned directly with a glass of wine. Placing it in front of Hardy Gibbs, he said, "You mind your manners, hear? Don't be riling them. Wait for that marshal."

Holding up his hands defensively, Hardy said. "Yep, of course." He took one sip and, as Hammond was turning away, said, "Where are your new guests?"

"Washing up. Going to the privy."

"Well," Hardy advised him, "you better tell them to hurry up or they're going to miss all of the fun. I can't keep these fellows laughing forever, you know. And they're not going to like it when the marshal tells them about your new house rule—"

"What new rule?"

"Hanging their sidearms up on the pegs over there when they come in, or stowing them behind the bar. Whatever you wish."

"Mister Thomas didn't say anything to me about this."

Hardy Gibbs grinned. "He will. Then again, maybe he won't have to." Leaning across the table, Hardy shouted over to the drovers, "Hey, do you think that fellow I talked to was joshing me? He said something about Mister Colby wanting shooters, but I thought he was talking about shooting varmints pestering his critters. Holy smokes, I wasn't thinking about two-legged varmints, no sir."

They chuckled again, and Tom Truscott said, "You better forget that job, son. It doesn't sound like your style."

"Nope, I reckon not," Hardy replied. "Say, you must be a shooter, carrying two revolvers like that. How do you do that? Why, you must be packing ten pounds of iron and lead around your waist! Whoee, doesn't that get burdensome, all that weight? I do declare, you must either be a poor shot or looking to scare people to death."

No one laughed, but the man called Caleb said, "Does it scare you? Or is your tongue flapping that way because of the likker?" And, calling over to Wilson Hammond, he asked, "Will, what the hell did you put in this kid's drink? Loco weed? Next thing you know, he'll be asking Tom to show him how his guns work."

Before Wilson Hammond could reply, Hardy Gibbs stood up and enthusiastically clapped his hands once, saying, "Now, I'd like that, I surely would! What I want to know is if he pulls out those pistols both at once, you know, or just shoots six rounds with one and then pulls out the other one. Damn, if he can hit anything, that's twelve varmints."

Wilson Hammond said, "Sit down, Charlie. Finish your drink."

"Charlie?" said Caleb, squinting curiously over at Hardy.

"Yep, Charlie, that's me," answered Hardy. "Charlie

the tit-nipper, that's what they call me around here," and he slowly moved out from behind the table and walked to the door.

"I can see why," Tom Truscott said. "You're a crazy kid with a big mouth, and you're no wire stringer, either."

"Oh, yes, I am," corrected Hardy Gibbs. "I strung wire this morning, patched up that whole section you boys tore out. I'm going back tomorrow with the marshal to check on it. If it's out of place, I'm coming over to see your bosses personally . . . with or without the marshal, and if I see any of you near that fence, I'll kill you—face on, not like you shot those two boys the other day. Yes, I'm Charlie the tit-nipper, Mister Truscott, and if I'm not mistaken, they call you Tom the Turd." Hardy Gibbs paused at the doorway, and staring back at the three awed men, he said, "If anything I've said upsets you, I'm sorry. I suppose I'll just have to wait outside in the street. Like Caleb says, waiting for you to show me how those guns work."

Hardy Gibbs walked out. The sun was low. Across the street he saw the drover who had come riding in earlier, and sitting behind him on a keg was Jediah Collins.

Back inside the saloon, Wilson Hammond went rushing to the rooms in back; the three drovers were standing around their table staring at each other in utter disbelief.

Caleb finally said, "Either he's crazy or he's a goddamned shooter."

Moving out the door, Tom Truscott shook his head. "No, he's a fool kid looking to make a name for himself. I've seen his kind before."

At the entrance to the bath, Wilson Hammond yelled, "Marshal Thomas. Marshal, you better get your ass out here fast! Charlie Parsons just called those Calhoun men outside—all three of them!"

A smothered cry came from behind the door. "Oh, shit!" and from another room, "Parsons!" Simultaneously, the doors flew open. Orlan Thomas, shirtless, grasping a revolver, came rushing out, and from the other door, Henry Burlingame emerged, slipping up his suspenders and following close behind, but by the time they reached the front door, Tom Truscott was already walking toward the middle of the street, Caleb and the other drover lagging behind.

Lifting his revolver and thumbing back the hammer, Orlan Thomas called, "Hold it, you two! Arms up. Slowly. Don't turn around, just back up here to me nice and easy. You boys stay out of it. This is no time to be making a foolish mistake."

The two men did as they were told, and once their heels had touched the porch stoop, Orlan nodded to Henry Burlingame, who quickly stepped up and carefully lifted both of the men's pistols. Orlan Thomas called again, "All right, Charlie, that's enough. You win. Call it off and I'll get this man out of town. Come on, now, let's drop it."

Tom Truscott shouted back, "Oh, no, Marshal, it's my game, not his. Fair and square. I'm only obliging the kid, teaching him a lesson."

Orlan Thomas cried, "Teaching him a lesson! For chrissakes, you don't stand a chance drawing on him! You damn fool, that's no cowhand out there you're facing. It's Charlie Parsons!"

If this alarming pronouncement had any effect, it

was lost on Tom Truscott, who was already poised, his mind transfixed by the moment at hand. He quickly drew his right revolver, had it midway in the air before Hardy's Gibbs Special belched flame and smoke. The bullet rocked Truscott back several staggering steps, and he stood there, mouth agape, staring down at the blood dribbling out from an eruption above his elbow. His arm was numb, paralyzed, broken, and he couldn't lift the revolver; it momentarily dangled, then dropped in the dust.

Back up the street, twenty paces away, Hardy Gibbs was holstering his revolver, and he shouted, "All right, let's see what you can teach me with the other one, Mister Truscott. You're not looking at any Willard Colby, you bastard, you're looking at his soul!"

Suddenly, from the livery, a man rushed out to the side of the street and leveled down on Hardy Gibbs. "Look out!" screamed Orlan Thomas, kicking at Caleb's backside and trying to bring his own revolver into play.

In this perilous moment, Hardy, half turning, swept his Gibbs swiftly from the holster only to hear a tremendous boom from somewhere inside the livery; the man poised in the street suddenly pitched over on his face, the back of his skull blown away. This unexpected diversion was enough; Truscott had his left gun fully extended. Two shots sounded as one, but Truscott was blown over backward, the bullet from Hardy Gibbs's weapon smashing him in the middle of the chest. Simultaneously, a sound of splintering glass signaled the impact of Tom Truscott's errant shot as the lead shattered the front window of the depot behind Hardy.

Jediah Collins, his shotgun over his shoulder, came

walking out of the livery, stopped, momentarily stared down at his victim, then looked over at Hardy Gibbs. "Didn't hesitate, did I? Didn't shoot you, either. Did all right, I reckon." He grinned and spat to the side.

"Ehyup, you surely did," said Hardy Gibbs.

Marshal Orlan Thomas, however, displeased that the law had been taken out of his hands, reluctantly admitted that young Charlie Parsons, at least for the present, had put a damper on the Calhoun brothers' unwanted presence in Oakley. How this would affect the fencing problem on the range above, he could only surmise, but he thought that after the two Calhoun drovers, Caleb Winston and Buster Chadwick, attested to Charlie Parsons's swift retribution and his grim warning to stay away from the Colby property, Quincy and Desmond Calhoun were more than likely to keep their distance.

Judge George Tubbs was irate; this wasn't his idea of a peaceful settlement, and he was further annoyed by the fact that no one had called him from the bath, where he had been luxuriating in the tin, when the shooting took place. However, the writer, Henry Burlingame, was elated. What did it matter if Charlie Parsons refused to talk with him? He had witnessed a spectacular shoot-out, had actually seen The Shooter in action, and after the saloon closed, he kept Wilson Hammond busy for several hours filing his dispatches over the telegraph in the depot.

Hardy Gibbs left at dusk for the Colby ranch, not too far behind the Calhoun drovers, Caleb and Buster, who were trailing two horses packed with the bodies of Tom Truscott and Hank Wiggins, the latter a victim of Jediah Collins's shotgun blast. Hardy left with an admonition from Marshal Orlan Thomas, who said even though Charlie was his friend, it would be better for the sake of everyone if he got out of the state of Kansas. The sooner the better.

My Dearest Julie:

I left John's farm several days ago and am now in a town in Colorado called Julesburg. I must tell you my leaving was very sad for I have never met two nicer people than John and Blackbird. That fellow Willard Colby I told you about last winter got killed down by his uncle's ranch. He was shot by some no-account and I went down to see his uncle Bill. When I learned all of the details I was pretty sore about it and it reminded me of back home when we had all of our trouble. One thing and another happened and I had a fight with this man who killed Willard and I ended up shooting him. It is all right. I am not in trouble about it but that newspaper man named Burlingame was there and I suppose by now you and Grandfather know all about it. Grandfather Amos is right. A man goes looking for trouble and he's going to find it in a hurry. I will not make this mistake again. That Bill Colby wanted to hire me for work on his ranch but I told him I had to get on the road or trouble will find me. I helped fix a wire fence. He wanted to pay me for this. It was no chore at all and I told him no. I just wanted to lend a hand. When I unpacked my saddlebag at John's farm I found a paper folded in it and $100. I suppose this is a lot of money for just fixing a Gates wire fence and getting my hands stuck by those sharp barbs. I thought this was better than thinking he was paying me for killing Truscott. I only did that because of what Truscott did to Mister Colby's nephew, Willard. Colby likes me and said he wants to stay in contact. I had no idea how this could be done so I gave him Uncle Paul's posting place and told him all about you. I will leave this Julesburg and go north to the old Oregon trail. I bought a new Winchester and a scabbard. John said I should do this. I trust plans for the wedding are going well. I will write to you and Grandfather at my next opportunity. Do not worry about me. I surely will miss your letters. I love you so much.

Yours forever, Hardy

TEN

Burlingame's Quest

The writer, Henry Burlingame, had reason to gloat—on three separate occasions now, he had been first on the scene to file dispatches on Charlie Parsons, and he was the only reporter who had witnessed The Shooter in action. Admittedly, the Oakley shoot-out had been a stroke of luck for him, but the editors in New York at the *Tribune* and *Harper's Weekly* didn't know this. It had established Burlingame as the most enterprising and authoritative writer on the mysterious Charlie Parsons.

When Burlingame saw Colonel E. C. Judson leaving the U.S. marshal's office in Hays, he knew the competition had arrived, for he suspected Judson, who wrote under pseudonym of Ned Buntline, was in Hays for only one reason—to get a background story on Charlie Parsons and solve the mystery. This dismayed Henry Burlingame, for he considered himself an objective, resourceful, and enterprising writer. He disliked Colonel Judson, whom he considered to be a fabricator of the first water, one prone to colorful distortions and sometimes, to Burlingame's notion, a horrendous manipulator of facts and an outright liar. This was not good journalism, but the financial remuneration the colonel had been reaping from his dispatches and short novels was considerable. This also annoyed Henry Burlingame. Ned Buntline had no integrity, but he was getting rich, while Burlingame *had* integrity and was just getting by.

And it was exactly what Henry Burlingame had surmised—Marshal Thomas, sitting back easily in his chair, confirmed it: "The colonel's heading out to Cheyenne. Like everyone else, he thinks he can catch up with Charlie on the trail somewhere. Said he smells a good yarn in the boy . . . the ultimate shooter, something like that."

"Good Lord!"

"Oh, I'm sure he'll come up with something." Orlan Thomas grinned. "He always does. Stretches the truth a little at times, but he always seems to find a way."

Henry Burlingame, smarting under his collar, grunted, saying, "His way, this time, is the wrong way. He'll get nothing out of that boy, even if he does catch up with him. Charlie knows only three words: yep, nope, and good-bye."

Orlan Thomas chuckled. "That's what's called keeping your mouth shut, Henry. Seems like the only time Charlie has much to say is when he's riled, and then he lets that damn Gibbs Special do his talking." Thomas leaned back, propped his boots on his desk, and clasped his hands in back of his head. "I like him," he mused. "He's a decent sort of a kid, but he has this look in his eyes, like he's lost something, like life has dealt him a bad hand. I don't know, he's touchy, a hair trigger, just like that revolver." Thomas sighed. "I'm glad he's out of my hair, Henry, I'll tell you that."

Henry Burlingame said, "He's not out of my hair. I

can't get him out of my mind. . . . Too many unanswered questions. How do you figure he learned to shoot that way? Who taught him? What does he do for wages? Where's he from? He's no cowhand, we know that."

"Wages?" Orlan Thomas laughed. "He got a thousand dollars for that Cadwell shooting. He doesn't drink. To my knowledge, he doesn't gamble so he's not hurting for money. His aunt has money, too. Said he holed up last winter on some farm up on one of the forks of the Republican, Benkelman country."

"All right," said Burlingame, "so I ask again, where is he going, and where is he from?"

Nodding, Orlan Thomas said, "He's from that way, and he's going the other way . . . west, that's all I know. 'Least, that's what he said last fall when he was through here. 'Course, he was heading for Santa Fe, too, but he didn't get very far. One of his ruses, I suppose. Surprised the hell out me when he showed up in Oakley that way." He glanced over at Henry Burlingame. "You tell *me* where he's going. Why don't you go find out?"

"That's what I've been thinking about doing. He's put a thorn in my side and I can't get rid of it. I made big mistake, you know, not getting to Jake Parsons's wife when she was here, but how was I to know everything was going to turn out like this?" Burlingame nervously drummed his fingers on the desk and said, "You know him, and I know him, but neither of us *really* knows him. Yes, I'm going, Orlan." He got up and smiled down at the marshal. "You take care, now. Keep the peace. I'm going to take a little ride on the choo-choo."

"And just where are you going?" Thomas asked.

Burlingame smiled, nodded as Thomas had done. "Not that way, not the way of that pompous ass, Buntline. That way, back down the line, maybe Abilene first."

"The widow, Missus Parsons?"

"Likely. You said Jake gave Charlie that Gibbs, didn't you?"

"I did," acknowledged Marshal Thomas. "He and the kid practiced with those forty-fours . . . 'fooling around,' the way Charlie put it."

At the door, Burlingame gave Thomas a doubtful look. "More than fooling around, I'd say. The finesse that boy has doesn't come from fooling around. Makes one wonder, doesn't it?"

It was raining the next day when Henry Burlingame got off the train at Abilene, and by the time he made it to the livery, his shoes were muddy, his hat soggy, and his temperament slightly ruffled. A drizzle was still coming down when he finally located the Parsons farm and pulled up in front of the big porch in his rented buggy. A big dog greeted him, then two children, a boy and a girl, then a woman, an attractive woman dressed in denims and riding boots, her long blond hair swept back fastened at the back with a tortoiseshell comb. Henry Burlingame had seen Rose Parsons twice in his life, once in the hotel dining room with her late husband several years past, the last time only at a distance when she was walking to the train station in Hays with Marshal Thomas and Charlie Parsons. That time, she was attired in a beautiful maroon suit and a matching bonnet. She was a good looker, and Henry Burlingame was a good reporter—he remembered all of the little details.

The widow Parsons was a very gracious woman, too. The boy called Timothy brought a rag, which Burlingame used to clean the mud from his boots. The young girl, also blond and pretty, gave him a towel to wipe down his soggy hat. Mrs. Parsons served him a cup of coffee and sugar cookies, and after some small talk, she discreetly dismissed the two children. From the moment Henry Burlingame had identified himself, she knew the purpose of his visit.

Rose Parsons calmly listened. Burlingame had worked diligently; he explained that in his preliminary investigative work, he had rummaged through the back files of two newspapers and found the obituary of Jacob Parsons—surviving relatives were listed. Jacob Parsons had a married sister, Mary Belle Hotchkiss up in Boonville, Missouri. Mary Belle had two daughters, no sons, and there was no mention of a brother to Jacob, no mention of a nephew, Charles. He didn't want to be intrusive, and if Rose Parsons so desired, she didn't have to explain this peculiarity. The writer also wondered if there were some connection between Jacob or the young man known as Charlie Parsons with the deaths of the Cadwell men and John Hartley—all were originally from Boonville, all reportedly had ridden during the war with William Quantrill. Wasn't this an oddity, too?

Rose Parsons finally set her cup aside, smiled, and said, "You, Mister Burlingame, gave Charles his name . . . The Shooter. I gave him his name, Charles Parsons. He was a friend of Jake's. He's a very nice young man. He was in trouble when he came by here and, quite simply, I helped him. It was only several months after Jake's death, and I had frequent visitors. Calling him my nephew seemed appropriate." Rose Parsons suddenly felt warm inside. Was she blushing? Calling Hardy her nephew Charlie was not only appropriate, it had been necessary, and conveniently deceiving. Oh, what a story she could tell about Charlie Parsons! The Shooter? He was a shooter, all right. That beautiful young man undoubtedly was the greatest lover any woman could ever hope to meet. Staring Burlingame straight in the eyes, she smiled and said, "Do you understand? It would have been rather embarrassing otherwise."

Henry Burlingame nodded, replying, "Yes, yes, but of course." He took a sip of his coffee, then asked, "You said he was in trouble?"

"I can't say anything more about that."

"I see," Burlingame said. Then, "Well what do you make of this Cadwell thing, the Quantrill connection? It struck me as rather peculiar. Or perhaps it was just coincidental."

"It may have been," Rose Parsons replied. "From what I read in the newspaper, it seemed to me they were looking for Charlie because he killed that Brewster. I don't think Charlie knew those men were among the raiders. The boy would have had some cause for what he did, though. His parents and sister were killed by some of Quantrill's men. Charlie was only seven years old at the time. He told me this, and I thought it was such a terrible burden to carry all of these years. Justice comes about in mysterious ways, doesn't it?"

This was astounding to Henry Burlingame. Good Lord, it was a story in itself, a young man on the vengeance trail after twelve years! But, truthfully, this wasn't so; it was just as Rose Parsons had described it—coincidental. Yet how bizarre, how chilling! Burlingame then asked, "You said Charlie was a friend of Jake's. How did they meet?"

"I'm sorry, I can't tell you that."

"Can't"—he smiled—"or you feel that it's improper?"

"It would break my trust with Charlie," Rose answered. "I realize your obligations, your work as a newspaperman. You must understand mine as a confidant and friend of Charlie. The young man has had a hard time of it already. Those Cadwells, they came here threatening me and the children. They made a terrible mistake and they paid for it. The very thought that I might do something else to make his situation worse is frightening. Oh, I understand your position, Mister Burlingame, but he doesn't deserve any of this notoriety. He's a wonderfully kind boy."

"Yes." Burlingame nodded. "But however faultless he may or may not be, he's become news. He's one helluva gunfighter, Missus Parsons, and no one can accumulate the experience at weaponry that boy has in a matter of two years. I don't know anyone around on the plains who can possibly stand up to him, not one man . . . not even two together."

Rose Parsons said sadly, "This is the problem, don't you think? Until he finds himself a new home, there's always someone around who'll think he can stand up to Charlie."

"You're very fond of him."

"Very much, yes. Until this, I had hoped he would return . . . work on the farm for me."

"Charlie told Orlan Thomas he got his Gibbs revolver from Jake," said Burlingame. "Is this true?"

"I don't know," lied Rose Parsons. "If Jake gave him that gun, I didn't know about it. I don't have any interest in pistols. I abhor them. I think you can understand why."

"Yes, I'm sorry. I was a friend of Jake's . . . everyone was."

"Do you care for more coffee?"

Henry Burlingame didn't. He said thanks, and pushed away from his chair. No, he had to be getting along, and he told Mrs. Parsons that he was indebted to her for letting him visit, that whatever he wrote about Charlie Parsons he would refrain from disclosing anything she had told him, nor would he mention her name. Henry Burlingame had integrity. His perception was very good, too; this woman's affection for Charlie Parsons was like still water—it ran deep.

The next day, Henry Burlingame was in Kansas City at the offices of the *Star*. He spent the late afternoon perusing all of the back editions of the newspaper prior to Charlie Parsons's arrival in Abilene, searching for regional stories pertaining to robberies or shootings in which the perpetrator or perpetrators had escaped. He finally found one item which immediately piqued his curiosity, one with a striking parallel—a shoot-out in nearby Sedalia the previous summer in which a former member of the Jesse James gang, Richard Biddell, had been shot by a young man by the name of Joseph Hollister. Biddell, according to the story, had once ridden with Quantrill's raiders! Joseph Hollister? Who in the hell was Joseph Hollister? Flipping back the pages on the wooden spindle, Henry Burlingame thoughtfully stared out the big window. Was Charlie Parson, in reality, Joseph Hollister? Was this another coincidence?

The following morning near noon, Henry Burlingame stepped off the stage in Sedalia, checked into a room at the Borden Hotel, washed, put on a clean shirt, carefully knotted his black string tie, and went to the sheriff's office, where he identified himself and asked about Joseph Hollister. Did Sheriff Wendell McDermott remember a young fellow named Joseph Hollister! He certainly did, and so did everyone else in town, particularly four or five men and several children who had been witnesses to the street shooting. Joseph Hollister had spent the night in Borden's Hotel; so had Richard Biddell. Everyone remembered this and what had followed.

And, Henry Burlingame asked, "What prompted the shooting?"

Sheriff McDermott scratched his head, tutted once, and said, "Well, that was damn hard to figure. Biddell was a robber. He hailed the Hollister boy in the street . . . tried to pull his gun and shoot him. Least, this is what those who saw it said. What it looked like was this Biddell thought young Joseph recognized him and was after him. And on the other hand, it looked like Biddell was trying to claim bounty on Hollister. Damn confusing, but we didn't have any paper on Hollister. We did have a wanted paper on Biddell, though. Five hundred dollars on his head for robbery."

"And this Joseph Hollister collected?"

"As a matter of fact, no," replied Sheriff McDermott. "As I recollect, he had a rendezvous with a brother up in Omaha. He rode on out. I did the paperwork, and when the draft for the five hundred came in, I sent it on to Hollister's stepfather."

"What did Hollister look like? Can you remember?"

"Nice-looking boy. About six feet tall, dark hair, brown, maybe. Polite, too." McDermott chuckled. "Was white as a sheet when I first talked to him ... sick about the shooting, you know." Fumbling around with a stack of papers, he finally pulled a sheet out and slid it across the desk. "Sent the reward to this fellow."

The address was for Paul LaBlanc.

Henry Burlingame looked over quizzically at the sheriff, who said Kirkwood was a rural community at the edge of St. Louis. After a moment, Burlingame asked, "Did you see the weapon this boy was using? What type of a revolver it was?"

Sheriff McDermott, rubbing his chin, shook his head. "No, I don't know what it was. It did have a long barrel like some kind of a horse pistol. That's about all I can remember."

"How about his horse?"

"Hah! Now, that I remember. Nice-looking horse, good blood. It was a black Morgan."

Henry Burlingame suddenly beamed, and standing, he pulled out a long black cigar from his inside coat pocket. He shook hands with Sheriff Wendell McDermott and handed him the cigar. "Thank you, Sheriff," he said, "you've been a great help."

"I'm obliged," McDermott replied. Rolling the cigar between his fingers and thumbs, he said, "You figure this Hollister is someone special? Planning to write a big story about him?"

Henry Burlingame was at the door; he paused and looked back at the sheriff. "Yes, I have a hunch he's very special. One of a kind, one might say, a clever young man, whoever he is."

Now Henry Burlingame was chomping at the bit. As had his famous counterpart, Ned Buntline, he smelled a good yarn; he was impatient to move east to St. Louis, where he knew he was going to get an answer on what had prompted the flight west of Joseph Hollister, alias Charlie Parsons. The life story of The Shooter was only one hundred fifty miles down the road, but Burlingame, at least for the present, was stranded in Sedalia like a hobbled horse, unable to move out until the next day. With a series of stage delays, one stopover, checking into a hotel in St. Louis, and renting a buggy to drive out to Kirkwood Town, when he finally did arrive at the post office he was a very tired and bedraggled man. He posed three questions to the clerk behind the caged window: does a Paul LaBlanc pick up his mail here? Yep. Does he have a stepson named Joseph Hollister? Nope. Where does Paul LaBlanc live? Farm, down the river road. It was as though he were talking to Charlie Parsons himself— yep, nope, find out for yourself.

Burlingame tried again. "My name is Henry Burlingame. I'm a newspaper writer . . . articles, stories, that sort of thing. I write for the *New York Tribune, Harper's Weekly.*"

The clerk was canceling a few letters, pressing a rubber stamp onto an ink pad, rhythmically smacking it down on the envelopes. He gave Burlingame a sidelong glance, a suspicious one, the writer thought, and said, "The LaBlanc farm is no place for a stranger to go poking around, and they don't take kindly to newspaper people."

Burlingame, usually loquacious, never at a loss for words, stalled. This was a stone wall. But he was curious and presumptuous enough to ask, "Why is this, my good fellow?"

"Good fellow" wasn't enough. The clerk replied, "Go see the constable. He might help you. He isn't welcome down there, either."

Without recourse, Henry Burlingame left; searched up and down the small street for some sign of a courthouse, thinking that this was what he should have done in the first place. Certainly if a Joseph Hollister existed and was in some kind of trouble, the law would be aware of it. But that post office clerk had already confirmed his worst fear—Joseph Hollister was nothing more than another one of Charlie Parsons's aliases. Damn clever kid! Not only could he shoot, he could lie like hell, too.

Henry Burlingame ultimately found a small building; a sign over the door said KIRKWOOD COURT; that was the extent of it, and once inside, he found himself in an office with two desks, and to the back of the office were three jail cells. The cells were empty; one desk was occupied by a mustached man wearing a white shirt with the sleeves turned up. He was reading a small magazine, and horrors upon horrors, when the man turned it over and looked up, Henry Burlingame saw it was a Ned Buntline novel! Once again, Burlingame identified himself, and once again the reception was cool. This man wasn't the constable; he was a deputy. His name was Michael Higgins, and he had never heard of Joseph Hollister.

Finally Henry Burlingame said, "I find this exceedingly strange. This Hollister doesn't exist, yet he said he had a stepfather here . . . one Paul LaBlanc. Hollister killed a fellow up at Sedalia last year—five hundred-dollar reward, and the money was sent to LaBlanc. Now, what do you make of this?"

For a moment, Michael Higgins just sat there silent, immobile, like he had been mesmerized, but then suddenly it was as though a hot poker had touched his backside. Leaping up, arms flailing, he exclaimed, "By me life, it's the lad himself—Hardy Gibbs!"

"Gibbs?" A tiny spark touched Burlingame's puzzled mind.

"Aye, Gibbs it is, Mister, Mister. . .?"

"Burlingame."

"Two summers ago, that would be the lad. Mister LaBlanc is his uncle, not his stepfather, and Hardy has taken himself another name . . . Hollister." Reaching for his hat, he said, "I'll have to get over to Shamus's place and tell him this."

Henry Burlingame, following the deputy to the door, asked, "What did this Gibbs boy do?"

"Killed three young lads over at a saloon on the road to town," answered Higgins. "Fight over one of the lassies. Aye, 'tis said the boys violated her, young Hardy's cousin, Julienne, and he shot the three of 'em."

"Good Lord" Henry Burlingame said in a hushed voice. Walking alongside Michael Higgins, he asked, "Did Hardy live with his uncle down at this farm? I'd very much like to talk with these people."

"No, no, no," the deputy returned. "He lived with his grandfather, Amos, at the south end of the town road, the big house. Mister Gibbs is the master gunsmith. Aye, and a fine one he is."

Burlingame stopped in his tracks beside the buggy.

The tiny spark that he had felt nipping at his brain suddenly flared into flame. By God, at last, here it was! Hardy Gibbs, The Shooter! Little wonder why? And what was it that Rose Parsons had said? The boy had been orphaned when he was a child, the killings by Quantrill. Of course! Here it was, like a wart on his nose—Gibbs, the Gibbs revolver—but why on earth hadn't he had some suspicion of this earlier? Of how Charlie had come to possess one of those expensive revolvers? On the other hand, there were any number of Gibbs Specials around, bought, stolen, traded, and the last thought in his mind had been the fact that Charlie Parsons could have any possible connection with the gun maker. But now, how wonderfully it all meshed. How incredible. Hardy Gibbs, from childhood to manhood, in the presence of some of the finest handguns ever made. By gadfrey, the boy probably had helped his famous grandfather make them!

As Michael Higgins disappeared down a small lane, the elated Henry Burlingame stepped into his buggy, settled himself, and with a snap of the reins, set out for the town road, the end of it, the place where Amos Gibbs lived. Even if the visit proved futile, it would be confirmation—the metamorphosis of the ultimate gunfighter. Ah, but this intrusion, it would have to be a delicate one, one of empathy and understanding on his part. On their part, well, he already knew—it would be either a "yep" or a "nope." Undoubtedly, as Rose Parsons had known, Amos Gibbs and his family already knew who Charlie Parsons was; there was no way they could have ignored his tumultuous journey across the plains, and they were probably sick at heart about it. Understandably, he couldn't fault Amos Gibbs if he refused an interview, even if the resulting story cast young Hardy in the role of a victim of circumstances, a defender of justice.

With these thoughts, Henry Burlingame approached the Gibbs house and gunsmith shop with a great deal of apprehension. And, as he brought the buggy to a stop near the front of the house, a large colored woman appeared on the porch. Burlingame thought she must be the caretaker, or maybe the cook, for she wore a white apron, a big flowing skirt, and had a bandanna swirled around the top of her head. She was a formidable woman, and Henry Burlingame politely tipped his hat to her, asking if Amos Gibbs were about. At this moment, the familiar sound of a revolver cracked the afternoon silence, followed closely by another explosion, and the colored woman merely pointed to the back. Yes, Burlingame nodded, just follow the sound. He did, and the sight he came upon gave him the second big surprise of the afternoon—a strikingly beautiful young woman dressed in a billowy blouse, denim trousers, and wearing western-style riding boots, was wielding the pistol. Henry Burlingame abruptly stopped and in utter amazement silently watched as she continued to perforate a small black target nailed on the wall of a big barn about twenty-five yards away—five shots in all, including the two he had heard from the front, from a Gibbs Special, a five-shooter. She deftly broke the cylinder with a snap of her wrist and turned back to a small table. She saw him, said something to an older man standing nearby, who turned, stared momentarily, then approached. There was no doubt in Henry Burlingame's mind that this was the master, Amos Gibbs, one of the greatest gunsmiths of all time.

Before Amos Gibbs could speak, Burlingame extended his hand and without a moment's hesitation said, "I came to pay my respects. I saw your grandson in Oakley, Kansas. I had the privilege of talking with him, and I wanted you to know that he's in excellent health and of good spirit. He calls himself Charlie Parsons. My name is Henry Burlingame. As you must know, I've written several stories about him, objective, I trust, and of course only this day have I learned his true name. I wanted you to know this at the outset. I presume you are Mister Amos Gibbs, Charlie's grandfather."

"I am Amos Gibbs, yes," was the reply. "I've read your articles in the weekly. I don't appreciate them, but I read them."

"Yes, I realize this," Burlingame said. "The boy is news. The public has come to fancy him, and, well, I have my job to do, too."

If Amos Gibbs understood this, he said nothing, only beckoned the young woman. After placing the revolver on the table, she walked up, and Amos, nodding at Burlingame, said, "This is the fellow who does all the writing about Hardy, Mister Burlingame. Says he had a talk with him at Oakley. Mister Burlingame, this is my assistant, Julie LaBlanc, my grandniece."

She only nodded.

Burlingame said, "You are an attractive assistant and, I must say, an excellent shot." How beautiful this woman was, even with her icy, calculating stare. He heard Amos Gibbs speaking again.

"Julie and Hardy are engaged. Still plan on getting married one of these days . . . despite the mess."

Good Lord, Burlingame thought, no wonder the boy

had gone berserk! Julie was Hardy Gibbs's second cousin, reason enough in itself, but she was also his fiancée! By gadfrey, what a story this was turning out to be, yet how depressing, how devastatingly sad. What could he possibly say? He tried, "I'm terribly sorry for all of your troubles, Miss LaBlanc."

This woman's beauty was as cold as her demeanor; she was unflinching, just as she had been while she was marking that black target directly in the middle. She replied, "It's men like you, Mister Burlingame, who don't make it any easier. How did you find us? What do you want here?"

Henry Burlingame took pride in his integrity, his honesty, and as much as it dismayed him to admit to the purpose of his visit, he did. "I plan on writing a comprehensive story, maybe a short novel, on Hardy Gibbs. I want it to be factual, not speculative or romantically dishonest. I want to write about the real Hardy Gibbs, from his perspective—your perspective."

Julienne returned, "The real Hardy Gibbs? The real Hardy Gibbs doesn't exist anymore." She gestured around. "His presence is here—down the road, along the trails, down by the river, in my uncle's heart, in my heart. This is all you'll find here, Mister Burlingame, memories." She whirled about, went back to the table, where she picked up her revolver, and brushing by Burlingame, she said, "Marksmanship runs in the family. Good day."

Amos Gibbs took a deep breath and sighed. Henry Burlingame saw the sadness in the old man's eyes; paradoxically, he saw something else, too, a glint of proudness intermingling with the sadness, yes, and a firm jaw set in iron.

"Julie has better steel in her blood than we put in those pistols," he said. "This about says it all, Mister Burlingame. Good day to you. You see that boy of mine again, you tell him we love him."

ELEVEN

Festus Cato and Little Bear

Traveling along the North Platte River, occasionally following the ancient ruts of the old Oregon Trail, was a new experience for Hardy Gibbs. He wasn't a pioneer, but he felt like one, for traffic along this abandoned migratory route was scarce: only an occasional freighter headed for some obscure ranching settlement upriver or one of those cavalry troops trotting along, for what reason Hardy couldn't figure out because he hadn't seen an Indian in his six days on the trail. In fact, except for those soldier boys and two wagonloads of sodbusters looking for a place to squat, he hadn't seen much of anything except big country, and this suited him just fine and dandy. It surely was less troublesome.

Late on the seventh day on the road, he rode into the old frontier trading post of Fort Laramie, now an army headquarters surrounded by a hodgepodge of decrepit one-story buildings, some stone, some log, and a few made of sod. He saw a few tipis, too, later learned these belonged to what some of the people called "fort Indians," friendlies who served as scouts for the army.

At the post mercantile, Hardy Gibbs also learned that despite the treaties and severe crackdown on the Indians following George Armstrong Custer's humiliating defeat, there were still a few so-called "hostiles" roaming the valleys to the north. While Hardy was replenishing his supplies, the bespectacled clerk in a blue apron advised him that it wasn't safe to be traveling alone. "Never know who's out there anymore ... hostiles, drifters, road agents, and the like, always someone lurking about looking to steal your outfit or take your hair. Have to watch your backside, too."

Hardy Gibbs smiled and began stacking his purchases to the side. "It's no different from where I've been," he said. "Not that hair thing, though. I don't take much of a notion to the thought of getting scalped. I'm no Indian fighter, you know."

The clerk chuckled, adjusted his spectacles, and replied, "No sane man is until he has to be, but I notice you've been consorting with them ... that buckskin you're wearing, the shirt. Cheyenne markings. Don't see many around with that quality anymore. The old squaws, they used to do that fancy beadwork. It's all cloth now, flannel, gingham, calico, brightest colors they can buy ... when they have money."

"You don't trade?"

"Here?" The clerk shook his head. "No, not much anymore. The army chased most of the Injun trade out of here a few years back. They built Fort Robinson over next to the Sioux reservations so they could keep them away from the white trade coming through. Less trouble. Just the sight of some of those Injuns scared the hell out of the white folks." He grinned at Hardy Gibbs. "Still does, especially after that Custer fiasco." There was a big bulge in the screen door where the knees of many supply-laden customers had pushed out of the store, but the clerk obliged Hardy and gave the door a shove. It swung open and the man said, "If you're looking to hire on with some cow outfit, best you be heading down toward Cheyenne. I hear that's where they're settling in these days. She's deader'n a doornail around here, son."

Thanking the storekeep, Hardy Gibbs went back to his quarters in Brown's Hotel, a hotel only by frontier standards, for anywhere else it would have been called a shanty. His small room contained one large bunk with a canvas-covered straw-filled mattress, a plank washstand, a chair, a pitcher and bowl, and one large chamber pot. Grubby and unkempt, there wasn't enough room to swing a cat. Close to the fly-specked window, there was a small mirror for grooming. It was dirty, too. Touched both by sadness and humor, Hardy thought of the old Watson homestead, how Julienne had swept the floor, brushed out all of the cobwebs, how she had scurried about like a little mouse building a nest. That woman surely would stomp her foot about this place. Damn, how he missed her! And this country—it was getting bigger and bigger, and he was getting lonelier and lonelier. Well, he mused, that storekeeper was right—this place was dead as a doornail. But at least, if the country were getting bigger and bigger, he was surely getting smaller and smaller. A fellow who always seemed to be getting into some fool shooting scrape had to take heart in this, and he certainly wasn't going anywhere near that big town of Cheyenne. He would keep heading up the river trail just like one of those old pioneers. It was Oregon or bust. But this horrible emptiness in his heart, this feeling of getting lonelier and lonelier, was beginning to give him second thoughts. Wasn't there some alternative?

If Brown's Hotel wasn't much for lodging, it was better for eating. Hardy Gibbs had a good breakfast the next morning—a huge stack of sourdough hotcakes, a slab of ham, and two cups of strong coffee. By the time he had saddled Sundown and packed his mule, he figured it was about eight o'clock.

Outside the fort, a few lines of horses were parading around, those blue-coated soldiers atop them, and he could hear someone yelling out commands. Riding slowly, he passed three big tipis, saw some people draped in blankets, a few squatted by a small fire, the others, as solemn as a church hymn, just watching him; but of course, those Indians that he and Willard Colby had seen down near Oakley last year didn't look very happy, either. This set Hardy Gibbs to thinking. There surely was a lot of misery around the country. Misery was a common affliction. Why, he had ridden all the way from Missouri, across Kansas, into the Colorado and Wyoming country, and he couldn't recall meeting anyone without some kind of misery or trouble, maybe excepting Curly Robe John and Blackbird. They were always singing or humming, but he hadn't heard anyone else doing this, not even himself. Every time he tried humming or even playing the harmonica, it always sounded like the lonesome blues, one of those moaning, wailing tunes. Adah used to sing like that sometimes. It had something to do with her childhood, her family and all, being slaves, and now the only kin she had left was Grandfather, and he wasn't blood. Dammit, he missed Adah, most likely he would never see that big woman and her wagging finger again.

Yah, yah, yah, Master Hardy, there's a bug buzzing 'round my stove, here. It's that ol' love bug, that's what it is.

Disconsolate, Hardy Gibbs plodded on.

Hardy spent the night curled up in his blanket and tarp near the Horseshoe Stage Station and, after breakfast at the stage stop, was away shortly after sunup. Now there were a lot of foothills to his left, some barren, some timbered with evergreens, reminding him of the piney woods below the Meramec. These hills reached up like long, twisting fingers to big mountains, the biggest he had ever seen. There was some good water around, too. A few of those creeks coming down from the mountains were as clear as glass. At one of these creeks when he stopped to rest and water Sundown and the mule, he caught a fleeting glimpse of a figure on the trail behind him. He thought this was kind of strange because, as he had been warned, he had been checking his backside regularly. Maybe he was just being overly cautious; maybe his eyes were playing tricks on him, you know, all of those stories about sneaky Indians and such, and after all, what he had seen, or thought he had seen, just seemed to melt away in the brush. Deer did this sometimes; so did turkeys. *Psst,* just like that they were gone, but he allowed this wasn't any deer or turkey; it looked tall and dark silhouetted against the midmorning sun. Well, he knew he had to do something. He felt a little tremble in his legs; he didn't like the notion of getting shot in the back. Nervously alert, he crossed the creek, leading his horse and mule into a small patch of aspen, where he quickly slipped off his bedroll, propped it up in the shade of one of the trees, and placed his hat atop it. With his Winchester in hand, Hardy Gibbs darted back through the brush and made a wide circle to his left, determined to get first look at whomever was following him, if, indeed someone were following him.

Hunkering behind a few sandstone boulders, he patiently waited; time sped, and just about the time he was beginning to feel foolish, he heard the slow, methodical clomp, clomp of a horse. Holy smokes, not one horse, but two—and here they came, right below him, two men leading them. Directly, they stopped, one of the men motioning ahead, and they began passing sign between each other. Hardy wasn't close enough to make out any of it, but after all of that time with Blackbird last winter, he could understand most anything she had flashed. After a moment, the men tied their mounts to some sprigs of brush alongside the trail and crept ahead as though they were walking on eggs. Well, it was more like crunching eggs because they were so busy looking ahead they were kicking up every rock and pebble in their path. What's more, the one in back was so bowlegged a hog could have passed under him without hitting his buckskins. *Buckskins.* Both of these men were clad from head to toe in buckskins, and the one in the lead had one of the biggest, floppiest hats that Hardy had ever seen. He also had a rifle. They surely were up no good, that was a fact, so Hardy Gibbs eased out from behind his rocks and crept along behind them.

Shortly, he was within twenty paces, and quietly stepping to the side of the rutted trail, he called, "Hey, you!" The men abruptly stopped and stared at one another. "Hey!" Hardy repeated, and this time they whirled about, only to stare at a rifle pointed directly at them. If they were surprised, Hardy Gibbs was even more surprised. Good Lord, it was two old codgers as old as Grandfather, one with big saddlebags under his eyes and a shaggy beard, the other a wizened, stooped fellow with more wrinkles in his face than a stale prune.

"Y'got us dead to rights," the man with floppy hat croaked. "We give up."

"The other man, an Indian, grinned and said, *"Hau."*

"I ought to shoot you," Hardy Gibbs said. "You damn fools scared the hell out of me! You're a couple of bushwhackers, sneaking up to kill me. Well, speak up, dammit!"

"Naw, naw," the grizzled white man protested, "no such thing. Mebee we'd count coup on ya, but killin' . . . naw, it's agin the law, and we sure wouldn't do that. No, sir, 'y'sure got it wrong, pilgrim. We's right peaceful, meanin' no harm."

Hardy Gibbs was flabbergasted. "Why, you're lying for sure! I saw you creeping along like a couple of snakes in the grass. Now, go on, get over there to the side and put that rifle against the tree. Go on, move!"

"Y'jest don't understand," the white man said, although by his dense whiskers, his shaggy beard, and dirty buckskins, Hardy could barely tell that he was white.

"Well, you tell me, then" retorted Hardy. "You just tell me what I don't understand. I may be a pilgrim, but I'm sure as hell not a blind one. Holy smokes, if you two don't take the cake!"

Obviously, the aged Indian didn't understand a word of what Hardy Gibbs was saying. He was still smiling, a funny little smile, all puckered at the corners of his mouth with wrinkles dancing in every direction. He sat down in the shade of the trees, looked up between his heavily lidded eyes, and said "Hau" again.

The other man, shrugging helplessly, wheezed, "Balls of fire, pilgrim, all we was lookin' for was a little grub. Been up there in the Medicine Bows nigh on a week eatin' straight meat, and our bellies are a mite onerous, that's all."

"Hah, and you were fixing to rob me!"

"Yassir, I reckon y'could say that," he admitted. "We's down on our luck . . . jest a couple of ol' timers down on our luck. We ain't beggars."

Hardy sniffed once, twice; they looked like beggars, and they also smelled like very ripe beggars. Moving upwind, Hardy said, "It's not begging if you just walk up and ask what's in the pot, is it? Sneaking around like that, you're liable to get shot, and I've had enough of people sneaking around looking for me. Damnation, now, what am I going to do with you two old farts?"

"On the run, too?" asked the white man. "Why, so is ol' Mato-Ciqala, here. Y'see, that's another reason we're pussyfootin'. Never know who yer friend is. Might be some headhunter fixin' t'take Mato's head back to Deadwood."

"Mato?" Hardy stared curiously at the old Indian.

"Mato-Ciqala . . . Little Bear," said the man. "Me? I'm Festus Cato, practically bred and born in these mountains, I am. He's a powerful medicine chief, he is. Lakota."

Hardy Gibbs sniffed again. Both of these culprits were a tad powerful. He said, "Why would anyone want his head?"

"Ain't been in these parts long, have ya, pilgrim?"

"Passing through, that's all."

"They's givin' two hundred and fifty dollars fer Injun heads up in Deadwood."

"That's ridiculous!" Hardy replied.

"Fer a fact, it is, so help me God," Festus Cato said. " 'Sides that, the bluecoats are looking fer Little Bear, fixin' t'take him back to the reservation. Fixin' t'string me up, too, aidin' and abettin' . . . stealin' a pony, too. Hell, pilgrim, we's at the end of the line."

Hardy Gibbs, with a long sigh, replied, "I'm at the end of my patience, that's what, all of this cock and bull."

"We's hungry fer some mealy mush," Festus Cato said. Turning to his silent companion, he said a few words in Siouan, and Little Bear, rubbing his stomach, nodded at Hardy Gibbs. *"Hau, hau."* Festus stared back at Hardy. "Y'see? I ain't fibbin' 'bout it."

Shaking his head, Hardy Gibbs sat down some distance away and rested his rifle across his lap. "I can't believe you two," he said. "You come sneaking up on me all ready to rob me, and now you want me to feed you a bowl of mush."

"We kin trade ya," Festus said hopefully. "We've got some venison—dried, it is, but good fer boilin' and stew makin.' Ain't spoilt, yet." Cocking his head around, he asked, "What y'on the run fer, pilgrim? Y'been partin' hair? Robbin' a stage?"

"Do I look like a robber?"

"Can't tell a man by his looks, can ya? Look at us."

"I have. You're a couple of old reprobates."

Festus Cato cackled. "Hungry ones, too. What's in the pot?"

"When's the last time you had a bath, Mister Cato?"

"Bath!"

"Yes, washing up, cleaning your leathers, that sort of thing."

"Why, I don't recollect, I really don't."

"I figured that." Hardy Gibbs thoughtfully drummed his fingers on the stock of his Winchester and, after a few moments, nodded toward the distant river. "Tell you what, Mister Cato, you and Little Bear go on down to the river and get yourselves all washed good and proper. I'll just keep your weapon. Yes, and while you're taking a bath, I'll see what I can find in my pack. We can have ourselves a picnic."

"Balls of fire!" exclaimed Festus Cato. "The river! Why, that water is cold, pilgrim! We'd be outright sinnin', that's what. Y'ain't joshin', are ya?"

"Nope."

Hardy Gibbs didn't prepare mush; he made a big pan of bannock, and this hot, fried bread, topped with generous portions of beans and bacon, had soon pacified the bellies of Festus Cato and Little Bear. Little Bear belched loudly; he was content, and fetching his blanket, he spread it in the shade, rolled over, and promptly went to sleep. Then Festus Cato, his clean, speckled beard now glistening, rested back against the trunk of a tree and began relating an astonishing story. Hardy Gibbs listened in fascinated awe. It was true, Mato-Ciqala was a Sioux chief, a holy one among his people, a man who made powerful medicine, a man who was revered and respected. But his confinement on the reservation had weakened his medicine, and this was the second time he had left without permission. This time it was final; the sacred Black Hills had been desecrated, their holiness destroyed by the white men who were tearing out the bowels of Mother Earth. Little Bear had done all he could. He made medicine, he prophesied the demise of the white man's village in the sacred Black Hills, he claimed fire and water would come and destroy the wooden lodges. Two winters had passed and the white man was still lodged in his village. Little Bear had lost his powerful medicine. The Great Spirit was calling him; he was prepared to go to a high place in the Big Horn Mountains and extend his empty hands to the Great Spirit, but if the bluecoats caught him, he would have to go back and die a dishonorable death on the reservation. This was not good—Little Bear was headed up to the Big Horns to die.

This was the crux of the stunning story told by Festus Cato, not necessarily in his exact words, but as close as he could remember the way Little Bear had told it. He said to a pensive Hardy Gibbs, "Y'have t'listen good, 'cuz sometimes it sounds like they're sayin' everythin' backwards. Tell ya, though, ain't no way of not gettin' the idea as to what they're meanin'. When it's time to die, it's time to die, so that's why we're goin', pilgrim, up to the big mountains, sneakin' around those bluecoats up the Bozeman Trail."

Hardy Gibbs sighed, saying, "That's the strangest story I've ever heard. What's more, it's pretty scary, him wanting to die this way."

"Says he traveled what he calls the 'Red Road' all his life," Festus Cato went on. "Sorta like our 'straight and narrow,' y'know, so he ain't got a bone of fear in him, that ol' boy. I reckon it's true, all right, 'cuz I've known

Mato nigh on forty years. Hells bells, I used t'trade with his brothers, sometimes traveled right along with 'em up into the River of the Tongues huntin' curly cows, some of the prettiest country God ever made." He paused, then grinned under his whiskers. "Hell, I don't know, if I feels like it, I jest may curl up and die with him. Ain't much left out here fer me, either."

Startled at such a bizarre suggestion, Hardy Gibbs said, "Why . . . why, that's crazy talk, going up on some mountain and dying. You're no Indian, Mister Cato. Jesus, what a notion!"

"Close to it, son. Lived and bred with 'em all my life, y'know, and I tell ya, ain't no better place t'go lookin' for the Maker than up on those big mountain valleys. Better'n down here in civilization with all the crazies, not meanin' no offense t'you, 'course."

"No, of course not." Hardy Gibbs stared thoughtfully over at the sleeping holy man who didn't look very holy, but, for a fact, looked downright disreputable even though he had grudgingly taken a bath in the river, the price of a meal. Looking back at Festus Cato, Hardy asked, "Where are these mountains? These Big Horns."

" 'Cross the river," Festus nodded, "up that'a way, a far piece, mebee six, seven days as the crow flies."

"This Bozeman Trail?"

"Same, pilgrim. Catch on to it, go all the way to the Yellowstone, up the Yellowstone to Bozeman City in the Montana Territory." He grinned at Hardy. "Damn sight better'n the way you're goin' if you're on the run, and I figger y'are. Nothin' but Injuns to the north till y'git to the settlements. Gold camps."

"And beyond the gold camps?"

"Rivers, valleys, till hell won't have it," Festus Cato

answered. "Once, I followed those valleys all the way to the Hell Gate, land called the Five Valleys. Me'n a feller named Jim Clyman, why, we hit in on trappin' beaver and dallyin' with the Injun women, ended up over with the Nez Percé in the Oregon country. Damnedest trip I ever made. . . . No whites 'round, then."

"Oregon?" questioned Hardy Gibbs. "You went that way to Oregon?"

"Hell, yes! No trails then, either. Why there's a reg'lar wagon road all the way now. Call it . . . let's see . . . yassir, the Mullan Road." He glanced over at Hardy. "Oregon? Is this where yer headed?"

Hardy nodded. "Had a notion about the place, yes, a good place to settle down and make a living, a new start."

Festus Cato squinted at Hardy. "There's better places, t'my notion, son. Y'don't look like a sodbuster. Y'look like a squaw man." He burst out cackling at this. "What's yer callin', pilgrim?"

Squaw man? Was this good or bad? Hardy Gibbs remembered when Blackbird had called him this, when he had proudly tried on his new clothes she had fashioned. His long hair had been tied in the back and bound with leather. Well, it still was. He surely didn't look like Hardy Gibbs anymore. He said to Festus, "I'm a gunsmith. A tinner, too. I can do about anything along these lines."

"Is that fact, or are y'braggin'? Y'look a bit young fer all of that."

"I started learning when I was seven years old."

"No brag, then," Cato replied. He thoughtfully stroked his whiskers several times, then put his fingers to his nose and sniffed. "I smell different." He grinned. "Sorta like a wet dog." He cocked his head; Hardy noticed Festus always did this, wondered if he had an eye out of kilter, or maybe it was just habit. "Y'know, pilgrim—say, what is yer handle, anyways?"

"Charlie."

"Well, y'know, Charlie, there's a callin' for gunsmiths 'mos anywheres, but now, tinners, well, that's a good trade. Y'get yerself set up in one of the settlements, and 'mos likely the swag'll come rollin' in. I'm not one for settlements. Y'see, I ain't got no callin' anymore, a reg'lar no-account. Civilization and ol' age done me in, I reckon. Got myself on a rail gang a couple of years back and they set me to fetchin' water. Downright humiliatin', kept yellin' at me, 'water boy, water boy!' " Festus Cato winked slyly. "Smart feller like you with some learnin' and a good trade can git himself lost out here. Change his name, git himself a good squaw for the workin' and beddin'. Know what I mean?"

Hardy Gibbs knew what he meant, all right. He had already changed his name twice; he already had himself a squaw, too, one-quarter, anyway, but he sure as hell wouldn't call her such a name, no more than he could claim to be an Indian. "All right, Mister Cato," Hardy said, "you've seen everything there is to see in this country. Now, say you have some learning . . . say you were about twenty-five or thirty years old—"

"I'd go crazy with the heat," Festus Cato cut in. "I'd even take a bath in the river. I'd fall at the feet of the first purty woman I saw. Mebee I'd git myself a job, too. Y'know, if'n I was young like you, Charlie. Hell, mebee I wouldn't mind workin. I'd sure like the lovin' part of it."

"I know, I know." Hardy sighed. "But where would you go? You just said there were better places than Oregon, where a man can get lost, find himself a good squaw."

Festus Cato tilted his head. "Did I say that?"

"You surely did."

"I tend t'fergit a lot, lately. Y'see, that's another sign of ol' age, fergittin' all the time. Oh, but I don't fergit the land, Charlie. No, I can remember 'mos every rock, tree, and river I ever did see, green grass in the meadows, sweet water. Yassir, I remembers things like this, I do."

"You remember any special place?"

"Did I tell ya 'bout the time Jim Clyman and me went cavortin' to the west? Followin' the Yellowstone?"

"Yes, I recollect you did mention that." Hardy Gibbs nodded.

"Well, I'll tell ya, Charlie, we hung 'round that Five Valley country nigh on to two weeks. Flathead Injuns lived there in those days—all moved north, now, but the land don't change . . . the people do. Whites there now, even a settlement and a fort. Don't even call it Hell Gate no more. Missoula, Injun name. Don't know if'n you'd find yerself a purty squaw in that place, but from what I hear there's a lot of sodbusters over there, and where there's sodbusters, ya ain't gonna find much trouble. Right peaceful lot, they are."

"I'm for peace," Hardy said. "Maybe I'd like to see this place . . . take a ride up that way."

Festus Cato cocked his head again, a quizzical look on his aged face. "That's northwest, Pilgrim, ain't west, y'know. Now, lookee here, y'ain't figgerin' on followin' along with me and ol' Mato, are ya? Goin' up the

Bozeman? Why, we can't be lookin' out for no pilgrim, Charlie. Hostiles, bluecoats 'round fixin' t'count coup on us. We got problems enough."

"No." Hardy Gibbs smiled. "I thought it would be the other way around, you two old buggermen following me. I'm the one with the rations. You're the ones with the onerous bellies, unless you're planning on eating straight meat again."

Festus Cato scratched up behind a weathered ear and slowly nodded. "Yassir, well, I reckon we could kinda show ya the way, all right, keep y'on the proper trail, mebee away from the hostiles."

Hardy Gibbs emitted a sigh of exasperation. "For chrissakes, Mister Cato, we're the ones doing the running! We're the damned hostiles!"

Hardy Gibbs paid fifty cents to use a spare bunk in the La Bonte Stage Station that night. Festus Cato and Little Bear were fortunate, too; with nary a complaint, they slept in the hay shed, and early the next morning, Hardy satisfied their hankering for mush. He took them two bowls of oatmeal and a small can of condensed milk from the station kitchen. Contented, they were all away in good fashion, Hardy contemplating the next stop at Fort Fetterman, where Cato told him he could purchase additional staples for the trek up to the Big Horns. About two miles along the trail, the men came to one of the old campsites used by the wagon trains that had once regularly plied the route, and among a pile of litter Hardy saw several rusted cans. Since he still harbored some mistrust about the two old rascals trailing along with him, he thought this was an opportune time to make a point—that he wasn't one with whom they could trifle. They stared at him curiously as he dismounted and went over and began kicking one of the cans into a clearing. Walking slowly away, he abruptly whirled around, drew his revolver, and in rapid fire sent the can bouncing all the way down the trail. Snapping open the cylinder on his Gibbs, he shucked the empties and began shoving in new cartridges. Then, with a small smile, he said to his stunned observers, "Practice. A man has to practice or he loses his edge."

Festus Cato's sad eyes were alert. Little Bear's crazy pucker of a grin was gone, his mouth rounded into a tiny oval of awe. "*Waśte, waśte,*" he finally mumbled, nodding.

"What's that?" Hardy Gibbs asked, looking up at Festus Cato.

"Mato says, 'Good, good'," answered Cato. "Phew-ee!"

And, going back to the packs on the mule, Hardy said, "Yes, not bad, not bad." He rummaged around for a moment until he found Festus Cato's small leather ammunition bag, which he had taken away from the old trapper the previous day. "Here," he said, tossing the pouch up to him, "you can have these back now. You better slide a few in that old Henry . . . help take care of this pilgrim in case I need it."

Slipping his rifle from its scabbard, Festus Cato replied, "I'm thankin' ya, Charlie, right proper, too, but by crackee, y'ain't no pilgrim. You're a goddamned gunfighter if I ever saw one." He began methodically pushing shells into his Henry, stopped momentarily, and guffawed. "If this don't beat all! We's three of a kind, all wanted by the law. A horse thief, a renegade, and a shooter, all lookin' for the Promised Land."

About four hours later, Hardy Gibbs finally saw the enfilade of Fetterman's towers jutting up, the river curling like a silver ribbon to the rear of the fort. At this point, Festus Cato and Little Bear stopped short; Little Bear spat disgustedly to the side, passed the edge of his hand across his throat, and said, "*Eyah, wasichu!*"

Nudging his horse to the side, Cato said to Hardy, "This is as far as we go, Charlie . . . me'n Mato. Meet ya over on the other side of the river, 'round a hill or two. That's the way we go, anyways. *Wachin ksapa yo*, pilgrim. Y'pay attention, hear?"

They rode off down through the trees and soon were out of sight. Hardy Gibbs gently kneed Sundown ahead, and five minutes later was riding across the perimeter clearing of the fort. Not much activity here, he observed, only several sheds, some corrals with big black and brown horses inside, their heads lowered in midafternoon dozes, and no tipis around. A lone soldier was standing in the shade near the gate, a rifle at his side. After a brief greeting, the soldier pointed out the sutler's store, a small log building in between two long barracks. Not much activity inside, either, two men sitting on a porch bench, and another one at attention by the screen door. This soldier had a rifle, too, and Hardy allowed this particular building was headquarters for the post. Festus Cato had told him to pay attention, but he certainly didn't see much around this place that required any attention.

Once inside the store, he found out why—most of the soldiers were on routine patrol duty, riding around the hills scouting for hostiles who, the sutler said, were few and far between. Hardy Gibbs bought his staples—"quite a passel" for one man, the sutler opined—took them outside in two separate loads, securely packed them on the mule, and rode out. The men on the porch were still there; the man on duty had moved to the other side of the door, and the soldier at the gate was still lolling in the shade. No one had paid Hardy any mind at all.

Two days passed. The rolling ridges to the left of Hardy Gibbs were now bulging like melons, reaching upward, blending into piney-wood forests and high-mountain meadows embroidered with white corn snow, the last remnants of winter. These were the lower Big Horns.

Festus Cato knew the land and Hardy never had to ask a question. Cato talked incessantly, and Little Bear prayed, every morning, every evening, off on a hill or a rise, chanting and singing. Old, ancient as the jagged peaks around him, Little Bear looked like a pile of prairie bones wrapped in a blanket, and thus in watching this decrepit old chief, Hardy Gibbs realized that the true worth and goodness of a person could never be measured by appearance. This old man was sad. He was in his twilight, but he was proud. As Festus Cato said of his dearest friend, Mato-Ciqala was going to die with his face to the sun.

The men traveled leisurely for another four days, keeping an eye out for roving troopers, always bearing slightly to the northwest in sight of the snow-capped mountains, and ultimately they came to a small stream called Little Goose Creek. It tumbled down from the canyons of the big mountains, leveled out, and coursed

through groves of fir, pine, alders, and cottonwood. The
new grass was yellow and green; the bushes were
freshly dressed in white and pink blossoms, and on
ripe mounds of moist earth, prairie dogs, erect, with
their tiny paws dangling across their breasts, were the
guardian sentinels. This was a beloved place for Little
Bear, for he had first come here when only a child. For
many moons thereafter, he had been here for the renewal rites of his people. He had made medicine on
the nearby hilltops and smelled the smoke of many
pipes. This was a good place to die.

Hardy Gibbs, however entranced by the glorious
splendor of the mountains, the invigorating air, this
wonderful breath of early summer, was sorely distressed at the idea of anyone coming to this wonderful
place with the intention of dying. And, once again, he
expressed his thoughts to Festus Cato. They were
stretching a tarp between two trees, making a little
camp not far from the stream. Little Bear had wobbled
away to a little ridge overlooking the plains below.

"This looks like a good place to *live*," Hardy said. "The
notion of him dying doesn't set well in my mind, Mister
Cato. It's the craziest thing I ever heard of."

"That's because y'don't have the mind of an Injun,
pilgrim."

"I have a little blood in me, you know."

" 'Mos everyone in this country does now," Festus
Cato said with a grin. "Never was much argument
'bout consortin' in the bedroll, but y'ain't got the
religion—the dreams, the visions. Y'ain't a piece of the
land and the big sky. Mato's ready t'give these pieces
back. Ready to fly, he is, more'n a notion." A piece of
rope dangling in his hand, Festus Cato stopped and

looked across the tumble grass, juniper, and sage. He's been ailin' . . . trouble gettin' on and off his pony, sometimes pissin' in his britches. Hell, I've been wonderin' if'n we'd make it this far. Wants me t'make him a scaffold, git things ready."

"Jesus," moaned Hardy Gibbs, shivering inside.

"Need some help, I will," Festus Cato said. "Ain't so fit myself, y'know."

"Well, of course . . . yes, I'll give you a hand."

"Mebee make it big enough for two," Cato added, grinning over at Hardy.

"Aw, for chrissakes," Hardy lamented, "will you quit talking like this? Here we are, free as birds in one of the prettiest places I've ever been, not having to think of squaring off against some fool shooter, and you two are making me feel like hell. Holy smokes, I can't believe it! I've been miserable enough without all of this. I should have left you two old buzzards on the North Platte and taken the long way around to the Promised Land."

Festus Cato cackled. "Look at it this way, pilgrim. You're our savior. Hadn't latched on with ya, we'd probably starved t'death and the varmints'd be pickin' our ol' bones. 'Sides, y'don't unnerstand nothin' 'bout death, the good parts of it . . . the peace, the freedom. I always thought when I come back I'll be one those snappin' turtles, git me a piece of every goddamned white toe that gits in m'way."

"A loggerhead?"

"Yassir, has its good points, y'know. Like everytime y'don't like what's goin on, y'jest go down and stick yer head in the mud and ferget it . . . come back up when ye're damned good and ready. When ye're tired of lookin' at what's happenin', how everythin' is turnin' to shit, y'jest go off and hide at the bottom of the world."

Shaking his head despairingly, Hardy Gibbs sighed and said, "That's some notion, Mister Cato."

They finished the shelter in silence, gratefully for Hardy Gibbs, who in between the talk of death and dying was thinking about life and living, wondering how and when he was going to get his Julienne out here beside him. Lord, Lord, what a pleasurable journey this would be, up through these beautiful mountains with her at his side!

Directly, he saw Little Bear waddling back through the brush, probing his way along with a dead branch as though he were a blind man. Pausing at the edge of the camp clearing, Little Bear threw aside his stick and began talking and making sign, some of which Hardy understood. Curved forefingers to the side of the old man's head, two hands, fingers flashing, the motion of shooting, and cupped fingers to his mouth. Buffalo?

Festus Cato confirmed it, saying, "Mato says there's a small herd of blackhorns up above us. Says we oughta go shoot one. Has a hankerin' for some liver, he does."

"Buffalo?" Hardy asked. Up until now, he hadn't seen any of these critters of the plains, not one single solitary buffalo, only signs of where they had been, or what was left of them, those hides back at Oakley a year ago.

"You wanna go shoot one?" he heard Festus Cato asking. "Have us a real feast t'night . . . liver, ribs, some hump, and y'kin roast some for yer pack. Make ol' Mato happy."

Hardy Gibbs thought this was a good idea, and after

some preliminary discussion, he and Cato, leading the pack mule, rode off through the edge of the timber in the general direction of the buffalo. About a half mile up, they came to small hill, went to the edge of it, and looked over. There, not more than two hundred yards away, were Little Bear's blackhorns, about thirty of them, grazing on the greening grama. Festus Cato cocked his head in his peculiar way and studied them for several moments, then told Hardy that they had two choices—they could ride out and charge the small herd and hope for a good shot, or pick out a yearling, make a stalk, and kill it. He said, "Don't wanna shoot those big ol' bulls, pilgrim. They're tougher'n a plank and got hides on 'em an inch thick."

From his hidden place in the trees, and the great distance, the animals all looked alike to Hardy Gibbs: big, ponderous beasts, most of them with their heads down. However, he could make out several that appeared to have larger horns. These, cautioned Cato, were the ones to avoid. The men elected to make a stalk. As Hardy suspected, Festus complained that his joints were too bothersome to go crawling through the grass and sage. Oh, he had the itch, all right, but he just wasn't fit, might spoil the whole game, so, with a fateful sigh of resignation, Hardy crouched and sneaked away by himself. He managed to get within about a hundred yards of the small band before he heard some nervous snorts. When he dared lift his head to take a peek, he saw several of the animals trotting around in a half circle with their tails lifted. Holy smokes, they were staring right in his direction! He surely didn't have much time to pick and choose, so coming to a knee, he aimed his Winchester behind the shoulder of the animal nearest him, touched off the round, quickly ejected, and threw in another, fired again, and stood up. He had heard the dull thud of the first bullet. The result was obvious; the buffalo bucked wildly several times, momentarily spun around in circles, and collapsed. The rest of the herd galloped off, but from behind, Hardy heard the triumphant cry of Festus Cato.

Dressing out that animal, a young cow, was one of the worst ordeals Hardy Gibbs ever experienced. With Festus doing the preliminary work, gutting the animal and carving away the liver and tongue, Hardy was left the dismembering of the hindquarters and the loin. Cato's small hatchet was dull from whacking too many pieces of firewood, and both the men's knives quickly dulled from slicing through hide and sinew. Hardy Gibbs, bloodstains up to his elbows, splotches on his belly (he had wisely removed his fine Cheyenne shirt), was a mess, and by the time they had packed the mule and returned to camp, he was exhausted.

Hardy Gibbs was also suddenly shocked; no sooner had the big liver had been set aside than Mato-Ciqala came with his hunting knife, carved off several bloody strips, sat on a nearby boulder, and began eating the meat raw. Chomping away with what few teeth he had left, and with blood creasing the corners of his mouth, Little Bear was nodding approvingly at Hardy, and Hardy, distressed, suddenly weak in his stomach, left the remainder of the meat preparation to Festus Cato. He hurried away to Little Goose Creek, where he found a deep pool, hastily undressed, and leaped in. Hardy Gibbs had a touch of Cherokee in him. The Cherokee never hunted buffalo; consequently, they never ate raw liver—reason enough, he concluded, to view old Mato's appetite as distasteful and appalling.

However, Festus Cato's promised feast on this evening was far from distasteful or appalling. It was delicious—several huge slabs of tenderloin and hump sprinkled with sage and salt, roasted over the fire, and cornmeal mush seasoned with red chili peppers. It was a night never to be forgotten by Hardy Gibbs. It was a night of prophecy, too. Hardy listened to Little Bear chant in monotone, a voice soft, flat, and dull like a frozen chord. Festus translated, saying it was about a dream of two gray foxes wandering aimlessly in a great circle, one fox always trying to catch up with the other. Sometimes the first fox dissolved, and when this happened, the second fox would moan and go around in smaller circles searching for his friend.

Festus Cato, staring across the fire at Hardy, said, "He says he finally figgered it out. Says it wasn't two foxes at all, jest one tryin' t'catch up t'its spirit. Says he thinks it was you, pilgrim. Yer spirit is runnin' outside yer body, and y'have t'git away someplace and meditate, wait fer a sign, git yer body and spirit t'gether again, become a new man." Festus Cato chuckled softly. "He's always havin' dreams . . . visions. Some of 'em don't make a lick of sense t'me, but I always listen right polite-like, y'know, like he's tellin' the gospel."

A chill coursed through Hardy Gibbs. He sighed. "Well, maybe that's me, all right. I surely have been chasing all over the place."

"Chasin' shadows, dreams," opined Festus. "Used t'do that myself a lot. Always came back t'right where I started. Mato says that's reality."

As the last flames of the fire flickered, Little Bear,

his words sometimes plaintive and halting, chanted a few old Lakota songs, Festus Cato keeping the rhythm, gently tapping the back of a saddle. Hardy played some lonesome songs on his harmonica. The wolves moaned at the site of the buffalo carcass. It was all very fitting.

Hardy slept late the next morning. Gray jays were flitting about in the trees, emitting their mellow whistles, cocking their heads, searching the ground for scraps. There was no fire, no smell of coffee, and this aroused hardy from his blanket and canvas. He saw no sign of Festus Cato or Little Bear; the bedrolls under their adjacent shelter were empty, yet their two horses were grazing peacefully with Sundown and the pack mule. Cato's Henry rifle was set against the tree trunk by the shelter. Perplexed, Hardy Gibbs quickly put on his boots, shirt, and jacket. Here, the mornings were cool, the air tinted with the pungent smell of sage and pine. Buckling on his gun belt, Hardy called out, received only an eerie echo. On foot the two old men couldn't be too far, and that scaffold—no, they wouldn't try building it without his help—yet he was suddenly gripped with apprehension. Taking up his Winchester, he began frantically searching about for some sign around the dewy perimeter, a gouge or two in the forest floor, anything. Oh, how poorly equipped in experience he was for this sort of thing! Yet he found a sign, a purposeful gouge scratched into the soft earth with a stick or the toe of a boot. It was in an ancient game trail twisting its way up the mountain, a pointed arrow, and Hardy Gibbs, his heart pounding, leaped away, following its direction. Then, farther, another arrow, and still farther, a stack of small rocks delicately placed alongside the trail. The ground was scuffed and trampled, and to the left he saw a single set of tracks embedded in the covering of dead leaves and pine needles.

The story was written here—Mato had collapsed; his climb had ended. Festus was carrying him, and unable to traverse the steep hill with his friend's body, had coursed away, attempting to scale the incline on an angle. Ah, these crazy, desperate old men! Hardy Gibbs hopefully called again, this time received the staccato bark of a pine squirrel. Pressing on, now in a jog, he followed the tracks along the hillside another few minutes until he came to a small rocky bluff, and here he stopped, for lying there in peaceful repose with the morning sun on their faces were Little Bear and Festus Cato. Walking slowly, gasping for air, Hardy Gibbs came to them and stared. Little Bear's eyes were closed, that little puckered smile barely discernible at the corners of his mouth. Festus Cato's eyes were open, little golden flecks in the greenish blue reflecting the early morning rays of the sun. The men were both covered with their blankets, and Hardy Gibbs, trembling, gently reached down, first touching the cheek of Little Bear, then the forehead of Festus Cato. They were cold, cold as the gray rocks around them. Both dead.

Fighting tears, Hardy Gibbs closed the heavy lids of Festus Cato, then slowly edged back the blanket. Cato's hand were clasped to his breast and were covered with blood from two huge slashes in his wrists. Hardy pulled the blankets over the men's faces, then staggered away to a great ponderosa pine, where under its shade, he sat down and wept.

TWELVE

The Lusk Shoot-out

Shortly after noon, Hardy Gibbs, weary and depressed, prepared to leave the small camp on Little Goose Creek. How despairing to experience this overwhelming sadness in such a beautiful and vibrant land. Yet paradoxically, as Little Bear had said, it truly was a good place to die. The two old men had passed on to another world as they had wished, happily together. Hardy had done his best; there had been no scaffold, but he had buried them on the high bluff side by side in shallow graves, had carried every rock and boulder he could find, and when finished, he thought the great stone mound was a fitting monument to two old souls who loved and revered Mother Earth as they had. Materially, they were poor, and had little more than their horses, saddles, and blankets. But they were rich in heart. Hardy scratched the names CATO and MATO on two flat sandstones, placed them high on the rocks. He turned their horses free to roam the broad valleys and lashed the saddles to the boughs of a pine. After a silent prayer along the rushing waters of Little Goose Creek, he rode to the north.

Following creeks, Hardy ultimately came to what he believed was a fork of the Tongue, which he crossed, and soon discovered the ruts of a wagon trail heading northwest. With darkness setting in, he made an impromptu camp near another slow, meandering stream, but troubled with intermingling thoughts of Festus Cato, Little Bear, and his beloved Julienne, his sleep was fitful. Oh, this land was spacious and beautiful— little wonder the Indians cherished it—but it was terribly lonely for a worried white man, a pilgrim. Hardy Gibbs spent a great portion of the night listening to croaking frogs, mournful wolves, and chirping crickets, and, of course, reliving his troubled life. When he awoke, his eyes felt as though they were filled with prairie sand.

Later this day, he came upon what once had been a very large Indian village, stretching out for several miles along the river bottom. From what he had been told and had read, he recognized this place; this was the Little Bighorn River, the Greasy Grass country, and this abandoned campsite was where Sioux and Cheyenne had gathered and surged out in angry hordes to demolish the Seventh Cavalry of George Armstrong Custer. There were still remnants of tattered cloth about, one small piece caught in a tree, fluttering eerily in the late afternoon breeze; there were rings of stone filled with gray ashes where the women had cooked, and along the meadows, toadstools were poking their shiny brown and white heads up through the dried droppings of thousands of ghosts ponies. The immensity of this old village was staggering. It took Hardy almost a half hour before he finally rode clear of the forsaken site.

Toward late afternoon, he was momentarily startled when he saw three men riding toward him, and when they approached within hailing distance, he saw they were Indians, young Indians riding bareback on multicolored ponies—"pintos," as Festus Cato had called them. Chattering and smiling, the boys curiously circled him until Hardy raised his hand and began making simple sign: Who were they? Where was their village? After some initial confusion, with everyone attempting to communicate at once, he learned these boys were Crow; Hardy was on the greater Crow reservation, and the agency, village, and Fort Custer were only several miles north. Wheeling their colorful mounts, they beckoned him, and Hardy Gibbs, relieved to be among friendly people, urged Sundown into a trot and gladly followed.

He soon discovered that the fort was a new one, and it was small, with only several barracks and a one-room administration building. It had no walls, no towers, nothing more than a pole fence and many corrals setting it apart from the Crow village, which, in contrast to the army site, was huge. Brightly decorated tipis, lodge poles jutting up from the tips of their cones like jackstraws, were everywhere, some arranged in semicircles, others in long lines, some along the flat meadowland, others tucked away in the shade of the trees. For the pilgrim, Hardy Gibbs, this was an exciting, invigorating sensation—for the first time, he was truly among the great people of the plains. He also saw people, in the distance, mostly children and women with their dogs and, farther below, hundreds of horses of all colors. Following his three young riders, he soon came to a small house, also newly built and fenced with poles. The three boys, once again whirling their ponies about, shouted several times and galloped off toward the village.

Directly, a man dressed in dark trousers and a white shirt, appeared on the small porch. Indeed, this was the Crow reservation, the man politely informed Hardy, and he was the agent, Stanley Cunningham. Could he be of any assistance?

Hardy explained that he was just passing through on his way west, had thought about spending the night, and wondered where he might camp without being in the way or causing any trouble. No trouble, the agent said, visitors were always welcome, and he directed Hardy to the fort. Hardy might not have to camp, Cunningham said—one barrack was empty awaiting a company of recruits coming up from Fort Keogh within another week.

Once at the post headquarters, a Colonel Justin Meeker confirmed this, and within ten minutes, Hardy Gibbs, accompanied by a Sergeant Stebbins, was stowing his gear in the empty building. He had his choice of thirty bunks; he took the one most convenient—next to the door. As he sorted out his belongings, Sergeant Halfred Stebbins, a most knowledgeable fellow in his mid-thirties, enlightened Hardy on these new surroundings. Normally there weren't this many lodges around the fort; the Crow were gathering for some sort of religious ceremony, a ritual they performed every year early in the summer. Most of the men, some women, and the older boys were up toward the Yellowstone for several days of buffalo hunting, thus explaining why Hardy had seen a multitude of women and children and very few men. Hardy also learned that the nearest civilization was about a seven- or eight-day ride to the west—Bozeman City, a growing community at the head of the Gallatin Valley. Sergeant Stebbins, a veteran of eight years in the army, had served one of these years at Fort Ellis, a post adjacent to Bozeman. He had also spent a few months at Fort Missoula, and when he learned that Hardy was headed to the Five Valleys to look over business opportunities, he had an opinion about this—Bozeman City was a better bet. The Northern Pacific rail line coming up the Yellowstone would most likely be into Bozeman two years before it reached Missoula. The Gallatin, as was the country north toward the Musselshell, was destined to be cattle country. A few spreads already had settled in, and Bozeman had become the crossroads for gold miners traveling south to Virginia City and north to Helena. Hardy Gibbs listened with interest to yet another opinion of the Montana Territory.

Stebbins said with a wry smile, "If you can tolerate a few cold months in the winter, any place up in this country is a good place to settle. Except for a few renegades over to the east, the Indian wars are over, Charlie. Tell you another thing . . . there's no hardware or metal shop in Bozeman yet, and if a man comes up with a broken firearm, he either tries to fix it himself or he buys a new one."

Sergeant Stebbins was knowledgeable in other ways, too, and very observant, Hardy quickly learned. As Hardy finished shaking out his hot roll and spreading it across the bunk, Stebbins went on, saying, "For instance, that pistol you're wearing, only a good gunsmith could fix that thing, maybe not even a gunsmith. You'd probably have to end it back to St. Louis where they're made. A Gibbs Special, ain't it?"

Hardy Gibbs cleared his throat. "Yep . . . yep, it's a Gibbs, all right, but nothing seems to go wrong with it."

"At the price of those things, I can imagine. Not meaning to be personal, but how in the hell did you come by it?"

"My uncle gave it to me," Hardy Gibbs answered. "Birthday present when I reached twenty-one."

"Damn fine present, I'd say," opined Stebbins. "Mind if I have a look?"

"Nope, not at all," and Hardy pulled it from the holster and handed it to the sergeant.

Stebbins just held it in the palm of his hand and gave a low whistle. Nodding, he smiled at Hardy and said, "This would pass inspection, Charlie. It's clean as a whistle. If I had something like this, I'd probably keep it hidden . . . maybe hang it on the wall."

"Yep," replied Hardy, dwelling momentarily on another man who had said those very same words, a dear man, now dead. Lord, it seemed ages ago. Hardy said, "It doesn't draw much attention, only the barrel. Most people think it's just a horse pistol."

"That's because they don't know anything about handguns in the first place. Hell, there was fellow killed down in Abilene for one of these . . . robbed and killed, and then some fellow came along and killed the robber."

"I know," Hardy Gibbs said. "That fellow from Abilene was my uncle—Jake Parsons."

Sergeant Stebbins, his brow suddenly furrowed, stared across at Hardy, then handed him back the revolver. "Parsons? I read about that. Parsons? Well, dadgummit, you must be Charlie Parsons! Jesus, you're the one who shot up those Quantrill boys down in Nebraska. Three of them!"

"Cadwell's kinfolk, the one who shot my uncle," explained Hardy. "Kissing cousins, and I found out that they take those things real personal-like."

"Well, if this don't beat all!"

"Yep, I figured maybe the way they get so upset, there might be a few more of those cousins around." Hardy Gibbs paused and grinned. "Maybe they might send four or five out the next time, and I just don't have any stomach for those kinds of odds, so I thought I'd come up here for a while. Sort of find a good place to hide."

"You realize what they're calling you? The Shooter, for God's sake!" Sergeant Stebbins said in a low voice, "Listen, if any of the boys around here start getting too friendly tonight, asking names and such, you find yourself a new handle, and damn quick."

"You mean they'd likely call me—"

"Oh, hell, no," Stebbins cut in. "But if this gets back to the colonel, he'll likely toss you out on your ass, or have you out there on the range demonstrating for these greenhorns—more likely the former, give you the old boot."

"I surely wouldn't like that," said Hardy Gibbs. "I want a good meal tonight, a good sleep for a change. Haven't had much of either for a couple of days. I had to bury two old fellows back in the mountains and it sort of riled my stomach . . . upset my appetite."

A stunned look on his ruddy face, Sergeant Stebbins slowly lowered himself and collapsed on the edge of Hardy's bunk. "You buried two men? You buried two men in the mountains! Were they following you? Some more of those kissing cousins?"

"No, no," Hardy Gibbs moaned. "These two old men—one was an old medicine man, the other, well, I reckon he was once a trapper, sort of a drifter of late— and, well, dammit, the poor old codgers just upped and died on me, had the whole thing planned, led me right up to their deathbeds." And Hardy Gibbs went on to explain, related the entire story, including the episode of killing the buffalo, and the delicious meal that Festus Cato had prepared that last night. After a weary sigh, Hardy asked, "Can you understand it? They knew they were going to die. It was just like they wanted to die. Holy smokes, I understood, but why me? More bad dreams. Just thinking about it, it makes me so damn sad I haven't slept hardly a solid wink."

"Fate," said Sergeant Stebbins. "Look here, Charlie, I've been out here now for going on five of my eight years, and I've seen some strange things, heard of more, too. Probably was fate. Somehow you were chosen, one of those medicine things. Maybe they wanted their spirits to touch you, give you some of the medicine they inherited, make a disciple out of you. Maybe it was like the Last Supper. Whatever it was, you won't forget it, I'll tell you this. Things like that never go away."

Hardy Gibbs knew all about that. He was already toting a burdensome pack of memories, some good, some bad, and for certain, they never went away. Lately, the load seemed to be getting heavier. Well, he felt a little better after telling this story about old Festus and Little Bear to Sergeant Stebbins. A man just couldn't go on mumbling to himself all of the time.

But then again, Hardy knew a man had to give trouble a good kick in the ass and get on with his life—grab life by the throat and shake the hell out of it. That was the gumption Grandfather was always talking about.

Hardy Gibbs stowed his gun belt and revolver under his bedding and went to evening mess with Sergeant Stebbins, where he met some of the "boys." He didn't do much jawing, just listened mostly, and discovered they did a lot of complaining—about everything, it seemed, from army food and patrol duty to itchy underwear and the lack of women. Oh, there were women around, all right, plenty of them, but trifling with those little Crow squaws was dangerous business—the colonel didn't like it, and neither did some of the Crow bucks. Later, Hardy got a good look at some of these women; Sergeant Stebbins took him for a walk after supper down through part of the village. He saw young, pretty ones, some not so pretty, some old wizened ones; he saw a few cooking meals, stirring big black pots. He saw children, some dressed, some naked, but he did not see one child whining or complaining. He also saw a few old men who were almost identical in appearance to Little Bear, all hunched over under their red and blue blankets, their faces a mass of wrinkles with sunken cheeks and those black, squinty eyes, and he couldn't help but wonder how many of these old fellows were going to wander off and die on some mountain with the sun in their faces.

Hardy Gibbs, for a change, had a good night. He had left the nearby door open, a back window, too, heard only a few bull bats making their funny little *beerups*, and was free from the bothersome, staccato whine of mosquitoes. He heard a bugle shortly after sunup, and later, the clatter of boots on the stairs of the adjacent barrack and a few voices. But it soon fell quiet again, and he rolled over in a half doze, dwelling on his lost love, Julienne. He thought it must have been a half hour later when Sergeant Stebbins arrived. He hadn't detected the sergeant's arrival, but sensing someone's presence, Hardy opened one bleary eye and there was Stebbins, hands on his hips, a pipe tucked in the corner of his mouth, staring down at him.

Hardy grinned. "Good morning, Sergeant."

Stebbins returned the greeting in a peculiar way. "Would you like a scouting job for a week or two? For two dollars a day and rations?"

Coming up on an elbow, Hardy replied, "A job? Holy smokes, in a week or two I plan on being over in this Bozeman City place! I can't be hanging around here, with all I have to do. If I don't get moving, I won't find myself a good hole until the snow flies, and then it will be too late for me to get my sweetheart out here." He sat up and rubbed a hand through his hair. "Scouting for what?"

"Horses," Sergeant Stebbins answered. "We lost damn near a hundred head sometime last night."

"A hundred head!" exclaimed Hardy. "Now, how can you lose a hundred head overnight?"

"They were stolen," replied Stebbins. "They were rustled off. Some of our stock and Crow ponies. Thought you might want to join the party—myself and a couple of troopers and some Crow scouts—and chase our stock down." He grinned and added, "We might have need of a good gunfighter."

"Nonsense! That's rifle work, and I'm no scout, either. I'd likely to go out there and get my fool self lost."

"You won't be going anywhere sitting around here," said Sergeant Stebbins. "At least, not for a while, you won't. Your black Morgan was stolen, too."

Hardy Gibbs, slapping a hand against the bed, moaned, "Aw, for chrissakes, what next! Soldiers all around this place, Indians, dogs, and you let some rustlers come in here and steal my horse." Grimacing, shaking his head, he gave Sergeant Stebbins a dour stare. "I knew it. I just knew it. When I came riding in here yesterday, I had a feeling I should just keep riding right on by."

Stebbins shrugged. "Surprised us, too, you know. We'll be leaving in about a half hour. One of the Crow brought up an extra pony in case you decide you want to ride along with us. Rustlers went east. Probably trying to get the horses over to Deadwood. Only place in that direction."

"East?" Hardy sighed. "I want to go west, not east."

"Half an hour. Better get yourself something to eat," said Stebbins. "Hard riding on an empty belly."

Without recourse, Hardy hurriedly dressed, went to the latrine, washed up, and had a quick breakfast. He also stuffed a few biscuits and some dried apples in his jacket pockets, and by the time he returned to the barrack, discovered one of the Crow scouts had already saddled his new pony, a stubby brown and white mare. Hardy finished up the job, packing on his blankets, tarp, and personal belongings, sliding his Winchester into the scabbard, and last of all, buckling on his gun belt. What Sergeant Stebbins had said was true—the party consisted of Stebbins, two troopers, and three Indians. Because his command was already shorthanded, Colonel Meeker could only spare three men; the three Crow scouts were already on call, and Hardy, the seventh man, the reluctant volunteer, considered himself a victim of circumstances. At two dollars a day for chasing rustlers, he didn't consider this a profitable venture, but the thought of Sundown being sold off to God only knew whom was appalling. Gritting his teeth, Hardy Gibbs rode off with the rest of the men, following tracks that Sergeant Stebbins calculated were six to eight hours old. Figuring the thieves had stopped at least once to eat and to rest the horses, he allowed that by now they were between forty to sixty miles ahead. By crow flight, Deadwood was a long four- or five-day ride.

At dusk, Stebbins's small party stopped on the other side of the Rosebud, made coffee, ate, and slept for four hours. Then they rode by night, two of the Crow, familiar with every landmark along the way, leading. Finally they crossed the Tongue River and, by midmorning on the third day, reached the Powder, where they once again napped, this time in a grove of cottonwoods. Examining the droppings left by the pony herd, one of the Crow scouts estimated the rustlers were about five hours ahead.

Alternately walking and trotting their horses, the seven men ultimately sighted the ranch land along the Belle Fourche River where a few squatters had settled. It was near sundown, and one of the scouts suddenly shouted excitedly and began motioning ahead— running horses, running men, too, two or three of them dashing across a clearing from a small cabin, but several other riders were already away, trying to push the stolen ponies up the river toward the settlement of Spearfish. Hardy Gibbs, charging ahead, saw a tiny puff of smoke, then another, and he veered to the side, yelling, "They're shooting at us!"

Waving a hand, Sergeant Halfred Stebbins shouted, "Spread out men. Spread out and disperse. Fire at will."

Well, Hardy heard this, all right, but he knew he wasn't going to fire at will and hit anything galloping along on his brown and white mare, so he laid his head up close to her neck and bore straight ahead for the little cabin where three rustlers were mounting their horses. They weren't firing now—they were doing their best to clean country. Three of them were riding around a pole fence when Hardy pulled up and leaped from the mare. Prone in the meadow, he took careful aim and set off his Winchester; he quickly jacked in another cartridge and fired again, then another. Two of the riders toppled from their mounts. Surprisingly, the third horseman booted wildly away in the opposite direction of his comrades with the horses, who by now were being outmaneuvered by the Crow scouts and their fleet-footed range ponies. Suddenly the herd of stolen horses made a big turn and came pounding back toward the corrals; the Indians had turned them. Sergeant Stebbins's two troopers, firing their pistols, went galloping toward the river bottom after the two escaping rustlers, while Stebbins himself rode over and checked on the men Hardy Gibbs had shot. They were white men, and they were dead.

By the time Hardy had remounted and reached the long pole fence, the Crow scouts were already riding among the milling horses. Hardy began searching for his Morgan, but it was nowhere in sight, and shortly, Sergeant Stebbins, cursing, told him why—at least forty-five horses were missing and probably had been herded into the security of Deadwood earlier in the afternoon. Horses in Deadwood were at a premium, and he said that in the morning they would be sold to the highest bidders at anywhere from fifty to a hundred dollars a head and then dispersed.

"Well," Hardy said, "we can stake these out here and go in and get the rest of them. Dammit, I don't like the notion of anyone selling my horse, not when he doesn't own it in the first place. That just rubs me the wrong way."

"Don't blame you, Charlie, but it ain't that easy. Deadwood is like a madhouse, a regular hellhole up there. People don't like soldiers and they don't like Indians, either, and the sheriff won't be able to do a damn thing about it, not without bringing the whole town down on his neck."

"Nonsense!"

"No, the gospel," retorted Sergeant Stebbins. "There's five or six thousand squatters in there on Sioux property digging gold. When they get careless on one of the trails, sometimes the Sioux pick 'em off, and vice versa. Those people are in town at their own risk. The army won't protect them because they've nested in there illegally. You understand? So they hate us and the Indians alike."

There was a clatter of hooves coming back from the river—the sergeant's two troopers. The two horse thieves had eluded them in the brushy bottom, and now dusk was setting in.

Sergeant Stebbins continued, "There's only four of

us, not counting the Crow—our Indian friends won't dare show their faces in Deadwood. And us? We'd get laughed out of town, that's what. No, we'll bed down here for the night, skedaddle back to Custer first thing in the morning, file a report, and see what happens."

Hardy Gibbs shook his head and said adamantly, "No, sir, I don't like it. First thing in the morning, I'm riding over there to get my horse. They won't be laughing at me . . . don't even know me. And if I find the man who has Sundown, he sure as hell won't be laughing." He gave the lower pole on the fence an angry kick. "What about those thieves? At fifty to a hundred a head they get rich and they get off scot-free, too. Why, that's . . . that's over three thousand dollars worth of horseflesh, and a lot of it government property. This is plain stupid."

Sergeant Stebbins began calmly stuffing his pipe. He said, "I understand how you feel about your horse, Charlie, but you just may get your hide tanned if you go poking around. Hell, no one is going to give you the time of day in that place."

Hardy Gibbs, burning inside, was thoughtful for a moment. He watched Stebbins flare a match with his thumbnail, and the following little *pup-pup-pups* sounded like a drum beat. He finally said, "I don't want the time of day. Damn few Morgans in this country, you know. And another thing, if I can get a line on who those fellows are, I might not get all of our stock back, but I'll bet I can claim their profit and get some compensation for us."

Stebbins smiled and replied, "You're a gunfighter, not a robber."

"Wouldn't be robbing, only getting back what rightfully belongs to us. That's the way I look at it."

Puffing on his pipe, the sergeant said, "Getting a line on them might not be too difficult." He nodded toward the end of the pole fence where the two dead men were lying. The Crow scouts were already stripping the men of their belongings, taking booty. "Those fellows look like Texans to me, big hats, Mexican boots, pants and shirts all cloth, no leather. Town is full of miners and gamblers. Their friends most likely would stick out like sore thumbs." Pointing his pipe, he added, "You'd be the biggest problem, if anyone found out you're Charlie Parsons, The Shooter."

At dawn, the following day came the farewell.

"Who knows?" said Hardy Gibbs. "Maybe I'll see you in a week or two. Or up in that Gallatin country this fall."

Sergeant Halfred Stebbins waved; one of the Crow scouts made a shrill outcry and shook his fist, and the sergeant's men moved out to the west, the band of horses trotting ahead of them. Hardy rode the other way, crossed some prairie and foothills, and by midmorning found himself riding alongside two freight wagons that were slowly winding their way up the canyon road to Deadwood. Shortly, dwellings of all kinds began to appear on the hillsides, shanties, tents, dugouts with canvas fluttering over them, and small log cabins, and then, for as far as he could see, the hills and gullies were pocked and gouged, and tiny, spidery trails led from one digging to another. Deadwood was a mess, a jumble of clapboard buildings, many of them with false second-floor fronts, roofs of planking and tin, and only a few of them graced with a coat of paint or whitewash. Half of the long, winding street was mud, the other half manure. Wagons of every description, a few carrying huge logs, clogged the main thoroughfare. Several new buildings were under construction, and the few people that Hardy saw were scurrying back and forth like prairie dogs. He reckoned that all of these holes in the hills belonged to them; most of these grubby people looked like they had been living in them all of their lives.

This was confusion at its worst, and Hardy Gibbs realized right off that he was going to have a hard time of it trying to find his horse. He wandered almost a mile up the wide gulch, and at every turn he saw trails leading off to both sides. Houses, shanties, and sheds were everywhere, and near some of them, men were digging. The ones not digging were sitting on a rock or a log with a rifle resting beside them. This place wasn't too friendly—no one he chanced to meet or pass offered so much as a smile or a hello. They had the gold fever. This is what it was all about, and it was just like Sergeant Stebbins said, no one gave him the time of day.

Once back down below, he saw a few signs painted on the storefronts, some hanging over doors—SALOON No. 10, PEARL'S, OVERLAND HOUSE, LONE STAR, CURTIS SADDLES AND HARNESSES. There were two mercantiles and a butcher shop. There were more solicitor signs here than anywhere he had ever been. Almost every other building had the name of an attorney on it, and not everyone was grubby white trash or poorly dressed. Hardy met a fellow dressed in a dark suit and wearing a derby in front of the mercantile where he had reined up, a fellow polite enough to point out the sheriff's office—down on one of the corners next to the bank.

Hardy thanked him and went inside the store and bought a few supplies to replenish his larder, then stopped at Zoeckler's Butcher Shop, where he purchased some smoked sausage and a slab of bacon. After packing these in his saddlebags and up under his canvas, he led his Crow pony down the street, carefully avoiding the mud holes and horse manure. He shortly discovered that not all of the people in Deadwood were so consarned unfriendly, either, for at this building called Lone Star he saw two young women leaning out one of the upper-floor windows. As he passed directly under them, they smiled and tossed him little waves, and one of them with long black hair, much like Julienne's, called him "Mister Handsome" and invited him up for a visit. Hardy Gibbs had to stare back at them and smile. These were the first white women that he had seen in a month of Sundays; maybe this is why they looked so beautiful. He mused that they were mining gold, too, only doing it in a more pleasurable way.

The sherriff's office was similar to the one at Hays, Kansas, the one Orlan Thomas had been in until he became a U. S. marshal. It had one room in the front, two windows, a cluttered desk, posters on the walls, and several jail cells in the back. It smelled the same, too, like old leather and stale tobacco. No one was in the place and the cells were empty. Despite what Sergeant Stebbins had told him about the law in Deadwood, Hardy Gibbs thought he would at least tell the sheriff about the stolen army and Crow horses, the fact that

one of them was his own. He believed if he chanced to
find his and got into a ruckus over it, the sheriff should
know what it was all about. After looking over the posters on the wall (none of which was his), he went over
to a small table by one of the front windows, pulled up
a chair, sat down, and picked up a few of the old periodicals. Resting back, Hardy Gibbs casually flipped
through the first one, cast it aside, and there on the
cover of the second one, smack-dab in front of his big
eyes and boldly printed across the bottom of the cover,
was his name, both of them—*Hardy Gibbs, Alias Charlie
Parsons*. Another smaller title said, *A Stirring Saga of
The Shooter* by Henry Burlingame.

Oh, that damn Burlingame, what had he done, now?
Feeling all queasy inside, a stunned Hardy Gibbs nervously thumbed over a few pages, and there it was, a big
drawing of him, too, all crouched over aiming his pistol, a puff of smoke coming out of the barrel, and some
poor fool in the distance standing there grabbing for
his revolver. Holy smokes! Hardy hurriedly read a few
paragraphs, and Jesus, there was grandfather's name,
Julienne's, too! Why, that Burlingame had gone all the
way back to St. Louis, knew the whole story. He
slapped the *Harper's Weekly* shut and buried it under
the pile of newspapers and magazines. He needed
some air, fresh air, and shoving the chair aside, he
straightened his hat and went for the door, only to be
met by a stocky, mustached man wearing a tan hat
with a broad brim, and a dark suit coat.

Before Hardy Gibbs could make his exit, the man
asked, "What can I do for you, son?"

Hesitating, reaching for words, Hardy finally said, "I

came to report my horse was stolen. Wanted you to know I came here looking for it."

"Stolen, you say?" The man went over to the desk and stood there looking curiously back at Hardy, who was still by the door, prepared to run or shoot, whichever he had to. "Where? When?"

Hardy Gibbs sighed. "Well, you won't believe this: Stolen over at Fort Custer, five days ago. A black—" And Hardy abruptly stopped here. He hadn't read all of that Harper's story, but he wouldn't put it past that Burlingame to mention his Morgan, Sundown.

"Fort Custer?" asked the sheriff. "And you think your horse is in Deadwood?"

"I know it is," replied Hardy. "I tracked it here myself, with a couple of soldiers and some Indians. Some rustlers stole a whole herd from the fort. Late yesterday, we got half of them back down below by the river. I think the rest of them, including mine, came in here. Probably all sold by now." The sheriff sat down behind his desk, and Hardy added, "I don't suppose you know about these horses? Some of them with government brands on them."

"As a matter of fact, I do," said the sheriff. "I didn't see them, but I heard some stock came in, some drovers herding them."

"Two less drovers now," Hardy said. "I killed two. They started shooting at us when we caught up with them, but it looks like they split the herd and were planning on moving the rest down south of here. We never figured that out. I want my horse back."

"You killed two! You should have come in here yesterday and reported this. That's Lawrence County down by the river ... Deadwood territory. Maybe we could have gotten something done."

"Not from what the soldiers told me. Too many hotheads here, they said. Squatters."

The sheriff stirred uneasily and replied, "That's a matter of opinion. Two sides to every story. And listen here son, those two you killed ... that should have been reported right off so we could try and identify them. What's your name?"

"Just call me Charlie," answered Hardy Gibbs. "The killing was all legal. I'm on the army payroll at Fort Custer. Those men shot first, made a run for it, and we did what we had to. They're outright thieves, and two or three of them are in your town." Crossing a leg and leaning against the doorframe, Hardy asked, "What's your name?"

"Seth Bullock."

"Well, Mister Bullock, that's my story," continued Hardy. "I don't have a notion what you plan to do about the stolen horses. They're probably scattered from hell to breakfast through these hills by now, brands blotted. But I suppose the army can figure this out. The sergeant in charge is filing a report on it. As for myself, I'm going to look about for my black. One way or another, I'm going to get my horse back."

"If you find it here, you come and get me or one of the deputies," warned Seth Bullock. "I don't want any trouble, not from you or the army. I've been having enough trouble trying to stop the shootings over disputes over mining claims. I'll make a report on this, fill out the papers, and if we get some time, we'll look around."

"Seeing half of the horses belong to the government,

seems to me you should find the time. What do you do with horse thieves?"

"If they're found guilty in court, we hang them."

"Jury of locals?" Hardy asked skeptically.

"In Lawrence County we go by the law, young man."

"Mister Bullock, if you went by the law in this county, no one would be here in the first place. Lawrence County! For chrissakes, you don't even own the land!"

"Is that all?" Bullock asked. "It's all I want to hear, I'll tell you."

"No, it's not all. I was thinking of how I can save your so-called county some money, though with all the gold you're taking out, I reckon it wouldn't amount to a bean. If I find the man who stole my horse, or any of those rustlers, I'll call them out. Save you the expense of a trial and hanging. If you see a few strangers wearing big hats, you tell them this. I figure my law is just as legal as yours."

"Ho, ho," snorted Bullock. "One of those big gunfighters, are you?"

Hardy Gibbs was out the door, and he called back, "Only when I have to be, Mister Bullock. Only when people like you can't do your job."

Sheriff Seth Bullock was irate. After several deep breaths, he began penning in a report. He had to. The army would file a report; the territorial government would get a copy, harboring army property, that sort of thing; the complaint would make a circle, come back to the mayor and city council, then right back in his lap again. Charlie? Charlie who? Seth Bullock leaped from his chair and went to the door—horses, wagons, a muddle of confusion on the street. No sign of Char-

lie, Charlie the cocky young gunfighter. He stood there
for a moment thoughtfully scratching behind his head,
for some strange reason troubled, wondering if he had
missed something in the conversation with Charlie.
Charlie the army scout? Charlie the gunfighter? He
studied the plank floor, stared up at the wall, from the
wall over to the wanted posters, then quickly strode
over and began examining them. Somewhere . . . And
then it hit him—Charlie Parsons! My God, could it be?
Bullock rushed over to the pile of periodicals, quickly
shuffled them, and there it was—*Hardy Gibbs, Alias
Charlie Parsons*. The description fit perfectly—
handsome, long dark hair, mustache, six feet tall, quiet
spoken but deliberate. What else? The hat, a drover's
hat with a small brim. The eyes were hazel-colored and
could look straight through a man. The pistol? Damn—
Bullock cursed under his breath—he hadn't noticed.
But then again, he had noticed the long holster hiding
the barrel of that revolver. Why, it must have been a
Gibbs. By God, Bullock thought, the boy was a cool
one, all right. Seth Bullock groaned. And here he had
been sitting on his fat ass, listening to a complaint
about a herd of stolen shitters, talking to the best gunfighter on the plains. What a fool! Snatching up his
hat, adjusting his gun belt, he strode from the office.
But hell, he couldn't go telling anyone about this. Why,
he'd make a jackass out of himself! Worse yet, what if
he tried to face this Gibbs boy head-on? Nine men, the
story said, some of them shot right between the eyes—
and that wasn't counting those two rustlers the boy
said he had shot down on the Belle Fourche. Seth Bullock looked up the street, then down the street,
thought he ought to go and find a deputy, just make a

routine check of the saloons, see if any drunks were causing trouble.

Hardy Gibbs knew that his visit had annoyed Seth Bullock. It was only an outside chance, but he was hoping the sheriff might spread the word that a gunfighter was in town, looking for someone who had stolen his horse. What he hadn't counted on was reading that after two summers, his true identity had been discovered. That big cur Henry Burlingame had been on his scent like a coon hound, and most likely within a month everyone on the frontier who could read would know Hardy Gibbs and Charlie Parsons were one and the same. And if in some crazy way he were recognized, some fool might try to collect the thousand dollars riding on his head. He didn't like the notion of getting shot. Once was enough; it was a painful experience. If he had to die, he wanted it to be like old Festus and Little Bear, with his face to the sun, not in the dust.

Well, he wasn't going to give up on poor old Sundown. He was going to get his horse back under him, but discretion had seized him, and this wisely brought about a change in his plans. It wasn't prudent to go roaming around Deadwood looking for those rustlers, not now. Hardy Gibbs rationalized if that Sheriff Bullock couldn't flush them out, most likely they'd come out on their own, anyhow. Those men were drovers, not miners. They probably detested working with picks and shovels, would rather ride horses, make an easy living stealing ones that belonged to someone else. With all that money, where would they go? Sure as hell, they wouldn't stay in Deadwood and freeze off their asses all winter. Nope, if they were Texans or good old southern boys, as Sergeant Stebbins had reckoned, they would go south, and in a hurry. They'd take their fat wads and go home and settle down for the winter.

So, taking a chance on this speculation, Hardy Gibbs left Deadwood and rode south along the stage route to Lusk, Wyoming. Fearful of being ambushed by renegade Sioux, he rode by night and dozed a safe distance off the road during the day. From his hiding places, he always peeked out at the sound of traffic, horses or wagons, and he saw them coming and going, but he didn't see any floppy hats of Texans, or any riders, in pairs or threes. Three days after he left Deadwood, he rode into Lusk. It was shortly after dawn; he took his horse to the livery, rented a room in the only hotel, the Yankee Dollar. After a bath, he went to bed.

Hardy didn't hang around the saloon, not inside; he found himself places in the shade: in the mornings at the far end of the porch, in the afternoons across the street under a big cottonwood tree. He read a rag-eared book with stories by Charles Dickens; he played lonely tunes on his harmonica; he waited hopefully. This was the only watering hole for miles, the only way south without riding through the great Lakota reservation and chancing upon hostiles. At two dollars a day for his room and board, he could afford to wait a few days, and on the third afternoon, he pocketed his harmonica, stood up, and adjusted his gun belt, for riding in across the street were three men, two with floppy hats and the other one wearing a sun-bleached derby—it was gray. And miracles of miracles, the man in the derby was riding a black Morgan—good old Sundown. Just as Hardy Gibbs had assumed, Sundown was too good a horse to sell, and one of the rustlers had claimed the horse for his own.

When the three men disappeared inside, Hardy went over and gently patted Sundown on the neck, talked to him, and apologized for all of the agony of the past ten days. His next move was to the door of the Yankee Dollar, where he stuck his head in and said, "Hey, whoever owns these horses better get out here in a hurry. Someone's about to steal them." And with this said, he walked briskly out to the middle of the street. Several men sitting on the porch heard this, and two across the street at the livery saw Hardy come to an abrupt halt and face off toward the saloon. They all knew what was about to happen, and they all took cover.

When the drovers emerged, Hardy Gibbs yelled again, "Hey, the one who claims the Morgan, step out first."

Those were the only words said. Gunfire suddenly erupted, breaking the afternoon quiet, three shots in rapid succession, and two of the men in front of the saloon went flying backward as though they had been struck by a railroad tie. A bullet from one of the rustlers ricocheted away from a splintered post in front of the saloon and went whining away, and the third man, cringing, slowly raised his arms.

Hardy Gibbs, walking toward him, said aside to the startled onlookers, "Horse thieves . . . rustlers."

The men said nothing, only began whispering among themselves; several were edging toward the door of the saloon.

Hardy Gibbs addressed the young man who had his hands in the air. "You bastards have caused me a lot of time and trouble. I had a hunch you'd come along, sooner or later, I surely did. Now, listen carefully. shuck your gun belt, and get over there and shake the saddle from the black. Then gather up all of the money belts, search every pocket, and drop everything right here in a pile. Understand?"

When this was done, Hardy ordered him to ride back to Deadwood to tell Bullock that, ". . . Charlie is taking your profit back to the army and the Crow at Fort Custer." Hardy gave the boy a sound kick. "Yes and one other thing . . . I'll drop him or anyone else who dares to follow me . . ."

The boy protested he could not make it there alone. Hardy told him he was lucky he had not killed him. Pointing his gun, he added, "Now get riding before I change my mind." The boy got riding.

A few minutes later, Hardy was ready to ride. Mounted on Sundown and trailing the Crow pony, he sidled up to the porch where several witnesses were standing. Hardy paused, fished out a ten-dollar gold piece, and tossed it on the porch. "Cheaper than Indian heads . . . only worth five dollars each. Bury them and have a drink on Charlie." He rode off.

The men only stared. One of them, a drifter by the name of Charlie Rollo, had recognized Hardy Gibbs, had once seen him shoot a man between the eyes in Hays, Kansas. Rollo walked back into the saloon with his drifter friend, Red Lockhart. Over a drink, they discussed the situation. They both knew the Bozeman Trail up to Fort Custer. They also knew some good hiding places along the way. They decided to take a little ride and get ahead of Hardy Gibbs. Hardy Gibbs was worth a thousand dollars, dead or alive, and besides, he was packing a lot of loot in that saddlebag.

Hardy's load of trouble was getting heavier. He knew it. Some confounded problem seemed to be cropping up and crawling in his bag like an ogre at every bend in the trail. Damn the hide of that Henry Burlingame! That wily scamp surely had made the situation worse for everyone concerned: Julienne and the Gibbs family. Just one big load of humiliation and worry. As Rose Parsons had said, fate wasn't smiling down at Hardy; fate was laughing at him. For once, however, he knew exactly what he was up to—he wasn't finished with Sheriff Bullock, not by a long shot, and he was going to do something for old Mato-Ciqala, too. So Hardy instead of riding toward the Bozeman Trail, made a big circle and rode the opposite way, making straightaway like a crow for Fort Robinson to get in one last blow before he took up his own mangled flight again.

The next day, he rode into the fort, and as at Fort Custer, there were Indian lodges all around the place. These belonged to the Lakota, Little Bear's people, who came here mostly to trade and complain about the squatters taking over in the Black Hills. He didn't have any trouble finding the headquarters building, didn't even have to ask. Directly in back of the parade grounds was a big flag waving, and behind it, a long flat building with a big porch, chairs all arranged neatly in the shade, and two soldiers standing at attention by a big doorway. This was no Fort Custer; it was a big place with buildings clustered all around the perimeter—houses, sheds, barns—and troopers walking, riding, exercising horses, and pounding hot iron.

Hardy Gibbs, after stating his business, had to wait only a few minutes on the porch before an officer came out and greeted him. Once inside, he went directly into an office and exchanged greetings with General L. P. Bradley, a very proper middle-aged officer resplendent with an immaculate mustache and mutton-chop sideburns. It was hot, and General Bradley was coatless, working at his desk in shirtsleeves. Hardy quickly got to the point of his visit: he had hired on with Colonel Meeker at Fort Custer to retrieve a herd of stolen horses. The trail had ended at Deadwood, where about half of the horses were ensconced, and his few men had been unable to do anything about it. Neither had Sheriff Bullock, who, Hardy claimed, had been uncooperative.

"That stock belongs to the army and the Crow," Hardy said. "If that Bullock had given me some cooperation, I could have rounded up every one of those critters within two or three days. All of them have markings. He told me I'd only cause a lot of trouble, and he didn't want any trouble in his town, so to my mind, General, he's just condoning the rustling, and those miners are no better than horse thieves themselves, buying government property that way. He told me if I brought my Crow scouts in there, most likely someone would shoot them on sight."

To Hardy Gibbs, the commandant looked a tad warm, like the heat of the day was getting to him. A few pebbles of sweat had popped out on his forehead, and he blotted them away with a red handkerchief. He made a few notations with a big quill pen and handed the paper to an aide. The junior officer glanced at the paper, saluted sharply once, and left.

General Bradley said to Hardy, "Young man, Mister . . . what was it?"

"Charles, sir," replied Hardy. "Paul LaBlanc Charles. Everyone calls me Charlie."

"Mister Charles, you can't imagine the trouble those people up in Deadwood have caused the army. It's absolutely preposterous. We built this fort to pacify the Sioux. We're building another fort below the gold fields to pacify the miners, and there've been a half dozen government commissions through here in the last two years shuffling meaningless papers and we still have anarchy. It so happens I have two companies going up to Fort Meade tomorrow morning. I've made out an order. Every horse in Deadwood without a paper of ownership or with a blotted brand will be confiscated and taken to Colonel Meeker up at Custer." Standing, General Bradley extended his hand to Hardy Gibbs. "I presume you'll be returning to Custer before our men accomplish this task, so give my regards to the colonel. And please tell him to tighten his duty watch. A hundred head! My God, Mister Charles, that's inconceivable!"

"Yes, sir, it surely is." Hardy Gibbs firmly shook hands with General Bradley, turned on his heel, and left.

Hardy was elated; this was far more than he had expected, and whistling a little tune, he leaped on Sundown, and with the Crow pony following, headed for the distant Sioux lodges. He was a disciple; he was going to tell the Lakota about Little Bear's honorable death in the Big Horn mountains. This he did, smoking pipe with a few of the Lakota elders in front of a large lodge, while many of the tribe watched Hardy and the chiefs making conversation by sign. At the conclusion, one of the chiefs placed his hands on Hardy's shoulders, then stepped back and made more sign. Hardy Gibbs wasn't certain about the meaning, but it was something to the effect that the spirit of Mato-Ciqala would ride along with him and help guide his destiny. Hardy felt good about this. Watching his backside, he rode off to the south to find sanctuary, a place where he could meditate.

THIRTEEN

Orlan and Henry

U.S. Marshal Orlan Thomas and the esteemed writer Henry Burlingame arrived by stage in Lusk, Wyoming Territory, four days after the departure of Hardy Gibbs. The news that Hardy Gibbs, alias Charlie Parsons, was back in the plains country had brought them both running. Orlan Thomas, because of his acquaintance with Hardy, was sent to apprehend him, and Burlingame hoped to write a conclusion to the saga of The Shooter.

The trail was cold, but not too cold. Marshal Thomas, after a preliminary investigation, revealed that Hardy had been in Deadwood, was now convinced that his young friend was on the run, probably headed south toward Colorado, Nebraska, or Kansas. The fact that Hardy Gibbs had been seen riding south on his black Morgan and trailing a brown and white horse was a starting point, and Orlan followed his hunch to the nearest big settlement, Julesburg, Colorado.

Two days later, at the Vickers Livery in Julesburg, his hunch paid off. Nate Vickers nodded. "Yes, indeed, a young fellow came in, oh, I reckon about a week ago," he said. "Had a Morgan, all right. Had an Injun pony, too, nice fat mare. Came back the next afternoon and rode out. Didn't talk much, no, and didn't say where he was headed."

Orlan Thomas asked, "Do you remember which way he rode?"

Nate vickers pointed, "Down the river . . . east."

Orlan smiled over at Burlingame. "That kid is probably going right back where he started from: Oakley, maybe even back to Abilene."

"Preposterous! Everyone along the line knows him."

"He'll ride at night," Orlan Thomas said. "He does this frequently."

Henry Burlingame questioned, "Abilene? The widow, Missus Parsons?"

"Why not?" Marshal Thomas smiled. "Hell, she took him in once, didn't she? She fooled the dickens out of us all. That young rascal was more than her nephew, and he has good friends in Oakley, too. Any of them will take the kid in and hide him."

It was Burlingame's turn to grin. "Especially Missus Rose Parsons. You're probably right about that lady. I could tell by the way she looked, the way she talked about him. She had some strong feelings about the boy. She was very protective, I can tell you that."

Nate Vickers, attentive to the conversation, asked, "Who was the fellow? Someone important? You know, there was two other men in here asking about a fellow riding a Morgan."

Perking up, Orlan asked, "Bounty hunter types?"

"Can't say about that," Vickers replied. "One an older fellow, the other a youngster. The young one said this fellow killed four of his friends up in the Dakota Territory, 'round Deadwood. He made off with all of their money from a Texas cattle drive. Three thousand dollars, if you can believe it."

Henry Burlingame stared over at Marshal Thomas. "Three thousand!"

And Nate Vickers said, "I kinda thought it was a tall tale, too."

"The young man with the Morgan is Hardy Gibbs," Orlan told Vickers. "The men he shot up along the way were horse rustlers, and it's damned possible they had over three thousand dollars on them."

Vickers stared back and forth at the two men. "Oh, I remember reading something about that Lusk shooting. Charlie Parsons, that's who it was, so the newspaper said. No mention of what caused the ruckus. Nothing about money, either. Gibbs, you say?"

"One and the same," Henry Burlingame said. "Parsons, Hollister, Gibbs, all the same."

"Humph, well I'll be damned!" returned Vickers. "All dressed in buckskins. Seemed nice enough. Like I said, he didn't talk much."

"Yep and nope?" asked Burlingame.

"Yes, I suppose that was about it, all right."

Orlan Thomas laughed. "He talks when he feels like it. Other times, he lets that revolver do the talking."

After thanking Nate Vickers, Orlan and Henry Burlingame walked slowly back down the long street into the dusty traffic of Julesburg. The fact that two men with a grudge had come into town inquiring about Hardy Gibbs didn't sit well with the marshal. Orlan Thomas liked Hardy; so did Henry Burlingame. As they walked along, they both agreed it would be a tragedy if Hardy ended up getting bushwhacked. Thomas had come on this trip because he had been assigned to the task of bringing in Hardy Gibbs. He could talk and reason with him. Both he and Burlingame adhorred the thought of Hardy taking a bullet in the back somewhere along the trail.

But the investigation in Julesburg was only beginning. Both Orlan and Henry were astounded by Vickers's story, or the story told to him about Hardy making off with three thousand dollars. And Burlingame said, "The boy's not a bandit, never was. It doesn't run in the family. The family has some money, his grandfather a wealthy old man, and Hardy, from what all I've uncovered in this story, hasn't been in any great need of money."

Grinning, Orlan Thomas said, "No, not if he's still on the payroll of his Aunt Rose. She's backing him, too. Charlie . . . Hardy said she was going to hire him on as soon as he got the traveling itch out of his system. 'Course, I can see why, now, and it wouldn't surprise me if he hightailed back there. He's always doing the unexpected. Abilene? Sure as hell no one would suspect it . . . except us."

"I never wrote about her," Burlingame said. "I kept my word, but I can't back off now, not if the boy takes this route. It would have to come out. She's not his aunt. She's his—"

"*Benefactor*," suggested Marshal Thomas. "Let your readers draw their own conclusions, Henry. She felt sorry for him, and don't forget that little woman Hardy shot up those boys over—his sweetheart, something like that."

"His cousin," Burlingame said. "That's the problem with this whole story. Everyone feels sorry for the smart little bastard." He grinned and added, "So do I, but this is the best yarn I've hit upon in years, Orlan, and I can't write around it forever."

Orlan said, "You're right. He's smart. He knows now he's in bad trouble, and he's not going to be packing around three thousand dollars. He's too smart to pull a fool stunt like that."

"You mean *if* he got three thousand."

"Those two fellows trailing him aren't bounty hunters. I'd say their story is true. So what are they after? Their own money, not reward. If they shoot him in the back and go claiming reward, too, they've written their own death sentences. They'd be dead in a week if they did that, the reputation that kid has. And you can sure as hell bet they won't take him on in a shoot-out. Even at two-to-one odds it's a poor bet. Hell, you know that. He took down three at Benkelman, remember?"

"So what do we do next?"

"Make some inquiries around here. A boy dressed in buckskins and riding a Morgan isn't hard to follow, Henry. When you see that kid, you don't forget him, either. If some fellow doesn't remember him, some woman sure as hell will." He chuckled, adding, "That little chambermaid in the Palace Hotel, Mary Lou, told me later she almost fainted when she was in his room cleaning and he looked her over, said something about wanting to go dancing with him, for beginners, eh? Yes, we'll make some inquiries, pay our respects to the sheriff, and catch a stage south out of here. If Charlie . . . Hardy is riding that way, we'll catch up with him between Oakley and Abilene somewhere. This is my best guess on it. He's running in a circle."

Orlan Thomas and Henry Burlingame began their rounds. A young man answering Hardy's description had been in one of the mercantile stores; he had stayed in the Grand Hotel one night, and when the clerk checked back in the register, he pointed to the name— Paul L. Charles. Orlan Thomas's next stop was the Julesburg Wells Fargo Bank. A teller remembered Mister Charles, and why not? The man had an account with the bank—he had deposited three thousand dollars in an assortment of bills and twenty-dollar gold pieces, and he had made a joke about it, telling the clerk he had just robbed a bank. What was the name on the account? Paul LaBlanc Charles. Orlan Thomas told the bank vice president that when Paul LaBlanc Charles returned to withdraw the money, bank personnel should immediately advise the Julesburg sheriff's office.

And later, after a visit with Sheriff Isaac Holman, the men went back to the hotel, where they took rooms for the night. The next morning, Orlan Thomas and Henry Burlingame boarded the Overland for the train junction town of Oakley, Kansas.

FOURTEEN

Sanctuary

My Dearest Julienne:

This will be hard for you to understand and disappointing, too. I am back at John Peltier's farm for a while. I had planned on writing from somewhere far west of here. I was headed for Oregon by way of a less traveled and safer route up through the Montana and Idaho territories. It was safe enough but as has been my misfortune I ran into trouble right off. I met two old men who were going up to this land to die. I know this sounds crazy but I swear it is true. One was a white man and other one a Sioux Indian. They died on me and I had to bury them. It was one of the saddest times in my life and then I was at Fort Custer by a Crow Indian reservation and a herd of horses was stolen including Sundown. A few of us chased after the thieves. We got most of the horses back but I had to kill two rustlers in a place called Lusk to get Sundown. They had more than $3,000 on them from selling the horses. Since all of the stolen horses are being retrieved I consider it my good fortune to have come into all of this money. I did not return to Fort Custer. I rode south. I deposited $3,000 in the Julesburg Wells Fargo Bank under the name of Paul LaBlanc Charles. I put your name on the papers as a co-depositor in case some bad luck befalls me. It seems strange to me that of late I have been trying to avoid trouble and it keeps following me wherever I go. I read part of that story in Harper's Weekly by Burlingame. I know you and Grandfather must be as unhappy about it as I am. To make matters worse, I saw a poster of me in Julesburg and it has a new drawing and the name of Charles Parsons as well as mine. I spent the night there and left the next day. I kept thinking men were following me and I did not feel safe until I was on the road out of Benkelman. I wish I could have been at Andy and Micheline's wedding. I will be here until I receive a letter from you and we can decide on what we must do or where to meet when it is safer. This is the best place for me now. I surely do miss you and I surely do love you.

Hardy.

As before, send your letter to John Peltier.

It was depressing; in six weeks he had made a gigantic circle, almost reaching the Yellowstone, riding across the high plains to the Black Hills, then south into Wyoming and Colorado country, and finally was right back where he had started. He had left rejuvenated with high hopes, had returned weary and sick at heart. He couldn't reveal all of his feelings to Julienne, not when she already was grieving over his welfare and safety, but at least once she learned he was back at Curly Robe John's farm, she might breathe a little easier. The disclosure of his true name was troublesome enough. Now that Hardy Gibbs and Charlie Parsons were the same man, he was fair game for the law, bounty hunters, or any fool seeking glory. This was a frightening thought, not of dying facing someone, but of dying from a shot in the back, for he knew by experience no one but an idiot would dare challenge him head-on. More frightening, ever since he had killed Tom Truscott over the hills in Oakley, he hadn't given a second thought about shooting anyone. There was no

remorse, none of that feeling sick in his stomach anymore. He hadn't even bothered to look at those dead
Texans. On the outside, he was growing a shell as
tough as a terrapin's; on the inside, he was getting all
hollow like a dead one. Just as old Mato had said that
night, it felt like his soul was floating around loose
from his body. He needed rest; he needed time to plan
his next move.

John Peltier and Blackbird, surprised as they were to
see Hardy, had welcomed him like a son. And this, in
a way, was home to him; it was sanctuary, a good place
to heal both body and soul. It was a good place to receive wise counsel, a place where he could go and sit
on the bank of the river, play his harmonica, and meditate. Oh, he worked, too, and he didn't mind farm
work, always had thought it was good honest labor. He
took up a shovel and a hoe and worked in Blackbird's
big fields and her garden; he heaved on poles, stripped
them of bark, and made a new corral; he milked the
two cows, and moved Curly Robe John's forty head of
cattle back and forth to better grass.

Every time he thought about riding out into civilization, his senses burned and crackled like dead willow.
Something—what, he didn't know—was compelling
him to wait. One thing he did know was that he could
no longer go around relying solely on that revolver on
his hip. He would have to learn to rely more on his
brains now, his wit. He was going to have to get on
that train and clean country, ride it as far as he could,
and send for Julienne. Lord, Lord, he surely was a hog-
tied man, so damn lonely for that woman.

One day, Curly Robe came back from Benkelman
(Hardy had wanted to go along on the wagon with him,

but both he and John knew it was no longer safe) with a big sack of full of clothes. He plopped the sack on the porch in front of Hardy. With a grin, he said, "There's your new trappings, Charlie." John couldn't get used to calling him Hardy. "Not exactly what you ordered, but it'll make do." And, digging in his pocket, he withdrew a few dollars and handed them to Hardy. "Even got you some change, I did."

Thanking John, Hardy pulled out the first item on top—a straw farmer's hat, big and yellow. He grinned back at John. But when he began to withdraw the rest of the clothing, he was more appalled than amused. A pair of big bib overalls, two blue work shirts, a pair of red longjohns, and, holy smokes, a pair of ugly sodbuster boots. Hardy Gibbs didn't know whether to laugh or cry. He just mumbled, "Yep, they'll make do."

Blackbird, however, didn't cry. She started laughing. She held up the overalls to her lithe body; only her head stuck out at the top, and using one of her husband's favorite expressions, she said, *"Mon Dieu!"* draped the trousers over Hardy, and shaking her head, disappeared back in the house.

John Peltier shrugged innocently. "What can I say?"

Hardy Gibbs smiled weakly. "How about maybe you're sorry?"

"But *mon ami*, if one works like a farmer, one should look like a farmer. *Oui*, a good, what you say . . . disguise. Who will say 'Aha, there is the gunfighter, Charlie Parsons,' eh? Or this fellow Hardy Gibbs?"

Hardy placed the yellow straw hat on his head, and trudging away with the rest of the clothing, he groaned, "Charlie the scarecrow is more like what they'll say."

* * *

Near the beginning of September Blue Hammond and her daughter, Lucinda, came riding into the farmyard in their wagon for an overnight stay and to buy some produce from Curly Robe John. They were flabbergasted when Hardy came up from the barn, first by his very presence at the farm, and second by his appearance: whiskers sprouting all over his chin, baggy overalls all cinched tightly around his waist by a big leather belt, and last by the fact that he wasn't wearing his revolver.

"Gracious, I'd never have known it was you, Mister Charlie," Lucinda said, brushing back her long black hair. "Papa's going to be surprised when I tell him you're working here. He says every stranger that comes along is asking about you. Even that lawman from Hays and that Burlingame man, the one who writes all of the stories about you. They came looking around, too. Papa tells them all you went to that Oregon country. Some of them just don't believe a word of it . . . say you're still hanging around somewhere, hiring out someplace to shoot rustlers. One of them even went up to Colby's ranch. My Joseph told him to get the hell out."

"Joseph?"

"Joseph Bemis," she said, glowing. "Don't you remember? You and Joseph put up the wire fence . . . still standing, too. And those Calhoun brothers don't come around anymore, either."

"Well," said Hardy, "I surely do remember Joe—"

"Everyone remembers you, too, Mister Charlie. All surprised to find out about you being Hardy Gibbs. Gracious, I knew it all the time, didn't I?"

"Yes, I reckon you did, Lucinda." Hardy smiled. "Our secret, just the two of us, but it got out, anyway."

If he had changed, so had Lucinda Hammond— either her blouse was too small or she was sprouting like a weed inside of it. Her tits were almost escaping and she was all grins like she was damn proud of it.

Hardy Gibbs said hesitantly, "You and Joe, you two . . ."

"That's my news for Blackbird and Mister John," she said proudly. "Joseph started calling regular right after you left the last time. We're getting married, and Mister Colby, why, he's going to fix up the line cabin on the upper Solomon for us, make another room, a regular little house."

Blackbird, her face radiating pleasure, came over and hugged Lucinda. John Peltier said, "*Mon Dieu,* I've never been to a wedding in my life! I have no clothes for such an affair."

Hardy Gibbs said wryly, "Don't worry about it, John. You can wear mine."

"Could you come, too?" Lucinda asked Hardy.

John quickly answered this, saying, "Not unless you want a funeral for someone the next day. The boy isn't taking to much to traveling of late, eh? Too hot to travel. *Oui,* he's waiting for things to cool off a bit."

Hardy Gibbs's mind was wandering off. He was thinking about the Colby line cabin, dwelling on the pleasant days and nights that he and Willard had spent together up there, talking about everything under the sun—mostly about the future. Strange, Willard's future had been so positive, his own so precariously tentative, and now Willard's had been etched in stone, and Hardy Gibbs, well, he was still searching.

* * *

The next morning, Hardy Gibbs was washing up at the big basin on the porch that Blackbird had put there for both him and John to use during the late summer weather. There also was a small mirror tacked on to a porch post, and here he was, staring at himself, dismayed at how he was beginning to look more like Festus Cato every day—a young Festus Cato, true, but nevertheless just as scraggly and unkempt. Thank the Lord he had soap and plenty of water, the river close by, for had he smelled as badly as Cato, Blackbird most certainly would have put him in the barn. Hardy heard a giggle behind him, turned, and stared sheepishly at Lucinda Hammond. She had on a long nightgown; her hair was all over her shoulders; her feet were bare. She was a pretty young woman, and that Joseph Bemis surely was a lucky young man. What a wonderful sight to wake up to every morning, Hardy Gibbs thought. How lovely, young, and vibrant, this Lucinda Hammond, this quarter-breed, this beautiful blend of red and white. And then a sudden feeling of nostalgia and loneliness coursed through his whole body, from the top of his shaggy head right down to his sodbuster boots. Jesus, this could be Julienne standing here, that cute little smirk on her face, poking fun at him in all of his homeliness. *Why, I declare, Hardy Gibbs, you are a mess if I ever saw one!* Did it matter? *Hardy Gibbs, I love you.* Yes, he thought, Julienne was liable to say that, too.

Instead, Hardy heard Lucinda Hammond saying, "Mister Charlie, you need a shave and a haircut. You aren't so handsome anymore, you know. You look like one of those hide hunters you chased out of Papa's hotel."

"I know." Hardy sighed. "I surely don't smell like one, though." He turned around and gave her hair a friendly tousle. "Looking at you, Lucinda, makes me feel lonely. It surely shouldn't. Looking at a pretty woman in the morning should make a man feel like going to work whistling."

Lucinda Hammond's smile turned sad. "Looking at me makes you think of that girl in the story, doesn't it? The one you were going to marry up with?"

"Yes, I suppose you're right."

Lucinda touched his arm, and with a little blush, she said, "When you first came to Oakley, I didn't want you to leave. I didn't know you had a sweetheart. . . . I had dreams, thinking about you—you and me. When you kissed me, I wanted to get on that horse and ride away with you. I didn't even care if you were Hardy Gibbs."

"I would have enjoyed your company," Hardy Gibbs said with a smile. "You're a beautiful young woman, and Joseph is a lucky man. It's worked out the best for you. I'm very happy for you, too."

Lucinda toed up and kissed Hardy Gibbs on the forehead. She said, "That story in the magazine about you . . . Mama and I thought it was nice . . . sad, too. Mama couldn't understand. Said if someone violated a woman like that in a Cheyenne village, he likely would be castrated or get his pecker cut off, and to my notion, that's worse than getting killed."

She was sincere, but Hardy Gibbs couldn't help but smile. He agreed, saying, "Yep, that's some powerful notion, it is."

Hardy began drying his hands with a big towel hanging from an iron ring. Leaning up against the post, Lucinda went on, saying, "I don't see much sense in you hanging around here pining and she's back there pining. You should do what Mister John says. Get on one of those trains, go someplace, and bring her out there. Looking the way you do now, ain't no one who's going to know you're Hardy Gibbs or Charlie. Papa says you leave love setting around too long and it turns into stale gravy."

"Wilson said that?"

"Yes, sir, he told that to Joseph." She giggled. "We aren't letting it set around. Papa just wants to get me married proper before I swallow a watermelon seed. That's my notion."

Hardy Gibbs momentarily reflecting back on the advice once given to him by his grandfather about those "powerful seeds," smiled at Lucinda, and said, "That's some notion, too." Then, pointing to the washbasin, he asked, "Want second water?"

Lucinda giggled, scooped up a handful, and threw it on him. Hardy Gibbs laughed again, thinking Julienne would have done the very same thing, or then again, she might have dumped the whole damned basin over his shaggy head.

Three days after Blue Hammond and Lucinda left, John Peltier came back from his weekly trip to Benkelman bearing a letter with a St. Louis postmark on it, and just looking at the fat envelope brought a glaze to the eyes of Hardy. Opening it, he found not one letter, but two, the second a letter of sorts. He dropped it in his lap and first began with the letter from his beloved Julienne.

My Dearest Love:

I received your letter and I am not disappointed. I am thrilled and so happy you are all right. After all these weeks of not hearing from you, I cried and cried, after hearing you are well and safe. When I showed the letter to Uncle Amos he said we must make plans soon to come out and meet you. He is worried and so am I. I cannot wait any longer. He says three heads are better than one. He says you should dress up like a preacher man and go to Denver. We looked on a map and Denver is not too far from McCook. We did not find Benkelman on the map but it cannot be too far since your letters are always marked McCook. Uncle Amos got this idea after we received the letter enclosed. It came to Papa. We do not know what it is all about but it looks official and all. Uncle Amos says you must have an important friend in Denver to send you a paper like this.

The wedding was nice. We all were dressed and had it on the front porch at Uncle Amos's house. We had some fiddles and a big supper and Andy and Micheline rode off in the surrey and stayed at a big hotel in St Louis. The new house at the Watson homestead is almost finished. They are already living there and I stop by on my way home when I leave the shop. I always call out because I never know what they are doing in there and once they were doing something and Andy was angry with me. Uncle Amos is planning on selling his patents to the Colt people for a great sum of money. He is tired of working. He says he might make a rifle or two just for the fun of it. Please write immediately about meeting us in Denver. We can come anytime but Uncle Amos does not want to wait until winter. It will not matter to me. I told him you can keep me warm. He said he knew this but asked me who was going to keep him warm. Adah misses you. She sends her love and her prayers. I love you so much and hope to see you soon.

Julienne.

Hardy Gibbs's dark eyes were so misty he could barely read the other letter. Actually he soon found it wasn't letter, but some kind of an official document with a note attached. The note was to his Uncle Paul and simply directed him to forward it to wherever Charlie Parsons was living, and below the directive, it said, "Charlie will understand. I read in the *Harper's* story that Charlie said he was the soul of my nephew, Willard. Every soul needs a body." The note was signed by Bill Colby.

Initially, Hardy couldn't imagine what this was all about. He slowly unfolded the piece of paper, and the printing across the top of it said, "In the District Court of the First Judicial District of the State of Colorado, in and for The County of Denver." Well, there was so much writing below this, so many of those "wherein" and "wherefore" words, it was difficult to understand, but he kept seeing the name William F. Colby II, and after a while at the bottom, it said that William F. Colby II was the son of William and Emma Colby of Colby, Kansas. A birth date was written there, and it was signed by a district judge whose name of was Clayton McKernan.

Suddenly struck by the document's significance, Hardy Gibbs swallowed hard and reread the bottom part again. It was as though he had been smashed by a bolt of lightning. Trembling, he handed the paper to John Peltier, saying, "Is this . . . is this what I think it is? Is such a thing possible?"

After John had scanned it for a while, he said, "You told me Bill Colby's brother, Willard's father—the one over in Denver—is one of those attorneys, eh? I tell you, *mon ami*, he is a very good one. *Oui*, this is a certificate of birth. You have a mother and father again. *Oui*, this is what it says. You are William Colby the second. Your father has a big ranch over the hills about a one-day ride from here. The one where you fixed the fence, eh?"

Two big tears suddenly rolled down and hid in the whiskers of Hardy Gibbs. Visions flew through his fractured mind—visions of his father and mother, his sister, flames, smoke, death, and then the flames and smoke of an ebbing night fire up in the Big Horn Mountains, two old men, chants, visions, and death again. With a great sob, he stared up into the purple of the evening sky and whispered, "Thank you, God."

John Peltier, gently patting Hardy on the shoulder, said softly, "Welcome to the farm, William Colby."

The big red rooster crowed at dawn, but Hardy already was up and about, first coaxing a fire in Blackbird's iron range, then bringing in two mules from the pasture, hitching them to the wagon. He went down to the lower meadow near the river and talked with Sundown and the brown and white Crow mare. This was a good place to live, he told them, plenty of grass and the water was good. He had been happy, here; so would they. He said that he had to leave for a while and that he would sorely miss their companionship. And later, after embracing Blackbird on the porch, bidding her a fond but sad farewell, Hardy Gibbs and Curly Robe John rode down the lane toward

Benkelman to meet the northbound Overland stage to Julesburg. Hardy was wearing his yellow straw hat, his bib overalls, a denim jacket, and his sodbuster boots. But he was naked—his most valued and cherished possession, his Gibbs Special, he left behind; he had given it to John Peltier as a parting gift. Curly Robe John, touched by this sentimental and significant gesture, had taken the pistol from its holster. He hung it from a wooden peg high above the fireplace. It was much too precious to carry.

Toward noon the following day, a disheveled Hardy Gibbs stepped off the stagecoach in Julesburg with several things on his mind: first, getting his money out of the Wells Fargo bank; second, buying a train ticket; and third, ridding himself of his old sodbuster clothes and straw hat. Despite his unkempt appearance, he was still suspicious and wary, and without his revolver, deception was the only defense he had.

At the bank, he withdrew the three thousand dollars he had deposited under the name of Paul LaBlanc Charles, immediately went to the railroad depot, and purchased a ticket for Corrine, Utah, the junction stop for stagecoaches running north into the Montana Territory. He entered the first haberdashery he saw, bought two suits, shirts, ties, underclothes, and new shoes. Changing into one of the new suits at the back of the store, he left by the rear entrance and, once in the alley, discarded his old clothes in a trash barrel. Hardy walked back to the main street almost a new man. Well, almost—he stopped by a barbershop, had his hair cut, his beard and mustache trimmed. Cocking his brown derby to the side of his head, he went to the

Grand Hotel, where he registered in as William Colby II and also immediately recognized the clerk, the same fellow who had registered him earlier in the summer. Hardy went to his room smiling; the clerk hadn't recognized him. William Colby shed his new clothing, took a bath in the washroom down the hall, went back to his quarters, and collapsed on the bed.

Meantime, Sheriff Isaac Holman, alerted by one of the staff members at the bank that Paul LaBlanc Charles had withdrawn his account, rushed over to get a description of the man. All that he learned was that it was a bearded fellow wearing overalls and a big straw hat. Did anyone notice if the man had a black horse hitched out in front? No one knew, nor had they noticed which direction the young man had gone, either. Sheriff Holman and one of his deputies immediately took to the streets of Julesburg, visited the saloons, but they saw no one remotely resembling their quarry. No one at the three hotels and rooming houses had seen anyone answering the description of such a man, and Nate Vickers at the livery, who surely would have remembered Charlie Parsons and his black Morgan, simply shrugged. However, the lawmen had better luck at the train station. Yes, a farmer wearing a straw hat and overalls had purchased a ticket on the westbound leaving in the evening. His destination? The stage junction stop at Corrine, the departure point for the gold mining camps of the Montana Territory.

Sheriff Holman, aware of the quick hand of Hardy Gibbs, picked up an additional deputy, and the three lawmen stationed themselves at the depot a half hour before the train was scheduled to arrive. It was dusk. They cautiously waited. Several dozen finely attired people gathered. The puffing train arrived, departing passengers stepped off, milled about with greeters on the platform, and boarding passengers got on, but there was no sign of Hardy Gibbs. Swearing softly, Sheriff Holman shook his head, then stared at his two deputies. "If he's on that train, he didn't get on it looking like a farmer. He's not a farmer. He's a goddamned fox, and he can shoot, too. That's a helluva combination."

"He outfoxed us, all right," one of the deputies said. "You know what I think? I think he got on the train from the other side."

Sheriff Holman sent the deputies back to the office, and he headed for the telegraph office. He sent two messages: one to Corrine, Utah, the other one to U.S. Marshal Orlan Thomas in Hays, Kansas.

It read: "Hardy Gibbs bought ticket for Corrine, Utah. Will alert sheriff in Corrine to check all passengers. Apprehend Gibbs with all due caution. Isaac Holman."

FIFTEEN

Julienne

It was a beautiful Sunday morning on the Meramec, the green river curling lazily down through the brushy bottom, the woodland stillness occasionally broken by the call of quail and the subdued laughter of Julienne LaBlanc and her sister-in-law, Micheline. They were sitting together on a blanket near the bank, a large picnic basket beside them, André LaBlanc, a contented smile on his face, stretched out nearby. Next to André was a cane pole propped up against a big rock, and below, a cork bobber was slowly moving back and forth in a quiet eddy. The fish weren't biting. It didn't matter. This was a time to relax, to count blessings, to contemplate. The new house was finished, and André and his father, Paul LaBlanc, had cut through a new road connecting the old Watson place with the LaBlanc farm. André had plowed over a hundred acres of the new land, thoroughly tilled it for planting in the spring, had a coop full of laying hens, a pen of pigs, and milk cows were in the lower meadows. It was harvest time, the skeeters and chiggers were gone, and there was a good sweet smell in the early autumn air.

A time of contemplation—a time of anxiety, too, for Julienne LaBlanc. This was the last picnic of the fading summer, a farewell picnic of sorts, for she and Uncle Amos were now only awaiting word from Hardy regarding their planned trip west. Julienne could barely contain herself. The past several weeks had been fraught with consternation and fear. This proposal to meet Hardy in Denver had been Uncle Amos's idea, and although he didn't say so, Julienne knew that since Henry Burlingame's revealing story, he feared for his grandson's life. The Shooter, Charlie Parsons, had met too many people some whom he considered his friends; but some of these friends could be friends only as long as it suited their purpose now that he was Hardy Gibbs. A one-thousand-dollar reward was apt to sever a friendship in a hurry. This was what Uncle Amos was thinking, and Julienne knew it. No wonder poor Hardy had to flee back to John Peltier's farm. Uncle Amos was trying to make light of it, though, always looking on the bright side, despite that latest shooting in the Wyoming Territory. That one had brought another one of those writers knocking on the front door, the man who called himself Ned Buntline. He didn't get any more out of Uncle Amos than did Burlingame, but he hung around Kirkwood Town for several days, talking to people and listening to gossip. Someone was always snooping around. This was one thing that Uncle Amos wasn't taking lightly—if Hardy did agree to meet in Denver, she and Uncle Amos were going to have to sneak out and take the night train. He didn't want anyone to tell one of those nosy writers; they had done enough damage already.

Julienne and Micheline went swimming, André took a nap, and later they feasted on fried chicken, cold cornbread, and berry pie. But the picnic ended on a

sour note. André hooked into a big catfish and lost it;
he thought it was Big Mama.

The next afternoon, Julienne saddled up the gray
mare and rode up to Uncle Amos's house, not to work,
but to visit her uncle and Adah. This had become almost a daily ritual for the past several weeks, everyone
anticipating some good news from the west, or what
they all dreaded, bad news in some dispatch in the *St.
Louis Daily Post*. Outside of a few daily chores and
tending the three horses Amos owned, there wasn't
much to do but talk. Amos Gibbs had only a few orders left to fill. The transaction with Colt Arms had
been completed, and Amos had a CLOSED sign on the
shop door. Amos Gibbs was a very wealthy man; he
was ready to do anything possible for his grandson and
Julienne. He wanted them married, and he wanted to
be a great grandfather. This made an otherwise unhappy Julienne happy.

She left Uncle Amos's house at sundown; she never
rode in the dark, and she always carried her Gibbs .32
Special inside her belt. It wasn't any secret around
Kirkwood Town that Julienne LaBlanc had become an
expert pistol shot. The children who sometimes came
running at the sound of practice shooting knew this,
and thus, so did everyone else in the community.
Micheline Bonet LaBlanc thought this was good—it
served as fair warning to anyone who might dare to trifle with her sister-in-law, and she knew Julienne
wouldn't hesitate to use her weapon if provoked.

As Julienne approached the road leading down to
Andy and Micheline's new house, she saw a small
cloud of dust, then the dark form of a buggy making a
circle in the road, and it took her a few moments be-

fore she got close enough to make out who the driver of the buggy was. Her face quickly came to a flush. Good Lord, she cursed under her breath, it was that buffoon, Shamus O'Leary! In the dusky twilight she could see that derby perched on his head, and that old black buggy. After all of these months, the idiot was still sneaking around, probably had found some chicken bones alongside the road. Now what was he doing? Blocking her way? Why, he surely was! As she rode closer, Julienne saw Shamus stepping out of the buggy. Thank God he wasn't carrying a shotgun. But no, this wasn't the constable—it was a taller man, dressed in one of those long suit coats, a vest, and shiny black shoes, and dammit, he was hailing her, waving his derby. Another one of those nosy newspaper people? How could she be certain? She wasn't, so pulling back her jacket, Julienne protectively grasped the handle of her Gibbs and shouted, "All right, stranger, that's far enough. I don't know what you're up to riding out here this time of the evening, but don't you dare even think about fooling around with me. I have a pistol here, and I know how to use it."

The man threw out his hands and replied, "Good Lord, woman, my name is William Colby. . . . Don't shoot! I'm just passing through on my way to Philadelphia to an engineering school, and I was looking to meet a young woman named Julienne LaBlanc, that's all."

My God! Why, this fellow's voice sounded just like Hardy's! But he didn't look like Hardy all dandied up this way, whiskers, too, and those little spectacles. But that voice! Heart suddenly pounding, she shied her gray to the side and gave the man a hard stare. "Hardy? . . . Hardy Gibbs?"

"No, ma'am," he answered. "Will Colby, a friend of Hardy's, and if you're Julienne, why, that Hardy was surely lying . . . said you were right homely, but damn, I think you're beautiful."

Julienne LaBlanc suddenly shrieked, "Hardy! Oh, my God, you crazy fool!" And, jumping from her horse, she leaped clear and threw herself into his open arms. And she just couldn't help it, but she started bawling like a baby, bawling so hard she couldn't even talk or kiss him. But he was kissing her, all over the top of her head, then her forehead, and then he just lifted up her chin and kissed right through her crying.

Julienne was still shaking inside as they rode together in the buggy down the lane to the Paul LaBlanc farm. Yes, it was true, William Colby was going to some college in Philadelphia to take examinations, and it was true that he knew Hardy Gibbs, had heard that Hardy had gone to the Northwest Territories. William Colby had bought an extra train ticket down at Union Station, too, and he was wondering if she would like to take a little ride in the comfort of one of those fancy sleeping cars. Julienne heard that old train whistle calling, *wha-oo, wha-oo,* and she said she would indeed like to ride in a parlor car. William Colby was also wondering if he could sleep in André's former back bedroom at the farm, said he thought he could find his way back there in the black of night. Julienne replied she could find her way back there in the black of night, too.

William Colby, looking down over his spectacles, said, "I surely would like that, ma'am."

Epilogue

About the prophecies of the old holy man, Little Bear—in 1879, exactly one year after Little Bear's death, a disastrous fire swept through Deadwood, Dakota Territory, destroying most of the town.

In 1883, a flood severely damaged the town. In both cases, residents rebuilt, but fires and floods continued to plague the citizens up through 1888. By this time, however, the gold rush had ended.

About the writer, Henry Burlingame—in December 1878, en route to New York City to assume a new position with *Harper's Weekly*, Burlingame stopped in St. Louis for a day and went out to the Amos Gibbs small arms plant. It was closed. Amos Gibbs, the colored caretaker told Burlingame, was away on an extended trip. Burlingame's visit was almost identical to his first, when the beautiful young shooter called Julienne LaBlanc had said that he would find nothing but memories of Hardy Gibbs in the area. Now Julienne LaBlanc was gone, too. Henry Burlingame knew the saga of The Shooter, Hardy Gibbs, had ended.

**Watch for the next exciting
Paul A. Hawkins novel
THE SEEKERS
coming to you soon from Signet.**

*Excerpts from a September 1904
interview with the writer-editor
Henry Burlingame of* Harper's Weekly.

Now, the notion that life on the frontier was a romantic, rewarding experience is balderdash. I have to call it "frontier" for want of a better word. It was a misnomer. It was only a frontier to invaders, who put their stakes down in a land that had been settled by a native civilization hundreds of years before we ever arrived. . . . During the period that I worked out there, there wasn't a more dangerous and unpredictable countryside that I could imagine. And I shall say the same about many of the men and women I met while on assignment. They, too, were often a dangerous and unpredictable lot. Survival—that's what it always came down to. . . . Women? Yes, there were a few women, several I chanced to meet in my tenure of fifteen years. Jane Canarray was a notorious one—indeed, a regular harridan. She had her own set of rules. She was "Calamity" personified. but even so, this woman had a heart for humanity. The other one you mentioned, Katherine Coltrane. Well, she was one of the most complex human beings I ever met. A beautiful woman, too, make no mistake about that, and some say as nefarious as "Calamity Jane." There are dozens of stories about Katherine Coltrane, but she and Jane were as different as night and day. There were only two things these women had in common. At one time, they were both mule skinners, and they were both "soiled doves." Jane, penniless, ended up in a pine box in Deadwood. Kate Coltrane? She was a miraculous survivor.

May 1876. Fort Fetterman, Wyoming Territory

They entered the fort late in the afternoon, a troop of twenty-four mounted soldiers, two supply wagons to the rear with seven Indian women and two old men perched on top. Amid the furor of General George Crook's preparations for his campaign to the north against the Lakota and Cheyenne, the small party attracted nothing more than a few curious looks.

The captives riding on the two wagons were from one of Crazy Horse's bands. One, a white woman, had been missing for five years. Except for Katherine Coltrane's tall stature and greenish blue eyes she appeared to be just as much Indian as any of the other unhappy, blanket-draped, women with her. The Indian captives were taken to a large tent shelter for food and additional blankets and clothing. But Katherine Coltrane was taken to the headquarters building where she sat on a chair outside Colonel Benjamin Bradford's office.

Inside Colonel Bradford's office, Lieutenant Thomas Clybourn made his report. Lieutenant Clybourn's troopers captured the small Sioux group on the Little Powder River. In the unexpected encounter with one of Crazy Horse's bands, many of the Indians escaped across the river after pinning down the troopers with a barrage of rifle fire from willows on the opposite shore.

Two of Clybourn's men had sustained superficial wounds before the Indians retreated and disappeared down the river in the dusk. Lieutenant Clybourn had been unable to estimate how many were in the moving village—probably no more than a hundred—but the braves who had opened fire were equipped with repeating rifles, and he though any pursuit on the following morning was ill-advised. The famed Indian scout, Porter Webb, and a Miniconjou breed, Joseph Brings Yellow, volunteered to follow the band to ascertain the native's intentions, but other signs and distant sightings already had indicated an exodus of many Indians toward the valleys to the north.

"They definitely aren't moving back toward the reservations," Clybourn said. "The Coltrane woman says the tribes are gathering somewhere to the north for their annual renewal ceremonies . . . Sun Dance . . . Sacred Arrow renewal rites, things like that. She didn't say much more. In fact, she's pretty upset about this whole affair."

"Upset?" Colonel Bradford said. He drummed his fingers on the desk. "Well, who in the hell isn't upset around here, Mister Clybourn? Coltrane did you say? Coltranes were once a freighting family. Parents passed on. Good people. . . .

"You know her, sir?"

"Personally, no," said Colonel Bradford. "I am surprised she's alive. A train her older brother was leading was attacked back in seventy-one or seventy-two below Laramie. Looted, burned by renegade Oglala. There were no survivors . . . not until, now."

"She's distressed," Clybourn said. "Half stunned, like

maybe in a state of shock. For a while I had a hard time of it talking to her. Shall I bring her in?"

Colonel Bradford shook his head. "No, Lieutenant. It's bad enough sometimes trying to understand a sane woman out in this infernal land, much less one in distress. No, I'll wait until tomorrow, until she gets her new bearings, gets herself adjusted to being a white woman again."

"That may take some doing, sir. She just seems to be staring around but not seeing much of anything. You want me to put her with the rest of those women . . . those two old codgers, bed her down in that squad tent for the night?"

Colonel Bradford replied, "She's a white woman, isn't she?"

"Yes, sir, and even in that Indian garb, a quite attractive one, too."

"Well, take her down to Slaymaker's boarding house," Bradford said. "Put her up there for the night, and tell Manny the army's paying for it. See if you can get anything more out of her. I'll talk to Miss Coltrane tomorrow morning, find out what she wants to do, where we can send her. Back down to Cheyenne, I suppose. That's where the Coltranes based their freighters."

"Yes, sir," answered Lieutenant Clybourn. "But begging your pardon, sir, I don't think that's where she'll be wanting to go."

"And why not? She can't stay here."

Lieutenant Clybourn paused at the door and saluted. "She wants to go back to the Powder River country, sir. During the fracas, she got separated from her family. Her Indian family, that is. She says her mother-in-law is a sister to Crazy Horse. Her mother-in-law has her daughter, a four-year-old, and she wants the little girl back. Says she knows what the bluecoats do to women and children when they raid villages."

Lieutenant Clybourn and Sergeant Marvel Hansen escorted Katherine Coltrane down to Manny Slaymaker's boarding house, a small hotel consisting of eight rooms and dining facilities. Manny and his wife, Mary, were already doing a booming business, housing several officers and four members of the press who had come to follow General Crook's campaign into the northern valleys. They quartered Katherine in the one remaining room left, a small cubicle to the back of the building, nothing fancy, a cot, commode, table and chair, and a tiny mirror. The lone window faced north toward the North Platte River, away from the confusion of the overcrowded fort.

Katherine's attention remained on the room briefly. "I understand everyone's concern," she said haltingly, "but it would have been just as well if I had been left with the others. Some of them don't understand any of this. They're afraid."

Standing at the tiny doorway Clybourn said, "Afraid? Afraid of what? They have nothing to fear. They're being taken care of . . . fed. Even sleeping rolls being put in for them . . . good food, coffee."

"You don't understand," Katherine Coltrane said. "They've heard the stories."

Clybourn knew the stories as well. It began with a failed attack on Two Moon's and Little Wolf's hunting village on the Powder. Colonel Joseph Reynolds had believed the camp to be that of Tashunka Witko—Crazy Horse—the elusive Sioux chief who had consistently dodged the reservation, making the unceded lands his home for more than eight years. The mistake was compounded when the Cheyenne, recapturing their entire pony herd from Reynolds' command, escaped to the north and took refuge for the rest of the winter and spring with Crazy Horse's people. General Crook, humiliated and incensed, had Colonel Reynolds court-martialed. And now it was no secret that General Crook was obsessed with capturing or destroying Crazy Horse, his Oglala people, and, indeed, the whole Indian nation. Lieutenant Clybourn said, "That was a terrible blunder, Miss Coltrane, a big mistake. . . ."

Katherine smiled bitterly, "They're always mistakes, aren't they? Sand Creek . . . Washita. I want my daughter back. Don't you understand? I want Julia back before she becomes another tragic mistake in the whole bungled affair. She's all I have now."

Clybourn nodded. "Yes . . . yes, I understand, and maybe it will all work out. Once everyone is back on the reservations, we can help you get it sorted out, eh, find your daughter."

"No, Mister Clybourn," Katherine said, "none of you seem to understand. The government has broken the treaty again by ordering these people back. They're not going back peacefully. It's already been decided. Mato-Nazin told me himself. There's going to be another big war, just like with Red Cloud and Dull Knife. Many people are going to die."

"Mato-Nazin?"

"Standing Bear . . . the father of my daughter, Blue Star . . . Julia. I call her Julia. They call her Wicapi Hinto, Blue Star. Crazy Horse is my uncle-in-law. He tells everything to the family. He says, 'We are going to fight the white man, again.' Now, everyone is saying it. Good Lord, Mister Clybourn, this is what few seem to understand."

"I understand their plight," confessed Lieutenant Clybourn. "I do."

"And mine?"

"Yes, of course, Miss Coltrane, I'll do what I can for you, I promise."

"I want Julia back," Katherine Coltrane said determinedly. "Get me a horse and I'll ride up there myself."

Clybourn shook his head and gave Sergeant Hansen a pathetic look.

Marvel Hansen, a veteran soldier, shrugged and said, "That's impossible, Miss Coltrane. Against orders for one thing—and another, it's a foolish act of desperation. You'd likely perish before you ever got up there."

"Would you have me perish down here, instead?"

"The Army will see to your well-being," Clybourn said.

"Fundless . . . without family. Good heavens, I'm destitute!"

"Your place in Cheyenne, we'll get you back there," assured Clybourn. "By the end of the summer we can check the reservation, work out a thorough search through Fort Robinson, the agents there."

Katherine, sitting on the edge of the small bed, stared disconsolately down at the plank floor. "Cheyenne . . . our house?" she asked. "Lord, if the neighbors haven't looked out for it, it's probably full of pack rats, by now. Five years? My brother's dead. So am I, as far as everyone knows. Our wagons are gone, all except three Kern freights we left behind, and I suppose they're useless from neglect."

Mary Slaymaker arrived and pushed through the small doorway. She was carrying a big hot kettle of water, towels and clothing draped over her other arm and shoulder. "Let the woman get herself washed up right proper," she said to Lieutenant Clybourn.

"Yes." Clybourn nodded, stepping aside.

Sergeant Hansen said to Katherine, "You speak Siouan, Miss Coltrane?"

"Yes . . . enough, I suppose."

"Well, if you want, I'll go down later with you, and you can talk to your friends at the big tent and explain to them that everything is going to be all right. We'll be taking them to Fort Robinson tomorrow sometime—back to their own kind on the reservation at Pine Ridge."

Tears suddenly rolled down Katherine's tanned cheeks. "How can I possibly explain that? Their families . . . children . . . all are up north where my own family is? They know what's going on around here. They know all about preparations for war."

"This is all so inconceivable, so strange," mused Clybourn. "Yes, your daughter I understand, but that you should feel this way after what they did . . . to you, your brother. If you'll pardon me, it's damned confusing, Miss Coltrane. You should feel relief being here."

"Mister Clybourn, do you know what it's like to wait year after year for someone to come and get you? Do you realize how it feels to be forsaken by your own people? . . . abandoned? At first, it was just surviving. But when I was with child I knew I had to do more than survive. I had to live. So, you see, I adapted. Oh, I knew this day was coming . . . sooner or later, I knew it was coming. I just wasn't quite prepared for it. Not for losing my child this way, for losing Julia."

"I'm sorry," said Clybourn. "I'd better go like Missus Slaymaker says. I'll be back later if you need me, or if you want Sergeant Hansen to go with you to your friends. I'll be back in about an hour. I'll escort you down to supper, Miss Coltrane."

Katherine watched him leave, then looked at what Mary Slaymaker had brought. A large pitcher of water stood on the commode, and beside it, in a small dish, lay a bar of yellow-colored soap; beneath the commode was a big tin wash pan, Katherine sniffed at the soap; she hadn't seen a bar of white man's soap in ages; it had a tint of lye to it; she would smell like medicine, but it was a clean odor. She carefully inspected the clothes Mary Slaymaker had brought: a long cotton skirt, two blouses, one frilly at the top, with ruffles, full at the front to disguise her bosom, long sleeves to hide her tanned and well-muscled arms, a pair of black stockings wrapped around a tortoise comb, white drawers, too—bloomers—everything used, everything appropriate, and everything clean.

Katherine removed her moccasins, draped her buckskin skirt over the back of the chair, and slipped out of her faded calico blouse. The tears in her eyes mingled with the warm water as she poured it over her head, let it course down the length of her body, past her middle, down her legs onto her feet. It puddled in the tin basin. Her toes were dirty, and with a large cloth she methodically began washing, a foot and a leg at a time, finally pouring the last of the water over her head, then gouging away at the crevices inside her ears. This was her bath, an impromptu bath, but she felt clean enough to slip into her white bloomers. She then sat on the chair near the window, and began combing out her long curtain of dark brown hair. It was still damp when she parted it in the middle and pulled it tightly behind her head and fastened it with her strip of leather. Katherine thought the frilly blouse was much too prissy. She chose the simple, pale blue one; it had white, pearl-like buttons on the sleeves that matched three buttons on the small collar. Twisting her Lakota blue and white beads into a smaller loop, she hung these around her neck. Finally, staring at herself in the small mirror, she smiled for the first time in days. She approved of her looks. She was a pretty woman, and only because of this had the glimmer of a smile shown. Without Julia, her new freedom meant nothing.

As he had promised, Lieutenant Clybourn returned in about an hour. When she opened the door, Katherine immediately saw the look of surprise on his face. She knew that her appearance pleased him, and she in turn was relieved that he had come back because, except for a few words with Sergeant Hansen, this young man was the only white man with whom she had spoken at any great length during the three days since her capture on the Little Powder. She liked him. He was understanding, and at least he was trying to be helpful, whether out of pity for her or just in the line of his assigned duty. And, if he were surprised to see her as a white woman, she was likewise surprised when he handed her a box. He smiled at her under his black mustache, a mustache well-trimmed, one that curved up under his ruddy cheeks.

Presenting her the box, he said, "You look nice, Miss Coltrane . . . the beads and all, not much like a squaw,

I should say." Nodding at the box, he added, "I hope these fit. Only two pairs of them at the sutlers and I took the biggest . . . not that you have big feet, mind you, but the other pair was pretty damn small."

That brought the second smile of the day from Katherine. "I'm not a small woman," she replied. "I do have big feet." Upon opening the box, she discovered a white shawl and under it a pair of very shiny brown shoes with pointed toes and buttons up the sides. "My gracious, Mister Clybourn . . . this is very gallant." Her glistening greenish eyes looked up at him. "Out of your salary, or does the army pay for these?"

"I have good credit at the mercantile," he said. "Please don't cry. It's my pleasure, a welcoming back gesture."

Katherine Coltrane pulled off her moccasins, fitted the shoes to her feet, and stood. She was a tall, slender woman . . . the high heels made her even taller, and her smile of appreciation was almost at a level with Lieutenant Clybourn's. He placed the white woolen shawl around her shoulders. She shook her long hair over it in the back as he escorted her out the door. "Don't be nervous," he said with a grin. "No one should be nervous about eating cornbread and stew."

"How do you know the bill of fare?"

"I stopped and asked," he returned. "I thought you might like chicken and dumplings for your first meal . . . something like that. It's stew, boarding house stew."

"No one but my brother ever took me to supper."

"I'm honored to be the first, Miss Coltrane."

"I am nervous, you know . . . they'll look at me, wonder all kinds of things . . . whisper."

"You shall ignore them. Be attentive to me. I'll tell

you my life story. It will captivate you, Miss Coltrane, and if anyone whispers about you, it will be because you're a very attractive woman. Just pretend they desire your company."

"Ridiculous, Lieutenant! A woman who has consorted with Indians for five years? . . . an unwed mother? Such a notion! Such a notion, indeed. Except for her daughter, Julia, five years of her young life had been wasted on the prairie, and at twenty-six, she felt twice that age.

There were four men at the middle of the table. Pausing in their conversation to nod politely, they quietly went back to the glasses of wine and talk without casting another glance her way. Writers, Thomas Clybourn told her, reporters from the east out on war assignments. No other women were present—none of General Crook's command had brought their wives with them. Crook anticipated this campaign would be a short one, and departure for the unceded lands to the north was imminent. Clybourn thought that by midsummer, Katherine would find her daughter on the reservation below the Black Hills. Katherine wanted to believe Clybourn, but she had lived with the Lakota. She knew the Indian mind and sense of purpose, and she was much less optimistic.

Mary Slaymaker soon came; she had white plates, and utensils. She came back a second time with a platter of hot cornbread and a steaming bowl of stew. There was coffee, bread pudding, and a small pitcher of condensed milk.

Clybourn did tell Katherine his life story, about his home in Columbus, Ohio, his parents, his graduation from West Point, his short tenure at Fort Buford, a transfer to Fort Laramie, and now, his temporary assignment at Fort Fetterman. He was twenty-five years old; he was an engineer, loved the army, and intended to make it his career.

Through the tangled web of her thoughts and mixed emotions, she listened, and by the time supper was over, Katherine felt like his mother. Two glasses of Burgundy wine arrived. The four men at the middle of the table stood and raised their glasses in a toast, and a stout man, coatless but with a bulging vest and a gold watch chain dangling from it, spoke for them. He said, "To your return, Miss Coltrane, and the very best of luck to you."

This writer tarried, and after the other three had left he came over to Katherine and introduced himself. His name was Henry Burlingame. He was on assignment for *Harper's Weekly*, and was interested in hearing about her life with the Sioux, if she was so inclined to discuss it. Katherine thanked him, but no, she had no inclination whatsoever to discuss it. It was much too personal, too bizarre, to grievous to her scarred soul. How could she possibly describe something like this, her capture, the inner struggles, the eventual capitulation, how she had survived? Biting her lip, Katherine shook her head. Henry Burlingame graciously bowed and left.

By dusk some of the tension, the fretful anxiety of the present and the unpredicatable future, had dissipated, and Katherine, draped with a blanket and once again wearing her Sioux moccasins, walked back to the fort with Thomas Clybourn. She would talk with her Lakota friends, but in their present pitiful plight, wear-

ing her new shoes and her pretty white shawl was more
than she could bear. She had been one of them for
these past few years, and she abhorred the thought of
sitting among them newly adorned as a white woman.
It bordered on humiliation, something she had once
felt herself when some of these same women had attempted to befriend her, to teach her the customs and
rituals of an alien society, one she detested, didn't understand, and one of which she wanted no part. Smiling wanly, Katherine looked at Lieutenant Clybourn.
Did he understand? Could he understand that despite
the animosities he had questioned her about, that despite her afflictions, the pain in her heart, she still had
some empathy for these people? That, unlike the white
man's government, she considered them her friends,
not her enemies, and felt they were being wrongfully
persecuted. Without prejudice, did he perceive? He
nodded—he perceived. He knew all about the historic
clash of cultures. They were as ancient and scarred as
the jagged peaks to the west, now stark black against
the dying sun.

The entry of the big squad tent was open and the
flaps to each side raised. A lone soldier was standing
near the front, and he saluted at Lieutenant Clybourn's
appearance. The guard's presence was customary, not
for precaution, for these few women and two old
men had no thoughts of escape. They had no place to
go, had no provisions, no weapons, and they were without their most prized possession, horses. They were
pitifully alone, but they had been well fed and were
now sitting toward the back of the tent, listening at-
tentively to one of the old men who, cross-legged and
staring into a tiny fire of smoldering juniper and sage

twigs, was chanting low, his hands extended, palms upward. Katherine entered, sat near the opening of the tent at the front.

Clybourn, sensing something spiritual in the fragrant aroma of juniper and sage, was hesitant to follow, dared not intrude, so he stood behind her in the shadows. But curious, he whispered down to her, "A ceremony? . . . some kind of ritual? Can you understand it?"

Katherine whispered back, "Maza Blaska . . . Flat Iron. He's an old holy man, once a warrior. No, not a ritual . . . not in an unholy place like this." She listened for a while, then whispered again, "He's telling them stories . . . stories in song. He says east is the white man's country . . . west is where he belongs. His old friends are now dead, and he soon may be with them, but . . . but he's not afraid. In this new place, this white man's lodge, they should not be afraid either, for Wakan-Tanka has given the women the Blue Elk to watch over them . . . the Blue Elk is out there watching over all the females. If they have faith . . . if they have faith and listen, they will hear the song, the inner song, the song from within, and it will give them peace."

"Putting them at ease, is he?" asked Clybourn. "This is what you came to do, isn't it?"

"Realistically," she returned. "I'll tell them no harm will come to them, not reassure them spiritually. Only men like Flat Iron can do such things. Standing Bear . . . the man I had, says Flat Iron has had many visions in his time." Pressing a finger to her lips, she said, "Shh, listen, he knows you're here."

"He never paid any attention to me on the train down. Three days and he barely noticed me."

"Old men like this one miss nothing, Mister Clybourn . . . nothing."

"Who is this Blue Elk who's watching over the females?"

"A spirit elk given big medicine by the Great Spirit."

"Interesting," mused Clybourn. "If one is a true believer, this has promising possibilities. A ray of hope, I should think. Perhaps this Blue Elk spirit thing will look out after your daughter until you find her."

"I don't know what to believe anymore," she whispered back. "Now he's singing about battle . . . the Oglala, he says are powerful, never defeated in battle . . . *ai ya he ye, ai ya he ye, okcize iyotan micilagon, miye sni se, ityotiyewakiye-lo'*—he was once mighty in battle . . honored. How he is old and wretched. He says he was never afraid to die young . . . to die in battle when one is young is honorable." Katherine turned and whispered up to the lieutenant. "For your benefit, Mister Clybourn—or General Crook's—he's letting you know in a roundabout way that you're going to lose if you battle the Oglala. You won't die with a toothache."